STORM WARNING

When the jotunn moved to sit on the other end of his bench, Rap called, "Careful! The stone's hot!"

The man turned to stare at him over a silver mustache large enough to sweep out a stable. The rest of him had been put together from knotted rope, brown leather, and wet polar bear combings. His pale eyes gleamed.

"Too hot for me, but not for you?"

"No! Sorry, sir! I didn't mean that at all."

"Ah. You mean I'm being stupid?"

"No, sir. I should have seen that you know exactly what you're doing." Rap had never expected to sweat so hard. "I meant well, sir."

The jotunn shrugged, disappointed. He sat, spreading his arms along the backrest, carefully not flinching at the heat.

Rap wished he had remembered that the nomadic sailor types were all homicidal maniacs.

By Dave Duncan
Published by Ballantine Books:

A ROSE-RED CITY

The Seventh Sword
THE RELUCTANT SWORDSMAN
THE COMING OF WISDOM
THE DESTINY OF THE SWORD

WEST OF JANUARY

STRINGS

A Man of His Word
MAGIC CASEMENT
FAERY LANDS FORLORN
PERILOUS SEAS*
EMPEROR AND CLOWN*

*Forthcoming

FAERY LANDS FORLORN

Part Two of
A Man of His Word

Dave Duncan

A Del Rey Book
BALLANTINE BOOKS • NEW YORK

The author gratefully acknowledges receiving a grant from the Alberta Foundation for the Literary Arts to support the writing of this novel.

A Del Rey Book
Published by Ballantine Books

Library of Congress Catalog Card Number: 90-93573

ISBN 0-345-36629-8

Manufactured in the United States of America

First Edition: April 1991

Cover Art by Don Maitz

Dedicated with thanks and appreciation
to Lester del Rey,
grand master of fantasy

A Man of His Word: Part Two
Faery Lands Forlorn

❲ CONTENTS ❳

The voice I hear this passing night was heard
In ancient days, by emperor and clown:
Perhaps the self-same song that found a path
Through the sad heart of Ruth, when sick for home,
She stood in tears amid the alien corn;
    The same that oft-times hath
Charmed magic casements, opening on the foam
Of perilous seas, in faery lands forlorn.

Keats, *Ode to a Nightingale*

❆ ONE ❆

Behind the veil

1

Eastward from the bare crags of the Agoniste Mountains, the land fell off in scabby ridges and gullies, sere and drab. Rare oases like green wounds pitted the valleys, but otherwise that desolate country was fit only for antelope and wild goats, watched over by buzzards drifting in the thin blue sky. Below the hills, a roasted desert stretched away to meet the surf of the Spring Sea.

In the main, the ironbound coast of Zark was as deadly and inhospitable as the interior. Yet, at long intervals where some trick of the landscape caught the nourishing sea wind or cool springs gushed from the rocks, life erupted in abundance. There the soil yielded crops of uncountable variety. The people dwelt there, on islands encircled half by ocean and half by desert. Whereas in other lands the earth spread its generosity widely, in Zark it hoarded all its goodness into these few green enclaves, like rich emeralds knotted on a string.

Richest of them all was Arakkaran, a narrow land blessed with twisting valleys of deep soil and legendary fertility. Its wide bay was the finest harbor on the continent. Many trade routes met in its markets, depositing wealth there in heaps to be fondled by the soft-fingered merchants: dates and pomegranates, rubies and olives, costly vials of perfume, intricate rugs, and the silver fish of the sea. From distant lands came gold and spices, elvish arts and dwarvish crafts, pearls and silks, and merfolk pottery unequaled in all Pandemia.

The city itself was beautiful and ancient. It was noted for its cruelty, and for fine racing camels. It boasted of a history written in blood. Near the close of Ji-Gon's Campaign, the young Draqu ak'Dranu had turned back the Imperial legions at Arakkaran, and there they won their revenge nine centuries later under Omerki the Merciless. During the Widow War, the city had withstood a siege of a thousand and one days.

From the loud and overscented bustle of the markets, it climbed by slope and precipice, in a tapestry of nacreous stone and flowering greenery. Trees had wedged in every unused crevice, hanging welcome shadow over steep alleyways and winding stairs. On the crest of the hill, celebrated in many ancient stories, the Palace of Palms was a marvel of domes and spires and towers, graced with lush parks and exotic gardens, as widespread in itself as many a respected town.

Throughout recorded history, a sultan of Arakkaran had ruled in that palace. There had been many sultans; their names and deeds were uncountable as the shells of the beaches. Some had held sway over half of Zark, while others had barely controlled the docks. A few were celebrated for justice and wisdom; many had been despots of a savagery to make the Gods recoil. No single family had ever dominated for long, no dynasty prevailed; old age had rarely troubled them.

Whatever he had been—warrior or statesman, tyrant or scholar, poet or giver of laws—every sultan of Arakkaran had invariably been renowned for his ferocity and for the number and beauty of his women.

2

From the dark cold of Krasnegar, Inos stumbled through a curtain of jewels into blinding light and a heat that took her breath away. Her willful feet carried her several paces farther before she felt them returned to her control.

But Rap and Aunt Kade were in danger—without even pausing to take stock of where she was, she spun around and rushed blindly back to the drape.

There was nothing there to stop her except many dangling strands of gems, flickering and tinkling in the breeze. A moment earlier she had passed between the strings with no trouble at all, but now she bounced off, stubbing her toe and almost falling. From this side, apparently, the curtain was as impenetrable as a castle wall. Yet it still shimmered and rippled. *Infernal sorcery!* She thumped fists on it furiously.

"Anger will not help," said a harsh male voice behind her.

She wheeled around, screwing up her eyes against the glare.

He was big, as tall as a jotunn. His pale-green cloak billowed and danced in the breeze, making him seem even larger. Yet in a moment she could make out his ruddy-hued face, and the thin line of red beard framing it. He was a djinn, therefore. Of course.

Under the cloak he wore voluminous pajamas of emerald silk, but she doubted he had just climbed out of bed. The scimitar hanging at his side, for example, its hilt glittering with diamonds—not a comfortable sleeping companion. The miscellaneous gems scattered from his lofty turban to the curled-up toes of his shoes, and especially the wide cummerbund of solid emeralds encircling his waist . . . no, those were not believable bed wear. And no matter how slim he was, that incredible belt must be excruciatingly tight. It was a wonder he could breathe in it.

His face was thin and intense, his nose aquiline, and his eyes hard as rubies. He was not very much older than herself. The size of him! Those shoulders . . .

The arrogance! He was enjoying her inspection. Whom had he intended to impress?

"Your name and station, wench?"

She drew herself up, miserably aware of her ruined leather riding habit, bloodstained and filthy; aware also that she must be haggard with fatigue—eyes like open sores, hair in yellow tangles. "I am Queen Inosolan of Krasnegar. And you, lad?"

Her insolence made fires flicker in his crimson eyes. Her head would barely reach his shoulder, and that emerald sash alone would buy her whole kingdom, even if the gems did not go all the way around him.

"I have the honor to be Azak ak'Azakar ak'Zorazak, Sultan of Arakkaran."

"Oh!" Dummy! Had she expected him to be a cook or a barber, dressed like that? The diamond medallion on his turban was worth a fortune in itself. Remembering in time that she was wearing jodhpurs, not skirts, she bowed.

The young giant studied her disapprovingly for a moment. Then he swept an expansive gesture with a large, red-brown hand and doubled over as if to touch his turban to his knees, making Inos wince. Obviously that emerald cummerbund was not tight at all—his waist really must be that narrow, and his back was even broader than she had suspected. He flicked himself upright again as if such gymnastics were no problem at all, but she could not tell if they were a compliment or a mockery.

Sultan! Rasha had claimed to be sultana, and this lad was far too young to be her husband. Of course that was assuming that Rasha was what she had seemed when she had first appeared in the tower—middle-aged and thick-bodied. There had been an even more revealing glimpse later, when Sagorn had replaced himself with Andor. Startled by the occult transformation, Rasha had momentarily become an ugly old woman. The svelte maiden image would have been the illusion, obviously. Sorcerers lived a long time, but most likely this very tall and youthful sultan was Rasha's son, or grandson.

A surge of exhaustion closed over Inos like a dark wave. She was in no state to deal with sultans, or sultanas, or sorceresses.

And then the jeweled drape tinkled. Inos spun around as Aunt Kade came through. Kade! Short and plump and blinking watery blue eyes at the brightness, but oh, how welcome!

"Aunt!" Inos hugged her fiercely.

"Ah, there you are, dear!" She sounded tired, but quite calm. She seemed blissfully unaware of her disreputable appearance— rose and silver gown all stained with tea, bedraggled snowy hair fluttering in the hot breeze.

Inos took a deep breath and forced herself to display suitably ladylike behavior. "How nice that you can join us, Aunt! Let me present you . . . the Princess Kadolan, sister of my late father, King Holindarn of Krasnegar. The sultan . . . er . . ."

"Azak!" snapped Azak.

"Sultan Azak." Inos was not at her best at the moment.

"Your Majesty!" Aunt Kade curtsied, with no perceptible wobble. She was again demonstrating her astonishing durability.

The sultan frowned, registering aristocratic surprise at these two waifs appearing in his domain. When he clenched his jaw, the fringe of red beard rippled. Of course he could not possibly be as stupendous as he thought he was, but Inos decided she would go so far as to class him as noteworthy. Again making his curious gesture, he bowed to Kade—deeply, but less deeply than before. Then he went back to staring at Inos.

"Your father? You are a queen in your own right?"

"I am."

"How extraordinary!"

Indignant, Inos opened her mouth and then firmly closed it

again; a queen with only two loyal subjects should be discreet. Which reminded her of her other loyal subject—

"Aunt, where is Rap?" She turned back to the curtain of jewels and pushed at it. It was still immovable from this side, a one-way curtain.

"Still in the chamber, I expect, dear."

"The slut is in there, I presume?" Azak inquired.

Inos and her aunt both turned to stare at him.

"The woman who calls herself Sultana Rasha? You have met her? She is beyond that drape—wherever that may be?" He folded his arms imperiously.

"Beyond that drape is Krasnegar, my kingdom!" Inos shouted, feeling her threadbare self-control starting to rip. This ordeal had been going for a whole day and night, and she just couldn't take much more. "I want to go home!"

"Indeed?" He seemed skeptical. "You have no magic of your own, either of you?"

"None!" Inos shouted.

"Inos!" Kade frowned disapprovingly.

The djinn shrugged. "Well, I am no sorcerer, merely the rightful ruler of this domain. For sorcery you must deal with the bitch."

"Is she not your . . . Well, if you are sultan here, then what is she to you?" Inos demanded, still ignoring glances from Kade.

The djinn scowled grotesquely at the magical drape behind them. "You have met her, I presume?"

"Queen Rasha? I mean Sultana—"

His already ruddy face darkened and reddened even more. "She is no queen, no sultana! She was a dockside harlot who illicitly acquired occult powers. Now she styles herself sultana, but there is no truth in that! None!" Just for a moment, his anger betrayed his youth.

But Inos knew that Rasha had not truly impressed her as royalty. She had not sounded right, or moved right—

"What a marvelous view you have here!" Kade exclaimed, firmly changing the subject.

For the first time, Inos took a serious look at where she was. The room was big, much larger than Inisso's chamber of puissance, but not unlike. It was obviously located high up, it was circular, and it had four windows. If those similarities were important and not just coincidence, they must mean that this also was a sorcerer's chamber. A sorceress's, of course. Rasha's.

The walls were of white marble, supporting a huge bulbous

dome of the same milky rock. There were no windows in the great shell, but light flooded it from somewhere, apparently through the stone itself. Moreover, that strange brightness pulsed with inexplicable, eerie movements that Inos could see perfectly well out of the corner of her eye, but not when she looked straight at them. Then the shiftings ceased and there was nothing there except smooth translucent marble; while the haunting would have started somewhere else. Creepy!

And the view that her aunt had mentioned—the four wide openings were larger by far than the casements in Inisso's tower, triple-arched and not merely unglazed, but lacking even shutters. Obviously Arakkaran's climate was kinder than Krasnegar's.

To her left, the austere yellow light of morning streamed in from a newborn sun, aiming a golden sword at her across the sea. All through her childhood, seaward had meant northward— the Winter Ocean. At Kinvale, although it was well inland, seaward had meant westward, toward Pamdo Gulf. Sea to the east was wrong, horrifying. It told her she was appallingly far from home.

Southward, towers and more pointed domes obscured much of the view, but she could tell she was high in some castle or palace. Beyond them she glimpsed a coastline of dry brown hills falling to white surf, stretching off to meet the sky. Craggy peaks to the west were already almost lost in a heat haze. They were much higher and rockier than the Pondague range, and obviously desert.

Fatigue and despair crushed down on her. She struggled to recall childhood lessons from Master Poraganu, wishing she had been more attentive. Djinns were tall, fierce folk, with reddish skin and hair . . . djinns lived in Zark . . . desert and sand. Those mountains looked bare as any desert she could imagine. But Zark was somewhere in the extreme southeast of Pandemia, about as far from Krasnegar as it was possible to be. Which would explain why Master Poraganu had not gone into details, and why she had not listened.

Her eyes went again to the shining water eastward. That must be the Spring Sea, and she remembered Mistress Meolorne talking about silk once, long ago.

"Is this truly Zark?" Kade exclaimed. "How thrilling! I have always wanted to see more of Pandemia. This will be a very informative and educational visit." She beamed warningly at Inos.

"Arakkaran is a small, poor place compared to the Impire," Azak proclaimed, "but its people are a proud and noble race, jealous of their own ways and their independence. We draw our strength from the desert, scorning the decadence of those who dwell in milder climes."

Oh, just juicy! Barbarians.

Again Inos tried the infuriating drapery of gems; again it refused to admit her. What was Rasha doing? Was Rap all right, or had the impish legionaries finally broken down the door? Her legs wobbled with weariness, but she must stay close to this impossible sorcery in the hope that somehow it would lead her home again.

Azak's eyes had made her think of rubies on first sight, but now they had darkened to garnets and were regarding her with a haughty stare that reminded her of Firedragon, the stallion.

"You truly have no occult power . . . your Majesty?"

Inos shook her head, feeling weary now beyond speech. A whole world between her and Krasnegar, and Rap. Rap? Suddenly she realized that, more than anything else, she wanted Rap here beside her. Solid, dependable, reliable Rap. How strange! Rap?

The sultan fingered his beard thoughtfully. His feet had not moved since she entered. They were enclosed in very soft-looking shoes that curled up absurdly at the toes. Certainly not desert wear. Rather decadent, in fact.

"That is indeed curious."

"In what way?" Aunt Kade inquired, casting another worried glance at Inos.

"Because the sorceress slut has cast a spell upon me. By rights you should both have been turned to stone before now."

"Turned to stone!" Inos and Kade echoed in chorus.

He nodded. "Anyone who grants me my correct honorific . . . I wonder if the curse works only on my own subjects, not strangers? No, the ambassador from Shuggaran was smitten."

It would have been kind of him to have mentioned the matter sooner.

"This petrification," Kade murmured, obviously deeply offended by the idea, "is it . . . reversible?"

He glanced in surprise at her—Kade's queries were often much sharper than her appearance led one to expect. "In the beginning it was not. The first half dozen or so victims are still statues. Now the jade usually restores them to life after a week or two."

"That is the most disgustingly stupid thing I have ever heard of!" Inos said.

"I told you—she is a whore, an evil woman, and spiteful."

"She must also be half-witted, if she did not see what would happen with a spell like that loose! Six people died before she changed to a sorcery she could undo?"

He shrugged. "But why were you not immobilized when you gave me my legal title?"

Obviously he had expected it to happen. That realization left Inos at a loss for words.

"The effects of the curse are limited to the palace itself," the big man mused. "Can it be that this odious sorcerous chamber is excluded?"

Again Inos looked around. She could see nothing obviously sorcerous, only an excessive amount of bright-colored furniture, much of it ugly and garish, intermixed with ill-suited statuary. Nor could she see any doorway. The floor, where it was visible, was a spectacular mosaic of vines and flowers, all intricately intertwined and as brightly hued as a swarm of butterflies, but the effect was ruined by a litter of rugs, as gawdy and mismatched as the furniture. Everything looked expensive, but nothing fit or blended. Whoever had assembled the collection had been sadly lacking in even the rudiments of taste. One glance at this warehouse would give Duke Angilki a seizure.

But being turned to stone . . . Was this oddly youthful sultan trying to be humorous? As Inos was planning a suitable query, the drape jingled again. A huge gray dog bounded through, skidded on the polished tiles past both Inos and her aunt, and came to a stop facing Azak. The dislike was immediate, and mutual.

The dog bared teeth, flattened ears, and raised hackles. Azak put hand to sword hilt.

Inos was about to speak, then her courage failed her. Rap had called the monster "Fleabag" affectionately, as if it were a cuddly lapdog instead of an overgrown timber wolf. It had obeyed him eagerly, but dogs were always happy to go along with Rap's suggestions, and Rap was not present now. It had not noticed Kade or Inos, apparently, and even to speak its name might attract its hostility.

Moreover, something about Azak's stance suggested that he did not believe he was in much danger, and Inos decided that she was more concerned for Rap's dog. True, it had overpowered Andor and then savaged the giant Darad. The djinn was not as massive as the jotunn had been, but he was almost as tall; he was younger and probably faster, and Darad had been hampered by entering the fight when he was already on the floor with the monster's teeth in his arm . . . Shocked to discover that she was assessing the contest as she might weigh an upcoming skittles match at Kinvale, Inos looked to Kade, and Kade was very obviously not going to interfere, either.

Azak's slim, curved blade slid into view. Inos glanced around at the drape in the hope that Rap might appear. If Rasha had allowed his dog through, surely she would not leave Rap himself to the unlikely mercy of the imps? The sword was out now. The wolf had begun to growl. Was that a good sign or a bad?

It gathered itself to leap; Azak drew back his elbow. The dog turned to stone. Kade recoiled, moaning, and Inos reached out to hug her, but more for her own comfort than her aunt's, probably.

May the Good be with us! There was no doubt—stone it was. No mundane sculptor could ever have matched the detail of the coat so well, nor achieved the cunning fit of the grain of the rock to the gleam of light over muscle and bone, but otherwise what had a moment before been a living, breathing, and highly dangerous predator was now only a graceful ornament. Inexplicably, that felt wrong. Inexplicably, that sorcery impressed Inos more than all the miracles she had seen and experienced since the terrors began, so many hours before.

Azak, on the other hand, sheathed his scimitar quite matter-of-factly, as if petrification were no more remarkable in Arakkaran than shampooing, or ladies entering rooms through windows.

Before anyone spoke, the jewels tinkled again, signaling the arrival of Sultana Rasha. Light flared up behind her and there was no longer an impossible night beyond the drapery. She was wearing the face of a mature woman, an imperious matron in her thirties—not conventionally beautiful, but striking. In Inisso's chamber her appearance had flicked back and forth from age to youth, from ugliness to beauty, and her flowing white raiments had varied similarly, from coarse white cotton to silks embroidered with pearls and gems. Now, like her face, her dress represented a compromise, rich but not ostentatious. Her fingers glittered with gems, though.

She stopped abruptly, frowning at Azak. "What're you doing here, Beautiful?" She spoke to him as Inos would to a wayward horse.

Azak scowled. His teeth were large and regular and very white. "You summoned me." Again the dislike was obviously mutual.

Rasha laughed. "Well, so I did! I'd forgotten. I was feeling bitchy and wanted some entertainment." She turned to Inos. "You've met Prince Azak, dearie?"

"He's not the sultan?"

"Oh, never! Don't believe a thing he says. He's a notorious liar."

A jotunn would have struck her for that remark, even had the act meant suicide. Azak almost did. His lips paled, his neck bulged, but he managed to control his fury, just barely.

Rasha was enjoying herself. "All men are liars, my dear," she said with affected sweetness. "Whatever they tell you, they only want one thing, and lots of it. Don't call him 'sultan' inside the palace, either—I'm trying to stamp out that nonsense. Here's all right; nowhere else. Now come, move your little buns." She led the way, marching like a legionary, her vestments floating out behind her. As she went by Azak, she reached up and tweaked his beard. He recoiled with a choking noise.

"Wait!" Inos cried. But the sorceress kept going, weaving between the furniture. Inos ran after, dodging overstuffed divans and bronze urns and porcelain animals. "What about Rap? And Doctor Sagorn? And the goblin?"

She caught up with Rasha at a circular balustrade in the center of the room. Here a grand staircase spiraled down to a lower chamber. That was why there were no doors, of course.

"What about them?" the sorceress asked, not looking around.

"You just left them there? Left them for the imps to kill?"

The sultana walked around to the top of the stair and paused at the first step, where the way was partly obstructed by a life-size carving of a black panther, seemingly poised to spring at any intruder coming up toward it.

"This is Claws," she muttered absently, but she was studying the great shimmering dome overhead. Or possibly she was listening to something. A small smile played around her mouth, registering satisfaction. Then she set off down the stairs, stroking the basalt neck in passing. "Isn't he gorgeous? I think I'll put him on one side and the wolf on the other."

Chasing down after her, Inos said, "It's real?"

"When I want it to be. Lucky I remembered to warn it that the Meat Man was coming."

Inos was becoming more bewildered by the minute. "Who?"

"Azak," said the sorceress. "I've got lots of names for him, but that one really twists his nose. It fits him, though—he's got biceps like the humps on his camel. I'll have him show you sometime."

Halfway down, she suddenly slackened her pace, as if the urgency—whatever it was—was over. Azak was padding down the stairs behind Inos in his kidskin slippers. Aunt Kade was just passing the panther.

"But Rap!" Inos exclaimed. "Doctor Sagorn? You can't just leave them there for the imps!"

Rasha continued down the stairs without replying. The lower chamber was as overloaded with furniture as the upper had been, mostly innumerable chests and tables of random styles. Two windows added little to the light spilling down the central stairwell. The walls were poorly lighted, therefore, and yet cluttered with ornate mirrors and bright tapestries barely discernible in the shadows. Musk and flower scent hung in the air like syrup.

Despite her worry over Rap and the others, despite her bone-deep weariness, Inos was intrigued by these exotic, alien rooms. They were like nothing she had ever seen, not even in the Duke of Kinvale's collection of lithographs; a collection that he had amassed from all over the Impire, and had inflicted on her during several mind-numbing afternoons. Neither in art nor reality had she ever seen decor so alien. Double doors vast enough to admit a coach and four stood shut; against the opposite wall was an absurdly huge bed, the largest four-poster in the world, wide and high, draped in filmy gauze. Then her eyes had adjusted to the gloom and the nature of some of the statuary penetrated her fog-shrouded mind. She took an incredulous second look at the illustrations on the walls and was suddenly very glad that such obscenities were so poorly lighted. Kade would have an apoplectic fit.

Hastily Inos turned her attention back to the sorceress. Surely the legionaries would be breaking down the door by now?

"You must save them!"

Rasha spun around. "Must? You say *must* to me, child?"

"I'm sorry, your Majesty! But I beg of you—*please* save them!"

"Why should I?" inquired the sorceress, smirking.

"Because they'll be killed!"

"Better than what you'd have got, dearie, if I'd left you there! You know what gangs of men do to pretty girls?"

"No!" Inos had never even considered such a thing. Imperial legionaries? A band of raiding jotnar, certainly, but not the imperor's army! It had been Rap who had been in danger, and the goblin, also—not her! "Not that!"

"Yes, that!" the sorceress said, her mouth twisting in an expression Inos could not read. "I know more about men than you'll ever guess at it, sweetie girl. Believe me, I know!"

Inos was still a couple of steps up, staring down at her in horror. Possibly the sorceress thought she was not being believed, because she suddenly discarded about twenty years, to become again the gem-bedecked, sylphlike maiden who had so bewitched Rap, her flesh glowing hot and tantalizing through garments of mist.

She smiled mockingly up at Inos. "All men have to do is die, and they have to do that eventually, don't they? That's nothing compared to what a woman might get. What do I owe them? What does any woman owe a man, ever?" She glanced past Inos, apparently at Azak. "Well, Wonderstud?"

Receiving no answer, she chuckled and turned away, sauntering toward the great bed with her hips swinging, ruddy flesh and ox-blood hair shining through garments that seemed to have become flimsier than ever, over a body even more voluptuous.

Inos had heard of women who dressed like that and behaved like that—had heard of them mostly in whispered tales in the castle kitchens. She had never expected to see a queen do such things.

Shakily she descended the last couple of steps, fighting back tears, trying to scrape some last trace of strength from the bottom of her personal barrel. Her knees trembled with exhaustion. Her head told her that the sultana's palace was rocking gently, like a ship, and that was not very likely. Soon she would simply fall over. Oh, Rap! Rasha must be a very powerful sorceress, but she might be crazy, also. Was her hatred of men genuine? Had she endured the sort of experience she had hinted at?

Could anyone ever believe anything said around here?

Azak stepped past Inos and moved toward the door—head high, back rigid. Kade came to Inos's side and took her hand in a gesture that held only caution and sympathy. Those were not much use.

Rap! He was only a stableboy, yet he had been the only one to stay faithful. Even when Inos had spurned him in the forest, he had not wavered in his allegiance. He had endured the ordeal of the taiga for her sake, not once but twice. Her only loyal subject! Monarchs dreamed of loyalty like that. For Rap, Inos would brave even the fury of a sorceress.

She had just one arrow left in her quiver, and it might make things immeasurably worse, because despite what Rasha said, men as well as women could meet ordeals more terrible than a quick death.

"He knows a word of power!"

Rasha spun around, matronly dignity replacing nymph seduction instantly. "Who does?"

"Doctor Sagorn!" Inos watched the sorceress stalking back toward her like a hungry cat. "And Rap has one, too."

"So!" Rasha came very close, smiling dangerously. "So that was why you were holding hands with a stableboy? I wondered why the smell didn't bother the royal nose."

Queen Rasha herself reeked sickeningly of gardenia. Rap, Inos suddenly realized, had smelled of laundry soap, not of horses as he usually did. Which was irrelevant . . .

"His talent doesn't work on people! Just on animals. He's a faun."

Kade said, "Inos, dear!" in a warning tone.

Still somehow catlike, the sorceress smiled. "But words of power have side effects. Even one word would naturally make a man more successful at lechery; he would automatically collect any stray princesses around."

"That wasn't what—I've known Rap all my life! I'd trust him with—"

"More fool you!" Rasha sneered. "Don't ever trust a man, any man. *Muscles, you stay!* I'm not done with you." Her eyes had not wandered from Inos's face; she had spoken to Azak without looking at him. "Men keep their brains between their legs. Don't you know that yet, child?"

"Not Rap!"

"Yes, Rap." She considered Inos slyly for a moment. "Maybe I will fetch him for you! I could show you his real colors."

"Don't believe her!" Azak shouted from the door. "She can inflame any man to madness!"

Rasha raised her eyes to glare at him. She did not seem to do anything more, but the young giant screamed, clutched his belly, and fell writhing on the floor.

"Brute!" Rasha muttered, then went back to studying Inos. Azak was thrashing and whimpering. Inos had heard tales of animals caught in traps trying to chew off their own paws . . .

why was she thinking of such stories at a time like this? Appalled as much by the sorceress's casual indifference as by the barbarity itself, she fought in vain for words.

"No," the sultana said. "They're all after the same thing, and nothing else."

"Not Rap!"

Rasha seemed to grow taller, and her eyes redder. "You think so? What do you know of life, Little Palace Flower?"

"Enough!" Inos shouted. "I was about to be married to a man I loved and I saw him transformed into a monster!"

"Inos!" Kade said sharply.

"At twelve I was *sold* to a monster. He was old. He oozed."

"I watched my father die!"

"When I was younger than you I watched my babies die!"

"I crossed the taiga in winter!"

"I was cook on a fishing boat for five men. Can you guess what that was like, Butterfly?"

Kade was clucking like a panicky hen at Inos's side. To yell at a sorceress was certainly rash, but Inos ignored the warnings. Yet she didn't think she was going to win this crazy shouting match. Rasha sounded like one of the fishwives on the docks at Krasnegar, an expert.

"I can't help what happened to you!" Inos bellowed, louder still. "But you could help me now!"

Azak was still sobbing and squirming in agony on the floor, disregarded by everyone.

"Help you?" The sorceress glared. "Help your stableboy lover, you mean?"

Inos dropped her eyes. It was hopeless! Oh, Rap!

"On the other hand . . ." Rasha said more softly. "Which one was Sagorn?"

"The old man."

"One of the sequential set? But they must share memories, so they all know it?"

Inos nodded, looking up with sudden hope.

"Interesting!" Rasha had reverted to her matronly, queenly guise, which was encouraging. "A matched set with a word of power! That could be amusing. And two words would be worth salvaging. Come, then, dearie, and let's see."

She started back up the stairs. Hope leaping wildly within her, Inos brushed past Kade, ignoring her attempts to signal warnings, following the sorceress. As she rounded the curve, she saw the basalt panther watching her with eyes of yellow onyx, gleaming bright. They seemed to follow her as she approached, but it remained a statue, and she ignored it, staying at Rasha's side.

Before they had quite reached the top, the sorceress stopped, holding out a hand to stay Inos, also. Then she advanced cautiously, one step at a time. When her head was level with the floor, she paused a long time, seeming to be listening, as she had before.

"What—" Inos said.

"Sh! All clear . . ." Apparently reassured, Rasha strode upward again. Once past the panther she did not turn north, toward the magic casement, but headed instead to the southeast, weaving between bijou divans and tables and grotesque carvings, until she came to a large mirror hung on the wall. It was oval, bound in an intricate silver frame depicting leaves and hands and numerous other shapes, all vaguely sinister. Even the reflections seemed oddly distorted.

Inos stared in horror at the two images she saw there, shadowed and dim. She was a fright—face livid, eyes staring, honey hair awry, looking for all the world like flotsam washed up on a rock. Rasha, meanwhile, seemed as fair and regal as everyone's ideal of motherhood. She was observing Inos's reaction with cool disdain.

Then she frowned, as if in concentration. The twin reflections faded and the glass darkened. Shapes moved within it. Inos gasped at this new sorcery, seeing the mists coalesce into the forms of imp legionaries. Soon she recognized the chamber at the top of Inisso's Tower, dimly lighted, with snow swirling beyond the panes and settling on the leading. She could make out the shattered door, and the throng of soldiers milling around in the thin gray light. There was no sound, only the vision in the glass.

"See?" the sorceress muttered. "No sign of your lover."

"He was not that! Merely a loyal subject!"

"Hah! He'd have been slobbering all over you as soon as he got the chance. They all do. But I don't see the goblin, either; nor one of the set."

Inos blinked tears from her eyes.

"And look here!" Rasha said. The scene lurched sideways and steadied again. Several of the legionaries were leaning out the great south casement, staring down. "Either they had the sense to jump," Rasha said, "or they just got thrown. Thrown, I expect."

The scene blurred as the tears won over the blinking.

Rap and Aunt Kade—only two of her father's subjects had stayed loyal to Inos. And now there was only Kade.

3

Eastward, a faint glow rising from the sea was washing the stars from the sky, playing on waves that rolled in monotonously from the dark to lap a beach already shining like hammered silver. Westward, behind Rap, the jungle was wakening into carillons of birdsong. He had never heard melody like that.

He had never breathed such air—warm and affectionate on the skin, sweet with scents of sea and vegetation. The humidity stole his breath away. It made his head spin, seducing him like a hot bed. It felt decadent. He distrusted such air, and the soft warm sand, also.

Morning was coming, and he had not slept at all. His eyelids kept drooping, no matter how fiercely he told them to behave themselves. Not that he needed his eyes, for his farsight told him that no danger lurked nearby. Nothing larger than a raven stirred within that dense foliage, and whatever those jeweled birds might be, they were not ravens. He had already scanned carefully as far as he could reach, satisfying himself that the forest was not merely deserted, it was impenetrable, a tangle of lush vines, succulent leaves, and nasty fleshy flowers. It teemed with bugs and snakes. He had never known trees so huddled, nor so varied.

Three young men stranded on a beach . . . Oppressed by the sticky warmth after the brittle chill of Krasnegar, they had all stripped off their heavy clothes. Imp and faun sat with arms on knees; the goblin was stretched out on his back. They had established that they had nothing—no money and no weapon except Little Chicken's stone dagger. They had no idea where they were.

Rap had just finished telling Thinal of his two earlier encounters with Bright Water, witch of the north. He was certain that it had been the voice of the old goblin woman that had summoned Little Chicken to the casement and thus brought all three of them here—wherever *here* was.

Thinal made a shivery noise. "She's not around now, though, is she? I mean, you can't farsee her?"

"No. But she doesn't always show to my farsight, even when

my eyes can see her.'' Rap brooded a moment, and then said, ''Is it true she's mad?''

Thinal squealed. ''Don't say such things!'' He whimpered.

''Why not? She's either not here or she's spying on us, and that's not polite.''

''Polite? Rap, witches and warlocks don't give a spit about *polite*!''

''But do sorcerers lose their power as they grow old? If she's three hundred years old and she's been one of the Four for . . . how long?''

''Dunno.'' Thinal had turned surly, hunched very small. ''You wanna talk that sort of thing, then I'll call Sagorn.''

''No!''

They sat for a while, staring at the ever-rolling waves.

Little Chicken must have been following at least some of the story, for he muttered sleepily, ''Why Bright Water call me, not you?''

''I don't know,'' Rap said. ''It's certainly you she's watching over. She keeps warning me not to hurt you.''

Little Chicken chuckled softly, raising goosebumps on Rap's skin, despite the sticky heat.

But Rap could not deny that being magicked to Zark was preferable to being chopped up by a platoon of angry imps.

When there was enough light for the others to see, then they all must go in search of something to eat. He was impatient to be on his way, angry with himself for feeling so concerned about food and sleep when he had more important worries. His failure to aid Inos was maddening—he would never forgive himself. She had cried out to him, and he had stupidly fallen over, flat on his back like a moron, helpless in the sorceress's entrancement. It was easy enough for Thinal to say that no man could have resisted such a spell, but that was small comfort to Rap. He had failed Inos, his lawful queen, his friend, his . . . his queen.

''Tell me about Zark, Thinal. Have any of you ever been here?''

The thief brooded in silence for a while and then muttered, ''I hope this is Zark.''

Rap grunted.

''Rap, I was wrong. Don't be mad at me, Rap?''

''You said palm trees meant djinns, and djinns meant Zark!''

''Yes, but not those palms.''

Rap glanced up, with eyes and with farsight, to where the

frondy trees were clearly visible now, dancing in a pewter sky. A wide belt of them flanked the edge of the sand as far as he could scan in both directions. The jungle growth behind them was different: matted, denser. "What about them?"

"There are two sorts of palm trees. These are coconut."

"So?"

"The djinn type grows dates. They're very alike, Rap, and it was dark! I couldn't help it!"

Just when you think things are bad, they always get worse. "Then where are we?"

"Hear the birdsong? The dawn chorus?"

Rap could hardly avoid hearing it, even over the rush of the surf. It was glorious, still increasing as new entrants added layer after layer of song to the symphony. One of the innkeepers in Krasnegar had owned a canary and there had been larks in the hills. Ravens croaked, geese honked, and seagulls cried, but this was birdsong on a scale he had never dreamed of. Inos would love it. "You've heard it before?"

"Sagorn did," Thinal said. "Once. Long ago. I mean, there's lots of places where birds sing . . ."

"But not like this? Where?"

"Faerie. It has to be Faerie. Sounds right. Even smells right."

Faerie was an island, Rap knew, and there was something mysterious about it. "Andor's been there."

"Andor!" Thinal spat. "No, he hasn't. It was Sagorn, when he was much younger. A lot of those stories that Andor told you were really of the others. We share memories, remember."

Rap growled angrily at the thought of Andor and his lies.

"They . . . we . . . can't help it," Thinal said, whining as he did if Rap so much as frowned at him. "I mean . . . Well, he remembers Sagorn being here, so when he talks about it, he would say it was him." He fell silent for a while, then added, "It doesn't make any difference, really."

It did make a sort of sense, though. Sagorn had spent a lifetime in search of magic, seeking to understand the workings of the words of power. If Faerie had a reputation for being somehow uncanny, then he might very well have decided to visit it. "How far is Faerie from Zark?"

Silence.

"Thinal," Rap said gently, "I'm not going to bite you. I won't even shout. But I do need your help! You know so much more than I do."

Thinal was flattered. "Well . . . Faerie's 'way west. Kras-negar's north. And Zark's east . . . and south, I think."

After a minute he whimpered, "Sorry, Rap."

"Not your fault. We didn't have much choice, anyway, did we?"

"But I should have known. Where Inos went there was day-light, wasn't there? And here was still dark. So she went east and we went west."

"Huh?" Rap was only an ignorant clerk, a glorified stable-boy. He wondered if Thinal could read and write, and reminded himself that there was probably more to the little thief than he showed, or perhaps believed himself. His despicable whimper-ing was pure habit, part of his professional expertise.

"Pandemia's very big, see?" Thinal sighed. "Dawn doesn't come at the same time everywhere. Must get to Zark long before it gets to Faerie."

Much worse! So the problem was not just how to find Inos and help her. The problem was how to get to Zark, and then find Inos and help her. So now there was no great urgency, and Rap was furious to discover that just knowing that made him feel much sleepier. Waves fell and rushed up the gleaming sand and died with a tiny hiss. Then the next . . . It was hypnotic, soporific.

"But why would Bright Water have brought me here?" he demanded.

But it had been Little Chicken the goblin witch had rescued; Thinal and Rap had merely come along for the ride.

"How should I know?" Thinal sniffed. "I'm dumb, Rap. Just a dumb cutpurse. A city slicker, an alley thief . . . useless in the wilds. You wanna talk smart stuff, I'll call Sagorn."

"No, don't! I don't trust Sagorn."

The surprise of Thinal's face was visible even to mundane vision now—a nondescript imp face, young and unpleasantly spotted with acne; a pinched face; ratty and worried. His ribs stuck out. He was skinny as a ferret, but what would a profes-sional thief know of honest labor? He was as puny beside Rap as Rap was beside the husky goblin.

"You can trust Sagorn! The king told Inos that. Andor's a twister, and Darad would tear you apart. But Sagorn has honor."

"No!" Rap shouted. Lack of sleep was making him short-tempered, and that sudden insight made him angrier still. He lowered his voice. "Maybe the king could trust Sagorn. They were old friends. Maybe Sagorn wouldn't cheat Inos, for her father's sake—but he's got no scruples about me."

Thinal mused for a moment. "No, he hasn't. Sorry, Rap. I didn't think. I'm a fool."

When Sagorn had been in Krasnegar, ministering to the sick king, Andor had been there, also, alternatively. Andor had been cultivating Rap, befriending him in the hope of wheedling his word of power out of him. Sagorn must have known what Andor had been doing when he was present, yet Sagorn had kept on calling him back.

"Besides," Rap said, "you have Sagorn's memories, don't you? So you know what he knows."

"It don't work like that," Thinal said glumly. "He's a lot smarter'n me, a whole lot smarter. He understands more."

"I don't see why."

The skeletal shoulders shrugged. "Well, I can remember all the years he spent sniffing around libraries. But the books themselves I can't recall like he can. They don't make sense to me. Think of Jalon. I hear a tune whistled or sung—I don't remember it much. No more'n you would. But Jalon would know it, and be able to sing it next time he's around. He'd ring changes on it and craft a great ballad out of it. We each have our own tricks. Like the djinn said, we're a matched set—artist, scholar, lover, and fighter. All you've got in me is a common dip, and there's small pickings hereabouts."

"Sagorn said that you were the leader."

Thinal pouted and looked guilty. "Long ago! He meant I got the bunch of us into the mess; it was my idea to break into Orarinsagu's house. Anyway, that was years ago. We were all kids. I still am." He turned his face away.

After a moment, Rap said, "Why are you? I know—because you don't exist as often, or as long. So you don't age. But why's that? Don't the others call you?"

Thinal wiped his nose with the back of his hand. "Sometimes. If one of them is hungry, or needs something that can be stolen, I'll help out."

"But you don't stay around. You call him back in your place right away. Why?"

There was a long silence then, while Thinal stared at the sea, weedy chin resting on spindle arms. Finally he said softly, " 'Cause I'm no good, Rap. That's why."

Rap's head felt stuffed with feathers, but he knew he needed

Thinal and must not let him disappear. "Bunk!" he said. "Right now, I'd much rather have you here than any of the others."

Thinal's eyes widened and he smiled shyly, showing teeth as crooked as a stork's nest. "Really?"

"Really! I can't trust any of them—not even Jalon, can I?"

Thinal sniggered. "He'd get lost in listening to the birds. And he might very well call Darad. Of all of us, he's the most likely to call Darad. No, not even Jalon."

That was a great pity. If Rap could only enlist the willing help of Thinal and his four optional replacements, then he would have a whole gang of useful helpers. Five specialists, strengthened by a word of power, a handful of men. He wondered if he dared offer a bargain, remembering how Sagorn had said that their one common purpose was to collect enough magic to be freed from the spell that bound them. They would do anything to learn another word of power, so Rap could offer to share his in return for theirs. It would be ironic if Thinal was the one to gain Rap's word, after the other four had all tried to steal it without success. Now that Rap knew what his word was, he could share it if he wished.

Certainly he must keep Thinal friendly. "Well, then! So promise me, will you—promise that you'll not call any of the others without warning me?"

Looking flattered, Thinal nodded and accepted Rap's offer of a handshake. His fingers were unusually long, his palm soft.

Rap's own attitude toward occult power had just changed. Up until now even his farsight and his mastery over animals had been more than he wanted, but with Inos in the clutches of a sorceress, new rules applied. The more magic the better now! Anyone who knew a single word of power was a genius at whatever his talent was. Knowing two words made a man an adept, a genius at anything. So Andor and Sagorn had said, but did he really trust either of them?

He was too fogged by weariness to decide now. He must not open any doors yet. An admitted thief like Thinal would just take Rap's word and then not tell his own—the temptation would be irresistible. And even if he didn't cheat, one day he or one of the others would certainly call Darad. Then the warrior would come after Rap and knot his neck, as he had killed the woman in Fal Dornin. Thus he could gain the rest of the power from both words, becoming a more powerful adept. Sharing with Thinal would be suicide.

Rap's eyelids closed. Angrily he jumped to his feet and rubbed them open again. "It's light enough!" he said. "Let's go!"

The little imp shot him a scowl. "Go where?"

"Breakfast. We'll starve here. North or south?"

Thinal didn't know. Little Chicken wanted to go north, because it was homeward—his grasp of geography was even worse than Rap's—but north was as likely as south to bring them to some sort of habitation. They ripped themselves loincloths from King Holindarn's robe, and set off along the beach.

Thinal kept edging seaward. "You're casing the jungle, I hope?" he asked Rap anxiously.

"There's nothing there but birds and lizards and things. What did you expect? People?"

"Headhunters!" For a moment he showed the whites of his eyes. "And monsters: griffins and harpies and hippogriffs!"

"They're not home at the moment." The coming of daylight had revealed a wide, shallow bay, with beaches curving smoothly away north and south to headlands so distant that even the tall palm trees at their tips were barely visible. There were no signs of life, either human or monstrous. Nothing moved on land or sea, at the moment. Why would Bright Water have moved her precious Little Chicken to a refuge so isolated?

"Faerie's an island?"

Thinal hesitated. "Andor probably told you more than I can remember, Rap. He's the tourist. I'm the lifter."

"He said something about a town. Only one, I think. Milsomething?"

"Milflor!" Thinal grinned at this triumph.

"We can get on a ship there?"

Thinal frowned warily. "I dunno. Certainly you can get *on* a ship. The trouble would be getting off. Where're you thinking of going?"

"Zark, of course."

Thinal trudged over the sand in silence for a moment. Then he burst out, "It'll take months, Rap! Probably years. You got any idea how *big* Pandemia is? And that djinn sorceress may magic Inos right back to Krasnegar by lunchtime."

Rap's heart sank. "What else can I do? I must try to help her!"

"Go to Hub, maybe? Hub knows everything, and it's in the middle. You can find out there where Inos is and from Hub you can go anywhere. You can call on the imperor, or the witch of the north, if she's a friend of yours." He sniggered. "Or ask the imperial marshal why his legions marched on Krasnegar?"

"Queen Rasha used occult power on the legionaries!"

Thinal sucked his teeth loudly. "So she did! You think that'll rouse the wardens? Treading on East's turf?"

Certainly that seemed possible to Rap, but almost any schoolboy in Hub would understand occult politics better than he did. And would the Four care enough about Inos even to rescue her, let alone put her on her throne? The wardens—three warlocks and one witch—were the occult guardians of all Pandemia. What sort of people were they? What were their real motives?

At that moment, the sun hooked a fiery finger over the horizon. The sky had unobtrusively turned itself blue.

"Go to Krasnegar!" Little Chicken growled. "Find woman back there." His khaki-hued skin was slick with sweat already.

"You'd like a good roll in the snow, wouldn't you?"

The goblin grunted. Rap went back to prying information out of the imp.

"How about the fairyfolk? Andor said he didn't meet any. He meant Sagorn, didn't he?"

"Yeah. They're rare now." Thinal halted and peered all around, shielding his eyes from the sun with a skinny hand. The first two fingers on it were of equal length. He evidently found nothing and began to walk again. "And dangerous, too. Headhunters, it's said." He stopped, frowning. "Lots of troops in Milflor . . . ."

"What's wrong?" Rap asked.

"Just . . . something odd . . . ."

"Faerie, you mean? What sort of odd?"

Thinal scratched his unkempt mop of hair vigorously. "I don't know. Why would the Impire guard Faerie so closely just because it's dangerous to visit? Why post troops to protect tourists from monsters and natives? There's no guards around Dragon Reach."

Rap felt suspicious. "Odd? What sort of odd? Whose idea is that? Sagorn's? Andor never mentioned that."

Thinal's feral features were suddenly completely blank. "Nothing. Just a city boy jumpy in the jungle."

"Out with it!"

"Nothing, Rap."

"I thought we were partners? We shook hands."

"Yeah. Sorry, Rap! But it's really nothing. I just get sneaky instincts when I see something being guarded.'' He smiled shamedly. "I'm a thief, see?''

"So?''

Thinal laughed uneasily. "I getta sorta itch when I'm near something worth lifting. I nearly went batty when Andor called me to Kinvale. He needed me to thieve a special brooch, but I wanted to loot buckets, and—''

"What,'' Rap demanded, "is worth stealing here?''

The lump in the thief's scrawny throat jumped. "Nothing I can see! Maybe I'm just going weird. Scary!''

He didn't look scared, though—he looked excited. Had he sensed that Rap's word of power was available in a way it had not been earlier? Rap could think of nothing else around that was worth any more than one stone dagger. He shrugged and kept walking.

"Thirsty!'' Little Chicken complained, glaring sideways at Rap as if it were his fault.

"Coconuts?'' Apparently Thinal understood some of his dialect, but of course Darad had spent time among the goblins. "You can get milk out of green coconuts. The dagger'll open them. Not the ones on the ground. Them up there.''

"I couldn't climb those trees!'' Rap protested loudly.

Changing direction and trudging toward the nearest palms, Little Chicken ostentatiously flexed his thick shoulders and spat on his hands. He welcomed any chance to demonstrate Rap's inferiority—which was what Rap had expected.

"Quick!'' he said, grabbing Thinal's bony shoulder to stop him following. "Tell me! Little Chicken insists he's my trash, but—''

"Oh? You're a slaveowner?''

Rap felt his face grow hot. "Not my idea! He thinks it's his duty to look after me—feed me, and even dress me. Not much else. I know he'll defend me in a fight.''

Thinal peered at him slyly. "Who wiped the imp?''

Rap's stomach heaved at the memory. "He did. Yggingi drew his sword and threatened me. He ignored Little Chicken, I suppose because he knew that goblins aren't dangerous.'' Little Chicken had taken the proconsul from behind, body-slammed him, applied a brutal headlock, and then slowly sawn through his neck with the stone dagger. Even while that had been happening, though, Yggingi had been trying to reach his fallen sword and Rap had kicked it out of the way. So he had been an accomplice.

After a couple of hard gulps, he added, "But I don't know if he was defending me then, or avenging all the goblins Yggingi killed. He won't run errands."

Thinal nodded, frowning at the sand. "He wasn't gentle with Darad. That hurt—I know! All this because you wouldn't torture him?"

"Yes. Darad has goblin tattoos—"

"Don't tell me!" Thinal pulled a face.

"But he must know! Little Chicken's waiting for some signal or other, from the Gods. When he gets that, then he's released from bondage and free to kill me, as slowly and painfully as he can."

"They're a gruesome pack." Thinal picked his nose for a while in silence. "I ought to know, Rap . . . but I don't. Darad wasn't interested in the slave thing."

"He enjoyed the alternative?"

Thinal shuddered. "Yes. Gods! I still dream about what he did to that boy. Trouble with Darad, he's been banged on the head so often a lot of his details are fuzzy to me. To him, too." He pondered a while longer. "I think . . . it may be something like saving your life. Yeah! Never let the goblin save your life."

Rap started to laugh. The little thief looked at him in surprise, realized what he had said, and grinned ruefully, again showing his irregular teeth.

The conversation was cut off by a yell from Little Chicken. Faun and imp ran across to where he was sitting in the sand at the base of a tree, cursing intently. He had badly scraped his belly and one thigh, and seemed also to have twisted an ankle when he landed. His opinions on palm trees were fortunately being expressed in dialect so broad as to be unintelligible even to Rap.

Thinal walked along to another tree nearby and flowed up it like a squirrel. In seconds he had reached the top and was twisting off coconuts. Little Chicken's tirade died away and he glared up disbelievingly at the despicably weedy imp. Then he glared even harder at Rap's smirk.

Burglars had their uses.

4

In the more than eighty years since Sagorn had visited Faerie, Thinal's memories of the event had become vague. He was fairly sure that Milflor lay somewhere on this eastern coast, but he had no idea whether the castaways were right to head north.

The jungle contained nothing any of them recognized as edible, but they chewed coconut and drank the milk until they were nauseated, longing for fresh water. Even under the palms there was little shade, and already the sun was brutal.

The goblin had an old pair of moccasins that old Hononin had found for him two days before, but he limped and he had lost his smug air of unworried superiority. Maybe his twisted ankle was more painful than he would admit, or he was suffering from the tropical climate, or the unfamiliar surroundings frightened him—or all three. He was no longer the skilled woodsman who had shielded Rap in the taiga.

Rap limped, also, being pinched by his borrowed boots. Faun half-breeds were not as heat resistant as he would have hoped.

Thinal was in worse shape than either of the other two. Andor's silver-buckled shoes would have been too large for his brother even when new and they had been split apart by Darad's enormous feet. Thinal soon threw them away and struggled along barefoot over the sand, his skinny legs laboring harder than they had done in a hundred years.

The headland seemed to withdraw as they advanced. It was hours before the beach had turned to face south and Rap began to notice the jungle narrowing. His farsight told him there was only more sand beyond the cape, but farsight's range was limited. At last the jungle faded away and there were only palms left. Soon his eyes could see through them, to another wide bay, as vast and deserted as the first. He had not known there was so much sand in the world.

On the point itself, sand gave way to rock. Rap and the goblin sank down and leaned back against boulders. Thinal was trailing, several hundred paces back, already looking boiled and mashed, as Rap's mother would have said.

"We should leave him!"

Rap smiled, for that had been a credible attempt at impish, although spoken with a heavy goblin accent. "We mustn't!"

"Why? Him . . . he . . . worse trash than me."

"Because he might give up and call Darad."

Little Chicken scowled, then nodded understanding. Darad's

arm would still be bleeding from the bites of Rap's dog, his back burned raw, and his eye bruised by the goblin's finger. Even in a good mood, the giant would not be a welcome companion. Mad, he would be literal murder.

Thinal arrived and sank wearily to the ground. He slumped back against a palm, and yelped when it scraped him.

Rap let him rest for a while before he spoke. "There are mountains."

Thinal twisted around to stare at the peaks now visible over the jungle. "So?"

"You can't recall seeing those from Milflor?"

"No." Thinal wiped his brow with a bony arm and brooded in sulky silence.

So Milflor was some way off yet. North or south? There seemed to be no way of telling. Rap's feet hurt already and the thought of retracing all those steps was unbearable. He decided to continue north. If the coast swung westward, then he would know they had made the wrong choice.

Offshore lay a reef, and from the headland he could hear the surf quite clearly and see pillars of spray walking along it as the waves advanced. Faerie would be a glorious place, he thought, with proper water and food and shelter. For a moment he let himself sink into a fantasy of this beach and those warm waves and a picnic with . . . with a beautiful girl. *God of Lovers!*— how she would enjoy this place!

His head lolled sideways. He jerked it upright. "Come on, then!" He rose.

Thinal had also been dozing. He snarled. "What's the piddling hurry?"

"I have to find Inos."

Thinal patted the sand. "Siddown, Rap. Listen. I know you won't trow this, but you're potty. She's in the hands of a sorceress, and an all-fired, real, four-word sorceress at that! She's somewhere on the far side of Pandemia—east or north, an' you don't know. An' you find her, if you ever, she'll be a grannie, and you'll be older'n Sagorn. Come on, Rap! Lay off!"

"I am going to find Inos!"

Thinal stared up at him balefully. "I know you're stubborn— but that's screwball! You don't know what you're saying."

"Coming?" Rap said. "Or will you stay here and starve?"

For a moment it seemed that Thinal was not coming. Then Little Chicken rose and stretched.

"You try better now, imp," he said, spooning out his words with care. "More later I carry you."

Glaring, Thinal heaved himself to his feet and began hobbling over the sand.

They headed north. They had hours of daylight left yet.

Waves marched in to die upon the beach—wave after wave after wave . . .

Behind the veil:

When you and I behind the Veil are past,
Oh, but the long, long while the World shall last,
    Which of our Coming and Departure heeds
As the Sea's self should heed a pebble cast.

Fitzgerald, *The Rubaiyat of Omar Khayyam*
(§47, 1879)

❰ TWO ❱

This day's madness

1

Sunlight gleaming along marble wakened Inos. For a moment she stared up blankly at gauzy draperies, striving to separate out their soft reality from bitter dreams of the tent she had shared with Kade in the long weeks of trek through the forest. Then awareness returned with a rush—death and sorcery; betrayal and bereavement.

But reality was not all sorrow. It was an unfamiliar silken nightgown soft on her skin; it was gossamer sheets and a bed that could have held a family of peasants and their livestock, also; it was high-arched windows imprisoning cutouts of peacock-blue sky. Also, it was morning; she must have slept the clock around. She had vague memories of being awake in darkness, memories of fear and grief, and she repressed those quickly. Had there been a tray of food beside the bed? She raised herself on an elbow and peered. There was no food there now, if there ever had been, but there was a small bronze gong.

Palace life might be very enjoyable, but her kingdom had been stolen from her, and she must see about getting it back.

Besides, she had never been more hungry in her life. Parting the draperies, she reached out and tapped the gong quietly, with a knuckle.

The reaction was immediate and almost embarrassing. A lanky woman swathed in black swept in through the doorway, hastened across the soft rugs, and sank to her knees; abasing herself as if Inos were a God.

29

"Good morning," Inos said cheerfully. "This is tomorrow, isn't it? Who are you?"

The woman raised herself to sit on her heels. She was old, her face deeply scored, and a tiny wisp of white hair peeking from below her head covering of snowy white. Her gnarled brown fingers glittered with gems, so she was no minor flunky. She might be a housekeeper, except she bore no keys.

"I am Zana, may it please your Majesty."

Majesty? *Oh, Father!*

"What are the chances of something to eat?" Inos inquired hastily. "And possibly even some hot water?"

About once an hour for weeks and weeks, she had been promising herself a hot bath at the earliest possible opportunity. She might have offered half her kingdom for one, had soap and towels been included. Inos had crossed the frozen wastes on a flood of imaginary hot water, but her wildest longings had never come close to envisioning the long-delayed consummation of her dream as it now appeared.

She was conducted deferentially along a corridor to a meadow-size bathroom containing a gigantic green marble tub. A team of black-draped maidens stood ready to assist, and before Inos could explain that she was quite capable of attending to herself, they were applying soap and oil, scents, powders, and ointments. Even music! Kinvale had never approached this.

Holy writ might claim that there was evil in every good, but Inos could find no evil in that bathtub except that she was too hungry to stay in it for another month. Robed at last in cool flowing garments of ivory silk, with her hair encased in lace and her feet in golden sandals, she was led along bright, airy corridors toward a promise of breakfast. Her way wound past high-arched windows offering vistas of a great city tumbling away in layers down a steep hillside. The shiny blue bay beyond was speckled with sails. Krasnegar was a fleabite compared to this place, and its palace a chicken coop . . .

Crazy—given the choice, she would take that shabby little arctic rock pile every time!

Then she came to a garden, enclosed by shrubbery, high walls, and an air of secrecy. Branches overhead cast hard black shadows, dappling grass so smooth that it must in truth be a green velvet tablecloth, and the flowers could only be silk, or possibly enameled gold. The sky was a fierce blue, the sun deadly, and the swiftly swooping birds were colored like nothing Inos had ever imagined.

And talking of birds . . . in a grotesquely domed gazebo of fretted marble, Aunt Kade sat like a caged dove, calmly nibbling sliced peaches.

Gold lace lay over her snowy hair, but otherwise she, too, was enveloped in white. Inos recalled far-off days of helping Ido in the palace laundry, when sometimes they had draped themselves in sheets to play at being wraiths of evil.

Then Kade looked up. Relief flashed in her faded blue eyes and she made as if to stand.

"Don't!" Inos said hurriedly and stooped to give her a kiss. They held each other for a moment—dear Aunt Kade, who ought not be bouncing around the world in such sinister adventuring, who should be settling in comfortably at Kinvale, good for another thirty years of fruitless knitting and conspiratorial matchmaking.

"You look very . . . austere," Inos said, tactfully not mentioning wraiths. "I haven't felt like this since the masquerade ball."

"I'm sure you would win a prize now, dear." Aunt Kade's inevitable good cheer was still present, and only a very close scrutiny suggested that it might be a little forced. Her pink cheeks were perhaps not quite so pink as usual.

"Best of Breed anyway." Inos released her. "This is a very pleasant dungeon, is it not?"

"Most genteel!" Kade in turn was carefully inspecting her niece for signs of wear. "Like something out of a fairy tale."

"Angilki would turn green."

"He would raze Kinvale to the ground and start over. I take it that you slept well, my dear?"

Mutual scrutiny completed, Inos settled on a chair as it was moved for her by one of the tall young servants. "I must have. I don't remember a thing." No need to dwell on tears in the night. "And you?"

"Very well. I looked in on you a couple of times, but you were out cold as ice floes." Just for a moment there was a hint there of an old lady who had been worried about someone. Then it had gone. "This melon is delicious. The coffee is stronger than we are used to, but there are fruits and pastries; and this fish, while unfamiliar . . ."

Inos glanced at Zana. "All of it," she said firmly.

The garden was shaded by trees she could not identify, and enclosed by marble trellises. The dome of the sky was an incredible cobalt, the flowers much too brilliant to be genuine.

Then, just to confirm the unreality, a thing like a jeweled insect floated for a moment above the table before Inos's startled eyes. She had barely time to decide that it was a tiny bird before it had vanished in a flash of rainbow. She began her survey again, looking around, trying to adjust to this unworldly setting, trying to believe that this was all real and that she had not somehow been transmuted into a hand-tinted lithograph in a romance.

Unfamiliar delicacies were laid before her on dishes of translucent china, and she attacked them with zeal. They were all just as delicious as they looked. Yet her mind kept chewing away at her troubles. Father dead. Rap dead. Andor an imposter. An army of occupation in Krasnegar, and another about to invade. Her claim to the throne rejected by the leading citizens. And what could she possibly do about it all, stuck here at the other end of the world?

The black-clothed maidens had floated away. Zana hovered discreetly in the distance.

"We certainly cannot complain about the hospitality," Aunt Kade remarked. Her eyes flickered a warning.

"Yes, I think I could learn to tolerate this," Inos muttered between mouthfuls, decoding: *Complaints may be overheard.*

She ate swiftly, and in thoughtful silence. Again she wished she had listened more carefully to Master Poraganu droning away her childhood. She could recall nothing of Zark, and all she knew about djinns was summed up in one piece of folklore she had overheard in Kinvale: *As honest as a djinn.*

But how, exactly, was that comment meant to be taken? Every race had its stereotypes, however unfair those might be in particular cases. A dirty child would be called a *filthy little gnome*, or a man *as strong as a troll*. Usually such remarks were meant to be taken literally—*mean as a dwarf*—but some were ironic. *An imp's secret* was common knowledge. *Gentle as a drunken jotunn?* And another she had learned at Kinvale: *Tell it to a faun.* What did *Honest as a djinn* really mean?

Well, Inos could hardly ask her aunt that now. "Have you . . . have you spoken with the sultana?"

"No, dear. But I expect she will be informed that you are awake now."

Again there was a curious rhythm in the words. Ladies at Kinvale soon learned how to pass silent messages under meaningless conversation, especially warnings. Aunt Kade was repeating her caution that a sorceress could inform herself. Talk could always be overheard—anywhere, at any time. Inos munched for a while in silence. But a sorceress could probably read thoughts, also.

"Imagine me sleeping round the clock! I wonder what they're doing in Kras—"

Oh, that had been stupid! She smiled apologetically at her aunt. Today in Krasnegar there would be a royal funeral. For a moment, blue eyes and green eyes communed in silence—it had been a release. His pain was over. *All things include both the Evil and the Good.* Inos had been able to say good-bye, and that was what mattered. That was why she and Kade had endured the terrible journey through the forest. Funerals were not very important. At the last weighing his soul would have prospered, the balance gone to join the Good. King Holindarn would have left no wraith of evil to haunt the world.

And Inos had given him a promise.

She attempted a smile. "Politically, I mean, of course. I wonder what is happening politically in Krasnegar now?"

Kade fumbled with a snowy linen napkin. "The Powers alone know! If Doctor Sagorn was correct, then the imps will all run away before the jotnar arrive. They may be back across the causeway already." She did not look pleased at the prospect, but the fact that she would even admit to having thought about it showed that she was concerned.

If the Imperial troops had gone, then Krasnegar's own imps and jotnar might well be at one another's throats by now. The jotnar would likely win hands down, given a fair fight, but the fight would not be fair, for the legionaries were imps, and they would surely tip the scales before leaving. And when the jotnar of Nordland eventually arrived to put Thane Kalkor on her father's throne—her throne!—then the tip would go the other way.

Or the imp half of the population might have fled with the Imperial forces, a tragic band of refugees. Or the imps might have driven the jotunn half out into the snow. Families sundered, friends become enemies . . . or . . . or . . .

Inos realized that she had stopped eating. Her hands could not keep the food moving, because her teeth had clenched. "I promised Father I would do what I could! I must go back!"

"I am sure that Sultana Rasha will be willing to advise us," Kade said solemnly, "and possibly even assist us."

Us? *Me!*

Inos thought back to the strange scenes of yesterday. "I'm not sure I like the thought of being utterly dependent on the sympathy of a former scarlet woman."

"Inos!"

"Do you doubt that . . . that . . . he . . ."

"Mistress Zana refers to him as 'the Big Man.' "

"Thank you. Do you doubt that the Big Man's description was truthful?"

"I don't think, as guests, we should give credence to vulgar gossip!" Aunt Kade assumed a very prim expression that Inos both recognized and detested; she had seen it often during her first few months in Kinvale, but not much lately.

"The fact remains," Kade said, "that we are her guests."

"I am Queen of Krasnegar!"

"No, you're not! You claim to be, which is not the same thing at all. You know no more about politics than I do, and you don't have an army up your sleeve. Her Majesty rescued us from the imps and has provided this superb hospitality. Certainly we must trust her judgment and good intentions." Kade took a sip of coffee as if that settled the matter.

Inos resumed her meal with a show of calm that she found unexpectedly tricky.

"Furthermore," Kade added, "you did not exactly go out of your way to enlist her sympathy at your last meeting."

Recalling the rowdy scene in the dome, Inos was aghast—shouting, arguing? God of Fools! "No! I was no credit to your training, dear Aunt!"

Kade smiled approvingly at this show of repentance. "Her Majesty realized that you were overwrought. After all, she did take you up to see the looking glass."

Inos nodded, and nibbled. "I suppose I should be glad she didn't throw me in the dungeons. Or turn me into a frog?"

"Hardly! I am sure that a brief note of apology will be acceptable, and certainly not out of place. Apart from that, we can but wait until her Majesty is ready to grant us audience." Kade dabbed at her lips with her serviette and glanced over the table to make sure there was nothing she had missed. She sighed comfortably.

Certainly she had earned a rest after those awful weeks on horseback in subarctic cold. Perhaps it was even understandable that a woman of her age would be content to settle down to enjoy some decadence—but Inos was not. Write a letter of apology like an errant child?

Well, yes. Maybe she had better do that much. Pride would be an expensive luxury at the moment, and she had not been tactful. Then sit and do nothing? Impossible!

"What exactly happened afterward?" Inos frowned. "Everything seems very hazy after I'd seen the looking glass."

"She put you in a light trance, dear," Kade said. "And sent us both off to rest. Prince Azak guided us himself, you remember."

"Not really. She . . . she undid whatever she had done to him?"

Kade nodded, apparently to a purple-flowered bush just outside the gazebo. "He seemed quite restored. A little shaky, was all."

What sort of a woman was this Rasha? She had tortured Azak barbarically, right before Inos's eyes. There lay some mystery that . . . *"Great Gods!* What's this?"

Her aunt chuckled, as if she had been waiting for that. "It's curried pineapple. I asked. Tasty, isn't it?"

Inos took a sip of an orange-colored draft and blinked tears away. "It ought to have a warning beacon on it. Mmm. Yes, not bad, when it doesn't jump out at you. What's pineapple?"

"A fruit, I suppose."

"Really?"

"I'm sure our stay here will be most educational. Travel is very broadening."

"Fattening, you mean?" Inos nibbled at something that tasted nutty. True, Sultana Rasha had been much more tolerant of Inos than of the unfortunate Azak. If one believed what had been said, then Rasha did not approve of men—any men at all.

How far could one trust a sorceress?

"You think," Inos said, "that our royal hostess would support the notion of a queen regnant in Krasnegar?"

Kade nodded noncommittally.

"Especially if the male jotnar objected?"

"Perhaps, dear."

"So . . . if her Majesty will forgive the way I shouted at her . . . then we can ask her to start by driving out the imperor's cohorts—I imagine a good sorceress could do that? Two thousand men?"

"I should think so. According to the poets, the warlock Quarlin defeated three armies singlehanded. Inisso built the castle in five hours, it's said." Kade looked smug at this efficient recall of ancient schooling.

"Well, then! Rasha can drive out the imps, and if Kalkor and his pirates sail in, then she can blow them away again, also?"

Kade pursed her lips. "We can ask, dear, certainly."

"And then all we need to do is to persuade the townsfolk themselves to accept me! Perhaps they're now sufficiently scared by their narrow escape to be reasonable?"

Inos considered that program for a few moments. Somehow it lacked a sense of progress; it seemed to leave her back about where she had been two days before. "And when I explain that I didn't mean to bring the legionaries . . ." She paused again. "Of course a suitable husband would still be an important factor, I suppose," she admitted sadly. A cold wave of regret washed over her as she thought of Andor—not the real Andor, of course, but Andor as he had seemed to be. The husband problem was not going to go away.

Then she realized that her aunt was not cheering, or otherwise displaying patriotic enthusiasm. Inos eyed her crossly. Kade, unfortunately, did not recognize politics as an occupation suitable for ladies of quality.

Inos took a fruit knife and reached across the table to tap her surprised companion on both shoulders. "Princess Kadolan, I hereby dub thee our royal chancellor, chamberlain, seneschal, and . . . well, that will do for today." In the ensuing silence, Inos heard a boy's voice say: "And I will be sergeant-at-arms and master-of-horse both . . ." *Oh, Rap, Rap!*

Kade frowned at such levity. "If I am designated your chief advisor, Queen Inosloan, then my advice is to restrain your ambitions until you have consulted Sultana Rasha."

"Why, pray?"

"Well, even though Krasnegar isn't in the Impire, I do believe there's a rule against using magic on the imperor's army." She settled back on her chair, pouting as if annoyed at having revealed even that much intelligence.

Unfortunately, on the rare occasions when Kade made a definite statement about anything, she was invariably correct. Rap had said something along those lines, too. Evil take it!

"The throne is mine by right of birth!" Inos thumped a fist on the table. "And I want it! Not because I think being queen of Krasnegar is any marvelous honor, but because I have a duty! I promised Father! Gods! If comfort is all I want, then I should certainly choose Kinvale—or even Arakkaran. Why should I want to go live in the tundra? You know that, Aunt! I've got royal blood. That's a ticket into almost any noble family in the Impire."

"Inos! What a disgusting—"

"It's true, and you know it! I could easily find some witless aristocratic husband and settle down to growing fat and making babies in luxury for the rest of my life—if comfort was all I wanted. But our family has always given Krasnegar fair, honest government. Maybe the imps and jotnar don't exactly live in peace together, but at least they live and let one another live. They settle their disagreements with knuckles, not blades. Usually.''

''Yes, dear, but—''

''But without our house to rule, the imperor and the thanes of Nordland will both feel bound to protect their own, and the war will start soon. If it hasn't started already!''

And where would it end? If the Nordland jotnar won in Krasnegar, the imps might seek retribution against any other jotnar they could find, and there were jotnar scattered along every coast in Pandemia. If the imps won, then the Nordlanders might start their raidings again, as they had done periodically throughout history—as they still did, in a small way, all the time.

The trouble was, Inos decided angrily, that she had been cheated. Had she been a boy, then she would have been taught politics and strategy and tactics. She would not have been sent to needlework classes at Kinvale, but to fencing lessons. She might even have attended the Imperial Military Academy in Hub—her father had spent time there. Not singing madrigals, but drilling soldiers! Not the ladylike art of conversation, but intrigue, machinations, and unscrupulous scheming—those were what she needed! She knew nothing about sorcery or imperial politics or Arakkaran's relationship with the Impire. She wasn't even quite sure where Arakkaran was. In Zark, yes, but where was Zark? Bottom right, with Krasnegar top left . . . Master Poraganu, why did you not make me listen better?

''You are not quite of age, yet, dear.''

''I am a queen!''

''You are not behaving like one,'' Kade said sharply. ''At the moment you are a penniless refugee in a very distant land. Sultana Rasha is your only hope. And even if she is willing to help, as she promised, good manners require that you show decent gratitude for what she has already done, and also wait a reasonable time before you start pestering her.''

Inos glared; her aunt glared back—and Kade's normally mild and rather watery blue eyes were capable of chilling into a very icy stare at times.

Suddenly Inos was back in Kinvale again, a much grander

version of Kinvale. She was not of age, true. She was penniless, also true. Helpless—not a friend . . .

Then an interesting idea began to take shape. Not all of the skills she had gained at Kinvale were completely useless; now might be the moment to apply some. There was one person around who would certainly know a great deal more than she did about magic and politics and their dangerous combinations; even if he was a barbarian at heart. *If you don't ask, you don't learn.*

Evil! That had been one of Rap's many little homilies. Rap had always had more proverbs than the sea had fish. He—

Forget Rap! The point was that Azak could be a valuable and disinterested advisor, if he chose to be. His views on Rasha herself would certainly be informative—there was no love lost there, obviously. And Inos thought she knew how to supply motivation in such cases. There were no official lessons in that art at Kinvale, but in practice it came ahead of anything on the curriculum.

Kade might not approve, especially if she suspected Rasha would not.

Inos made a decision. "I am rightful Queen of Krasnegar! My kingdom has been stolen from me, and I swear by all the Gods that I will do—"

"Inos!" Kade's voice rang like a blade striking armor, with all the menace of her jotunn forebears. "Do not tempt the Evil!" She made the sign of the holy balance.

Inos glared stubbornly at her. Well, she wouldn't say it. But she meant it—*do anything!*

When she did not speak, Kade relaxed, and was at once apologetic for her unseemly outburst. "You must learn not to be so impetuous, dear," she said reprovingly.

Ha! Impetuous? Just wait!

"Will you approach the sultana for me, Aunt?"

Kade sighed. "If you wish."

And Inos would seek out the Big Man.

2

Having dashed off a brief note to Sultana Rasha apologizing for yesterday's ill temper, Inos passed the writing materials to Kade. They had settled down to letter writing in a truly charming sitting room decorated with frescoes of flowers and vines.

Wide windows looked out on the cool greenery of the garden, on its fountains and sensuously vivid blossoms.

Zana had been quite astonished when her charges had asked for paper and ink—so astonished that Inos at once suspected Zana herself must be illiterate. It had taken some time for the requested articles to be fetched, but now Inos had done her part, while managing to convince herself that she was doing it of her own free will. Kade had begun to pen a note requesting an audience with the sultana, and Kade could be counted upon to take at least an hour to do so.

A little exploration seemed called for, but if Inos should just happen to get lost, and just happen to find herself somewhere in the sultan's vicinity, then who could say what interesting conversations might ensue?

She slid quietly out into the corridor. She was not too surprised when Zana materialized in front of her.

So now she had two jailers, not just one?

"Something your Majesty requires?" Zana was close to old age, her face a sun-baked desert landscape. Although her eyes were the shade of a robin's breast, they were also sharp as flint, and they peered down at Inos without blinking.

"Ah, there you are, Mistress!" Inos said blandly. "Little notes are all right for ladies, but not for gentlemen. I wonder if you would convey my respects to the . . . Big Man . . . and inform him that I am anxious to wait upon him at his earliest convenience?" If Zana were indeed illiterate, then verbal messages would seem quite normal to her.

Zana smiled. She had a disconcertingly wise sort of a smile. It hinted that Inos was being much less subtle than Inos thought she was. On the other hand, it did not seem particularly sinister. "I shall see that he receives the message as soon as he returns this evening, ma'am." The upper part of her tall shape swayed forward, as if caught by an invisible wind.

"You are too kind!" Inos returned the bow and stepped past, intent on having a voyage of discovery, alone.

She had gone about six steps when the dry old voice said, "This is not the Impire, ma'am."

Inos stopped, turned, and considered. "Obviously."

"These apartments are very extensive, Majesty. It is quite easy to become lost. At least take Vinisha along as a guide?" Snapping her fingers, Zana produced one of the younger attendants in a feat of legerdemain that Rasha herself could hardly have bettered.

Vinisha was no older than Inos and no taller, short for a djinn. She wore the standard black garb, including a cloth over her hair, only her face and hands exposed. That face, already pink, was turning pinker as she waited for Inos's decision.

"Of course," Inos said cheerfully. She was being bribed with a chance to interrogate Vinisha, who would certainly have been chosen for her discretion, but it was a fair trade, and a guide would admittedly be advisable in a place this size. "If my aunt asks for me, pray inform her that I shall be back shortly."

All her life, Inos's closest friends had been the children of her father's servants. At Kinvale she had befriended the domestics quite successfully until Kade convinced her that it was kinder not to. She thought she might handle Vinisha better than Zana expected.

"I'm just curious to explore the guest apartments," Inos said, striding along the wide corridor. "No, please walk beside me."

Vinisha moved to her side obediently. She had beautiful features, and she moved with a sinuous grace that Inos knew she would never master. Even on skates, she could not move like that.

"Is there anything special I ought to be looking for?" she asked. "Any fine works of art?" There was nothing much to be seen in the corridor, unless stained-glass skylights were worthy of note.

Vinisha looked blank. "No, ma'am."

"Well, what's the best way to go? How many rooms are there?"

Blanker. "I don't know, ma'am."

Vinisha had not been chosen for her discretion. Vinisha had been chosen for her stupidity. Inos sighed.

"The sul . . . The palace must entertain a lot of guests?"

Vinisha's eyes flickered at Inos and then straight ahead again—blankly, of course, and now worried, also. "I don't know, ma'am."

Inos let two cross-corridors and a large hall go by before she tried again. "Well," she said as cheerfully as she could manage. "These are very extensive apartments for catering to visitors."

Relief! "These aren't normally guest quarters, Majesty. They were Prince Harakaz's habitation."

"Were?"

"Yes, ma'am. He died very suddenly."

"How sad! A close relative of the . . . the Big Man?"

"A brother."

"Tragic! This happened recently?"

"Just a few days ago." Vinisha was not reluctant to talk, once she was on a subject she understood. "His quarters and chattels had not yet been reassigned, and Mistress Zana thought we might enjoy entertaining royal ladies."

Inos paused at a junction and then headed for a shady cloister, flanking another jewellike garden. It led to a wide and promising flight of stairs. Vinisha floated along at her side. A group of women in black stepped aside and curtsied. The steps were wide, carved in sumptuous black and white stone. The walls were plain white marble; already Inos was becoming so inured to marble that she hardly noticed it.

"And who is Mistress Zana, exactly?"

"The Big Man's eldest sister."

Already halfway up, Inos glanced wonderingly at her companion. "Then she is a princess?"

Vinisha looked puzzled again. Inos waited patiently. She could hear voices up ahead, faintly.

"I'm not sure what a princess is, Majesty."

This was not the Impire, Zana had said.

"Then what is a sultan's daughter?"

"A woman, ma'am."

The conversation was making no sense to either of them.

The stairs led to yet another corridor, with large arched windows. Inos noted a dazzling view of the city and the bay, but she was not in the mood for admiring scenery. She was becoming extremely baffled and anxious not to show it.

"Zana looks old enough to be Azak's mother, or even his grandmother."

That observation won no reaction, so was apparently not remarkable. At the next junction Inos paused, then headed in search of the voices.

"Then by what title should she be addressed?"

"Just Mistress Zana, or 'ma'am,' ma'am."

Another bend brought the sound closer and also brought more windows, with a vista of a wide park. In the distance men were riding horses. Now that was promising!

"Oh, I love horses! Do you ride, Vinisha?"

Vinisha's beautiful eyes opened about as wide as was possible.

Inos sighed again. She swung away from the window and tried not to break into an unladylike march. She went back to personalities, as those seemed to be about her companion's limit for conversation. "Is she married—Zana, I mean?"

A puzzled headshake. "Not that I know of, Majesty."

"Funny. She sort of seems so . . . motherly."

"Oh, yes! She has borne five sons."

Inos gaped. "And how many daughters?"

The djinn blushed and did not answer. Evidently that question was improper.

Inos's view of Arakkaran as a larger, richer Kinvale was crumbling rapidly. "But never married? Who was their father?"

Vinisha frowned in thought. "I'm not sure, ma'am. More than one, likely."

May the Good preserve me! What would Kade say to all this?

Now they were passing doors, all leading to very splendid bedchambers—large and airy, furnished in fine furniture and silks. The beds were very large and looked comfortable. Kinvale had boasted nothing finer. Obviously the late Prince Harakaz had been a very important personage.

The corridor ended at yet another door. It was ajar, emitting sounds of children laughing and playing. A classroom? Inos hesitated, suddenly reluctant to push that door fully open; afraid of what she might find. Many children, obviously, and she could hear women's voices, also. Babies crying? A nursery?

She clutched at the one attractive idea that had come out of this bewildering exploration.

"I suppose if I wanted to go riding, that could be arranged? For a guest, it could? Couldn't it?"

Vinisha's face registered desolation. She seemed close to tears. "Riding, Majesty? On horses? But . . ."

"But what?" Inos snapped.

"But you'd have to go out!"

"Out of what?"

"Out of this habitation."

Inos took a deep breath. "Prince Harakaz's habitation? These quarters?"

Vinisha nodded vigorously, looking relieved.

"You mean you don't? Don't go out? Not even into the rest of the palace? Never?"

Each question brought a vehement headshake.

God of Mercy!

A word spoken earlier suddenly registered. "You said 'chattels'! Reassigned? You were . . . You didn't mean . . . You meant you! *Assigned* to him?"

Vinisha nodded solemnly, seeming more confused and worried than ever. And Inos could feel her own face burning; she must be the redder of the two now.

"Exactly what were your duties for Prince Harakaz?"

"*Exactly?*"

"No!" Inos said hastily. "In general."

A wide smile of relief restored Vinisha's face to its normal youthful beauty. She laid a hand on the door. "Would you like to see my baby?" she asked hopefully.

3

Inos eventually discovered the main door without having to ask. It was locked, and a peek through a window told her that there were armed guards outside. What she had believed to be the palace itself was merely a minor mansion assigned to the late Prince Harakaz, and he had been one of the junior princes—that much Vinisha knew. The whole palace complex seemed to be larger than the towns of Krasnegar and Kinford put together.

In a dark mood, Inos returned to Kade and found her happily inspecting the unfamiliar flowers in one of the enclosed gardens.

The day only got worse as it went along. The royal guests were welcome to enjoy all the comforts of these quarters, but no, it would not be possible for them to leave without the Big Man's permission—or Sultana Rasha's, of course, but Zana firmly refused to discuss the sorceress. Nor would she say much about "the Big Man," either.

Once Inos had thought of Kinvale as a prison. This place might be even more luxurious, but it was even more of a prison.

The note to Rasha brought no reply, and Zana explained patiently that the Big Man would very likely be off hunting, so he would not receive Inos's message until he returned at sunset.

Inquiries about Azak and Rasha—how long they had respectively reigned, what their relationship was, how the people felt about them—all were politely declined. Even Kade began to look restless. Her cheerful talk about enjoying a welcome rest after the rigors of the long forest trek started to sound hollow.

The day grew crushingly hot. Inos indulged in another protracted bath, reflecting that she had several dozen to make up.

Kade experimented with a wide variety of sweetmeats and unfamiliar foods. Inos counted forty women in the "habitation," some old, some barely nubile. They were polite, charming, and completely incapable of discussing anything except themselves and their children and the exciting prospect of being assigned to the household of some other prince in the near future. Vinisha had not been stupid; she had been typical.

Inos also tried counting babies and children, and lost track at thirty-something.

Zana admitted that she did not know how many princes there were in the palace. Hundreds if you counted all the boy babies, she said. Adults . . . maybe a hundred? But any royal male with a mustache was an adult, with a household of his own.

And yes, even those would have women *assigned* to them.

This was not the Impire. By all the Gods, this was not the Impire!

"Djinns are worse than jotnar!" Inos stormed to Kade when they happened to be alone for a few minutes.

Kade blinked her pale-blue eyes reproachfully. "Krasnegar jotnar, maybe. I don't know about the Nordland type, though."

Remembering the stories of Thane Kalkor, Inos quickly changed the subject.

Just after sunset, Zana excitedly informed Inos that the Big Man had received her message and would pay his respects to her the following morning. That seemed promising, although puzzling. Should not the visitor be paying her respects to the host?

After some thought, Inos went and told Kade of the appointment. To have kept it a secret would have been to admit that Kade was in charge, and Inos was determined that she was now queen, hence senior. Kade merely enthused, as was her custom, and did not inquire why she had not been consulted—thus making her niece feel infuriatingly guilty.

And a few minutes later Zana appeared to both of them with the information that they were invited to attend the state dinner that very evening, apparently a rare honor. If the formalities were to take place the next morning, dinner parties should have come afterward, surely? This was not the Impire.

Inos indulged in a third bath and reveled in the luxury of letting herself be dressed in an even softer, filmier gown. Dubiously she permitted a mantilla over her hair, but then the attendants produced a veil, intended to hide her face below the eyes. By now she desperately needed to score a point or two, and she adamantly refused to wear it. That led to an argument with Zana herself. The Big Man already knew what she looked like, Inos said, and this was the only face she had, and she wasn't ashamed of it. Zana yielded reluctantly, with deep disapproval. It was only needed until the guests arrived at the dinner, she protested—guards and other lowly men would see. Let them, Inos retorted. Kade stayed out of the discussion, which meant that she approved, and she did not wear a veil, either.

Zana herself was included in the invitation, apparently. She had discarded her black in favor of a fine gown of ivory silk, with much jewelry and a pearl-embroidered wimple that made Inos want to whistle in astonishment. Leaving their large band of attendants twittering in approval, the three ladies swept off to attend the state dinner.

Across parks and courtyards, they were escorted by six enormous guards, all armed with scimitars and extensive collections of other blades around their persons. Two of them even wore coiled whips on their belts. Their torches sent sparks whirling up into the warm night to meld with a breathtaking skyful of stars. Kade chattered about feeling excited, and Inos reluctantly agreed. This exotic land certainly had overtones of romance and adventure.

Would there be dancing? Inos inquired of Zana. Sounding rather puzzled, Zana assured her that almost certainly there would be dancing. Inos smiled in secret satisfaction, confident of her ability to impress on a dance floor. That gangling young sultan had moved with a slinky grace that promised he would be an admirable partner.

About a dozen other . . . er . . . ladies of the palace . . . had been invited, also. They were all young, all sumptuously over-dressed, and their excitement at the unusual honor of attending a state dinner soon overcame their shyness at being in the presence of strangers. Their conversation, regrettably, was confined entirely to domestic topics, such as childbirth and teething.

Rasha did not appear.

The food was excellent; Inos could not deny the quality of the food, unfamiliar though the dishes were. And the wine was superb. The service could not be faulted.

The banquet hall was magnificent, lighted by more candles than there were stars beyond the great dark windows. Azak himself was there, resplendent in the green of royalty, with his glittering emerald cummerbund plainly displayed. He lounged on a divan, one of a great circle of divans, all bearing princes. Inos counted twenty-five of them, from graybeards to striplings.

What ruined the evening for her, though, was that she and all the other women sat in a high gallery, shielded by a fretwork

screen so that they could watch the exciting events below them
without themselves being observed. The only females down on
the main floor were the scantily clad belly dancers who per-
formed at the end of the evening, right after the jugglers and
fire-eaters.

4

Inos was rarely at her best in the very early morning, and her
audience with Azak—or his audience with her—was set for dawn.
Had she still held any doubts that she had been transported far
beyond the bounds of civilization, an appointment for that hour
would have convinced her otherwise; but she was ready on time,
and so was Kade. And they did not wear veils.

When the royal guests set off for the audience chamber, they
were flanked by Zana and six of the older women, all veiled and
swathed in black. Eight of the fearsome brown-clad guards escorted them. Protecting them from what? Armed guards within
the palace itself? This time the journey was even longer.

But despite her early-morning sulks, Inos found the audience
chamber breathtaking. The great hall at Krasnegar would not
have made a pantry for it. High-arched windows stretched off
along both sides and the mosaic floor shone like a treasure chest,
wide as the Kinvale skittle field. Even the emptiness was impressive, letting the soaring stonework display its own naked
beauty. That was in striking contrast to the overfurnished mish-
mash of Rasha's chambers. Obviously the sorceress lacked taste.
The rest of the palace glowed with it, even on this enormous
scale, when grandeur could so easily have become vulgar osten-
tation. Inos glanced at her aunt and saw that she, also, was
mightily impressed.

The two of them were conducted to a low dais that seemed
designed to support a throne, but there was no throne in sight.
They stood in awed silence, instinctively edging closer. Zana
positioned herself and the other attendants at their rear. The
others were whispering excitedly, as if this were the first time
they had been allowed out in years.

Time passed. Inos felt the beat of her heart, and it was speed-
ing up as her anger began to grow. She did not understand the
backward etiquette. As visitor, she ought to call on the sultan,
but to keep her waiting when she had been placed in the position
of honor was deliberate afront.

Then the pale light slinking through the high arches blushed swiftly golden pink and brightened to proclaim sunrise. A trumpet blared, and a small procession wheeled in at the far end of the hall and advanced, with Azak's unmistakable height in the vanguard. Behind him marched at least a dozen other men, all of them clad in various shades of royal green. A squad of guards entered, also, but remained by the door.

The procession halted before the dais, and for a moment the two parties surveyed each other in silence. Inos took her first close look at Arakkaranian princes and was not impressed. They ranged in age from fresh-faced boys to grizzled elders, but those that could, wore beards. None was as tall as Azak, but they were all ruddy-skinned, red-eyed djinns, and despite their gems and the fine cut of their garments, they seemed a rough, fierce crew. To a man, they were scowling at her in shocked disapproval. She was not accustomed to having men disapprove of her appearance, but the distaste was mutual—she thought she would sooner trust a longshipful of unwashed jotnar.

There was no doubt who was captain of these pirates. His turban, glowing today with pearls, stood clear above all the rest. As he had when she first met him, two days before, he wore a loose tunic and trousers, plus the same wide jeweled belt that would have purchased a kingdom. But now his pants were tucked into high boots and his cloak was of heavy stuff, with a hood thrown back and long slitted sleeves dangling unused at his side. These were obviously outdoor garments, and his scimitar was a more serious weapon than the one she had noticed on him the previous morning. Azak, Inos assumed, was now in his work clothes.

Abruptly he snapped his fingers. A slim youth stepped stiffly forward a few paces and stopped. His red djinn complexion had paled to a sickly pink, his fists were tightly clenched, and something about the way his eyes moved told Inos that he was terrified. Sweat shone amid the fuzz of his mustache. He glanced around. Azak nodded impatiently. One of the older men frowned and nodded, also.

The boy turned back to face the visitors. He swallowed and licked his lips. Suddenly Inos knew what was about to happen, but before she could object, it had happened.

In a quavering tenor the youngster announced: "His Majesty, Sultan Az—"

He was gone; life was gone. His clothes remained, stirring in the eddies of the wind, but they enclosed only a statue of shiny pink granite. As a likeness it was superhumanly perfect, in every cruel detail—mouth still open, eyes inlaid in cinnibar and mother-of-pearl, staring fixedly at nothing. Kade stifled a cry, and Inos felt herself shudder. Azak ignored the transformation. He strode forward two paces and doubled over in one of his gymnast's bows, with the same elaborate gestures he had used before.

Then Inos saw that the older man in the background was beaming proudly, and she felt a moment's relief. To proclaim Azak sultan within the palace brought down the curse, so he was using it as a test of loyalty, or courage. It had been the boy's turn, that was all, and the others' lack of concern showed that the sorceress would remove the spell before long.

Inos was still much too icily furious to say a word. She curtsied. Azak was a step lower, but his gaze was level with hers, and for a moment they stared at each other, as if each were waiting for the other to speak. He had noted the absence of a veil, obviously, but she could read nothing in his expression except arrogance. There was plenty of that. Young Azak thought he was spectacular, and in a ferocious sort of way he was undeniably handsome. With his ruddy face framed by the trim line of beard, with his fierce hook nose and flashing red-brown eyes, with his overpowering height and physical presence, Azak clearly believed a woman should feel like swooning whenever she looked at him.

He might not be too far wrong, damn him!

His neck alone was remarkable.

On the other hand—gander saucing goose—his own inspection of Inos could not be described as desultory. At their first meeting she had looked like something washed up by a flood; now she was better prepared. She was not quite jotunn height, but taller than an imp. She wore no veil. Her lace mantilla did little to hide her honey-gold hair, which must seem as much a rarity to him as green eyes.

Show him! Even dressed in a tent, she thought she should be able to raise male blood pressure merely by fluttering her lashes. Thus.

Yes, his pupils dilated satisfactorily.

She wondered about her own pupils, and who had come out ahead. Evil take him! Barbarian!

Having expertly appraised her and allowed her a chance—however inadequate—to admire him, Azak bowed again.

"Your Majesty is an honored guest in this, the humble house

of my fathers. If anything at all is lacking to make your stay more enjoyable, your Majesty's whims command the nation.''

Without waiting for a reply, he bowed to Kade. "And your Royal Highness, also.''

Kade curtsied, while Inos struggled with her anger—and lost. Rashness won over caution. If this troll-size savage required his followers to suffer petrification just to soothe his bruised arrogance, then he obviously put a very high value on courage, and Inos was not going to be outdone in that, despite Rasha's warnings. A brief sojourn as a statue might be a restful experience anyway.

"We are deeply honored by this opportunity to visit with—'' She took a deep breath. "—our cousin of Arakkaran.''

Kade uttered a small cry of alarm, but nothing occult transpired. The royal courtesy had been too subtle for the curse to detect. Azak had noticed, though. His eyes widened, and something like a small smile flexed his beard.

With her heart still thumping madly, Inos pushed her luck a little farther. "And we welcome the chance to view the beautiful kingdom of Arakkaran . . . blessed with so noble a ruler.''

This time even the mob of lackeys caught the circumlocution. Glances were exchanged, lips pursed. Azak beamed and bowed again, lower than ever.

"Your Majesty is most gracious!''

Her Majesty was quivering with terror at what might have happened, but was determined not to show it. "I trust that you have fully recovered from your ordeal, Cousin?''

Azak's eyes glinted again, but he faked bewilderment. "Ordeal, Cousin?''

"Two days ago? When we first met, you seemed to be smitten quite severely for a while. An agonizing experience, I think?''

"Ah, yes!'' He waved a large hand dismissively. "The slut sorceress seeks to break my will with mere physical pain. She should know by now that the effort is wasted.''

Inos displayed shock. "It has happened before?''

Azak shrugged, but his face was bright with pleasure at this opportunity to inform his followers about the incident. "Many times. Pain is nothing. She also inflicts plagues upon me: vermin or suppurating sores, disabilities in major organs. I have been struck blind, crippled . . . I expect she will learn in time that no prince of Arakkaran can be swayed from his duty by such trivia.''

Uneasy expressions flitted over the faces of those princes of Arakkaran then present.

"But what can she hope to gain by such atrocities?" Inos exclaimed.

Another shrug. "Voluntary recognition of her ludicrous claim to an unmerited title. I will not submit if she chars my bones. But now, if there is nothing more that your Majesty requires at the moment . . ."

But there was! This futile little ceremony was all a fake, a game that Azak had accepted to suggest Inos was his guest and not Rasha's. Inos had played along for him, so now it was his turn.

"Well . . ."

"Yes?" Azak stopped halfway into a bow.

"I am most eager to view some of this beautiful kingdom—" Just in time Inos stopped herself adding "of yours." The narrowness of her escape took her breath away.

"Of course! A carriage and escort . . . some ladies of high station to accompany—"

She had already noted his high boots and drawn conclusions. "You are going riding, Cousin?"

Several hairy mouths behind him fell open in shock, and even Azak blinked. "You ride?"

"I do. Is that surprising?"

"Peasant women ride donkeys, I suppose."

"In the Impire ladies of the highest rank ride, many of them very well. And I could certainly use a little exercise right now." Plus a long talk about sorcery and politics and running kingdoms and military campaigns and things.

Kade uttered a small moan. "I suppose if we do not actually—"

Inos turned to her and smiled sweetly. "No need for you to come with us, Aunt."

"Inos! I . . ." Kade was shocked speechless.

"I am sure that I shall be perfectly safe in the company of . . . our cousin of Arakkaran. Is that not so, *Cousin*?"

Azak's hot eyes flickered from niece to aunt and back again. Inos hoped she was conveying challenge, not entreaty, but for the moment the sultan was obviously nonplussed.

"I shall be quite safe, Aunt. Surely you will not insult the . . . our royal cousin by implying otherwise?"

Kade stuttered, flushing.

Clearly Azak had other plans for his morning, but he was

aware of his debt to Inos. He swallowed hard, the corners of his beard flexing cutely. "Of course I shall be delighted to escort your Majesty in person." He was a terrible liar.

"Wonderful! Who else could better show a queen the kingdom?" Still Inos remained unpetrified—the curse was obtuse at detecting innuendoes. "If I may have about ten minutes to change? I hope that my riding garb has been cleaned . . ." She glanced around at Zana, who was quite boggle-eyed at the conversation, but who nodded in agreement. "Ten minutes, then?" Inos extended queenly fingers.

Azak shied backward as if she had stabbed him. For a moment his face showed something that Inos thought might be horror. She wondered what terrible offense against the customs of Zark could be represented by a lady offering her hand to be kissed. Then the huge young man jackknifed himself in another great bow.

He straightened with ill-concealed fury. "However long your Majesty requires . . . I am at your service always."

Of course he was! Inos curtsied demurely, rewarded him with a last flutter of eyelashes, and departed in search of more suitable clothes without another glance at her aunt.

Ally-gathering was about to commence.

5

Inos took longer than the ten minutes she had promised. She took even longer than the thirty minutes she had planned, but eventually she was ready and was led down yet another staircase to where the sultan stood with arms folded and toe tapping. The delay had been caused mostly by the need to find someone who could braid up a lady's hair—a rare art in Zark, apparently. Then Zana had insisted on waiting for a suitable cloak to arrive. Inos had protested that her riding habit alone would be much too warm for this climate and she wanted nothing more, only to be informed in firm, motherly tones that she must wear a cloak of dark material, loose and airy—not for warmth, but to keep off the sun. Wind and dust, also, but mainly sun.

Azak acknowledged Inos by folding himself in another acrobatic bow. She attempted to respond in kind—Ooof!—riding habits were not designed for such maneuvers. The princely gaze wandered arrogantly over her again in blatant appraisal. Then he presented the four companions who were all that remained of his earlier entourage. All four were princes with guttural-sounding names, but the relationships puzzled her. The eldest was one of Azak's brothers, much older than he, thick-bodied and bushy-bearded.

She caught the name of the next—Prince Kar—and decided at once that she did not like his blandly penetrating smile. He was clean-shaven, another brother, yet still older than Azak.

The other two were uncles, identical downy-faced striplings about her own age, obviously twins. She made mental notes to have Kade disentangle the royal family of Arakkaran for her; Kade was a genius at such genealogical investigation. The laws of succession might be worth knowing, also, to explain how a reigning sultan could have older brothers.

The princes and their guest set out for the stables—a journey long enough in itself to have justified horses. Azak did not speak and he deliberately strode so fast that everyone else had to scamper along breathlessly at his side. Inos concluded peevishly that this young giant still had a lot of growing up to do.

And again there was an escort of hard-looking guards armed with enough weapons to furnish a military museum. Her father had walked alone anywhere in his kingdom, yet this so-arrogant juvenile sultan needed protection within his own palace!

When they emerged from the last arched doorway and struck out across open courtyard, Inos felt sunlight hit her like a falling roof. It took her breath away—it would melt horseshoes. She knew she had been rash; now she wondered if she had been crazy.

Even the grandeur of the palace had not prepared her for the magnificence of the stables, whose tiled roofs seemed to cover a small city. An ocean of silken paddock stretched off to faraway fences and trees shampooed in pink blossom. Above them the crenelations of the palace itself gleamed against the distant sea. Many men and animals were standing around in the open glare, waiting, but there was not a woman in sight. Probably these royal boors were finding her behavior shameless and outrageous.

So it was mutual!

Among this crowd she made out several who had been with Azak earlier, and many other men in green—some already mounted, others inspecting steeds and equipment—and obviously they had waited around only to view the extraordinary phenomenon of a woman on a horse. Once that was concluded, they were going hunting. The unfortunate five, Azak and brothers and uncles, gazed with undisguised longing at this mob of

men and horses, grooms and kennelmen, bystanders and attendants. Dogs strained at their leashes and cadgers stood ready
with birds.

Inos felt a twinge of real guilt. "I see that I am intruding on
your sport, Cousin. I was very presumptuous. My sight-seeing
must wait until another day."

Azak glanced down at her with exasperation—a sultan who
had announced a decision could not then change his mind.
"There will be many more days for hunting, Cousin."

"I would almost prefer to come along and watch," Inos said
with maidenly innocence, "if that were permissible. I have never
witnessed hawks flown. Those are hawks, are they not?"

"Goshawks."

"Ah. We used gyrfalcons in the north, of course."

Ten royal eyes lighted up like signal lanterns. "Gyrfalcons!"
the two young uncles echoed in awed tones.

"You . . . yourself?" Azak said.

"Certainly."

Five royal faces went stiff with shock. Obviously a woman
on a horse was a minor obscenity compared to a woman hawking.

"My favorite was Rapier. Very fast, very responsive—oh,
how I miss her! Father flew a golden eagle for a while, but he
had very little luck with her. I tried peregrines a time or two at
Kinvale, but I learned with gyrfalcons. There are no others at
Krasnegar."

The princes exchanged glances that might have conveyed
doubt or outrage or both.

"Let us see you mounted first." Azak almost put a hand on
her shoulder and then withdrew it hastily, gesturing her forward.
With the four princes trailing behind, they paced over the springy
turf to where two horses stood apart from the others within a
cluster of stablehands. One was a gigantic black stallion, undoubtedly the largest Inos had ever seen, jerking and prancing,
stamping, keeping three grooms both busy and worried. Krasnegar's ponies were hardy, shaggy beasts, but she had thought
that Kinvale's were the best that wealth could buy. This polished
ebony marvel could have eaten them alive. She knew who would
ride that one.

She turned her attention to the sad little plug standing beside
it, and any residual guilt she was feeling dissolved in a wave of
indignation. A longer look turned indignation to fury.

"*Cousin!*" she said in a slender voice that would have frozen any member of the palace staff in Krasnegar. "What is the meaning of this? My father would have had his hostler flogged for that!"

"Your Majesty?" Azak stared down at her, his rosewood eyes filled wide with puzzled innocence. He really was a terrible actor.

Inos's voice went even softer. "Well, if you can't see from the way she's standing, then perhaps you should ask the groom to lead her around for you—if he can!"

The old mare was back on her heels, hopelessly foundered. With a rider on her back she would be as immovable as the palace itself. The quartet of princes exchanged glances of appreciation that Inos found both satisfying and infuriating.

"Ah!" Azak threw up his hands in sudden enlightenment. "My apologies, Cousin. I had not recognized . . . I thought it had been fed to the dogs already. The groom responsible was hard dealt with, I assure you. You! Take that rubbish away and bring a more suitable mount for the queen."

"Something more like that one," Inos said.

Error!

The watching princes guffawed. Hairy gibbering apes!

Azak's teeth flashed in the sunlight. "You are welcome to ride Evil if you wish, Queen Inosolan."

She had pushed too far. She had been angered by the cruelty of allowing a dumb horse to eat itself to death, and infuriated by the arrogant assumption that she would not know a foundered horse when she saw one—and so she had pushed too far. Eagles and gyrfalcons and now this. She opened her mouth to make a smiling refusal, and her anger said, "Well . . ."

Dare she try? She had just completed weeks of riding through the taiga—she had never been in better practice. She had ridden Firedragon once, although Rap had been present then and horses were always well behaved when Rap was around. *Stop thinking about Rap!*

But wait! Yesterday she had lamented the uselessness of her Kinvale training. She had forgotten that she had other training. She had been taught to ride by a young man who knew horses as no one else did, who could always tell you exactly what a horse was thinking. Here was a chance to pay tribute to his memory.

With her heart going insane inside her chest and every nerve screaming warnings, Inos walked over to take a closer look at

Evil, a mountain of shiny blackness without a single white hair on him. If Gods were horses, They would look like this one. She offered to pat his neck as Rap would have done. Evil lifted a groom off the ground and rolled a menacing eye at her. The men clinging grimly to reins and cheekstrap glared at her resentfully.

Inos glanced around the wide paddock. There was lots of room.

She was a queen now. They had tried to foist a decrepit jade on her first. What sort of hack or vicious beast might they try next? A sultan's mount could be nothing worse than high-spirited.

"Shorten the stirrups!"

Azak's stupid smirk became instant fury.

"No man has ever ridden that horse but me."

"That will still be true." Inos met his stare, trying to show much more confidence than she felt.

"Queen Inosolan, that horse is a killer!"

Possibly so, but she could not back down now. Besides, Rap had always insisted that there were no such things as one-man horses. Of course, Krasnegar's little herd had contained a couple of rogues that no one but Rap had ever dared approach—but that was irrelevant. Certainly Azak would be a superb horseman; in whatever he did, he would settle for nothing less than mastery. So the horse had been well trained. Anything more was just a matter of manners.

"Did you or did you not say I might ride him?"

Now Azak was boxed in, also. He was too furious to back down, but the ember-red eyes studied her for a long hot minute before he growled, "Do as she says!"

Grooms flocked around to adjust the stirrups, then retreated hastily, leaving one man waiting with cupped hands and another at the stallion's head. Both looked terrified. A third was poised on the far side.

Inos eased out of her cloak and passed it to someone. She stepped closer; Evil showed his teeth and laid down his ears. His withers were higher than her head, his saddle the size of a barn roof. How would her knees ever find a grip on such a monster? It was a type unfamiliar to her, with a very high pommel, but she had seen its like at Kinvale, and she remembered a trick she had heard mentioned there. Certain that an instant's pause would snap her nerve, she took the reins and reached up to bind her left hand to the pommel with them. She had to stand on tiptoe to do it. Evil rolled an angry eye. Inos raised a boot for the waiting hands.

She seemed to fly higher than the highest dome of the palace. Men grabbed her feet and thrust them in the stirrups, leaping out of the way in the same moment. The groom at Evil's head was hurled aside by Evil himself and the saddle rose straight up . . . Inos had never been hit by anything so hard as the impact of that saddle. She was staring down at a fleeing Azak, seemingly far below her, framed by Evil's ears.

Hooves hit the grass. *Impact!*

He bucked. *Impact! Impact! Impact!*

Then Evil was standing erect, front legs dark against the sky. With her face buried in his mane, Inos felt as if she were trying to climb a marble pillar. Her knees and thighs screamed at the strain. Came the sudden reversal and she hurled herself back to meet the rising rump . . .

Impact! More bucking . . . *Impact! Impact!*

Without warning, Evil took off, cracking Inos's neck like a whip. She was moving faster than she ever had. The paddock was suddenly tiny, the blossom trees at the far side rushing straight at her in a blur of white and pink. He would leap that fence or go straight through it. He would smash branches with her. She kicked and tugged to turn him, and the stallion stopped dead. Her knees slid, her shoulder struck in his mane, and only her hand bound to the pommel saved her from disaster. A moment later he tried to bite her and she kicked him in the jaw. Then he wheeled, bucked again, reared again, was hit again, screamed with fury and launched himself forward again. Grooms and princes scattered like leaves as she bore down on them. He turned in midair. He skittered sideways on four straight legs. He had more tricks than a prestidigitator.

Again she saw sky straight ahead. *Impact!* Then grass. *Impact!* Sweat was blinding her. Her spine was rammed into her skull. Then into the saddle. Skull again. Trees coming up ahead again. She caught glimpses of eggshell palace domes against blue, green turf, pink blossom, white fence, black horse, white, blue, black pink white black-blue-white-greenbluewhite . . .

Her legs were breaking with the strain of gripping. She was dead—nothing could survive this. How much longer . . . get it over with . . . back to bucking again . . .

The next few hours were all very exciting, but just when she had concluded for the hundredth time that she had lost, suddenly, inexplicably—shivering, dancing, foaming—Evil surrendered. He dropped to a trot. Feeling a great surge of triumph, Inos kicked him into a gallop. Again they rushed at the fence, but now she was in charge. Up they went. The top rail was higher than she was, but Evil seemed to grow wings and fly. Power!

He landed as gently as a falling petal. No wonder Azak did not want to share such a marvel! She circled him, flew him back into the paddock again, and cantered sedately over toward the onlookers, rejoicing at the steady leaden thud of the great hooves on the grass and the wilder beating of her own heart. Triumph! Now those hairy-faced boors knew that a woman could ride.

Now she would be one of the boys!

But there was no cheering. Spectators scrambled back, clearing a path all the way to Azak himself, who was standing with arms folded and red murder blazing in his eyes. Inos reined in, just as a thunderclap of reaction struck her. Suddenly she was shaking, soaked in sweat, fighting not to have hysterics. Any minute now she would bring up breakfast. She thought she had sprained a wrist and bruised every bone . . . But she had done it, damn it! Hadn't she? She was one of the boys now, wasn't she?

Evil was in no better shape—foam-flecked, white-eyed, every muscle jittering. Everyone else was cowering away in silence from the sultan's fury.

"Flogged, you said!" Azak roared, so loud that Evil shuddered. "Flogged? Any groom of mine who treated a horse like that would be buried alive!"

"Huh?" No praise? No congratulations?

"What do you plan to do with him now, wench? Oh, you stayed on! I admit you stayed on! But he'll not be fit to use for days, or weeks. Look at him! Would you like to try ruining one of his brothers next? Or perhaps you'll accept something you can handle?"

Inos slid unaided from the saddle, and it was a long way down. Her knees almost folded with the impact. She straightened and thrust the reins at a groom. With a great effort she straightened her chin and clasped her hands tightly behind her. Then she managed to look up into Azak's glare.

"Something I can handle, please," she said. "And then let's get on with the hunt."

6

Evening at last . . .

With her face politely frozen in a Kinvale-style smile of interest, Inos strolled along palatial avenues, mounted grandiose staircases, and crossed majestic parks. Despite the leisurely pace, she was straining every muscle and nerve in her efforts not to limp. Would she ever dare sit again? She moved within a worshipful company of at least a dozen princes. They gazed at her with wonder and admiration, this green-eyed, golden-haired woman who could ride a horse, fly a bird, shoot a creditable arrow, and who claimed to be queen in her own right. Arakkaran had never met such a marvel.

The marvel felt like a shipwreck. Her eyes burned with dust and sun, half the sand of the desert clung within her hair, and little more of this maltreatment would give her a complexion fit to smooth planks. But she had survived the day. She was one of the boys.

She had not obtained her confidential chat with Azak, so she could not claim total victory. However awestruck the rest of the royal princes, the sultan had ignored Inos ever since she relinquished Evil. Most of the time he had been barely visible in the distance, usually the far distance, leading suicidal charges over the rocky hills. So Inos could claim no victory, merely a draw that would let her fight again tomorrow. No hawking tomorrow; tomorrow the princes were going coursing. Revolting!

The aged and portly prince on her left was panting out an interminable tale about a dagger, a rockslide, and some unfortunate goat he had slaughtered long before she was born. A much younger one on her right was continually edging too close, fingers straying. Stars were appearing in the darkling sky.

Idly Inos swung her riding crop on her right and felt a gratifying impact. "Incredible!" she murmured to the left as the narrator ran out of breath on the stairs. That was wrong! *Fascinating!* had been next on her list. She must keep them alphabetical, and not be so gauche as to repeat herself. Still . . . not long now. The procession took off along flat ground, and the goat killer picked up his tale again. Fingers moved in again.

At last the Gods were merciful, and she reached the entrance to her quarters. Guards sprang to attention, eyes wide at seeing such an escort. The door opened on an unobtrusive signal. Inos turned and smiled at all the princes.

"Your Royal Highnesses, my thanks! Till tomorrow?"

Fifteen or sixteen royal turbans swung forward in salaam. Inos bowed in turn, suppressing a whimper of agony. Then— divine mercy! She was inside and the great door thumped shut.

She leaned back against it as a tidal wave of questions broke over her. She was facing what seemed to be the entire female population of Zark, all jabbering excitedly, with Zana vainly trying to restore order. But of course these were merely the late Prince Harakaz's women, all eager for news of the day's miracle.

For a moment Inos felt a great surge of annoyance. She wanted a bath and a massage, perhaps some food, and then lots and lots of sleep. She did not want to recount her life story! Then her annoyance gave way to pity. And it was oddly flattering.

She raised a hand, and the babble died down to a few wails from bewildered babies. "Later?" she said. "Yes, I did go hunting with the princes. But later, please! After I've had a bath and changed, I'll tell you all about it!" She smiled as sincerely as she could manage and tried not think about a long evening ahead.

With excited promises of hot water and food ringing over a renewed clamor, Inos limped off behind Zana in search of Kade.

Their way led through a chain of rooms, and then outside, to a high balcony. Flocks of gaudy parrots soared by, screaming mockery. The sky was a canopy of cobalt suede hung over the Spring Sea, and a couple of earlybird stars shone above the ever-dancing palms. Down in the bay, the white sails of dhows and feluccas glided toward their roost like ghosts of owls.

Nibbling dates and holding a book at arm's length in the fading light, Kade was reclining on a sumptuously overstuffed divan. A frosted carafe of some cold drink stood on a table beside her, and the very sight of it made Inos's mouth ache.

Every joint screamed as she sank wearily—and very carefully—onto the cushions at her aunt's side. She was suddenly aware that she had not thought about Father all day. Nor Andor.

Zana was already pouring something musical into a goblet. Kade disposed of the book and smiled with eyes like winter sky. "Had a good day, my dear?"

Inos made a guttural croaking noise and drank. Oh, glory! Ice! Cold lemonade! What sorcery was this? "Marvelous! And terrible. I feel like bread crumbs—dried out and mashed up. But I do think I made an impression, Aunt."

"I'm sure you did."

Zana tactfully floated away.

Gods give me strength, Inos thought. But she had certainly treated Kade rather cavalierly that morning.

"I'm sorry if I took you by surprise, Aunt. You know me—impetuous! It just seemed like a wonderful opportunity to, er, meet the local gentry."

"You always were good with birds, of course."

Inos almost choked on her second draft of the miracle elixir. "You saw?"

Kade nodded. "Her Majesty showed me in the looking glass—just a few minutes, while you were riding out. Did you catch anything worthwhile?"

Inos's hawk had reduced one unfortunate rock dove to blood and feathers, but that might not be what Kade meant.

"Nothing of any importance." About to mention that the chase would resume in the morning, Inos changed her mind. "Patience is the mark of the successful hunter, Father always said." She began tipping a third cool draft into her internal desert.

Kade was not amused, obviously. Her niece had been behaving in unladylike fashion. "When I was having tea with her Majesty—"

Inos spluttered again. Memories of Kade's pompous little tea parties at Krasnegar and the awesome dowagers' rituals in Kinvale blended into an image of her aunt sipping tea with a djinn sorceress, and together provoked a typhoon of coughing. As soon as she could breathe she said, "Then you have made better use of your day than I have!"

"Possibly. She showed me many things in her looking glass." Kade sighed as if she were discussing the latest outrage in dress styles. "I really had never conceived how *useful* sorcery could be! Imagine—here we are, in faraway Zark, and yet she could show me what was happening almost anywhere! Kinvale, for instance! We saw the duke supervising the bedding out. It's springtime in Kinvale. Yes, a looking glass is a wonderful device. Everyone should have one!" She considered her own words, then amended them. "Persons of quality, of course."

"And Krasnegar?"

Her aunt's face darkened. "We didn't . . . We were too late. The funeral must have been held yesterday."

Inos blinked, and nodded. "And the imps?"

"They're still there. They look as if they're settling in to stay." A rare expression of anger showed on Princess Kadolan's normally convivial face. "They've turned the great hall into a barracks! They're using merchants' stores as stables!"

Inos leaned back against the cushions, wincing. If Arakkaranians used smaller bathtubs, they could fill them faster. Raucous parrots swooped by again.

"And what happens now? When does Kalkor arrive with his jotnar? What—"

"I could hardly *cross-examine* her Majesty!"

"Of course." Inos sighed. Kade would keep the tale going all evening.

"Queen Rasha did confirm what we suspected, though. She can't just evict the legionaries for you. Only the warlock of the east is allowed to use sorcery on Imperial soldiery."

That closed off one path to sanity. "I see. And a warlock is stronger than a mere sorceress?"

Her aunt cleared her throat warningly, her we-may-be-overheard noise. "Their respective strengths would not matter, dear. Any sorcerer breaking that rule incurs the enmity of the Four combined. That's part of the Protocol."

"But the thanes can still use force, when they arrive?"

Kade pulled a face at the thought of violence. "Oh, yes. Force is mundane. No rules apply. I mean, that's what force means, doesn't it? But while the imp soldiers are the domain of East—Warlock Olybino, of course, is an imp himself—similarly, jotnar are reserved to the warlock of the north, and she's a goblin. I mean the warden happens to be a witch at the moment, Bright Water. Not all jotnar, just the Nordland raiders."

Inos had never heard her aunt lecture on politics before. It was a staggering development, but it must mean that she had won the confidence of Queen Rasha. She had therefore put her day to much better use than Inos had; no wonder she was so pleased with herself! However muddled the telling might be, the facts would be correct, for although Kade believed that well-bred ladies should appear scatterbrained, she could apply her wits well enough when she wanted to. Then the significance sank in.

Inos sat up straight, heedless of her aches. "You mean that imp versus jotunn means one warden against another?"

"Well . . . not just any common brawl, dear, but if the Nordland fleet clashes with the Imperial army, that does seem to be one possible result. Seapower and landpower. The sultana says that this has happened very rarely since Emine set up the Protocol, only once or twice in all history. It could involve the wardens. It could even split the wardens, two against two. That apparently can produce all kinds of disasters. The jotnar aren't there yet, of course. It may be a long time before their ships can reach Krasnegar. Queen Rasha says she could disperse any other army with no trouble—a good blizzard would not be difficult to arrange, she says. But in this case she dare not try to influence either side; not the imps there now, nor the jotunn raiders if they come. They're both out of bounds for her. Like dragons, she said."

"God of Turds!"

"Inos! *Really!*"

"Sorry. But this is awful! This is terrible! Remember when Andor brought the news to Kinvale, about Father? We talked? We wondered if the town would accept me? We thought neighbor might quarrel with neighbor. Then the imp army moved in, and it wasn't just neighbor against neighbor, it was thane against proconsul, raider against legionary, Impire against Nordland. Now you tell me it's warlock against witch?"

"It may come to that," Kade said cautiously. "The Four may not even be aware of the problem yet, of course."

"Who would win?"

"Impossible to say, apparently. Bright Water is very old, and . . . unpredictable, I'm told. Olybino is quite young by sorcerer standards, her Majesty says, but he has a bad temper and may do foolish things on impulse."

"That's wonderful news! Just wonderful!"

"And the other two may side with one or the other."

"Or split? Bad, bad, bad!" Inos noticed Zana hovering in the doorway, meaning that her tub was ready. But baths now seemed much less important than they had before. An account of the occult politics of the Impire—of all Pandemia—was very important indeed. Even Doctor Sagorn had complained how hard it was to obtain information about magic; the sorcerous did not normally take the mundane into their confidence. Kade had won a tremendous victory! The information could not be confirmed, but what reason could a sorceress ever have for lying?

"Tell me about the other two wardens?"

Kade nodded almost imperceptibly to show she had been expecting the question. "Both warlocks. South is an elf, Lith'rian. Queen Rasha was, er, rather disparaging about . . . about elves. Usually there are two witches and two warlocks, but West died about a year ago, and a warlock took her place.

Zinixo, a young dwarf. An extremely powerful sorcerer, the sultana says, and something of an unknown quantity.''

"Died?"

"Was killed."

Inos thought for a moment. There was must be more, but her aunt was apparently reluctant to volunteer any of her own conclusions.

"So what does her Majesty recommend?"

"She suggests we wait and see, of course. The imps may flee. The jotnar may or may not come. Hub may or may not interfere—the imperor, the Four . . . Meanwhile, we are welcome guests. She has invited me to visit her again tomorrow, and of course you—"

"I am going hunting again tomorrow."

There was still quite enough light to show Kade's disapproval. It would probably have shown up in total darkness. "How many other ladies will be there?"

"None, I expect."

"Inos, you are being very unwise! Very! Even in the Impire, a lady would not go hunting without some female companionship. Here in Zark they have even stricter—"

"It's all right, Aunt. I'm one of the boys now." Gingerly Inos started to rise.

"I am quite serious, Inos! Customs differ, and you have no idea what sort of impression you may be making."

"So they won't invite me to their dinner parties again, you mean?"

"So they may think you a complete wanton!"

What exactly was an *incomplete* wanton? How could she possibly get into trouble going hunting with a gang of *princes*? "What did the sultana think?"

Point to Inosolan.

Kade pursed her lips. "She was amused," she admitted. Rasha, of course, while a queen and a sorceress, was emphatically not a lady, and Kade must be having trouble reconciling that discrepancy.

"What is Rasha's interest in my . . . our affairs? Just aiding a poor defenseless woman?"

The question sprang another warning cough. "I'm sure that's part of it. The best hope, of course, is that cool heads will prevail. Surely Krasnegar is not worth a war to either the imperor or the thanes. The Four may simply agree to put you properly on your throne. That would be the status quo, as near as possible.''

So Inos was a pawn in a much vaster game than she had ever dreamed. If the warlocks themselves were involved, then anything might happen. Krasnegar might be melted down, or moved to Zark, or turned into chocolate pudding.

Krasnegar! She was homesick for Krasnegar!

She drained the last of the lemonade and pushed herself painfully to her feet. She certainly had enough to think about while she soaked.

This days's madness:
> Yesterday This Day's Madness did prepare;
> Tomorrow's Silence, Triumph, or Despair:
> Drink! for you know not whence you came, nor why:
> Drink! for you know not why you go, nor where.
>> Fitzgerald, *The Rubaiyat of Omar Khayyam*
>> (§74, 1879)

⟮ THREE ⟯

Some little talk

1

"No people?" Thinal said. "You're sure about no people?"

"No, I'm not sure!" Rap retorted. "It's right at my limits. I'm sure about the huts. I don't *think* there are any people. None on the path, anyway. And what choice do we have?"

It was late afternoon on their third interminable day. The sandy bays had followed one another without respite, some broad, some narrow, but all of them devoid of streams or rivers. The castaways had survived on coconut milk and a few meager sips of rainwater caught on leaves in the frequent showers, but they were all weakening fast. They needed food and, above all, they needed drinking water—copiously and soon. They needed rest and shelter. Little Chicken was furious that these woodlands were so unlike his home forests. In the taiga he could have survived indefinitely with no tool but fingernails; here his survival skills were little better than Rap's.

The scanty and unfamiliar diet had made all three of them ill. Thinal was close to collapse, and his feet were raw. At times he had allowed Little Chicken to carry him, and then they had moved faster, but even the brawny goblin was failing. His moccasins were worn away by the abrasion of the sand, his ankle was swollen, and obviously only his contempt for pain was letting him walk at all.

Rap's boots were no great advantage. He had torn strips from his loincloth to bandage his blisters, but then he had merely developed other blisters in other places. Walking on sand was worse than running in snow; his legs ached in every muscle and joint. The shallows provided firmer going, but sand and sea-water together were agony on raw flesh.

At least the westering of the sun let them walk in the palms' dappled shadow, but high tide had driven them up into shingle and shell banks at the top of the beach, with every step real torment for the imp and the goblin. And then Rap's farsight had solved the strange problem of where the rain went. The lushness of the jungle proved that rain was frequent; the absence of streams seemed inexplicable. Snapping out of an exhausted daze, he had realized quite suddenly that there was a river a short distance inland, paralleling the coast, a river that was capturing all the rainfall. A river meant fresh water and it must join the sea somewhere, although here it was unreachable, shut off by undergrowth as thick as hay bales.

And then, as he forced his farsight out to the limits of his range, he had detected a path, a narrow strip of bare reddish soil winding through the trees. One end opened on the beach just around the next headland, the other lay on the riverbank. There were buildings there.

"Tell about huts," Little Chicken growled. He was becoming surprisingly proficient in impish.

"Just huts." Rap's head was aching with the effort. "Eight or nine of them. In a half circle. And some things made of poles. Little buildings, thatched . . ."

"Headhunters!" Thinal wailed. "Fairyfolk are headhunters!"

"What choice do we have?" Rap said again.

Thinal glared at him, his foxy features sour with pain. "You don't have any. But I do."

"You promised."

"Then I'm un-promising! You get me into danger, Master Rap, and I call Darad! I said I'd warn you. I'm warning you now." It was astonishing, really, that the little guttersnipe had endured as much as he had.

"Okay!" Rap said. "You've done very well. More than I would have expected. You stay here, and we'll go ahead and scout. If it's safe, we'll come back and get you."

Thinal looked around the beach. Not much of it was visible at high tide, with the waves surging almost into the palms. No food. No water. No company. "I'll come," he said grouchily. "But I'm warning you—if anyone's head's going to decorate a pole, mister, it ain't going to be mine."

2

"People?" Thinal whispered, almost bumping into Rap as he stopped on the path.

"There's nothing alive in the village except chickens," Rap said. "And nothing moving in the jungle." He wasn't quite lying, but he hated even being devious. "Look behind that bush."

Thinal just stared mutinously where Rap was pointing; it was the goblin who pushed in and parted the leaves. Rap already knew there was a dead dog there, with an arrow in its hindquarters. It must have dragged itself away to die.

Snorting angrily, Little Chicken pulled the shaft from the rotting, buzzing carcass. He returned to the path. Thinal whimpered.

"It's a long arrow," Rap said. "Fairyfolk are small, aren't they?"

Thinal shrugged, but Rap was sure Andor had told him that fairies were black-skinned and little taller than gnomes. Long arrows would need long arms, surely. The point was made of iron, sharp and barbed. "It's like what the legionaries carry, isn't it?"

"Don't know," Thinal said. "Darad would."

"How far, Flat Nose?" Little Chicken asked.

Rap squared his shoulders. "Just around the next bend. Come on." He resumed the painful monotony of moving one sore foot in front of the other, leading the way.

Once there had been a dozen huts in the village, clustered in the shade at the perimeter of a clearing, but four of them were ruined, probably burned. The poles that had puzzled him at a distance were scaffolds for drying nets; a Krasnegarian should have recognized those. He could also make out wickerwork privies and chicken coops, a couple of boats—and a well. The thought of water was making every cell in his body scream.

Then he rounded the last curve and an explosion of cackling startled him; birds flapped across the ground in terror and vanished into the trees. Rap headed for the well, and his companions put on a spurt behind him.

Water! Praise the Gods! Water and more water . . .

Slaked inside and out, soaked and dripping, the three waifs forced uneasy smiles at one another. Very uneasy smiles—there was something terribly wrong about this abandoned settlement. Four huts burned, no people, a dead dog. Thinal's shifty gaze was even jumpier than usual; the goblin's angular eyes had narrowed to slits.

The little clearing was well hidden. The path to the oily dark river was short, but it was narrow and would be hard to detect from the water. Upstream lay other, larger, clearings planted with crops, but even those somehow suggested concealment. The calm jungle air was heavy and sticky; the insects numerous and savage. Rap slapped and flapped and cursed, as his companions were doing, and wondered why his mastery didn't extend to insects, and why anyone would choose to live in such a place when the shore was so much more pleasant.

"No people?" Thinal asked for the hundredth time. "You can't see anyone at all?"

"There's nobody moving," Rap answered cautiously. He tore his farsight away from one particular spot near the edge of the fields and began to scan the huts. The trouble was, he didn't trust Thinal as far as he could have thrown Little Chicken, which was no distance at all. The imp's nerves were as tattered as his feet, and any nasty surprise was going to bring Darad in his place in a flash. He had not replaced his canceled promise.

And the goblin was almost as bad. In the northern forest he had been doggedly insistent that he was Rap's trash, his slave and servant. He had not mentioned that recently. Here, far from his familiar haunts, his customs and habits were being shaken and undermined. He had always been a threat at Rap's back, but now the tradition that had stayed his bitter hatred was weakening. He was becoming less predictable by the hour.

Thinal ended his cautious scrutiny and hobbled toward the nearest hut. The goblin unconsciously drooped into a tracker's crouch as he began quartering the ground. Rap followed Thinal.

The cabin was small, its leafy roof low. The walls were made of flimsy wicker and no higher than Rap's waist, leaving an open space all around below the eaves. In that steamy climate this might be adequate shelter, however impractical it seemed to Rap's northerner's eye. He ducked in through the doorway, but then he had still to keep his head bent below hanging nets full of small gourds and tubers—the family larder, presumably. They reminded him how ravenous he was.

Woven mats covered the floor. Thinal was already rummaging through some rattan hampers in a corner. There was no other furniture except some clay pots, a couple of rough stools, and rolls that were likely bedding.

Thinal straightened with a sniff of disapproval. He flashed an unexpected grin. "A thief would starve to death here! Wouldn't he?"

"Dunno."

Chuckling, Thinal limped over to another corner and flicked aside the mat to reveal a wooden disk set level with the dirt. By then Rap had sensed the pot buried underneath.

"How'd you know about that?"

"Professional secret!" Thinal sniggered and hauled out a handful of beadwork. "Darkest corner. Necklaces . . . bangles? Junk!" He tossed it aside. "Coral and shells and pretty, pretty junk! No metal. No stones."

Rap left him to his petty pillaging and went out to look for the goblin, whom he found studying one of the hearths. He greeted Rap with a mirthless, disbelieving show of oversized fangs.

"No people, Flat Nose?"

"One," Rap said softly. "Ran for the woods. He's still there."

Little Chicken nodded, little mollified. He pointed at the charred ruins. "Anything in there?"

Rap scanned casually—and then more closely.

"Gods! Bones?"

"No boats. Marks of many. How many people lived here?"

A factor's clerk should be able to estimate that. "Forty? No, nearer sixty, counting kids."

Little Chicken nodded agreement and grinned again. "Now count the bodies." He chuckled at Rap's shudder and walked off, apparently following some sort of trail, despite the deepening shadows.

Rap sat down in the dust to ease his feet and began the gruesome task he had been given. Bone was hard to distinguish from charred timber, but two of the ruins seemed to contain none and he realized with relief that many of the remains were those of dogs. In the end he was sure of only three human skeletons. Even so . . .

He rose and went to report. Little Chicken was standing inside one of the undamaged huts, peering up at the rafters. Here the storage nets had been cut down and thrown in a corner.

"Three," Rap said, and was tempted to add, "sir." The

goblin was back in his element, evidently. Now his grin showed real happiness.

"See here?" He pointed at the flooring. "Blood!"

Rap knelt. The stains were barely visible in the dust, and quite dry. "Maybe."

"Is blood! Spattered. See on walls?" In his excitement, Little Chicken had reverted to goblin dialect. "And up here? Marks on wood? Rope!"

"What are you suggesting?"

"Flogged. People hung up here and flogged. Only whips would splash walls like that."

Rap heaved himself to his feet, feeling sick. "You have a gruesome imagination!" he snarled, and stalked out into the brighter light of the compound.

Maybe. But Little Chicken was an expert on torture.

3

Fire snapped and cracked, working on green wood, throwing nervous shadows around the tiny settlement and wafting pale coils of smoke lazily upward. It was certainly not needed for warmth. Little Chicken had said it would drive away insects; he had been wrong, and likely he just found fire reassuring. Overhead, the stars were hidden by cloud. Rain threatened.

An imp, a faun, and a goblin—all far from home, Rap thought wryly, and far from happy. In the gathering dark they sat on stools around the fire, too weary for the effort of making conversation. Now and again the others would start, glancing warily at the encircling jungle. Rap did not need to look at it; he was keeping it under surveillance constantly, but nothing was moving out there.

The imp had never been robust; now he looked wasted. Blotchy stubble made his narrow face seem dirty, yet did nothing to hide the pustules and blackheads. All his bones showed as he gazed despondently into the flames.

Firelight had given the goblin's skin the greenish tinge that Rap remembered from the winter nights. He was leaning his elbows on his knees, staring at the coals; worried and resentful at being out of his element. His sunken cheeks emphasized the breadth of his face and his long nose, but he was certainly in better shape than either Rap or Thinal.

And the faun? He at least had a purpose, and somehow that purpose had made him leader of this itinerant disaster. He felt woefully unqualified to lead anything, having achieved nothing with his life so far except a string of disasters. He had betrayed his king in a futile attempt to warn the king's daughter; he had failed Inos herself when he should have accepted two more words of power to become a mage. She had called out to him, and he had failed her again.

He needed help.

Rap coughed. Little Chicken looked up and Rap nodded: *now!*

The goblin rose, swatting bugs. "I will bring more firewood," he announced loudly. He was a lousy actor, but Thinal was engrossed in watching the embers and did not notice. The goblin faded away into the shadows.

Compared to Little Chicken, a butterfly was a noisy blunderer. Quieter than starlight, he circled around behind Thinal and took up position as Rap had requested earlier, raising a woodsman's ax high, as if poised to split the imp's skull. Rap rose stiffly, clutching a slender fishing spear. He limped closer to Thinal, who looked up with understandable alarm.

"Don't worry," Rap said. "It's not you I'm after. I want a favor."

Thinal flashed a nervous toothy smile. "What's that, Rap?"

"I'd like to talk to Sagorn."

Thinal grinned in relief. "Sure." He tugged at the thong around his waist, loosening the knot.

"About time!" Sagorn said.

Rap had been expecting the transformation. He had seen it done before, yet he was just as shaken by the instantaneous substitution as he had been the first time. He still felt there ought to be some sense of change, of one person melting into the other, but there was none of that. The swarthy little imp was gone and in his place sat a tall, gangling old man, calmly adjusting the loincloth to fit him.

His thin white hair was unruffled, as it had been when he vanished from Inisso's chamber. He was clean and freshly shaved. Somehow he could still project a sense of superiority, even wearing nothing but a rag. His skin was pallid and limp, hanging wearily on his bones, and he smiled an old man's thin-lipped smile. Firelight deepened the clefts framing his mouth to gashes.

Rap took a deep breath. "I want your advice, sir."

"You need it, you mean. You are a very determined young man, Master Rap. However, I give you my oath that I shall recall

Thinal. I assume that your henchman is standing behind me with another spear?"

"A stone ax."

Sagorn raised spikey white eyebrows. "Hitting Darad on the head would not be a gainful procedure. You could only make him madder. But I give you my word."

Rap had been very careful not to look toward Little Chicken. Sagorn had guessed he would be there. He was demonstrating his superiority, seeking dominance.

"But you will not mind if Little Chicken stays there? After all, I have no reason to trust you."

Sagorn's wrinkles deepened in the smile that always reminded Rap of an iron trap. "As you wish. But I bear you no grudge. Darad will not be called by me. I give you my word on that."

"Thank you," Rap said awkwardly.

"So you want my opinion of this village?" Sagorn's gaze wandered around briefly. "As Andor told you, I never met a fairy. Vicious headhunters, it is said. The city is well fortified."

"The doorways here are low, the beds short."

"So I saw—Thinal saw. Obviously this is a fairy settlement."

Rap had already come to that conclusion. "But what happened? Why is it deserted? Or is it?"

"Probably one band of fairyfolk attacked another . . ." Sagorn frowned, peering up at Rap's face, which could not be very visible to him against the fire. "You have reason to think otherwise?"

"Bedding, cooking pots, nets, food?"

The old man tugged his lip. "You are right. Those would be looted."

"There are bones in those ruins."

"So?"

"Three skeletons. Three skulls."

"Mmmph! You may be ignorant, but you are not stupid, my young friend. So if not headhunting, then perhaps it was a reprisal by Imperial troops?"

"Do legionaries flog captives to death?"

"Yes."

"But for what?" Rap said. "I thought headhunters used their victims' skulls as trophies? There is nothing like that here—no heads on posts, no posts to stick 'em on, even. Those things over there are for fishing nets. All the weapons we found look like hunting equipment. No swords. The arrows are small, bird size, not barbed. This is a fishing spear. Ask Little Chicken."

The pale jotun eyes glinted at him in the firelight. "You are more astute than I thought, Master Rap. When I first met you, in the king's study . . . I underestimated you. You have grown a lot since Jalon met you in the hills last year."

Rap had grown enough to resent the patronizing. "The fields are still being tended, in places. Ashes in one hearth had not been rained on. Little Chicken saw. Weeds are sprouting in doorways, but one hencoop still has occupants. Someone has been feeding them."

Sagorn twisted around carefully to look up at the goblin, who still held the ax over him without a tremor. "Things grow here faster than in your northern forest, young man."

Little Chicken said nothing, his angular eyes shining gold in the fire's glow. Sagorn turned to face Rap again, obviously disconcerted by this looming threat.

"If you allow for the tropics, whatever happened here was quite recent, a few weeks at the most." So far the famous sage had not said anything very profound, Rap thought, but now he flashed his grim smile again. "And if you detected survivors with your farsight, you did not dare tell Thinal."

"Someone ran away as we approached."

"Just one?"

"Just one. And he is still there, about two bowshots off." Not that an arrow would go far through these woods.

"Doing what?"

"Just sitting. He's been there a long time."

"Well? Describe him!" Sagorn glared impatiently. "I can't do your thinking for you if I don't have the information."

"About this high. Skinny. I can't make out much detail at that distance. No weapons, as far as I can tell. Dark, I think."

"Humph! That is not even gnome height. A child, then?"

Rap nodded.

"Then I think I agree with your guess. Imperial troops or jotunn raiders. One child survived the attack. Not knowing what to do, he has remained here and tried to carry on the work of the village in the hope that someday the others will return. You must catch him! Use your farsight, or your goblin." Again the old man smiled his sinister smile. "You did not risk calling me just for that obvious advice, did you?"

Sagorn rubbed his chin. "No, things are certainly amiss. Thinal's intuition is very interesting. As he told you, I was young when I came here. It was before we learned our word of power. I have spared no thought for Faerie since then, and Thinal has certainly had no cause to. If he now believes it holds something worth stealing, then it probably does."

Rap put his suspicion into words. "You mean that the fairies are protected from the visitors, not the other way round?"

"That would seem to be one possibility. There are certainly monsters, though. I saw a pair of sphinxes and a chimera."

"In cages?"

"Yes. I rode on a hippogriff. But you are right—there is too much protection if the purpose is merely to repel wildlife. Even Thinal saw that the Impire does not usually bother to defend tourists. No headhunting, you think? And the last remaining inhabitant of this village is frightened of you, of strangers. So who or what is protected, and from whom?"

Sagorn fell silent, slapping angrily at bugs.

Rap wanted answers, not questions. "Tell me about Milflor, sir. Where is it?"

"On the east coast, near the south, I think. The prevailing wind . . . Yes, far south. You came the wrong way."

"How big is it?"

"Not big, at least when I was there. Many Imperial troops . . ." He paused again. "And ships. Small, coastal vessels. Smuggling?" The pale jotunn eyes flickered with excitement. "Now why, I wonder? This is a very interesting little mystery, Master Rap! Trust Thinal to stumble onto this. If there is ever anything of value around, he will always find it. And steal it."

A word of power was a thing of very great value. Rap hoped that more than just his own word of power was triggering Thinal's acquisitive instincts. "What could there be here worth stealing?"

"I don't know. But I suspect that Thinal will find it."

"I just want to get away."

"Let me give you some real advice, then, as that was why you summoned me." The old man glanced down at Rap's feet. "All of you need rest. You must stay here for a few days to recover. No, hear me out! You will gain nothing by killing yourselves, and Thinal is at the limits of his endurance. I am astonished he has stayed. You have been flattering him, and I suggest you continue to do so. You are quite right not to want either Jalon or Andor around, and I cannot help with the traveling. So keep praising Thinal. It will help him, and you."

Thinal, of course, would remember this conversation.

"What's your interest in this?" Rap demanded suspiciously.

Sagorn chuckled dryly. "The occult! Why did the magic casement react so strongly to you? And Witch Bright Water—why, I wonder, is she so solicitous of our brawny friend here?" He gestured with his thumb at the goblin. "What have you done to rouse the wardens?"

"I only know what I told Thinal," Rap said.

"And Thinal believed you. Of us all, he is perhaps the best at detecting lies, so I shall accept his judgment."

"Then tell me about this Bright Water, sir."

"She is very old and said to be mad—a safe enough bet."

"Why?"

"Oh, work it out! Remember how horrified you were when I first told you about your own word of power? The sorcerous live a long time. They can have anything they want: power, riches, women—or men, of course—youth, and health. Anything! It must pall after a decade or two. And yet they live in perpetual dread of other sorcerers."

"Who seek to steal their words?"

Sagorn hesitated. "Possibly. Andor told you that, right? But no mundane really knows how their minds work. There is another possibility. A strong sorcerer can bind a weaker to his service with a spell of obedience. The wardens are reported to do that. Other sorcerers fear the wardens, because they are the strongest of all, jealous of rivals, and they always seem to have retinues of mages and lesser sorcerers at their command. I suspect each warden continuously scans his sector, hunting for sorcerers he can bind to his service. Inisso's castle at Krasnegar . . . remember the occult barrier you sensed around it? You told Andor."

Now Rap felt he was getting somewhere. "And the chamber of puissance was outside the shield, above it, like a watchtower?"

"Well, then! Sorcerers seem to have two options. Some build strongholds like that in remote places and become virtual hermits, cowering inside occult shells. Others just hide from view by not using their powers—that is the only way I can explain how sorcerers spring up without warning. History is full of such stories. The new warlock Zinixo, for example, supposedly inherited all four of his words from a great-great-grandmother who had used her abilities only to prolong her own life. No one had ever known that she had occult power."

Bright Water, Rap recalled, had claimed she could detect power being used, even his tiny talent. He shivered.

Sagorn twisted around toward the menacing figure of Little Chicken. "Would you mind putting down that ax, young man? I find it remarkably unsettling, even just knowing it is there."

Rap nodded, and the goblin slowly lowered his arms and stepped back a pace; but he did not relax, and he kept his angular eyes fixed firmly on the scholar. The fire was dying, giving less light and more smoke.

Still frowning, Sagorn turned back to Rap. "How much do you know of the other wardens?"

"Very little, sir."

"Well, we know more about their activities than we do of minor sorcerers', because it is they who make history happen. Again take Zinixo as an example. He is a young dwarf, little older than yourself, I fancy. His predecessor, Witch Ag-An, had been West for almost a century. Perhaps she had grown careless. About a year ago she attended a wedding in the Peacock Hall of the Imperial palace. She was struck down by a bolt of lightning. Five bystanders were killed, also, and many more wounded."

Rap grimaced. "Lightning indoors?"

"Certainly. But only moments later there was an even greater manifestation in the public gallery, around Zinixo himself. Parts of the balcony collapsed and the death toll was much greater—many people burned or crushed. I was working in the library, at the far end of the palace, and I felt the tremors and heard the blast. It was an awesome release of power, and Zinixo's survival is an astonishing tribute to his occult strength."

"Who did that?"

"Good question! Possibly one or more of the other wardens had aided him in his coup against Ag-An; probably one or more of the others then tried to retaliate. Or it was an attempted double-cross by one of his former allies. Or some other nonwarden sorcerer took the opportunity to make his own move before the newcomer could consolidate his position. You see the problem? We just don't know! But you were right last year to dislike the thought of being a sorcerer. It can be a dangerous trade."

It would be a disgusting trade! "Zinixo might have faked the attack on himself?"

Sagorn's mouth snapped shut with a click of teeth, and for a moment he just stared at Rap. The fast flickering of the firelight made his face impossible to read.

"Ingenious!" he murmured. "But I think not. A warlock has

no need to impress anyone, except perhaps other powerful sorcerers—and they would not likely be deceived. No, I think I prefer the popular belief, which is that the second attack was a retaliation by Warlocks Lith'rian and Olybino—South and East—who tried to smite the upstart in his turn. If so, then he withstood their combined efforts!''

"Is that possible?" Rap felt crawly and scratchy whenever the occult was discussed, but he knew that this information was important if he was to have any chance of ever helping Inos.

"Certainly! One warlock has often defeated two others in combination. On that score at least we have good historical records. That is why the Protocol needs the Four; one may withstand two, but never three. Never? Let us say 'rarely.' Who knows?''

Silence fell, broken only by fire noises and the muffled fall of surf in the distance. Scattered raindrops hissed in the hearth. Rap realized that Sagorn was regarding him quizzically, as if waiting for him to catch up.

"Zinixo is warlock of the west?"

A nod.

"West's prerogative is the weather?"

Sagorn flashed his gruesome smile once more. "No! I've heard that said often enough, but the records just do not bear it out. There are too many reports of sorcerers raising tempests and so on. I don't know what force is reserved to West. I assume there is one, though.'' He thought for a moment. "He may just have some special status within the Four. Possibly his prerogative is the imperor himself, although the official position is that the imperor is sacrosanct.''

"And we are in West's area?"

"I assume so. Faerie is certainly very far west. And south, too, of course.''

"So Bright Water had no business moving us here?"

Another patronizing smile. "Not without his permission.''

"She is a friend of this Zinixo?"

"She may be. She may even have aided his accession. Warlock Lith'rian is universally believed to detest him—elves and dwarves are rarely compatible. Warlock Olybino . . . this is just between you and me, young man, but I have seen him . . . Olybino is a pompous owl. Anytime South and East combine, then West and North are likely to become friendly—you understand?'' Sagorn frowned up at the sky, as if warning the raindrops to stop falling. "So North's inexplicable interest in your goblin ax-man may involve the warlock of the west, also. On the other hand, Witch Bright Water may just be confused. She may have made a mistake. She may have forgotten all about you by now."

Remembering the old hag he had seen slouched naked on the ivory throne, Rap felt attracted by that thought. "I hope she has!"

The old man rubbed his hands gleefully. "Or not! So you see why you can trust me, Master Rap? I find all this fascinating! At least you can understand that I do not want to let Darad get his murderous hands on you. I would much rather let you blunder along in your own way, just to see what happens to you and your goblin—a unique opportunity to observe power at work!"

"So we're nothing more than an amusement for you?"

"What more could you be? Or me to you? Friends?" The old man scowled; his voice became brittle and bitter. "Which of us would you want as a friend? We are five solitary people. You can trust none of us in a tight spot. We cannot even trust each other!"

"Not Thinal?"

Sagorn sighed and stared wistfully at the hissing embers. The drops were becoming unpleasantly frequent. "The last time I saw Thinal, I was ten years old, and trying to hide behind Andor—five of us facing an angry sorcerer."

Rap tried to imagine that long-ago scene. "How old was he?"

"Thinal? About fifteen, I suppose. He seemed very big and manly to me. Do you understand guilt, Master Rap? He has never forgiven himself for what happened that night. You are everything he would like to be—determined, self-reliant, honest. So keep on building up his self-esteem, and he will continue trying to be worthy of your friendship."

Rap did not think Thinal would agree with much of that. "Trust him, you mean?"

"You have no choice, do you? At least until you all get to Milflor and can start looking for transportation back to the mainland. That may be tricky . . . perhaps we can talk again then? Take a few days' rest. Keep your feet clean. Wounds become poisoned very easily in this climate, and you have a long walk ahead of you." The old man smiled sardonically. "Well, as the weather seems to be turning sour, and I have no desire to provoke my lumbago, I think I shall depart.''

Little Chicken raised the ax again.

''Wait! I have to find Inos—''

Sagorn laughed raucously and shook his head. ''So you keep saying. But it would take you months, or even years, to reach Arakkaran or Krasnegar. A few days' rest now will be a wise investment and can make no difference.''

''I have another question,'' Rap said. ''Why did the sorceress take Inos?''

The scholar fumbled with the knot on his loincloth. ''Who can say?''

''*Sir!*'' Rap took a step forward. The spear quivered in his hand.

Sagorn looked up, glaring. ''Threaten me, boy, and you will answer to Darad!''

''Then be helpful!''

''You have a brain—use it! I can think of at least four reasons, but I can no more decide among them now than you can.''

''List them!'' Rap demanded, still hot with anger.

''*God of Patience!* They are obvious! To steal her word of power—and if that was the cause, then Inosolan is dead or tortured into madness by now. Or to do her a kindness—she was in a dangerous situation, remember. Or thirdly, it may just be that the Rasha woman is bored and wants to meddle in politics like a warden. Even a sorceress is not omnipotent. Not the most powerful warlock could ever *create* a genuine living princess with an established lineage and a claim to a throne—only the Gods can do that. So Inos has rarity value.''

Rap had already thought of all this. ''What's the fourth reason?''

The hearth steamed and hissed. Rain drummed on the leaves; water dribbled down Sagorn's face. ''To use as a bargaining chip.''

''*What?*'' Rap roared. ''Is that the best you can do? Bargaining chip? If sorcerers are so powerful, then what can they ever need to bargain for?''

The jotunn's long upper lip curled in an arrogant, aristocratic sneer. ''Boy, if you need to ask that, then you have not heard a word I told you!''

He was gone. Only the haughty sneer remained, incongruous on the paltry Thinal.

4

Farsight was not like vision. Rap did not *see*, he just *knew*. Even in the dark, he knew where the rotten sticks lay, where the thorns and creepers tangled his path, where the mossy trunks and low branches waited; and even in cellar blackness he somehow knew of their intrinsic greenness, also. In daylight he would never be as skilled a stalker as Little Chicken was, but at short range on a rainy night with no light at all, he was unsurpassed. Step by cautious step, he advanced through total darkness toward a sleeping quarry curled up under a bush in the jungle.

Or perhaps not sleeping . . . When he was a dozen paces away, he sensed that the child was a girl, and then that she was weeping—lying under a bush, sobbing. She was slight and black-skinned, and very small.

Some members of her family had been brutally murdered, perhaps in front of her eyes, and the rest dragged away in bonds. Now other intruders had driven her from the village she had been haunting like a wraith, taking even that feeble comfort from her. Rap wanted to weep, also.

Deliberately he cracked a twig, and she sat up with a tiny, quickly stifled wail.

"Don't be frightened," he said. "I'm not going to hurt you. I brought some food. I'm a friend."

The child whimpered and huddled down, impossibly little.

"I can see in the dark, but I won't come any closer. I know where you are. You have your arms round your knees. There's a tree right behind you, right? And a trowel near your foot. I'm not moving, not coming closer. You can hear my voice, so you know I'm not coming closer. Don't be frightened."

There was no reply, no sound except the tramp of rain on the forest canopy high above and the steady drip of water. The air was thick with damp woodsy scents, the fetor of rotting leaves.

"I am going to lay down my bundle. I brought a blanket and a gourd of water and some food. There, I've laid it down. Now I'm walking away again. You can hear me going away, can't you? And now I'll tell you how to find the bundle I brought. Aren't you hungry?"

Still silence, but . . .

"You nodded. I saw you nod. So I can see in the dark, but

I'm not going to try to catch you. You can hear that I've gone farther away, can't you?''

The child nodded again. Rap thought he could even sense her hands trembling and her fast breath.

"Now I'll tell you how to find it. Move forward . . .''

The child merely clutched her knees more tightly.

"I can guide you to the food.''

She shook her head.

"All right,'' he said, "you don't have to. But I don't want to hurt you. Who killed the people in the village?''

Her lips moved at last. "Soldiers.''

"Well, I'm not a soldier. I have two friends with me, and they're not soldiers, either. We want to help you. If you crawl forward, I can tell you how to find the things I brought for you.''

But the tiny figure still did not move. Obviously Rap's efforts were only increasing her terror. He could have soothed a frightened foal, or calmed a puppy, but with people he had no occult skill at all.

"Then I'll go away and leave you. Do you want that?''

She nodded.

"Then you come and see me in the morning. I'll go out to the place where you were pulling weeds, and you come and see me, and we'll talk. In the morning. All right? And I'll leave this food right here, and the blanket. I'm going now.''

Whistling a sad tune, hating himself, Rap turned and walked noisily off through the invisible forest. The child stayed where she was, in the rain.

5

She did come the next morning, after Rap had been waiting in hot sunlight for nearly an hour. He had thought to bring a stool, for his feet were inflamed and painful, but he had no sunshade and all he could do about the insects was slap and swear. Thinal and Little Chicken sat in plain view at the edge of the clearing.

The girl had been watching them from the jungle all that time, but Rap had pretended not to know. He had spent his time studying the vegetables, trying to guess what they were. The only ones he knew for certain were beans.

His patience ran out at last. Turning to face her, he cupped his hands and shouted. "Come out! I won't hurt you. I'm not a soldier."

After a few minutes, she emerged, walking toward him with so light a grace that she might have been floating. At most she was twelve years old, but her head barely reached his chest. She wore a simple dress of brown homespun, with no shoes or adornments. Her hair was straight and hung loose. Like her skin, it was black, and her eyes were black—all black. Even the sclera were black, as if her face had been carved from a single block of ebony. Rap had not noticed that in the night. He hid his surprise with a smile and sat waiting for her, his hands held open to show that he had no weapon.

She came much closer than he had expected, stopping a few paces from him and trying to return his smile with a lip that insisted on wobbling. His pale-brown skin and gray-and-white eyes must make him seem just as uncanny to her as she was to him.

"I shall call you Food Giver," she said, her voice quavering. "How will you term me?"

Rap had already opened his mouth to tell her his name; he was nonplussed to be asked for hers instead. Then he remembered one of his mother's superstitions—that evil sorcerers sought out people's names in order to do them harm. Perhaps fairyfolk had the same belief.

"I shall term you Forest Sleeper."

His guess worked, she seemed to approve. She took a deep breath. "Food Giver, you are welcome to our hearth and spring. May the Good be prospered . . ." She hesitated and bit her lip. Black lips, black tongue. It was almost a relief to see the tips of her teeth and learn that they, at least, were white. She tried again. "We offer all we have, and may the Good be prospered by your coming. May your stay be joyful and your leaving . . . ah . . . not soon?" She smiled uncertainly. "Did I say that right?"

"I think so. You said it very well. But I don't know the right words to answer. Can you tell me what I am supposed to say?"

She shook her head apprehensively.

"Then I'll just say thank you, Forest Sleeper, and tell you again that I want to be your friend."

She smiled with relief.

"Will you come and meet my friends now? I have two friends, and we don't want to hurt you. They want to be your friends, too."

The child hesitated, then gave him her hand. The palm was sticky with fear, the fingers tiny as a baby's. He rose and led her back toward the huts, marveling at how she seemed to float over the ground. As she moved through rows of plants, the leaves hardly seemed to note her passage.

"When did the bad soldiers come?"

"A long time ago."

"And you were the only one to escape?"

She nodded. Rap thought she was going to start weeping. He cursed himself for questioning her so soon.

"Momma had sent me to the fish trap, for food to offer—" Her voice broke off in a near sob.

"You can tell me later. I expect you're hungry again? When you've met my friends, then we'll all eat, and then have a talk."

What was he going to do with this orphan? If Imperial soldiers had been responsible for the atrocity in the village, then he could not take her to Milflor. She might be in danger there, and she would certainly not be happy. So Rap would have to go in search of another fairy settlement—and that might take weeks. He certainly could not abandon her here alone.

"When the moon shines," she said timorously, "and I want to dance, will you clap for me?"

"Of course."

She smiled happily. "I have danced a little, as I could, but there was no one to clap. I will clap for you to dance!"

Rap thought she was going to have another disappointment then, but he promised he would dance.

She stopped suddenly, tugging his large hand with her tiny one. He looked down in surprise at her worried expression.

"Food Giver," she said, "what is nearest your heart?"

"Er . . ." Rap smiled as cheerfully as he could. "I don't think I understand, Forest Sleeper. I come from a long way away, and I do not know how things are done here."

"Oh." She looked alarmed.

"You tell me what I'm supposed to tell you."

It seemed that Forest Sleeper was not sure of the answer, nor why she was asking. She hesitated, fumbled for words, and then said, "Tell me your dreams?"

Rap felt inadequate and bewildered. He knelt down on the red soil to study the strangely haunting face, and even then his eyes were higher than hers. "My dreams?"

"What you seek." His inability to understand was frightening her again.

"What I want most, you mean?" Rap asked, and earned a vigorous nod. "Oh! I seek a lady, a friend of mine. She was taken away . . . She had to go away, and I want to find her."

The black-on-black eyes seemed to search his. The fairy child's skin was very shiny, as if polished, but her eyes gleamed brighter still—like black metal, oddly beautiful in spite of their strangeness.

"Why?"

"So I may serve her. Because she is my queen."

Another pause, and a sudden childish grin, as if this had all been a joke. "You do not know!"

Apparently that cryptic remark concluded the ritual, if it had been a ritual. Seeming greatly reassured, Forest Sleeper tugged at Rap's hand to make him rise, and then set off skipping at his side. But he did not think that curious episode had been a joke and he hoped that there were no more unfamiliar customs in store.

Her increasing confidence had changed her gait to a dance. Rap felt as if he were holding her down, that without his grip on her hand she might flit away into the sky. Andor had told him once that the elves were the most graceful of all the races of Pandemia, but Andor had never met a fairy. Few had. Her features were fine and delicate, and her jet skin had a strangely fascinating beauty. Even her fingernails were shiny black.

Thinal came forward a few feet. Perhaps he thought he might be less frightening than Little Chicken, but the girl's hand gripped Rap's very tightly as she approached him. Then they stopped, and for a moment no one spoke.

"I shall call you Small One," she announced.

Bewilderment crossed Thinal's face, and he looked to Rap.

"Name her," Rap said very quietly, almost mouthing the words.

"Oh. I shall call you . . . Dark Lady."

She giggled, as if that were funny. "Small One, you are welcome to our hearth and spring. We offer what we have, and may the Good be prospered by your coming. May your stay be joyful and your leaving . . . er . . . "

"Be long delayed," Thinal prompted.

Her eyes sparkled. "Be long delayed!"

Thinal bowed. "May the Good grow within your house and the Evil diminish. May your men be strong and your women fertile, your children wax in beauty and your elders in wisdom. May your crops flourish, your herds increase, and all your arrows fly true."

Forest Sleeper—or Dark Lady—clapped her tiny hands joyfully. She looked up at Rap in reproach. "He knows the words!"

"Then he shall teach me."

"It's a faunish greeting," Thinal said, with a smug glance at Rap. He repeated the ritual, line by line, and Rap in turn spoke it to the girl.

She laughed when he had done. Then she became troubled again, stepping very close to Thinal and giving him the same steady stare she had given Rap. "Small One, what is nearest your heart?"

Again Thinal's eyes flicked to Rap's for guidance.

"Your greatest ambition?" Rap muttered.

"Ah! Dark Lady, I seek to be relieved of a spell placed upon me by a wicked sorcerer."

The fairy studied him for longer than she had Rap. Then she gave the same reply, but hesitantly. "You do not know!"

And now obviously it was Little Chicken's turn, and the fairy was gaining confidence. She told him that his name was Big Ears, at which Rap and Thinal hastily suppressed grins. The goblin's slanted eyes widened slightly.

"I term you Beauty of the Night," he said in his heavily accented impish.

Rap was surprised and gratified. Not bad at all! Knowing how goblins disparaged women, he had been afraid of some surly rudeness.

Beauty of the Night rattled off her ritual welcome, and Little Chicken replied with Thinal's faunish formula.

Then he was given the close stare. "Big Ears, what is nearest your heart?"

Rap knew the answer to that. He wondered if Little Chicken would be truthful. He was, but he spoke in goblin.

"Kill Flat Nose. Long, long pain."

This time the scrutiny was longer still. Then the fairy child said, "Oh!" and held up both hands to the goblin. Rap was astonished to see that her deep jet eyes had brimmed over; her cheeks of polished ebony were glistening with tears.

"You do know!" She tugged at the goblin's arms. Puzzled and wary, he sank down to his knees. Even then she had to rise on tiptoe to embrace him, to reach up and kiss his cheek.

Rap and Thinal shot each other glances of mingled astonishment and amusement, Thinal rolling his eyes; but before either could frame a suitably ribald comment, Little Chicken cried out and clutched at the tiny form, suddenly gone limp.

He lowered her gently to the ground. Rap knelt to see, but even as he did so, he had no doubt. She was dead.

Just like that—dead.

Faun and goblin stared at each other across the body in mutual horror.

"Did not hurt!" Little Chicken protested. He scrambled to his feet and backed away, paler than Rap had ever seen him, livid green blotches highlighting his cheekbones. "Did not touch!"

"No, you didn't. I saw."

Thinal gave a choked cry and vanished. A thong snapped, a loincloth fluttered to the ground, leaving Sagorn naked and absurd—and paralyzed with shock, staring down at the body. All the color drained out of his already pale jotunn cheeks, turning them almost as white as the strands of hair still plastered over his face by the previous night's rain.

"He didn't touch her!" Rap said. "She put her arms around him. He did nothing! In fact, he had his hands behind him, like this."

Sagorn licked sallow lips. "I saw, too. Thinal did." His bewilderment seemed as great as Rap's.

"Well?" Rap shouted. "Doctor? You're the great scholar! Explain this, old man—there's a dead child here. What did we do wrong?"

"I . . . I have no idea." Sagorn gazed at Rap in frank dismay. "No cachexia or morbidity or trauma I have ever encountered . . ." He sank down and felt the tiny neck for a pulse. Then he closed the all-black eyes with fingers that seemed cruelly huge. He rose stiffly; seeming to notice his nudity for the first time, he stooped to retrieve the loincloth.

"I have never seen anything like that," he muttered. "I know of nothing to induce moribundity with such alacrity. Postulation of occult agency must—" He sucked in his breath.

"Well?"

The old man was staring at Rap with pure horror contorting his features. "Nothing!"

But there was something.

Then there was no Sagorn. He had vanished, calling back Thinal in his place.

Rap roared and stepped over the dead girl to grab the imp by the shoulders. "What did he remember?"

"What? Rap!"

Rap could barely restrain himself. He wanted to shake Thinal like a dusty horse blanket. "What did Sagorn think of, that made him leave like that? He remembered something, didn't he?"

"I don't know."

"Think, man! Think!"

"Rap, you're hurting . . . He thought of a book he read—"

"What did it say?"

"I don't remember! I don't know! It was years ago, in the Imperial library. Just a book, Rap. About Faerie, I think—"

He was lying. Rap was certain of it. But to bully Thinal was to risk Darad. To demand that Sagorn be brought back would be useless, for he would not remain if he did not wish to be questioned. With a great effort, Rap released the imp and swung around to the goblin, whose ugly face bore a strangely bemused expression.

"She spoke to you. Didn't she? She whispered something in your ear. What did she say?"

The goblin pouted. "Don't know."

"You're lying, trash!"

A dangerous glint shone in Little Chicken's eye. "Not impish. Not goblin. Didn't understand."

He was lying, also. In dismay, Rap stared around at the hot jungle and the pitiful cluster of huts, bereft now of their last pathetic inhabitant. Wanting to hide his tears from the others, he muttered something about a spade and walked away.

He wept.

There was a mystery here that he could not start to understand. He was only a dumb stableboy, or at best a factor's clerk—far from home and hopelessly out of his depth. Inos seemed farther away than ever and he more lost than ever, trapped with two companions he dared not trust.

He had brought an innocent child to her death. Somehow his blundering ignorance had killed her.

The world was a much stranger place than he had expected.

Some little talk:
> There was the Door to which I found no Key;
> There was the Veil through which I might not see:
>> Some little talk awhile of ME and THEE
> There was—and then no more of THEE and ME.
>>>> Fitzgerald, *The Rubaiyat of Omar Khayyam*
>>>>> (§32, 1879)

❰ FOUR ❱

Destiny with men

1

"Steady there, lady," Inos said. "Steady! Now I take a look at your hoof. All part of the game." She slid from the saddle, then tried to comfort Sesame, patting her neck and cooing. "Sorry, girl! Sorry!" Sesame champed her bit and backed away rebelliously, clattering on the wind-polished pebbles; she kept that up for several minutes before allowing herself to be soothed. She was one of the sweetest-tempered mounts Inos had ever met, but at the moment she was very mad, and with good reason.

The only vegetation in sight was thorny scrub, useless for tying reins to. Apart from that there was sand and stone as far as the eye could see, hot enough to bake bread. Heat lay on the desert like a lake of molten lead. It shimmered in silver mirages and blurred the rocky ridges, even the closest. It poached the eyeballs. The Agonistes were barely visible ghosts, snowcapped and remote.

Sesame was still fretting, perturbed by the lack of other horses, perhaps not trusting Inos to find the road home again. The last of the hunt had just topped the ridge ahead, disappearing after the hounds; the beaters and dog handlers were leagues back. Timeless silence had returned to the barren hills; the air was still and cruel, too hot to breathe, and smelling of dust.

Inos unhooked the canteen and dropped her veil to drink. She had no objection to covering her face out here in the hills, because everyone did, even Azak. She ought to pretend to inspect

89

Sesame's shoes, but at the moment there was no one in sight,
so she could just say she had done so. She shook the canteen
and scowled at it for being so near to empty. The sky was fright-
eningly huge, and she could imagine herself as a God might see
her, an insignificant dot on a great barren expanse of rock.

She replaced the canteen, wiping her face with her sleeve. It
had been a tougher day than usual—she wondered again what
on earth she was hoping to achieve, broiling herself in the desert. For more than two weeks now she had been imprisoned in
Arakkaran, Pandemia's most luxurious jail, and in those two
weeks she seemed to have accomplished nothing at all. Nothing
for Krasnegar; nothing even for her own satisfaction, for she had
not achieved that monarch-to-monarch talk with Azak that she
had set out to win.

Likely it would have done her little good anyway, for Sultan
Azak seemed to spend all his days in hunting, all his evenings
at state dinners with his brothers and uncles and cousins. When
had he ever had the time to learn anything about world politics?
He was only an untutored savage, who probably knew less than
she did.

"Stubborn, I am!" she told Sesame. "I just don't want to
quit! I don't want to crawling back to Kade, admitting that I
can't even back a man into a corner when I try. Stubborn!"
Stubborn as a certain mule-headed faun she had known once.

As far as she knew, Kade was not making much progress,
either. She seemed to pass her days in teaching the palace women
how to run tea parties and ladies' salons, and the sorceress had
been encouraging this importation of Imperial customs. There
had been no change in the situation in Krasnegar—so Rasha had
told Kade. Of course news took a month or longer to travel as
far as Kinvale. To cross all Pandemia might take years, so what
the sorceress had not heard, no one had.

"So why do I bother, lady? Tell me that!" Inos patted the
pony's sweaty neck. "I'll tell you why I bother—because I don't
want to waste my days lounging around with Kade drinking tea
and eating cake and growing old and fat!"

Sesame blew a loud breath of disbelief.

"Well, you've got a point," Inos admitted, scanning all
around again without seeing any change in the empty land. "It
would be more comfortable, and I'm probably aging much faster
out here. So you're absolutely right—I do it because I want to
show I'm as tough as any of these hairy-faced baboons."

Sesame shook her head and backed up a few steps.

"No? Well, I suppose I'm not, am I? And they don't care now anyway, do they?"

The novelty had worn off, and the princes were mostly shunning Inos. Perhaps they resented her, and the example she was setting for their womenfolk. Some of the younger men still spoke to her, although what they wanted to discuss would have been unthinkable in Kinvale. Only one of them had actually offered to include marriage in the arrangement, young Petkish, and she had not seen him around lately. She hoped there was no connection between his marriage proposal and his disappearance.

Still, at least she had learned that a woman could get married in Zark. Marriage was unusual, and it brought very few rights, but it was possible. Nice to know.

"You're absolutely correct," Inos told her horse sternly. "I do this because I don't like being snubbed by an ignorant oversize savage. He knows I want a private word with him and he's deliberately staying out of my way, and I'm going to chase after him until he's sick of the sight of me."

Sesame sighed disbelievingly.

And then a horse came into view in the distance, one of the hunt returning. It was heading straight for Inos, so obviously the rider had already seen her. In a few minutes she recognized Kar's big gray. Surprise! To see Kar farther removed from Azak than his own shadow was very rare.

As usual, Azak had outridden the entire court, vanishing over the horizon with uncles and brothers straggling in pursuit behind him. Often he even outrode his brown-clad guards, known as the family men. Kar's return meant that the kill had been made; the others would be along shortly.

In a moment he flowed up effortlessly beside Inos's still-restless mare and simultaneously slid from his saddle with a grace that suggested descent from a thousand generations of horsemen. He dropped his own reins brashly, snapping a word of command at the gray. Then he reached out to stroke Sesame's neck, and she stilled as if soothed by magic. Azak had the same knack. It wasn't quite Rap's magic, but it was almost as impressive.

"It was just a rock," Inos said. "Then I thought I'd give her a rest."

"Which foot?" Kar inquired, with a smile.

Kar always smiled. Kar had probably been born smiling and most likely slept smiling and would be acting out of character if he did not die smiling. Alone among the full-grown princes, he was clean-shaven, his face round and boyish. He was shorter and slighter than most of the others, probably in his late twenties, a little older than Azak. He was another ak'Azakar, either brother or half brother to the sultan. His eyes were wide and innocent, as red as any, and yet the coldest eyes Inos had seen outside a fish market. There was something sinister about Kar that she could not place, and yet she had never heard him raise his voice or even seen him frown. Or stop smiling.

"Right front," she said.

"It looked more like back left." The smile grew broader, buckling his cheeks without touching his eyes at all. "But it doesn't matter, does it?" He stooped to run his hand down Sesame's fetlock and then lift her hoof. "It was quite realistic."

"Who is telling lies about me? You could not have seen it yourself."

"I see everything."

Inos had preferred not to watch the antelope being pulled down and torn apart. Coursing was low on her list of favorite sports.

"It fooled most of them," Kar remarked to the hoof he was studying. "The Big Man didn't notice, luckily. But this frog does seem a little tender. Did she have any trouble earlier? Real trouble?" Even when he was bent double, there was something very irritating in Kar's manner.

Tempted to lash out with her boot at so profitable a target, Inos regretfully refrained. "Not that I noticed. I mean, no! She was fine."

He grunted, released the hoof, and went for another. Sesame tossed her head as he ducked below it. "Don't ever try it when he might see."

"I have more sense than that."

"I thought you had more sense than to try it at all. You think your sex would protect you?"

Inos rejected her first choice of response and framed a more civil reply. "Certainly not. I expect I should receive much the same lecture as Prince Petkish did."

Kar made a scoffing noise. "*Lecture?* You think that was all Petkish got, a lecture?"

As huntmaster, Azak was a fanatic. Princes who muffed a chance at game or displayed anything less than total mastery of their mounts were certain to receive royal reprimands, which were usually long and invariably savage. No matter how senior the culprit, or how many lowborn attendants might be within earshot, Azak would bellow out his scorn and contempt for all to hear. He wielded an enormous vocabulary without pity—ridicule upon humiliation, insult upon sarcasm—irony, scorn, and scurrility. Frequently the tongue-lashing would continue until tears dribbled down the victim's cheeks, and days might then pass before he dared come again into the sultan's presence. A public flogging would have been kinder and less feared.

Azak, in short, treated the princes with undisguised contempt. He was reasonably patient with the lowborn—with grooms, falconers, and other attendants—but he made no allowance for human fallibility in royalty. It was not a style of leadership that appealed to Inos. The third or fourth time she witnessed one of his brutal tirades, the victim had been young Petkish, just two days after he had started inserting marriage into his frequent offers of cohabitation. His horse had balked at jumping a wadi, a very nasty little gully, rocky and deep, its edges crumbling. Azak had somehow seen what happened behind his back and had returned to berate the culprit with a fury of invective that continued until the lad dismounted and threw himself on the ground before Azak's horse, rubbed his face in the dirt, and begged for forgiveness. He had then been sent home, and Inos had not seem him since.

Within a few minutes, Azak had been leading the remainder of the hunt at full gallop over terrain that would have caused any reasonable man to dismount and proceed on foot. The remaining princes had clung to him like fleas, with Inos in their midst, heart in mouth—if mere princes could do it, then a queen must not fail. By a miracle no horse or rider had come to grief, but that night she had awakened several times sweating and shaking; and understanding a little better.

She understood, also, that such leadership did not permit Azak himself ever to fall below perfection. His mount must never stumble, his arrows never miss. And apparently they never did. It was small wonder that the younger men worshipped him, and even the oldest cowered below his frown.

But now she felt a stab of alarm. She had liked Petkish. Almost alone among the princes he had seemed to appreciate that a woman might be human once in a while. "What else happened to Petkish, apart from the lecture?"

"He was banished."

Kar was still doubled over, but Inos kept her face schooled anyway, hiding her distaste. Banished—for a single refusal, or because he had been too friendly with the visiting royalty? Poor

Petkish and his tiny ginger beard! Either way, he had learned a hard lesson.

Azak couldn't banish Inos, because she was Rasha's guest, but if he learned that she had faked a lame horse in order to avoid the sight of blood, then she would no longer be one of the boys. She would be back doing flower arrangements with Kade.

"You were misinformed, Highness," Inos said. "My horse did pick up a stone. Had I known I would be doubted, I should have saved it as evidence. Surely you are too much of a gentleman to tell tales?"

Kar completed his deliberate inspection of the second hoof, then straightened up. He rested one hand on Sesame's withers and turned to Inos with quiet amusement.

"I always tell tales," he said. "I tell everything. I am his chief of security. Did you not know?"

"No. I didn't."

Kar shrugged. "He trusts me. I am the only man he trusts."

Inos felt very much aware of being alone in an empty desert with this smiling, baby-faced enigma. She had never spoken with Kar before, and he made her scalp pucker. She wished the rest of the hunt would come into view. "The only one he trusts completely, you mean? He must trust some of the others somewhat?"

"How can you trust anyone *somewhat*?"

"Well . . ."

Kar's smile widened. He moved around to check Sesame's rear feet. "Why do you wish to speak with him?"

Ah! So this was business? She should have guessed! Obviously the straightforward approach was suspect and she was supposed to do things in devious ways. Faking a lame pony might be the correct form of address when seeking audience, and now Azak had sent Kar to open negotiations.

"I wanted his advice, as one monarch to another."

"Why should he give you advice?"

Nonplussed, Inos snapped, "Why should he not?"

Kar was scratching at the hoof with the quillon of his dagger and he spoke without raising his voice at all. "You are in league with the bitch sorceress. She brought you here for some purpose of her own. Your aunt spends half her days drinking tea with her, spreading dissent and sedition among the women of the palace."

"I bear no malice toward Arakkaran!"

"What evidence do you offer, apart from your own word?"

Idiot! She should have expected this suspicion. She had not been thinking about local politics at all, only her own.

This was not the Impire. It most certainly was not Kinvale, and she had been playing games. Azak might indulge in sport, but he would never play games. "Do I look like a threat to Arakkaran?"

Kar straightened and regarded her with less smile than usual. "You look like an Imperial spy."

"That is rubbish! I no more look like an imp than you do."

"There is a scent of war in the wind."

"Yes, there is. The imps stole my kingdom!"

"So you have been telling the women. You have also been asking questions," Kar said softly. "Strange questions. You asked how the sultan is chosen, for example."

"Yes! How is the sultan chosen? That can't be a state secret, yet no one will tell me. Azak has many older brothers. Why him? In Krasnegar, and in the Impire—"

"In Zark it is done otherwise." Kar bent to the fourth leg. "By election."

"Very democratic!"

"Yes. When a sultan dies, then the imam calls the princes to assembly."

"Imam?"

"Bishop. He asks who is to succeed. If more than one steps forward, the imam dismisses them. The next day he calls them again."

She felt sick. "Until there is only one claimant?"

"Exactly."

Election by elimination? "And how many stepped forward with Azak?"

Kar completed his inspection and straightened. He was still smiling, if redder-faced than usual. "How many would you have expected?"

"I think I understand."

"That is good. Lead the mare around."

"I'm sure she's all right."

"*Do it!* You never know who may be watching."

Did he mean mundane eyes or occult? Inos led Sesame around in a small circle, wondering if the sorceress had driven the whole palace mad or if all Zark was like this. Even Kade had become strangely tight-lipped and jumpy lately.

"She is fit to ride," Kar said.

"The previous sultan—"

"Zorazak. Our grandfather, of blessed memory."

"And how—"

"Extreme old age." Djinn eyes darkened in bright sunlight, and Kar's were now the color of dried blood. "Very sad."

Despite the brutal heat, Inos shivered. Now she knew why no one had been willing to discuss this. "How old?"

"Almost sixty. His passing was slower than we expected, but quite painless."

"I am greatly relieved to hear that." *Honest as a djinn!* Now she knew what it meant.

Kar nodded. "The sultan said to tell you that you have made your point, and your continuing presence on these hunts is no longer necessary." The smile grew more loving. "And I give you some advice from myself. Stay out of politics, Inosolan. They are an art too dangerous for women—even queens *regnant*!"

Slender and lithe, Kar strode across to the gray, which had hardly moved a hoof since he left it. He vaulted into the saddle without using the stirrups and instantly was gone, cantering away over the gravel, leaving Inos standing beside Sesame.

Sesame snickered loudly.

2

Alone and early, Inos returned to the stables; there were no guards available to escort her. With a snort of indifference, she gave Sesame a farewell pat and set off by herself, striding along a well-known route through halls and cloisters, shady groves and narrow short-cut alleys. She moved within a glow of anger that burned worse than the sunlight, that seemed to be still increasing. Perhaps it was easier to be angry on foot than on horseback.

She had been a complete imbecile! A child! She had charged into Arakkaranian high society like a mad bull, expecting all those royal princes to change their entire way of thinking just because a slip of a girl could ride a horse—expecting the sultan himself to change!

She had been wrong and Kade had been right, and that hurt worst of all.

Imagine Azak at Kinvale? Impossible! Azak at Kinvale was unthinkable. Inosolan in Arakkaran was unthinkable, too. She must have seemed brash and wanton and insolent and . . . Ugh! Immature!

A queen must always think politically! She would remember that in future.

In a scorching open courtyard, about fifty small boys were doing sword drill under the raptor eyes of a couple of elderly family men. She swept by them, staying close to the wall, and no one paid any attention to her. Fifty more princes in training, fifty more arrogant, women-hating, pig-headed . . . Bah!

Rasha was absolutely right!

Now Inos had thrown away her chance to enlist an ally, a disinterested advisor. She would have to rely entirely on the kindly intentions of the sorceress and somehow she felt less inclined to trust that shape-changing old hag than she did to trust Azak, even if he did treat women like livestock and had murdered his grandfather. Anyway, that story had come from Kar, whom she trusted less than anyone.

Still, *Mastery is made of mistakes*, as Rap had always said, and she must try to learn from this one. She stalked along a cool arcade, hearing her bootsteps echo in odd patterns from the arches of the roof. The second day . . . That was where she had gone wrong. The audience with Azak, the riding of Evil, even the first day's hunt—all those had been sound strategy. Her presence that first day could almost have been passed off as an accident. Exactly who had invited her to hunt again the next day she could not recall—one of the graybeards, she thought—but she should have declined. Politely, of course. Very gratefully . . . but declined. Then they might have come to her. Azak might have. Out of curiosity. Instead she had turned herself into an everyday spectacle, a curiosity instead of a marvel.

Do anything! she had vowed, do anything to recover her kingdom. And all she had done was play games and flutter eyelashes. Well— *no more games!*

But the first order of business must be to apologize to Kade and admit that she had been right. Grrr!

Inos swung around at the sound of feet running. One of the family men was chasing after her. She stopped and waited until he arrived, flushed and gasping in the heat. He was shorter than most, very youthful. He wore a scimitar and at least two daggers and an odd sort of conical cap that she had noticed before among the guards. His face was round and innocent, and very, very red.

"Came . . . escort . . . Majesty . . ." he gasped, chest heaving.

Inos was practically at her destination and quite obviously in no real need of an escort, but she nodded graciously. "That was very kind of you. You need to rest for a minute?"

He shook his head, and she would not have been suprised to see drops of perspiration fly off him like rain. In some way this earnest young guard reminded her very much of the banished Petkish, with his well-meaning offers of protection; and he did need to catch his breath.

"Tell me something," she said, not moving. "What do the rings on your hat mean?"

He raised coppery eyebrows in surprise. "Mean? These? Nothing, your Majesty. They're a weapon." He raised a hand and hooked the top ring off his cap to show her. The outside edge was honed like a razor. "It's called a *chakram*, Majesty. I throw them. Off a finger." He raised a free finger and twiddled it around to illustrate.

"Deadly?"

He nodded, grinning, and drew the finger across his throat.

Inos shivered. "Thank you."

He replaced the ring, and the two of them started to walk.

Get them alone—that was the secret! Kar had talked when he was alone with her. They didn't like to be seen talking with a mere woman. She smiled over her shoulder, and the coppery eyebrows jumped nervously.

She did a little dance step that put her at his side instead of in front. "Tell me something, then. Why are you guards known as 'family men'?"

He had recovered most of his breath, so he was able to puff himself up proudly, even if for only a moment. "Because we have sworn our loyalty on the heads of our sons!"

Which was what she had been told before. Allowing for the beard, he looked about seventeen. With a sudden glint of devilry in his eye, he added, "Three, so far, your Majesty."

Inos hoped she did not blush. She was almost at her quarters. She might get one more question in before they came within sight of the sentries and her informant became tongue-tied again.

"And how does one become a family man?"

The question puzzled him, and he frowned for several paces before he worked out what she wanted to know. "Royal birth, ma'am."

"A prince?"

He went redder still. "Not always. I wasn't quite. Palace born, but too distant. Great-grandnephew of the Sultan of Shuggaran, your Majesty."

So that was what happened to all the excess princes—palaces exported swordsmen.

"Thank you," Inos said sweetly once again and let him drop back a pace as they rounded the corner and the apartment doors and its guards came in sight. Ex-prince Petkish, she assumed, might well be practicing *chakram*-throwing in Shuggaran right now. That would teach him to propose marriage to an Imperial spy.

Just a few minutes' friendly chat with an anonymous guard has been enough to put Inos in a much better temper. By the time she had stormed up a long staircase and thrown down her hat and veil and gloves and cloak and slammed a couple of doors, her fury was back again. And she knew why, too! She was going to have to confess to Kade that she had failed utterly. In two weeks of bone-grinding effort, she had obtained not even two minutes' private talk with the sultan. Perhaps such a discussion would have done her no good anyway—that was not the point! The point was that she was feeling like a complete fool. It was not a totally unfamiliar sensation, but it was not a common one, either, and it was certainly not welcome.

Wondering where everyone was, she threw open another door, heading for Kade's favorite balcony. And there everyone was.

The little salon seemed to be crammed with all the residents of the habitation, from wizened old crones down to dampish babies. Everyone turned toward the door and fell into an excited, expectant hush when they saw who had just entered—back early, of course. Kade was there, in the middle of the excitement, and Zana was overseeing everyone with her wrinkles wrapped in a grandmotherly smile.

Swiftly women and youngsters cleared out of the way, so Inos could see the strikingly beautiful woman quietly blushing in the center of it all. For a moment Inos just gaped, causing a couple of small girls to start giggling. It was Vinisha.

But her gown was an Imperial-style ballgown. Thralia was putting the final touches to her high and elaborate coiffure, and Vinisha's hair was revealed as a stunning auburn. She had not yet put on any jewelry. Perhaps she had none. But the gown! Enormous masses of shining samite were gathered around her, cascading out from a very low waist, and above the waist . . . remarkably little, just a low-cut bodice. Very low-cut! Vinisha had a striking figure; there was no doubt about *that*. It had been months since Inos had seen a décolletage anywhere near that daring, and then the dowager duchess had ordered its wearer from the hall. For a moment Inos thought of strolling into a gathering of Arakkaranian princes in that outfit, and her mind reeled.

The gown was a miracle. It set off a djinnish complexion perfectly, but it was also the exact same shade of green as Inos's eyes, and the gold thread in the samite would match her hair, near enough. Vinisha was the same size as Inos—near enough. The bodice was too tight on her . . . but certainly near enough.

The tragedy of a figure like that buried in a sack all day!

Uneasily aware that she was filthy and dusty and stinking of horse, Inos tore her eyes from the gown and looked at Kade, who beamed opaquely.

"Where did you get *that* wonder?"

"You like it, my dear? Sultana Rasha showed us some functions in progress in the Imperial palace. She adjusted the color of the material for us. Then Mistress Thralia, and Mistress Kasha, and . . ."

Of course the design would have to be from Hub, or at least one of the major cities of the Impire. A provincial backwater like Kinvale would be shocked speechless by that neckline, and the fabric alone would buy a coach and four.

Inos gave her aunt a hard stare. Kade fell silent.

"Vinisha, you look absolutely enchanting!" Inos said, earning a stammering blush. "Now, Aunt, let's you and me go and have a little chat?"

Kade nodded in innocent surprise. "If you wish, dear."

3

The town was shadowed now, the sun just setting. Inos leaned on the cool marble balustrade and stared down at distant sails on the enamel blue of the bay. She felt uncomfortably aware of her own grubby stickiness as Kade came to stand beside her, ignoring the comfy divan she normally favored on this balcony.

"Zana found me an Imperial breviary today!" she said brightly.

Inos muttered congratulations. Kade liked to offer a prayer each night before retiring, but her illuminated pocket prayer-book had remained behind in Krasnegar. Its loss had wounded her deeply, because it had been a gift from her mother and one of her most treasured possessions. Worse, she had discovered that the prayers in Zark were different—and therefore wrong, of course. Kade was old enough to believe that the Gods had the same traditions that she did and would prefer to be invoked in old familiar words. Inos suspected that They might enjoy a little variety after so long. Kade must know most of the prayers by heart, anyway.

To business! "Pray explain that gown," Inos said. "If I appear in the palace in that, then nothing will remain for me in Zark except a career in belly dancing. Or have you already arranged for my first lessons?"

"Gracious! Certainly not, dear." Kade looked shocked and sounded slow-witted. Kade, therefore, was choosing to be inscrutable, and that meant being a good deal less scrutable than a cupful of tea leaves. "Her Majesty planned it all, of course. She has asked that you call on her this evening, and she wants you suitably dressed."

"Suitably for what?"

"Suitably for a queen, I suppose." Kade peered up blankly.

Inos felt baffled. Zarkian hunting she thought she now comprehended, but she had not yet got around to learning all the niceties of social life; if there were any, which she doubted. But her ignorance was her own fault. She had seen little of her aunt lately, probably because she had not wished to confess to lack of progress in her pursuit of the sultan. Most evenings she been so exhausted by a day of persecuting wildlife that she had just tumbled into bed as soon as possible.

The royal guests had been granted a standing invitation to Azak's daily state dinners, but after the first experience had shown what was involved, Inos had pettily declined, protesting that she was not a devotee of belly dancing. Kade, however, had been attending regularly, and must thereby have befriended many of the senior palace ladies in their spectators' gallery.

Moreover, Kade had been spending her days nibbling cookies with a sorceress. Could she have become so used to the situation that she saw nothing sinister in this odd development with the gown? Or was it Inos who was missing the point? Kade had never been a gossip and in their few brief chats she had volunteered little information about Rasha. Possibly this mysterious appointment would turn out to be just an innocent get-together.

And yet . . . a full formal ballgown for a private chat? It made no sense. It was wrong for Zark, it was out of character for Rasha. Rasha was quite capable of magicking Inos to a grand Imperial ball in Hub itself in that gown, or she might be planning a ball of her own under the great alabaster dome, a coven of sorcerers and sorceresses from all over Pandemia.

Why bother with a real gown when sorcery could make Inos look like anything or anyone? That question suggested a possible explanation for tonight's activities that roused whole legions of internal butterflies.

"She didn't say what she had in mind?"

"She wants you to meet someone, I believe."

But that time Inos heard a wrong note. "Aunt!" she challenged.

Kade laughed and reached out to squeeze Inos's hand where it rested on the balustrade. "I'm sorry, dear! I just couldn't resist teasing. You are to be presented! Such an honor!"

The butterflies took flight again. "Presented to who . . . whom?"

"His Omnipotence Warlock Olybino, my dear! Warden of the East." Kade began exuding copious ladylike excitement. "There is news of Krasnegar! Not all good news, I'm afraid, but now the imperor knows what has been happening, and the Four do, of course, even if the capital itself has not officially been informed—mundanely informed, that is—or so her Majesty tells me. Just think, Inos, you and I, here in faraway Zark, know things about Krasnegar that even the Senate in Hub hasn't heard yet!"

That had been true ever since they arrived. Inos listened with half an ear to the preliminaries, while running her mind's eye over the possibilities. Surely the warlock would not be coming here? So she must be going to Hub.

Escape from Zark!

Why did that prospect make her feel so uneasy? It should be good news!

Kade was at last getting to the point.

". . . Hub yet, not by post, but apparently there is a sorcerer somewhere in northwest Julgistro, and he, or perhaps she, reported what was going on to one of the wardens, Witch Bright Water, because that area is within her sector. She's North, you see? So the Four met with the imperor." Kade lowered her voice and glanced around. "His Imperial Majesty is very upset! It's never happened before in the history of the Impire, the sultana says."

"What hasn't?" Inos inquired sweetly.

"Goblins, dear! They've burned Pondague and they're raiding over the pass! Raiding inside the Impire!"

"Good for them!"

The odious Proconsul Yggingi had not only taught the goblins how to ravage, he had moved the entire Pondague garrison to Krasnegar. He had left the door unbarred.

"And of course the imperor . . . Inos? Inos, did you say—"

"The goblins want revenge, Aunt. Wouldn't you? If you'd been burned and pillaged?"

Kade blinked uncertainly. "I suppose so. I hope they don't do any serious damage!"

"I expect they'll try. Now, what of Krasnegar?"

"Well, no real change, dear. No signs of the jotnar yet. The ice is not out of the bay yet."

"And what exactly is the sultana planning for tonight?"

A faint hesitation . . . Kade gazed for a moment at the other bay, the harbor of Arakkaran, a bay that would never know ice.

"Just a meeting with Warlock Olybino, dear, to discuss how you may be restored to your throne."

Kade was clearly holding back now, and yet what she had said was enough to stir the tiny hairs on Inos's arms. "What is there to discuss? He has two thousand men in the town, doesn't he? The warlock of the east controls the legions, doesn't he? He need do no more than send me back there with a letter to Tribune Oshinkono. Need he?"

"That wouldn't solve everything," Kade said firmly.

No, of course it wouldn't. Not with Kalkor and his raiders due any day, a population divided and perhaps disloyal, a queen who could certainly not be trusted to choose herself a husband.

Now it was Inos who scowled out at the exotic city below her, the waving palms, the moon wakening to silver as day retreated in somber tones of mauve. She ought to be enjoying this adventure at the far end of the world. She ought to be excited at the thought of accompanying the sorceress to great Hub itself, to play the royal role, a queen making a state visit. Or at least she ought to be sighing for the safety and comfort and peace of Kinvale. But instead she was merely very homesick for dowdy little Krasnegar—Krasnegar as it used to be, without invading imps and the looming threat of Nordland. Without sorcery!

Father dead. Rap dead. Possibly many others dead now, if there had been fighting. But it was Krasnegar that stuck to her heart. Like a molasses sandwich, Rap would have said.

"A visit to Hub?" Inos mused. No more need to fret about Azak and Kar and family men. That should be exciting—why wasn't it?

"Isn't it wonderful?" Kade enthused. "I have dreamed all my life of visiting the capital, as you know, dear. And you are very fortunate to have a powerful sorceress like her Majesty to act on your behalf like this!"

Again a wrong note. Inos peered hard at her so-cheerful aunt.

"What gown will you be wearing?"

A momentary flicker of worry crossed her aunt's face and disappeared. "I'm not invited. Just you."

So that was what Kade was hiding!

Inos turned and hugged her, tightly. "I'm not going anywhere without you, Aunt! Absolutely not! After all, you are my chancellor and chamberlain, and so on!"

Kade gave an almost imperceptible sigh. "That's very kind of you, dear, but of course you must be guided by her Majesty."

Meaning that a mundane could not resist a sorceress. Whatever Rasha wanted, Inos would have no choice but to comply. Why was Kade not included in the invitation?

Inos released her, suddenly remembering that she was not in a state for closeness, not even polite company. She must certainly wash up and make herself presentable before she was presented to a warlock.

Kalkor the fearsome thane of Gark . . . Foronod the factor . . . imps and jotnar . . . even the imperor himself . . . none of those mattered now. If the wardens wanted Inos to be queen of Krasnegar, then she would be queen of Krasnegar.

And if they refused to support her, then nothing in the world would help.

4

At the third hour of the night, Inos draped her revealing gown in a voluminous cloak, covered her face, and set off across the palace grounds, escorted by four grim family men. They were all fierce, husky types bedecked with things for slashing, stabbing, or throwing; one bore a battle-ax slung on his back. They looked collectively capable of dismembering an Imperial legion, but when they came to the entry to the sorceress's quarters, they stepped aside to let Inos pass without even trying to conceal their relief that they need not accompany her farther.

She acknowledged their salutes with a regal nod, lifted her skirts, and started to climb the long stone staircase, her heavy train rustling over the treads behind her. She went quickly, so that she could attribute the thumping of her heart to exertion. At the top, she paused to discard the cloak, then set off along the wide corridor, her progress lighted by the restless flames of torches in golden sconces. She must have come this way on her first day, but she had no memory of doing so.

The voluminous samite gown was heavy and awkward, and yet a comforting reminder of similar, lesser gowns she had worn at Kinvale. She felt much more assured in it than she would have been in a Zarkian chaddar.

This was not a game, she reminded herself. This was not like calling on the fearsome Ekka, dowager dragon of Kinvale. This was politics, an affair of war and death.

But how to deal with the sinister Rasha? Kade had reported what little information she had been able to glean about the sorceress. Rasha had been the only daughter of poor fisherfolk in a tiny coastal village. At twelve she had been married off. *Sold* had been the word she had used to Inos herself, that first day, and a poor family with seven sons and one daughter had probably needed money to feed those more-valuable sons. Small wonder that Sultana Rasha hated men!

Her life had undoubtedly been hard and horrible in ways that Inos could not imagine, and yet somehow she had gained occult power. Now she was effectively ruler of a kingdom and could negotiate with warlocks. There was a great mystery there.

The corridor was barred eventually by massive double doors of metalwork and carven wood, inlaid with bright-fired jewels. Inos paused, irresolute. Should she knock or try to enter? Nestling amid writhing serpents and clawed reptilian monsters, the centerpiece of each great flap was a hideous demonic face with ivory tusks and eyes of some bright yellow stone that gleamed ominously in the wavering light. Inos reached for one golden handle, and the two faces sprang into life. Four eyes rolled around to regard her. She froze.

Lips of mahogany writhed over sycamore fangs, and a sepulchral voice boomed from the face on the left. "State your name and business!"

Kade had warned her, but it was a moment before she found her voice. "I am Queen Inosolan of Krasnegar."

The faces faded back into inanimate carvings, and the doors creaked open on their own.

She blinked, momentarily blinded by light that seemed as bright as noon. Then her eyes adjusted, and she blinked again. This was the same great circular bedchamber she had seen before, but now the jumble of ugly furniture and grotesque statuary had been removed.

Filmy draperies still floated around the same enormous four-poster bed at the far side, but everything else had changed. The wide expanse of mosaic floor was no longer concealed by rugs. Chairs and tables were few and elegant, vulgar clutter had been replaced by restrained good taste, and the tapestries on the walls now depicted landscapes or demure rural merrymaking. Inos recognized Angilki's touch, even if at secondhand. Now she knew what Kade had been up to in her days with the sultana.

The moon hung beyond the windows, but its rays were drowned in a flood of what seemed to be sunlight streaming down the central stairwell. Rasha was not present and must therefore be waiting in the upper room. Determined that a queen would not be intimidated, Inos raised her chin in defiance and set off toward the stair. She heard a gentle thump as the doors closed behind her.

Climbing purposefully, she looked up and saw that the white dome itself was the source of the light, blazing as if the sun were directly overhead and shining through the stone. Evil-begotten sorcery! Her curving path brought her within sight of the top, and it was flanked by the basalt panther and the glittery gray wolf, their front paws hooked over the uppermost step, their shiny amber eyes fixed upon her. They continued to watch as she approached and passed between them, but they remained statues.

Kade had been busy in the upper chamber, also, transforming cluttered ugliness into elegance, letting the intrinsic beauty of the great circular space speak for itself. A few simple divans and tables assisted, and did not argue. Inos was impressed, thinking that the duke of Kinvale himself would have been hard put to do better, even with the same occult resources. She could see evidences of sorcery: a potted palm whose fronds were writhing more than the usual breeze could account for, a bronze bust that represented a different person every time she looked at it, a device like a blue birdcage that buzzed and hummed. She decided to ignore those.

Three windows imprisoned stars and moonlight within their darkened arches, while the fourth was obscured by the jeweled drapery of Rasha's magic casement. Inos turned away quickly, oppressed by a sudden jolt of memory. Automatically she glanced over to the big looking glass in its silver frame—the glass that had told her of Rap's death. Now it was reflecting a distant image of Inos herself, her fine gown of pale green, her golden hair piled high and seeming strangely alien in Arakkaran now, even to her.

A tall girl was standing near it, waiting in solitary grandeur. Inos took a deep breath and walked toward her.

It was Rasha, but so transformed as to be barely recognizable. She seemed little older than Inos herself, but now she was using youth and beauty to depict ice-maiden innocence instead of voluptuous seduction. The high-prowed djinn nose seemed somehow less conspicuous but no less arrogant; thick rosewood-colored hair was piled high and pinned with gems; her gown was a luxurious miracle of yew-green silk, patterned in scrolls of a million tiny rubies. When selecting a style for Inos's gown, Kade had apparently held back from the extremes of Hub's current fashion, but Rasha had not. Her scanty lace bodice did nothing to conceal the jutting curves of large and shapely breasts, nor their hot djinn coloring.

Inos could not imagine herself ever appearing in public like that—not in Hub, nor Kinvale, nor Arakkaran.

She can inflame any man to madness, Azak had said. Would men would prefer this challenge of haughty majesty or the previous brazen inducement? That might depend on the man, of course, and either would be effective. Much less allure than this had reduced Rap to a babbling jelly.

Inos stopped and curtsied.

Rasha nodded approvingly. "It suits you to perfection, child. You are a great beauty." She had lost her harsh Zarkian accent.

At a loss for words, Inos curtsied again and then blurted, "I shall not be noticed beside yourself, ma'am."

Rasha registered faint amusement. "I certainly hope not! You know why I summoned you this evening?"

"To call on the warlock of the east, I understand." Inos wished her mouth was not so shamefully dry, wished she dare clasp her hands to restrain their need to tremble.

"Oh, hardly!" Rasha's laugh was a genteel tinkle, not the raucous mockery she had used before. "I would not fall into that trap! No, his Omnipotence will be calling on us!"

So Inos need not demand that Kade be summoned to accompany her! A deluge of relief told her how tense she had been at the prospect of arguing with the sorceress. That discovery annoyed her.

Rasha continued her calculating inspection of Inos. "However, he may send a votary in his place. As long as whoever comes is male, you will impress him, in that splendid Imperial-style costume." There was more than a hint of sarcasm in her tone.

Inos curtsied again.

Rasha sneered. "Think you can impress a warlock, do you?"

Well . . . yes! Inos was a far more genuine queen than this upstart slattern before her. She had been trained to wear finery and converse with cultivated gentlemen.

"I repeat, your Majesty, that he will not even see me in your company."

"That depends. If he materializes fully he will. That is why I arranged for your gown—your beauty is mundane and genuine, mine only occult artifice. Even if Olybino does appear in person, he will probably send only a projection of himself, and in that case his ability to penetrate my glamour will be very limited. He will also be harmless." She shrugged perfect shoulders. "It works both ways, of course. I hardly expect him to reveal his true appearance. What good is sorcery, if it will not nurture vanity?

"Come," she said, and led the way across to a pair of divans, upholstered in ivory silk and set at an angle to each other. "Don't be too proud, child. Warlocks are accustomed to gratifying their whims. If you do too good a job of impressing him, you may find yourself . . . surprisingly eager to accommodate his wishes, shall we say?" She laughed softly, but her eyes were mocking Inos's shock. "Do sit, though. We have a little time to kill. Wine?"

"Er . . . thank you." Inos sat and fussed at arranging her train, but eventually she forced herself to lift her chin and look across and meet the sultana's scornful gaze.

"Your Majesty, I behaved very badly the last time I was in this room. I did not thank you for rescuing me from the imps. Truly I am grateful and I apologize again for my discourtesy."

A slight movement of Rasha's lip seemed to convey more than a whole shrug might have done. "You were overwrought, and besotted by a man. Girls are subject to such fits of insanity. I hope you have recovered by now?"

"I shall never forget Rap. What he did for—"

"Your aunt told me. Whatever he did, he did for one reason only. Everything men do is aimed at possessing and using women!"

In Zark that might be more true than Inos had first thought. Rather than argue, she just smiled.

"You don't believe me?" The sorceress stretched out a hand and cupped the crystal goblet that stood on the table beside her. There was another on the table beside Inos, who had not previously noticed even the tables.

"You have much to learn, child," Rasha said. "Now I must warn you of something." She stabbed a stiletto fingernail toward a small rectangular rug. "Our visitor tonight will appear there."

Inos might have guessed that, for the mat was so positioned that anyone standing on it would be facing the two women, putting the three of them in a logical triangular grouping. She wondered why no chair had been provided; that seemed very inhospitable.

It was a curious mat, patterned in metallic tones of gold and silver and fiery copper, but as thin as paint. Even the knife-edge joints in the smooth mosaic floor seemed to show through to its surface, yet Inos could imagine that this strange carpet was not resting on the floor at all, but was somehow suspended above it, and the shiny spirals in the metallic surface went round and round while a faint, high note like a distant viol—

She jumped.

Rasha had snapped her fingers. "Don't look too hard at the mat, Inosolan. It's powerful stuff for a mundane."

"Er . . . yes. Thank you." Shakily Inos took a mouthful of wine, still aware of a faint singing in her ears. The patterns seemed to have daubed themselves on her eyes, dancing faintly in the air between her and anything she looked at.

"They're known in the trade as welcome mats," Rasha remarked. "So much power tends to leak a little. As I said, our guest will materialize there. There could be danger."

"Danger?"

"Yes, danger. And not just to your precious virtue, either!"

Why did she keep raising the stakes? Of course there were old tales of sorcerer wars and battles where occult powers had been loosed, but Inos had never paid them much heed.

"The sorcerous rarely trust one another." Rasha lowered her long dark lashes, and for a moment looked as untrustworthy as could be imagined. "Olybino may attempt a strike at me."

"Oh?" Inos wondered darkly which team she should be cheering.

"He may seek to lay a loyalty spell upon me. The wardens are particularly fond of that abomination—I expect they all do it. Of course, I might prove to be the stronger, and then he would be mine.'' Rasha smiled in thoughtful silence and sipped her wine.

Inos debated which question to ask first. Apparently she was expected to ask something. "Is there any way of . . . Can you judge in advance who—''

"Who's stronger? Not usually. It would require extensive intelligence work, and of course a sorcerer will normally seek to invoke the aid of his votaries. Battles between sorcerers can mushroom into occult wars with dozens involved on each side. That was what destroyed Shing Pol, and Lutant. Even the water in the harbor boiled at Lutant, so they say . . . I'm sure Olybino has been around long enough to have collected quite a few votaries.''

"Slave sorcerers?''

Rasha smiled, catlike. "But he has not had time to bring any to Arakkaran by mundane means, and I haven't detected any occult intrusions. I might have missed them, of course.'' She did not seem very worried; indeed, she seemed to be looking forward to whatever was going happen. "As I said, he may be too cautious to come himself. Even if he does, he will probably materialize very faintly, just a transparent wraith. In that case we shall merely have a civilized little chat, and he will depart again. If we wants to use any sorcery here, then he must project more of himself, and if he steps off the welcome mat, we can be sure his intentions are hostile—he will be trying to bring in help. I doubt that even a warlock can manage to do that and hold me off at the same time, but you had best take cover if it happens.''

"Take cover where, your Majesty?''

"Downstairs. Run like hell,'' Rasha snapped. That was the first real flaw Inos had detected in the aristocratic impersonation. The accent was still pure Hubban aristocrat, but the words did not ring true, even as humor.

"Run swiftly,'' Rasha said crossly, "to the stairs and get below floor level—understand? Apart from this chamber, the palace is shielded. That doesn't mean he can't come after you, of course, once he has dealt with me.'' She took another sip of wine, again regarding Inos carefully as she did so. "Or he might try to steal you away from me. Refuse any invitations or instructions to approach the welcome mat. Your aunt would miss you.''

So that was why Kade had not been invited! Inos was a token in the evil game, and Kade was a hostage for her good behavior.

Inos reached for her glass again, conscious that her hand was shaking again. She hoped that was only from anger.

"Tell me about him," she said.

Rasha smiled like a satisfied cat. "He is about my age, and an idiot. He likes to play with soldiers, and yet he has no more sense of strategy than a pigeon. About a year ago, the dwarf Zinixo appeared out of nowhere and slew Ag-An, the witch of the west. Had Olybino had any sense at all, he would have hailed the new warlock and tried to make friends. Instead he let himself be talked into a counterattack with Lith'rian, the elf. Elves hate dwarves, of course, but what had that to do with East? Nothing! Anyway, they failed miserably! So East has made a dangerous enemy. Whatever he may tell you, just remember that he is a very worried warlock!"

"Worried, ma'am?" What on earth could worry a warlock?

The sorceress nodded gloatingly. "He fears the dwarf's grudge. Only his alliance with Lith'rian protects him; he certainly can not trust mad old Bright Water to take his part, especially now his legions have despoiled her fellow goblins. So he needs the support of the imperor. He can vote, too, remember, if the Four split evenly."

Inos nodded dumbly, wondering what this had to do with her.

"Olybino has two thousand men stranded in Bright Water's sector, likely to be destroyed by jotnar as soon as the ice goes out. What will the imperor say to that, mmm?"

"I know that, but where do I come in?"

"You," Rasha said with obvious relish, "are extremely important!"

"I am?" Inos felt a tremor of excitement and hope.

"Yes, you are. If the warlock aids his troops against the jotnar raiders, then he violates the Protocol, because they are reserved to the witch of the north. If he tries to withdraw his men, then the goblins will attack, and Bright Water may come to their assistance. Again, he would provoke an occult war between wardens."

"So he needs a peaceful solution!" Inos cried. Who would have dreamed that events in tiny Krasnegar could have such far-flung repercussions? But Kade had been right all along to trust Rasha! Cool heads must prevail, she had said.

"And a peaceful solution needs you, Inosolan. If the wardens agree to put you on your throne, then they can force Kalkor to withdraw his claim, and the imperor, also. You are the only solution that may be acceptable to both sides."

Foronod and the hometown jotnar could not resist the wardens, either. They would just have to accept a reigning queen
whether they liked it or not! Wonderful! Inos took a drink in
celebration.

The sorceress lifted her own glass and sniffed, testing the
fragrance of the wine while regarding Inos carefully over the
rim. "Azak lusts after you."

Damnable woman!

"You blush, so you already know that."

"I have seen no evidence of it; he avoids me utterly. And any
lady would blush at such a statement."

"Lady?" the sorceress muttered. "What exactly is a lady?
Never mind. Give me your opinion of our self-styled sultan."

"He is crude and violent, a barbarian!" Of course, if all a
woman cared for was muscles and size, then Azak was unsurpassed. But what sort of woman would want a human stallion?

Red fire burned within the ice—Rasha's eyes glittered at Inos
over the top of the glass. Inos wondered nervously what she
might have provoked, and why, but all the sorceress said was,
"You have not told me what you think of my wine."

Inos reached for her goblet. "It is quite delicious, ma'am.
Elvish, is it not?"

"No, it's only the local rotgut, but I upgraded it. Glad you
like it. Where have you tasted elvish?"

"At Kinvale, at Winterfest. Well, my father let me try it
once . . ."

Rasha sipped thoughtfully, still playing the part of haughty
aristocrat to perfection. In what way was this cryptic sorceress
hoping to impress the warlock? Inos could imagine her floating
into any ladies' salon at Kinvale without ruffling a single eye-
lash—except of course the conspiratorial mothers and duennas
would indulge in mass suicide on seeing their marriageable wards
and daughters so utterly outclassed. A mere adept, knowing
only two words of power, could master any skill with ease, so
Kade would have found a sorceress a miraculously quick pupil.

Coursing after hounds with Azak suddenly seemed like a very
relaxing occupation compared to this sinister soiree.

"Your quarters are satisfactory, your Majesty?" Rasha laid
her goblet carefully on the table and smiled.

So now it was conversation time? Inos hastily gathered her
wheeling wits and began enthusing politely about her quarters.
The small talk danced rapidly around Arakkaranian horses,
Kade's life in Kinvale, and comparisons of climate. To babble

such trivialities with a sorceress was a weirdly unexpected experience, but Inos was quite willing to cooperate. Peaceful solution! Extremely important!

If Rasha was now seeking to put her at ease, then she was being very skillful, and of course even the Imperial gowns, more familiar than djinn costume, might be designed to help. Alternatively, the sorceress might just be practicing her own acting technique. Or both.

Inos prattled on in the approved Kinvale fashion, saying nothing, playing the game. When she had first been introduced to small talk, she had found it a deadly boring pastime. Then she had discovered that it had little rules, and she could keep score, and play it as a contest. She had confessed this once to a couple of other girls at Kinvale and discovered that they were doing the same. Even their respective sets of rules had turned out to be similar.

Rasha was holding Inos to a tie.

"Your aunt Kadolan is a remarkable woman."

Ah! Two points for compliments about a relative.

"I love her dearly. She is all I have left." One point for sickly sentiment.

The sorceress nodded and for a moment seemed to brood. "There is something about her . . . She is a lady, I suppose. So she regards herself. My experiences of so-called aristocrats have rarely been pleasant, Inosolan. I was prepared to despise her. I thought that 'lady' meant 'parasite.' I deliberately told her something of my history and background. I expected contempt."

Silence fell. Lose the match for going serious . . . Inos said softly, "She pitied you. She still does."

"Yes, she does. And that surprised me, I admit."

"Despite her affected ways, Kade is a very genuine and sympathetic human being. There isn't a mean bone in her body."

"No, there isn't. I have learned much from her in the last two weeks. As you have noticed?"

Inos took her courage between her teeth and said, "You can read my thoughts?"

Rasha glanced at her quizzically, then laughed. "You can usually tell when someone is lying, can't you?"

"I . . . I may suspect."

"A sorcerer knows. Mundanes give themselves away all the time, as obviously as dogs wagging tails or cats arching backs. That is most of it, a talent called *insight*. Sorcery can go further, of course, but I don't like to pry, because it takes all the fun out of things. Other people's minds turn out to be as disgusting as one's own, and mucking about in them is depressing. It also tends to addle their brains. Torture is cleaner.''

Inos shivered, and Rasha chuckled. Then she glanced over at the east window and frowned. "He is late!"

She was forgetting her illusion of youth. No woman of her apparent years, a mere girl, could ever radiate confidence as she did. At Kinvale Inos had met maidens of great beauty and such elevated breeding and self-esteem that they could hardly breathe, but none of them had been as assured as this seeming innocent. And she was criticizing a warlock, no less.

The wine was superb. Inos was grateful for the warmth it poured through her. Despite the white glare of the dome overhead, this was nighttime in Arakkaran and the sweet-tempered wind was cool now on her arms and shoulders.

"It is nearly three weeks since your father died."

Inos sobered. "Yes, ma'am."

"Three weeks since he gave you his word of power."

Very sober! "I don't think he did give me a word of power, your Majesty. I think he tried, but he was too ill, too weak. He said something, yes. It was only gibberish."

Rasha eyed her thoughtfully. "They are all gibberish. No one knows what language they are in or what they mean, if anything. If you heard it, you must remember it. Can you remember it?"

"No, ma'am, I can't. I mean I can just remember bits of it. Like a long 'ooo' sound near the end."

What if Rasha demanded the word of power and Inos couldn't tell her? What if the warlock did? Red-hot hooks or addled brains? Inos's hand tightened around her goblet, and she reminded herself yet again that she was a queen and must play politics with truly royal nerve.

Now the scrutiny was longer. "Everyone is good at something."

"I beg your pardon?" Inos said politely.

"Everyone has a talent for something. Gulth's was thinking like a fish."

Inos peered carefully to see if the sorceress was trying to be humorous. "Did you say, 'Thinking like a fish,' your Majesty?"

"When I was twelve, my parents owed much money to an old man called Gulth. He took me in part payment."

"Kade told me. Tragic."

Kade might not have a mean bone in her body, but Inos was uncomfortably aware that she herself had quite a few.

"Mmm. Gulth had a word of power. His native talent was a skill at fishing. Even without the word, he might have been a success. With it, he was a genius. Always he knew where the nets should go, where the fish would be that day. Had he also had any real brains at all, he might have grown rich. He didn't. Even so, he was the least poor man in the village."

"Least poor! You are being ironic, Majesty?"

"Meaning he had two blankets and his roof was the only one that didn't leak. He taught me what I must do to please him. It was better than being beaten."

"But not much better, I expect? Not at that age."

"Very much better. Obviously you have never been properly beaten. And I had a natural talent for it."

For being beaten? Surely not! Inos wished that the warlock would arrive soon and interrupt this dangerously personal conversation. "Talent for . . . ?"

Queen Rasha's lip curled in either contempt or sarcasm. "For pleasing men, your aunt would call it. Gulth was old and weak. He was also greedy, once he understood what he had in me. He told me his word of power!"

Inos didn't think she understood that, and might prefer not to.

"Shared it. He whispered it in my ear one cold, damp dawn, and I, too, became a genius, a genius at pleasing men. But he was old and sick. I expect the word had been helping to keep him alive. He weakened his power by sharing it, you understand? And then he overexerted himself."

"Doing what?"

"Being pleased."

"Oh."

"So I was a widow and just turned fourteen, but I was a genius at pleasing men."

"Ah!"

"And my talent was even stronger after he died, of course. A self-defeating talent most of the time!"

"Why that?" Inos inquired foggily, thinking of Azak for some reason. Did big men need more pleasing than little men?

"Babies."

"Oh."

"And what is your natural talent, Inosolan?"

"Not politics, certainly. Perhaps riding and hunting—"

"No," said the sorceress firmly. "You used no occult power on Evil that first day. I saw that episode. You ride well, but only as a mundane."

Shocked, Inos said nothing. The sorceress stared at her darkly.

"You don't seem to have one, do you? You're certainly not hiding anything from me. You just don't know the answer. I've watched you from time to time, but I don't know, either!"

"Could I have a talent for just being a good all-rounder?"

Rasha laughed abruptly and took a sip of wine. "That's a contradiction in terms, I think. We shall have to wait and see. Perhaps one day you'll discover you're the world's greatest ventriloquist, or vase painter—but when you say you don't remember what your father said, you're lying."

Inos started to protest and the sorceress raised a hand to stop her. "It adds to your value. Let us talk of pleasanter things."

Shaken by that ominous mention of value, Inos racked her brains for a safe topic. Perhaps Rasha was not too dangerous when there were no men present and the conversation was kept well away from men. And how many people ever had a chance for a heart-to-heart talk with a real sorceress?

She must try to learn about magic, of course. "How did you learn the rest of your words, ma'am?"

"From men!" The sultana scowled dangerously, but her gaze was on the sinister mat, not on Inos. "A word makes you lucky, they say, and I suppose mine did—at times. A widow's lot is never easy, and yet I lived in a palace for a while."

She glanced up momentarily. "No, I was not assigned to a prince. A commoner's cast-off is not worthy of such an honor!"

Inos felt herself blush and saw the sorceress sneer faintly in response.

"I entertained important guests! Oh, it was a fair living. But one word won't stop you aging. I was out again when I was twenty-two. When I was sixty, I was one of the lowest-price whores on the Arakkaran waterfront. And that is low."

Kinvale training faltered. Inos could think of nothing to say. She could not even imagine such a life, so any sympathy she offered would be as phony as Prince Kar's smiles. She hoped the warlock would come soon.

Rasha, too, was becoming impatient, glaring out at the stars beyond the windows, absently scratching at a cushion with a long carmine nail. "Then there was a sailor they called Nimble. He was old, like me. Older. It may just be that our words attracted each other, but he was still nimble, and I still had my genius. He had much joy of me, and he shared his scanty fare."

She seemed almost to have forgotten Inos, seemed almost to be talking to some long-forgotten invisible ghost. That was creepy enough, but to hear a young girl speak of times long ago, of disease and poverty and suffering in the seaport slums of Zark, was even more unnerving.

In his last illness, she said, Nimble had told his friend of a lucky word he had heard once, long ago and far away, in Guwush. "So he died, and I was an adept."

"I don't know much about adepts, your Majesty."

The sorceress hesitated and then laughed her discreet Kinvale laugh. "I didn't either, then. And I don't know why I'm telling you all this now. Could that be your talent, Inosolan? Your genius—to worm out confidences? But I detect no ripples."

"Ripples, ma'am?"

"The use of power sets up ripples in the ambience. The more power, the more disturbance. At this range, I could detect almost anything you were doing, perhaps even just using one of the sights. But your power would not work on me anyway." She took another sip of wine and pouted again.

"Your magic casement behaved very oddly that night. When you first opened it, the whole of Pandemia rang with escaping power, and yet such devices are valued precisely because they are usually discreet. Something had charged it with power, and I don't know what would do that. You were very fortunate that most of the sorcerous were safely asleep in their shielded little beds. I was awake and felt the shock, even here."

The ruddy eyes slid sideways to watch Inos. "I was pacing the floor, waiting for someone."

Inos took a sip of wine. The talk was again becoming dangerous.

Rasha went back to frowning at the rug and picking her nail on a silken cushion. The noise felt like sand under Inos's skin.

"So you want to know about adepts? An adept rarely has much occult power, but give her a lesson or a few hours on her own to practice and she can become expert at any mundane skill. Like acting, for instance!

"When I understood what I could do," Rasha went on, "I headed for the nearest palace, which happened to be this one. I moved in."

"No one stopped you?"

"No one saw me. At least, they didn't see what they should

have seen. You don't know what slums are like, child, but I knew palaces. Much nicer!''

That was funny—that the harlot from the docks should walk into the royal palace and not be questioned by anyone. Inos risked a chuckle.

Even Rasha smiled. "Yes, it was amusing. I helped myself to whatever I wanted. I ate and drank, joined in the conversations, slept between silken sheets, and no one ever questioned why a toothless crone should be living among the undistributed maidens. They saw me otherwise, and assumed I was an instructor of some kind. Until I ran into the sultan one day.''

"Sultan Zorazak?''

"Zorazak." Rasha sighed, then. "He was an adept, too, you see.''

Suddenly everything became very clear. For centuries the kings of Krasnegar had known one word of power. The sultans of Arakkaran had known two. Well, not quite everything . . .

"So you didn't fool him?''

"Not for an instant. He demanded to know who I was and what I was doing. So I told him.''

"What happened then?'' Inos asked, bracing herself for some more horrors, dreading that now she would hear of some final fiendish experience that had completed Rasha's hatred of men.

"He sat down and laughed until he cried.''

In the silence that followed, Inos felt goosebumps rising on her arms and she hugged herself against the playful teasing of the wind, rich with the scents of night flowers. Two adepts in a palace, and one of them the sultan? She must not let her suspicions congeal into thoughts lest her face betray her. Which one did she trust less—Azak or Rasha?

Rasha just sat and brooded.

"They used a slow poison on him," she said at last. "They weren't sure about the magic, you see, but there had always been rumors in Arakkaran, and they wanted to give him time to pass along whatever he had. At best they hoped for a single word.''

And the old villain had bequeathed both his words to Rasha instead of Azak, the obvious successor. Rasha had then been a full four-word sorceress. But what had Rasha been to Zorazak? Friend? Occult companion? Or much worse? How long had she lived in the palace after the sultan discovered her, and had she used her sorcerous wiles to make the old man bequeath her his words of power? Inos wondered if she dared ask any of those questions and vacillated between them like a donkey between hay piles—and in the end she got to ask none of them.

A soldier stood on the welcome mat.

5

On one particularly bad afternoon at Kinvale, Proconsul Yggingi had cornered Inos between a spinet and a hydrangea and delivered an interminable sour-breathed lecture on military insignia. She recalled only that the color of the helmet crest was important; white for a centurion and so on. Purple for the emperor himself, scarlet for the marshal of the armies—who else but one of those two would wear a cuirass inlaid with the Imperial star in gold and jewels?

There were more gems inset in his greaves and the hilt of his short sword, but the helmet now being tucked under that muscular arm bore a crest that looked more like spun gold than dyed horse bristles.

She was on her feet and did not recall rising. Rasha was lounging back at ease on her divan, but yet she was watching the newcomer tautly. He had already saluted her. By removing his helmet he was making the visit unofficial, informal. He was smiling.

He was tall for an imp, square-jawed, dark-eyed, and astonishingly young. Teeth flashed as he glanced around the big dome and made some complimentary remark to Rasha. Black curls.

He looked solid, not in the least transparent.

Then he seemed to notice Inos for the first time and stopped speaking in midsentence. His bright eyes widened in wonder.

Corny, yes, but still effective when well done.

"*You* are Inosolan?"

Inos curtsied low. When she rose, he bowed—gracefully, of course. No absurd Zarkian flourishes, either; just a good, solid, Imperial bow. Rasha had said he was old, but he didn't look old. Bronzed and lean, and sparkling eyes . . . even Andor would not have competed with him in looks.

Or youthful charm: "They told me you were a great beauty, ma'am, but I was making allowances for the usual exaggeration. All imps cherish romantic ideals of royalty. Queens are wonderously beautiful by definition!" He grinned. "You redefine the standard!"

Marvelously done, with just enough humor to carry it off.

Evil take it, but she was blushing like a child!

"Your Omnipotence is most gracious."

He chuckled. "No, I'm genuinely impressed, and it takes a lot to surprise a warlock." He seemed to tear his eyes away from her in order to address Rasha. "You did us all a favor, mistress, when you rescued Queen Inosolan from that rabble. God knows what might have happened!"

"I know exactly what would have happened," Rasha said coldly.

The warlock lifted eyebrows that reminded Inos of a poem about ravens' wings. "Yes, I'm afraid I do, too. Well, we are grateful for what you did. And we must certainly undo the damage, and see justice done and her Majesty installed on the throne of her fathers."

He turned back to Inos and gave another long sigh of wonder. "Tomorrow is Blossom Day in Hub and the Blossom Ball in the Opal Palace. The imperor will be there. Everyone will be there! Consuls, senators, the aristocracy of the Impire. And you will amaze them all! Queen Inosolan, would you wear that gown for me tomorrow and do me the very great honor of letting me escort you to the Blossom Ball?"

Inos stammered. She was being bribed. Flattered. Seduced. She must remember that he had no more right to look youthful and handsome than Rasha had. But he was making her heart pound, and she recalled how Rap had been unmanned by the sorceress. Unwomanned? It didn't feel like being *unwomanned*. He made her feel very womanly. Charm! Even his renewed grin seemed to admit what he was doing to her, a naughty-boy, isn't-this-fun grin. She must remember Kade.

He held out a hand.

She took a step. Another. Remember Kade. He's not a boy. He's old. Remember Kade. Remember Kade . . .

"That will do for now!" Rasha said.

Cold bath!

Inos stopped, feet frozen to the floor. Her hand was stretched out to the warlock's, the fingers almost touching.

The warlock shrugged. "Something wrong, ma'am?" he asked the sorceress, while flickering a hint of a wink at Inos.

"You forgot to leave some coppers on the dresser."

He pursed his lips disdainfully, yet he did not lose his amusement. "Then by all means let us discuss what reward we can offer. The Four always repay debts, usually manyfold!" He smiled apologetically to Inos. "Do please be seated, Inos. You don't mind if I call you Inos? I'm sure this won't take long."

By the time Inos had returned to her couch and adjusted her train, a seat had appeared behind Warlock Olybino—a chair like crystallized sunbeams, a throne raised on a dais, with sculpted gold ablaze on arms and back, encrusted in rainbow jewels. Inos had never seen its like, even in picturebooks or paintings. She wondered what it weighed, and if it was real, and whether the floor would support it. Everything else in the great dome seemed suddenly dull and shabby. In one lithe movement, the warlock stepped up backward and sat, placing the crested helmet on his lap, smiling down at the two women.

Puzzled, Inos glanced at Rasha and caught a hint of a sneer. What had she said about Olybino knowing no more strategy than a pigeon? The throne was *wrong!* Did warlocks forget how to handle defiance?

Rasha had hardly moved since the warlock arrived. She conveyed ease and yet wariness, like a watchful cat. "That looks like a very uncomfortable seat. I can recommend a good physic for piles, if you feel the need."

His smile faded to sad reproof. "Perhaps you do not understand the situation, mistress? We are talking justice here! We do not buy and sell queens, or kingdoms! You are not bargaining in a bazaar for a poke of dried dates."

"And you are not dispensing judgment in Emine's Rotunda."

He frowned. "Take care that I do not!"

Inos sensed a pompous man trying not to bluster.

Rasha sat up suddenly. "Enough of this nonsense! I have the girl, and you need her!"

"Need?" He shook his head and favored Inos with a brief glance of what-does-she-mean perplexity.

But Inos knew what Rasha meant. Help had its price. She was going to be sold! *Kade had been wrong, and she had been right!* Rasha was no friend. Rasha was a whore and thought like a whore. And what mattered except price when these two evil old sorcerers wanted to bargain?

"Need, mistress? I am a warlock. I *need* nothing."

The sultana snorted. "You need protection from West!" Her polished accent was starting to sound scratched. "You and the elf can't handle him. You can't count on Bright Water to keep the peace, because she doesn't always find her mouth with the spoon these days. You dare not antagonize the imperor by losing those men in Krasnegar, and you can't solve the Krasnegar problem without *her*!'' She jabbed a fingernail in the direction of Inos.

Raven wings swooped low—the warlock scowled. ''What strange rumors have you been hearing, mistress? I need no protection from Warlock Zinixo! Young West is doing splendidly. I've been giving him pointers. He's an apt pupil, and grateful. South doesn't like him, but that's to be expected. Everyone knows you don't invite elves and dwarves on the same evening.''

Rasha yawned. ''Meet my price, or go away. I can peddle my wares elsewhere.''

Peddle my wares! Inos shivered with an urge to unsheath claws and slash with them. How dare this phony old strumpet speak of her like that!

The warlock smiled slyly, narrowing his eyes. ''Besides, even if I suggested restoring the girl to her homeland, how could we be sure of Bright Water's cooperation? Her agreement is essential, for it is a jotunn matter, and in her sector. Her feet do not always point the same way these days, as you said, and she has always had a soft spot for butchers like Kalkor. It's her goblin blood.''

Rasha shrugged. ''Let her choose the husband. He will have to be neutral, and she must have hundreds of relatives scattered around.''

Olybino nodded, suddenly thoughtful.

Inos did not believe it. ''What!'' she shouted. ''Marry me to a *goblin*?''

''Quiet!'' Rasha snapped, without looking away from the warlock. ''They're all the same color in the dark, dearie, and no one's going to let you go back home without a husband.''

''Such a waste,'' Olybino muttered. ''But intriguing! Yes, it might just work!''

Married to a goblin? Inos felt sick. At least the Krasnegarians would unite to oppose *that*—and yet their resistance would be useless against the Four. And her only option would be to kill herself.

''Definitely a possibility,'' the warlock said. ''And your price, Mistress Rasha?''

''The red palace, of course,'' Rasha said.

''Impossible!'' Olybino roared. In one fast move he donned his helmet, sprang from the throne, and landed nimbly back on the mat. The throne and its dais vanished at his back. ''Completely impossible!'' He put his fists on his hips and somehow seemed to swell, grow thicker, older, larger. He no longer re-

sembled the urbane military officer who had sipped tea in Kinvale drawing rooms. Now he was much more like the rough
soldiers Inos had known on her journey through the forest—
dangerous, ruthless. He glowered, huge and menacing, embodiment of the Imperial legions, the armored bullies of all
Pandemia. "Think again, sorceress!"

Rasha was on her feet, also, although Inos had not seen her
move. The room seemed to shimmer, like water approaching
the boil.

"That is the price, Warlock!"

Olybino hunched his shoulders, glaring. "Fool! It is incon-
ceivable."

"Then I keep the girl, and Kalkor will have your cohorts
and—"

"Let him! Do you think it matters? Pondague was a penal
posting. They are the scum of the army, they had deserted their
post, and the imperor will be well rid of them. Jotnar or goblins,
it does not matter. And who cares about Krasnegar, anyway? It
was never of any importance—as you would have realized, had
you known any Imperial politics at all!"

"Begone!" Rasha screamed.

Just for a fraction of an instant, Inos thought she saw them as
they were: old, squat, ugly—Rasha short and fat, Olybino
paunchy and balding . . .

Lightning flashed, thunder roared.

And the lights went out.

6

The sun, which had completed its daily rounds in Zark some
hours before, was now winding up in Faerie, also. Already bird
headed for nest and bee sought hive. Night beasts stirred from
their slumber, while welcome shadows crept outward from
the edge of the jungle and spread across the fields . . .

Hugg was a troll and therefore not nearly as stupid as he
looked. He was not especially bright, either, but he knew he
had laid his supper on the dirt beside him only a moment before.
Now it was gone. While he thought about that, he linked his
fingers together around a coconut and cracked it. Munching the
pieces, Hugg came to the firm conclusion that he had been
robbed. That meant he would get nothing more tonight except
probably a beating for losing the bucket. He had brought his
meal to the edge of the field so he could sit in the shade. He had

not seen the thief out in the open, but there were bushes behind him.

Hugg rose, reared to his full height, and turned around. Trolls' ears and noses were much more acute than those of most other men, and their strength let them move through thick jungle faster than almost anything else. They could also do so in eerie silence if they wished, despite their size and ungainly appearance. In fact, trolls were unsurpassed as woodsman, and the wind was in his favor.

He put his head down and lurched forward like a charging behemoth. He did not bother with stealth, because he could tell that his quarry was still in motion, bearing the precious lunch bucket farther away all the time. Furthermore, he had not removed his clothes, and they caught and tugged and ripped on thorns and branches. Stripped, Hugg could have slid through the undergrowth as silent and unscathed as a fish in water.

Under the lowering rain clouds of their native valleys in the Mosweeps, trolls haunted forests of perpetual gloom. Although their doughy hides were durable as pigskin, they were very susceptible to sunburn, and any good overseer knew enough to provide his trolls with a complete covering of clothes. It was an extra expense, but trolls were worth it.

Hugg was twenty-four years old. When he was fourteen he had wandered into a village to trade some bright stones for a chisel. Trolls were much given to erecting massive edifices of raw masonry among their jungle-quilted hills, usually choosing a site that straddled a stream, so that they could have running water in every room. A troll might spend years on such a construction and then just walk away from it before it was complete, only to begin another two or three valleys over. Hugg had begun to feel restless and unsatisfied with the tower his parents were building. He had decided to go off and begin work on one of his own rather than continue to help on theirs. Perhaps, when he had completed two or three rooms by himself, some wandering trolless would come along to help. Meanwhile, the first thing he needed was a chisel, one of those shiny bronze ones and not the junky steel kind that rusted away in a week or so.

Ever since conquering that part of the Mosweeps fifty years earlier, the Impire had been striving to gather the inhabitants out of their dark, damp forests into specially designed model villages, hoping to civilize them and keep an eye on them and encourage them to increase their numbers. Out of the trees and into one of these villages wandered Hugg. He was at once arrested for indecent exposure and for not possessing a permit. He did not know what a permit was. He did not know why clothes were necessary. He explained patiently that he would cover himself until he departed if that was required, but normally he never saw anyone except his own reflection; and in the forest, cloth or even leather would certainly rot away to pulp within a few days. He did not understand why his offer was not an acceptable compromise.

Nor did he understand the courtroom proceedings, short and simple though they were. He was sentenced to two years' hard labor and led off for a three-week introductory course in the value of docility. His bright stones had been taken from him, but they were not mentioned in the court records.

Ever since the reign of the Impress Abnila, slavery had been illegal in the Impire; but the army had to find some way to cover the cost of its occupation of the Mosweeps, and graft was as widespread and inevitable as weather.

As soon as Hugg had learned to do exactly what he was told as fast as possible and never to speak unless spoken to, his place of confinement was changed from Hamlet 473 to the town of Danqval, and from there he was marched in an ever-increasing brigade of other convicts down to the market in Clamdewth.

Later he and a few others enjoyed a brief sea voyage, Hugg having an oar all to himself on the basic principle of *two men or one troll*. He arrived at last at a plantation somewhere to the north of Milflor and was then provided with a chance to escape, which he did.

They always did.

He was run down with hounds and horses and given a lesson that left him ever after with a slight limp and a ringing in one ear. Even trolls could learn from that sort of teaching, and they healed quickly. Never again did he try to escape.

At twenty-four, Hugg was still there. He did not know that he should have been shipped home after two years. Had he known that, and asked for an explanation, he would have learned that his file had been mislaid and he must pen a formal petition to the marshal of the armies, in Hub, as his area had been under military rule at the time of his offense. But he did not ask, and no one told him, and nothing would have changed anyway.

He dug and tilled and harvested; he chopped wood and bore burdens as he was told. He grew to be the largest and strongest troll on the plantation, and no one ever stole his supper.

Following the scent and unmistakable sounds of flight, Hugg

plunged through the trees and bushes, smashing and breaking and even uprooting as required, heedless of his own noise or the damage to his clothes. After a few minutes, he realized that there were two or three persons ahead of him and he remembered old stories of headhunting fairyfolk. Perhaps he had been rash, therefore, but he had never heard of any natives coming near the plantations, and the fugitives were obviously running away as fast as they could. That was good, because their scent was not troll scent, and therefore he could outrun them in this undergrowth. Furthermore, if they were running away they were probably unarmed, and then he would not hesitate to accept odds of three to one, or perhaps even four. Trolls were placid by nature, but they could be roused to anger like anyone else. Hugg enjoyed his daily bucket of slop. He intended to win it back.

He heard a few loud oaths ahead of him, a couple of shouts, and knew from the sounds that his pursuit was to be contested. Two kept running—still carrying his meal, doubtless—but one had turned back to challenge. A moment later Hugg crashed through a dense wall of shrubbery and saw him. He was a husky youth, but shorter even than the average imp, and half the size of a troll. In the dappling shade of the branches, he seemed a very odd color. He smelled strange and his eyes were curiously angular. He was standing in a half crouch, holding out his hands and waiting for Hugg with a big toothy grin.

Trolls preferred action to thought. Roaring with joy and never breaking stride, Hugg swung a fist that should have stoved in the brat's chest. The last thing he saw was a tree trunk, dead ahead.

"God of Mercy!" Rap shouted. "Did you have to kill him?"

Little Chicken folded his arms and turned his smirk into a sneer. "You think he wanted to talk?"

No, the giant had not wanted to talk; and now he would never talk again. The bark of the tree bore more obvious damage than did his head, but his neck was undoubtedly broken. Abandoning futile efforts to find a pulse, Rap rose shakily to his feet and glared across the corpse at the goblin.

The situation was a creepy echo of the time they had faced each other across the body of the fairy child, but then Little Chicken had been as distraught and bewildered as Rap. Now he was showing his huge goblin teeth in a satisfied grin, proud of having beaten an opponent so much larger than himself.

Since the castaways had left the fairy village and headed south, Little Chicken had changed ominously. He now spoke passable impish and thus could express himself better, but there was more to it than that. He had grown in confidence. He swaggered now, he often smirked as if relishing some secret joke, he patronized Rap again, as he had in the taiga, and he treated Thinal like an unwanted and unpleasant child. He was obnoxious and unnerving.

"Used a leg throw on him," he said, nudging the corpse with his foot. "Didn't see the tree there. Not much time to plan ahead when you're about to be smeared, Flat Nose."

That was not quite what Rap had seen with his farsight. Admittedly his attention had been mostly on his own undignified flight through the shrubbery, and he had not seen the throw, but he was fairly sure that Little Chicken had then picked the troll up bodily and rammed the tree with him. In fact the evidence was clear—the man had obviously made a right-angle turn somewhere on his journey.

Thinal was creeping back through the bushes, at the same time gobbling whatever was in the pail he had stolen. Using two fingers, he was scooping mush into his mouth, spreading it liberally on his chin, also. Rap shouted to say it was all clear, then went back to scowling at Little Chicken's self-satisfied smirk.

Time had ceased to mean very much, but the moon was almost full now, so the refugees had been in Faerie more than two weeks. Their journey south had been aided by the equipment salvaged from the deserted village—nets and waterbottles, hats and boots made by Little Chicken, backpacks jammed with food. Those supplies had lasted them all the way to the edges of the impish colony around Milflor. Here they had been forced to detour inland, staying in the fringe of the jungle and gradually replacing the fairy kit with whatever Thinal's quick eyes fancied. Their passage through the settled lands had been marked by a steady pilfering of local garments and foodstuffs, as the little thief looted larders, clotheslines, and even ovens.

So Rap had a good pair of boots at last, and a fine cotton shirt. Little Chicken wore nothing at all except a soft and frilly pair of silk pants. He was extremely proud of those, not having realized that they were actually a woman's undergarment, as Thinal had sniggeringly confided to Rap.

Now Thinal himself squeezed cautiously through a canebrake and gulped at the sight of the corpse. "By the Powers!" He looked at the goblin. "How'd you manage . . ." He shot a scared glance at Rap, who knew what he was thinking, although none of them had ever yet put it into words.

"Little Chicken is a skilled wrestler."

"Skilled?" Thinal shook his head in wonder. "That's a full-blooded troll!"

"He's big."

"Big? They're just about indestructible. Even the half-breeds . . . Listen, officially there's no such things as gladiator contests anymore, right? But some of the big houses round Hub . . . Darad's made money fighting at them."

Little Chicken looked interested. "They wrestle?"

"Not usually." Thinal shoveled more of the paste into his mouth. "But a troll with a club against men armed like legionaries—that's a popular match. Big stakes."

"How many imps?"

"All together, usually three. One at a time, it may take five or six to wear him out, sometimes more. And you just knocked off a troll singlehanded?"

The goblin chuckled. With a lightning snatch he relieved Thinal of the bucket, then held it out to Rap. "Eat!"

"I don't want any."

"Eat, Flat Nose!"

"No!"

"I will stuff it down your throat. Have to keep your strength up, faun."

He was mostly just mocking, Rap thought, flaunting his superiority; but perhaps he still regarded himself as Rap's trash, who must care for his master. Either way, Rap had no doubt that he had best do as he was told, for clearly Little Chicken's blood had been roused by the fight, and he would love an excuse for another tussle.

So Rap took the bucket and stepped back from the huge corpse. Flies were buzzing around it already.

"Let's go somewhere better, then. None of this poor guy's stuff will fit any of us." In fact, only the troll's boots were worth a second glance. He had pretty well stripped himself naked coming through the undergrowth, ripping even his leather breeches in a dozen places. His fungus-colored hide was barely scuffed.

"Let's get well away!" Thinal said, wiping his mouth and then licking his hand. "Someone'll come looking soon . . ." He gaped at Rap in sudden horror. "Hounds! When they find his body, they'll put hounds on us!"

"Leave hounds to me," Rap said, gagging at the sour taste of the slave's mash. "But they may have more trolls, and this one was following our scent."

Thinal nodded with disgust. "I'll remember in the future." A city thief had not expected a victim to trail him that way, nor thought to check wind direction. Even an occult genius was not infallible.

"Leave trolls to me," said the goblin, with another satisfied gloat at the dead one.

Destiny with men:
>   'Tis all a Chequer-board of Nights and Days
>   Where Destiny with Men for Pieces plays:
>   Hither and thither moves, and mates, and slays,
>   And one by one back in the Closet lays.
>   Fitzgerald, *The Rubaiyat of Omar Khayyam*
>   (§49, 1859)

❲ FIVE ❳

Slave and sultan

1

The moon was all wrong in Zark. It rode much too high in the sky and it seemed to have been tilted sideways, so its face was strange and unfamiliar. Not that Kadolan was looking at the moon, but she was aware of its beams shining on the floor below the windows, and those bright patches were much smaller than they could ever be in Krasnegar. Such unleaded windows would be unthinkable there at any time, while here even in the middle of a spring night, the wind was no worse than cool. Reflections of moonlight on marble gave ample light.

She huddled on the edge of her bed in her flounced robe, a frilly nightcap pulled down low to hide her curlers, and her feet snug inside goatswool slippers. Her niece was pacing the chamber as the cheetah in Duke Angilki's zoological garden paced its cage. Just as the cheetah made a sort of half rear at the end of each length to start its turn, so Inosolan swept her train around in a swish of samite before retracing her steps.

She was on the third or fourth telling now, still very upset, understandably. "Aghast" might be a more exact word. Kadolan had not even grasped the enormity of it all herself and had not experienced the terror of it firsthand, as Inosolan had. Small wonder that now she need talk herself down from an emotional high that had flown perilously near hysteria. ". . . so here's my choice except that I don't even get to choose but apparently I'm either to be married off to a goblin or else the imps and the jotnar will fight each other to the death and the goblins move in to finish up the survivors and everyone I know'll be dead and there won't be a kingdom left to rule anyway and as for me I'll probably end up entertaining important guests down on the waterfront . . ."

The windows opened on a balcony overlooking one of the many moonstruck gardens of the palace. Kadolan worried that many ears were listening, but Inosolan had ignored all suggestions that she lower her voice. The sorceress certainly wasn't listening, she said; she was occupied otherwise. That bit had not been explained yet.

What Inosolan really needed was a good, long, motherly hug, but Kadolan was not skilled at such intimacies. Her strong point had never been children, and she had not known Inosolan as a child. By the time she had reached Krasnegar after Evanaire's death, the chance for closeness had gone. They had not shared more than two or three hugs, ever.

". . . maybe should be glad I *don't* get to choose! I mean, suppose they line up a dozen or two bristle-faced goblins and . . ."

Kadolan had never borne children of her own, or she might have learned better how to cope with them. Adolescents were her specialty. She knew by instinct how to deal with adolescent girls, or at least she could never remember when she did not have a knack for them. There was no great magic involved, only clear rules and endless patience. One had to set an example as best one could, for those quick young eyes spied out hypocrisy at once; so one stood up honestly for one's principles, like a lighthouse at the end of a difficult strait. One encouraged, one explained, one kept one's temper, and in the end, usually without much warning, the strait had been traversed, the ship was in the harbor, and another young lady was available for matchmaking. Very distant cousins, or just friends . . . Inosolan had been merely the last of many, many girls who had called Kadolan "Aunt" at Kinvale. Kadolan had failed none of them, but none had been a keener or a more gratifying pupil than her own niece. None had met with more success, or less good fortune.

Inos was still wayward and impetuous, of course, but those traits were part of her jotunn heritage, and she would not likely ever outgrow them. They cropped up frequently in the family.

"A goblin? Can you imagine? A goblin king in Krasnegar? What do you think—would he amuse the guests by carving up the servants or entertain the servants by cooking up the guests?"

That was better. Murderously unfunny humor, but humor. Inosolan's voice was steadying, too.

And she had seen that lost kingdoms were not returned like misplaced parasols, that there must be a price to pay—perhaps not as much as marriage to a goblin, but a price. What price would Inosolan be willing to pay? Would she be given the choice?

The irony of it all was that Kadolan, having guided her niece through to womanhood, should now feel so completely useless as an adult confidante. She was too old for this wild adventuring. Her life had been much too sheltered for her to know anything at all about women like Rasha—who, despite her incredible occult power, was still only a woman, a hard, twisted, bitter woman, a woman who had fought for every crust she'd ever eaten, a woman abused and maltreated by men in ways Kadolan could not imagine and did not want to.

Inosolan was younger and stronger and had been coping amazingly well, considering how very little room she had to move at all. Now came this latest outrage—warlocks and warfare. No one could be expected to cope with this. Kadolan was out of her depth. She felt she was being left behind. That was old age, she supposed.

Suddenly Inosolan fell silent and still, a beauty's dark profile against the moon-drenched sky within the arches.

"I do talk a lot, don't I, Aunt?"

"Come and sit down, dear."

"Yes." Inosolan came across and joined Kadolan on the bed, and put an arm around her. "Thank you for listening. I feel better."

"I wish I could do more than listen. What happened after the warlock left?"

"Rasha threw a tantrum. I suppose she can see in the dark. She started tossing thunderbolts at things—the welcome mat and then the furniture. I ran."

"Wise!"

Inosolan gulped, then laughed shakily. "It was so childish it was almost funny! I was too scared to feel scared, somehow. I slipped on the stairs and hurt my ankle—Rasha healed it for me later—but I crawled over to the doors, and they wouldn't open, and I just crouched there until the thunderstorm stopped. Until the noise stopped and the smoke cleared and Rasha came down."

"How terrible!"

"Well . . . ." Inosolan shivered. "The worst part was that I was afraid of the panther and the wolf—they were roaming around somewhere in the dark, I thought. And maybe demons? Something flapped overhead a few times . . . Or maybe it was worst when the torches blazed up in the sconces and she came slinking down the stairs. Your Kinvale lacquer was very thin, Aunt. She was back to being a brothel seductress again.''

What is a lady? Rasha had asked. Kadolan had tried to explain that being a lady was a discipline, a way of life. A lady was considerate of others' feelings. A lady was the same to all people, of high rank or low, at all times, under all conditions.

Those, the sorceress had said with a believing sneer, might be useful things to know. "Show me!" she had commanded. "For I must deal soon with the wardens, and these impish manners may impress them.''

So Kadolan had shown her, and she had learned amazingly fast.

"Yes, dear, I know. I knew she was too old to change, of course. I knew it was only affectation. But she was so very convincing I found myself believing in her. Forgive me!''

"Nothing to forgive, Aunt! You did a much better job with Rasha than I did with Azak.''

Kadolan had been wondering why she had heard no news of Azak.

"Imperial lady, sultana, dockside slut,'' Inosolan said reflectively, "but I fear her most when she plays seductress. *Inflame any man,* Azak said—remember? It sickens me. It frightens me. She's a man-eater, wriggling her body around like a worm on a hook. That's how she was—young and gorgeous and shining through gauze, promising love, and yet burning inside with hatred and contempt . . . That's the hook.''

Kadolan tried to find something to say, but couldn't.

"Had I been a man . . . If there was a man there, I thought, he would be driven mad. Am I wrong?''

"I don't think so, dear. It is an evil magic.'' After a moment Kadolan added quietly, "Lust is not love, but I don't think her Majesty has ever been taught the difference.''

Inosolan shivered again. "She cured my ankle and my bruises. Then I wanted to go, and she made me stay longer. She talked. She insists she was right and Olybino was lying. He really is in league with Lith'rian of the south against Zinixo. He really does need to find a peaceful solution to the Krasnegar problem. They're all afraid of the dwarf. So she says.''

Kadolan squeezed her, but she was still rigid as a statue, trembling slightly even yet.

"I said, 'So I must marry a goblin?' She laughed and said she would bespell me so that I was crazy about male goblins! Ughh! Can you imagine?"

"It's all over now, dear, and you should try to get some rest."

"Gods! It must be halfway to morning." Inos fell silent, and her aunt realized that she had not heard it all yet. There was still more to come.

Inosolan rose, started to pace, and then stepped to a window. For a moment her hair and shoulders were washed in silver by the high moon. Then she turned and spoke. "I won't marry a goblin. But I *will* get back my kingdom!"

This time she did not swear any oaths about doing anything at all, Kadolan noticed. She had learned about costs.

"So I can't just rely on Rasha!"

"That's obvious, dear!"

"So what do we do now, Chancellor?"

This was where Kadolan felt so inadequate. "Why not discuss this latest development with the Big Man, Azak?"

"I didn't tell you earlier . . ." Inosolan had dropped her voice, at last. "Kar told me today—yesterday. I'm not welcome on the hunts anymore, he said. I never did get to talk with the Big Man alone, Aunt. Anytime we stopped, to eat or anything, he was always surrounded by princes. So I never did get to talk with him." She wandered back to the bed in a rustle of fabric. "You did better with Rasha than I did with him. He never gave me a chance to speak with him. And now he certainly never will!"

Kadolan held her breath. In a moment Inosolan continued.

"Rasha kept me there, talking. We were downstairs by then, in her bedchamber. She'd healed my twisted ankle. She just kept talking, saying nothing and repeating it over and over."

"Yes, dear?"

"I could hardly bear to look at her. I would have minded less if she'd been naked, I think. What she was wearing was worse! Gems in . . . well, never mind. And then, suddenly, she put a finger to her lips . . . It's a funny room, that. Only two windows. It looks like it ought to have another, over by the bed, doesn't it? Well, what it has there is a hidden door. Behind the hangings."

Kadolan guessed what was coming and knew that Inosolan had seen her twitch of shock.

"The hinges creaked. He pushed aside the tapestry and stepped in. And saw me there!"

"The Big Man?" Not that Kadolan doubted it.

"Azak, yes. She'd done it deliberately, of course. She must have summoned him and been waiting for him. She told him to come in and make himself comfortable—can you imagine the tone?—and then she told me I could go now. Oh, the look in her eyes!" Inosolan shivered.

Tremors of distaste ran down Kadolan's arms. "Well, we did sort of learn when we arrived, didn't we? I mean, she did drop broad hints—that she summoned him, and so on."

"Oh, yes! But why?"

"Because she hates men, dear. Gods know, I suppose she's had reason enough."

"And he's everything she hates in men—young and handsome and royal! Big and strong, and unbeatable at everything!"

The sudden enthusiasm in her niece's voice made Kadolan uneasy. "And a murderer!"

"Is he?" Inosolan's voice rose higher. "Think of this, Aunt—Rasha the adept was living in the palace. Uninvited. Freeloading. Then she met the sultan, and he was another adept! He saw through her disguise. She hinted to me that they became friends, or even lovers perhaps, two adepts together—and I suppose it must be hard for the sorcerous to be friends with mere mundanes. How sweet! But really she was in terrible danger, Aunt, because although they were both adepts, he had temporal power, also. He could have tortured her to learn her words of power—but instead he died! Azak got the throne, but she got the words."

Kadolan gasped. "You think it was Rasha who killed him?"

"Or helped. How do mundanes kill an adept? Maybe Azak made promises he hasn't carried out? She can force him to do anything, but he'd promised . . . Oh, I don't know!" Inosolan rose and began to pace again. "It doesn't matter much, does it? If I can't rely on Rasha, then he's my logical ally, because he hates her. *My enemy's enemy is my friend*, but—"

"Who ever said that?"

"What? The thing about enemies? Oh, it's just an expression I heard from . . . from an old friend. A friend I never really appreciated. But Azak wouldn't talk to me before, and he certainly won't now, because I've witnessed his shame. Because I know Rasha summons him to her bed so she can torment him and humiliate him as men humiliated her. He'll never set eyes on me again!''

Kadolan took a deep breath. Inosolan was grasping at straws, but straws were all she had, and perhaps her incompetent, inadequate chancellor and chamberlain could help out a little; and even if it did no good in the end, it might give her something to hope for while her spirits were so horribly crushed.

"You want a private talk with the Big Man? That's all?"

"It would be a start."

"Well, we can certainly arrange that, dear," Kadolan said cheerfully. "You go and try to get some sleep now. First thing in the morning, I'll ask Mistress Zana to take him a message. I promise you, he'll come running!"

2

Inos spent a miserable day. For the last two weeks and more, she had been rising before dawn; now she managed to sleep until almost noon and left herself feeling frowsy and off-key. By the time she was bathed and dressed, both Kade and Zana had already departed for a tea party with the sorceress, and that was a terrifying development—how could anyone keep secrets from a sorceress? Surely Rasha would learn at once of the note that had been sent to intercept Azak as he left on his hunt at daybreak.

Kade had designed a cryptic message, in the best traditions of conspiracy, but she could not have made it cryptic enough to deceive Rasha without making it unintelligible to Azak. And if Rasha did learn of it, she might well resent Inos seeking an alliance with Azak, whatever he was to her.

Inos worried and fretted and tried to seem calm and relaxed. The habitation felt more like a prison than ever. She spent a couple of hours exploring it, just for something to do. In need of an excuse to keep moving, she worked her way systematically from dingy, stuffy wine cellars up to the divine glory of the master bedroom. Then she went down and played a few games of *thali* with Vinisha and some of the other women. They all wanted to hear about Inos's visit to Rasha's chamber of puissance, and that was the very thing she did not want even to think about. They must be wondering why she had abandoned hunting so suddenly, and that was a humiliation she preferred not to discuss. The conversation was stilted and pointless.

Why could a person's memory not forget things to order?

Every now and then, just when Inos was least expecting it—admiring the late Prince Harakaz's collection of hunting boots, or in the middle of a coup at *thali*—she would be struck by a spasm of mental agony. It was like having a broken bone somewhere, or a torn muscle, and accidentally putting weight on it. It was remembering the one most awful thing that had come out of the previous night's horrors, the one she had tried to store away deepest in her closet of Things Not to Think About. And it kept falling out and hitting her: *Marry a goblin!*

It was unthinkable.

She was of royal blood. Queens or princesses were rarely fortunate enough to marry for love. Dynastic marriage was their lot. A year ago, facing exile in Kinvale, Inos had refused to admit that obvious truth. Now she could see that the best she could ever hope for was a husband who was relatively decent, agreeable, and not too absurdly old. But a goblin, any goblin—that was carrying duty altogether too far.

The trouble was, it made so much sense from everyone else's point of view. It would placate the witch of the north, who was a goblin herself. It would favor neither the imps of the Impire nor the jotnar of Nordland, so no one need lose face. The citizens of Krasnegar might resent the idea at first, but now that tempers had been roused, the jotnar among them might even prefer to see a goblin on the throne than an imp; the imps might rather have a goblin than a jotunn. Winning was less important than not losing. And the old men of the council would be happy, because a goblin king would have no interest in actually running the kingdom. From what little Inos knew of goblins' social habits, he would certainly not allow his wife to do any real reigning either. He would leave that to the council, while he concentrated on . . . On what? What in the names of all the Gods did goblins do all the time?

They bred ugly little green babies, that's what they did.

And tortured people.

The afternoon dragged on, hot and desolate. The sorceress's tea party seemed to be lasting a very long time.

Inos was having her third stroll around one of the many shadowed gardens when Thralia came hurrying through the magnolias and honeysuckles in search of her. Apologizing abjectly for having forgotten earlier, she offered Inos a book. The princess had left that for her, she said, when she went out.

Well! Inos kept her temper, smiled icily, and retreated to a shady bench to see what Kade might have in mind. The volume was huge and very tattered, and obviously ancient. Its faded ink must have been hard on Kade's old eyes, but Prince Hakaraz had certainly been no patron of literature, so perhaps this was the best she had been able to find to read. The cover was torn and the title unreadable. What remained appeared to be a collection of quotations and extracts from other volumes. On her first, fast flick-through, Inos saw how the writing changed, from labored and straggly at the beginning to a heavy, arrogant scrawl near the end. The final few pages were blank.

Clearly this tome had been some long-ago prince's commonplace book. He might have chosen the passages himself, or they might have been selected by his tutor. Perhaps he had been expected to memorize them afterward, as many seemed to be concerned with princely decorum. There were lists; there was history, and religion, and philosophy. Some pages held very sickly sentimental poetry that might have been original; a few extracts near the end were so erotic that Inos discovered she was not as unshockable as she had thought. She wondered what Kade had thought of those!

On a second, more careful leafing-through, she found a fresh flower petal. It lay near the middle, among a group of passages on history, but the vellums were only inscribed on one side, so there was no ambiguity—Kade was directing Inos to an extract from a drama, and specifically to a long and very turgid speech attributed to a man named Draqu ak'Dranu. Alongside the petal she read:

> He who smites mine foe is my friend, and he who turns a blow from me I shall embrace. To aid my enemy is to offend me; to stay him, nay yet to hamper him, shall win my praises and rich gifts. Know then that the white and the blue befriend us when they harry the gold, for the claws of the gold rake hard upon our flesh; our women are made to weep, our children starve and cry out. And though the white and blue may not stay the claws lest a greater evil befall, yet will they suffer not that doors be opened, nor the ways smoothed.

There was more, much more. But that was enough to explain why Kade had been so certain that she could win Inos an audience with Azak. It even explained how she had dreamed up the cryptic message she had been planning to use: *I have met a man with a golden helmet.* That would mean a lot to Azak, she had insisted, but would likely make little sense to any commoner who might intercept the note. The palace of Arakkaran would not have changed its princes' upbringing much in the last few centuries, and the Big Man would have been reared on the sort of fare represented by this book.

"Gold" meant the warlock of the east, of course, and the four claws would be the legions; the imperor's symbol was always a four-pointed star. White and blue were the wardens of north and south respectively. The Protocol forbade any sorcerer but East from using magic on the legions; Kade had said so, and Rasha had confirmed it. That prohibition included the other wardens. If they wanted to help the imperor's opponents, which in the example quoted had evidently been some Zarkian confederacy led by the verbose Draqu, their help would have to be very limited and indirect.

What Inos had not realized was that there was a subtle exception to those rules. The extracts that preceded Kade's marker made the point more clearly: The other wardens were within their rights in stopping East from *aiding* the legions with magic. Obviously the best that the imperor's enemies could ever hope for was that their battles would stay mundane, but obviously they often did, else the Impire would have conquered all Pandemia ages ago. Of course most lands had fallen to the legions many times, only to win back their independence in due course. The tide flowed and the tide ebbed. Guwush was part of the Impire now, but the old map on Inos's schoolroom wall had shown it as a collection of independent gnomish commonwealths. Zark had been conquered and liberated repeatedly—she'd learned that much since she arrived.

She went back to Kade's curious digest, and a few pages later found an account of a battle in some other century. The Imperial forces had been driven back against a ravine. A bridge had appeared by magic to save them. A few minutes later it had vanished again, and stayed away. The resulting carnage was described in loving detail.

How typical of Kade to have discovered something like this! *My enemy's enemy is my friend,* as Rap had said. And Kar had spoken of a scent of war in the wind. The Impire had a new marshal of the armies.

The warlock of the east would never be a popular figure in Zark. *My enemy's enemy!* If Rasha was now Inos's enemy, then

Azak must be her friend. And Olybino was another common foe. Kade had seen it.

What could Azak do about it, though?

Kade and Zana returned at last, looking weary, but the tea party had to be described for everyone, so it was an hour or more before Inos managed to get her aunt to herself. Once again, they drifted out on the balcony to watch the city and the bay darken into night. Inos leaned on the balustrade; Kade sank into the soft divan, sighing like a contented puppy.

No, Rasha had not seemed suspicious, Kade reported. No, she had not mentioned the previous evening's meeting. There had been many palace ladies there, of course.

"So when will we get an answer from the Big Man, do you suppose?" Inos asked.

Her aunt blinked up at her. "Oh . . . of course you didn't hear! He answered at once. You are invited to go sightseeing with him tomorrow."

Aha! Inos laughed gaily. "You are a sorceress, Aunt!"

"Oh, no, dear!"

So Inos would get that private chat she had been seeking for so long. And now she had even more reason to talk with the sultan. Surely together they could find some way to frustrate the evil Rasha?

Then Inos saw that her aunt was staring at her with an oddly concerned expression. "Something wrong?"

"Oh, no, dear, nothing. Nothing at all. But . . . have you ever met Prince Quarazak?"

"I don't think so," Inos said suspiciously. Kade was being devious. "Describe him."

"About this high. Handsome young lad, sprightly, reddish coloring. The sultana presented him to me a few days ago. And a couple of his brothers, also."

"Oh?" *Oh!* "Tall, like his father?"

"Yes, dear."

It took Inos several seconds to work out the connection. Then she burst out laughing. "Really, Aunt! Surely you do not imagine I am seriously interested in . . . I mean, my interest in Azak is purely political."

"Of course, dear."

"Anything else would be absurd!"

"Of course. I didn't mean to suggest . . . Of course."

But Kade had been thinking it. Azak? Admittedly a djinn was

more appealing than a goblin, but that was certainly not what Inos had in mind. No, just politics!

"Oh, you needn't worry about *that*, Aunt. Barbarians are not my type at all. I'm not attracted to that one!"

"But how does he feel about you?"

"Really, Aunt! If he has that on his mind, then he has a very strange way of showing it! This young prince . . ."

"Quarazak. Quarazak ak'Azak ak'Azakar."

"Yes. How tall did you say?"

Kade gestured vaguely. "About so. He says he's eight, but he looks older because of his height."

Azak was twenty-two.

For a moment Inos's mind refused to believe the necessary calculations. "Fourteen? Or maybe *thirteen*?"

"I suppose so."

"Gods!" Inos muttered. "That's disgusting!"

"Yes, dear," Kade said quietly.

3

The air was cool and clammy, color still undefined. Even the skylarks must still be snoozing in their nests.

In the pearly light of predawn, Inos sat and shivered on Sesame in a stable yard. At her side, Kar was still as a statue on his favorite gray, watching his brother inspect the honor guard of family men.

Inos had expected a confidential chat during a ride in a coach, not a state procession.

She had burned her mouth on her coffee and six coarse Zarkian biscuits lay like lead in her belly, but now she was ready for whatever surprise the sultan was prepared to spring next. At least, she hoped she was. There were no other princes in sight, only wary grooms on the sidelines, and the twenty-five guards with their mounts. Azak was examining them like a trader planning an offer.

"Family men are royalty from other cities?" she asked.

Kar smile without turning his head. "Mostly."

"Is this what happens to unwanted princes?"

"Some sink even lower."

"How much lower?"

"They sell their skills for silver and serve *commoners*!" Kar said with infinite contempt.

"But when a throne changes hands somewhere—"

"Thrones change buttocks. In Zark, monarchy is denoted by a sash. Sashes change men."

"Very well. If a new sultan succeeds, might some of these guards then be summoned back to their homes?"

Kar started to nod, then suddenly frowned. It was gone in an instant, but that was the first frown she had ever seen on him. One of the family men had been dismissed and was leading his horse away. Friend Kar had missed something, perhaps?

"Explain, please," Inos said meanly.

He beamed. "A poorly fitted shoe. I thought it would pass, but the Big Man's standards are higher than mine."

"The man will be punished? How?"

Kar turned his smile full on her for the first time. "One of his sons will be beaten."

"That's wicked!"

"They all knew what their oath meant when they swore."

"How much of a beating?" she asked queasily.

"Probably just one lash for each year of his age."

"I suppose the man himself has to choose which son?" She was beginning to understand the sadistic thinking.

"Yes."

"And he must watch, I suppose?"

"He must do it."

That ended the conversation.

Azak completed his inspection. He swung up into the saddle of one of his black stallions, which put up a small show of resistance and then calmed. He had at least a dozen of those beauties, and Inos recognized this one as Dread, one of the least cantankerous and therefore something of a disappointment to him. He walked it over to her as Kar rode off to line up the guard.

The last time Inos had seen the sultan he had been summoned to an old crone's bed like a gigolo, and yet his gaze was steady and unashamed as their eyes met. It was Inos who blushed. She felt her face grow hot—where was her Kinvale poise when she needed it?

The jeweled belt he always wore was missing. Instead he bore a gleaming baldric across his chest, a narrower strip of the same silver mesh studded with emeralds. Then she realized that it was the identical piece, that normally he must keep it wrapped four or five times around his waist, out of the way. This was probably how it was supposed to be worn, the symbol of kingship. His clothes were the finest she had ever seen on him, so embroidered and emblazoned with precious stones that they might hold half the wealth of the kingdom.

The mutual scrutiny ended. Inos had brought a riding crop expressly so she could salute him with it, and she now did so, wondering if the curse would interpret that as an admission of his status. All that happened was that Azak arched one shapely auburn brow almost into his turban—an annoying trick she had seen him use before.

"You will have to cover your face in public."

"Of course. I am sorry you find my appearance distasteful!"

She should have known she would never embarrass him. As she moved to adjust her headcloth, he said, "Not just at the moment, but later. We princes have heard of Imperial ways and enjoy admiring feminine beauty as much as imps do."

Princes also enjoyed seeing how much blush they could provoke.

"But the common folk would be shocked," he added imperturbably.

"Then you should educate them, Cousin."

"But in what ways? Imperial ladies uncover their faces, but merwomen expose their breasts, and Arakkaran is much closer to the Kerith Islands than to Hub."

Following the vanguard of family men, Azak rode out from his palace. Sesame paced smoothly on his right, and Kar's gray on the left. The route ran southward, through olive groves and shady hollows, still shiny with dew.

"I am glad to be spared another day in the desert, your Majesty," Inos said, able to give him his title beyond the palace grounds.

Azak glanced down—he was very high above her. "You haven't seen true desert yet. It is hard and cruel, but it brings out the strength of a man. It does not tolerate weaklings. Farmland feels soft and decadent to me. Please call me by my name, Inosolan."

His ability to take her by surprise was infuriating. "Of course, Azak."

"No one else in the kingdom may."

Again taken by surprise, she looked up, and he was regarding her with amusement.

"I want to talk about Rasha."

He scowled and shook his head. "Not now. You wanted to see my kingdom. This is a good chance. I thought you might also care for a brief lesson in kingship. You may find it useful when you come into your inheritance."

Before she could find a reply to express her annoyance, he laughed. "Our ways seem strange to you."

"They seem unnecessarily cruel."

"Anyone who tried to change them would be regarded as a weakling. Not that I want to change them, of course."

He was baiting her, and she was not going to be browbeaten like one of his princelings. "You killed your grandfather?"

"Kar did, on my orders. The old rogue knew his time was coming. He'd tried to kill me several times."

"Rasha said he was an adept."

"Then he was a mighty ineffective one."

Or else Azak had been aided by another adept.

"This shocks you, Inos."

"It is not the custom of my people."

"It is old here. You think like an imp. Many imperors have died by violence."

"But never a king of Krasnegar."

"Truly?" Azak said skeptically. "You cannot be certain. Kar can slide a bodkin under a sleeping man's eyelid. That leaves no mark."

Inos felt sick. "How many men have you killed?"

"Personally, you mean? In fights or in execution? Fair fights or cheats? Or do you also count those I sent Kar after—Kar or others? I suppose a couple of dozen. I don't keep count."

"I'm sorry! I should not have asked. It is none of my business, and I should not judge Arakkarn by the standards of other lands." She turned her attention to the arid and dusty countryside—the goats roaming the dry hills, the greener valleys falling seaward. Now the haphazard little road ran between dry stone walls and thorn hedges, landscape new to her.

But Azak had not done. "I had no choice."

"What?"

"Even as a child," he said softly, his voice almost lost in the clatter of hooves, "I was obviously superior. I had to try for the top or be killed myself. The first attempt on my life was made when I was six years old. There have been two attempts on Quarazak already and he is rubbish, barely above average. His brother Krandaraz has survived three tries so far, and even he does not compare to what I was at his age."

She was horrified. "Kill children? What good would that do?"

"It would belittle me, of course."

"It is a barbarous custom!"

"It is very efficient. We measure a man by many things, but his virility and the number of his sons count high. So . . . always many princes. Princes cannot work in the fields. It costs money to support the royal family. This is one way we reduce the burden on the country, and we make sure that the ruler is a strong man."

"Strong?" she said with her heaviest scorn.

"Strong. He must be able to win loyalty, and that requires excellence. He must have iron nerves. He must be cunning and treacherous and totally ruthless. I am all these things. I may kill or banish Krandaraz eventually, if I think one of my younger sons is better. It is an efficient system, good for the land."

Before Inos could find an answer to this outrageous rationalization, they rounded a bend and there was a village ahead.

"Cover your face," Azak said, "and do not speak."

The mud-brick houses had low doors and no windows. Possibly the massive walls kept them cool in this blistering climate, but Inos had seen pigsties with more grandeur. The hamlet merged in all directions into olive trees, and there was a scent of oil in the air, barely detectable under the other stenches. The drone of insects was a constant low undertone.

The royal visit had been expected. The single street was blocked by people, obviously the whole population—every man, woman, and child crouching with face in the dirt as the sultan arrived. He reined in Dread, and Inos halted Sesame a few paces back on his right. Prince Kar's gray drew level on Azak's left, and the family men spread out on either hand. Then there was a pregnant pause, while everyone listened to the flies and the muffled coughing of the sick.

"Azak ak'Azakar ak'Zorazak!" Kar proclaimed in an astonishing roar, "Sultan of Arakkaran, Increaser of the Good, Beloved of the Gods, Protector of the Poor. You may greet your lord."

The village surged to its feet and cheered until it was hoarse.

Kar raised a hand for silence. An ancient headman came limping forward and held out a tray to offer Kar a selection of fruits, pastries, and insects. The prince selected a fig, bit half of it, chewed for a moment, and then passed the rest to Azak, who raised it to his lips. Inos thought he palmed it.

"His Majesty has graciously accepted your hospitality," Kar announced.

The headman scrambled out of the way as Dread moved forward, Kar's gray following. Uncertain what to do, Inos stayed where she was, sweating behind her veil but very grateful for its concealment. Apparently she had made the right choice, for the family men did not move either. Azak and his brother rode slowly around—Azak inspecting the village, Kar guarding Azak. The sultan took his time, scrutinizing everything out as far as the trees on either side of the road, although he did not dismount and enter buildings. The inhabitants shuffled their feet in apprehensive silence.

Insects buzzed. In the distance a donkey brayed.

A sudden eruption of barking from inside one of hovels cut off in terrified yelps. Inos realized that there were no dogs in sight.

At last the royal inspectors came back to the same place as before, and the headman returned warily to Kar's stirrup.

"His Majesty congratulates you on the condition of the trees."

"His Magnificence is most gracious."

"His Majesty inquires when the pits were dug?"

"Pray inform his Beneficence . . . about three months ago."

Kar's riding crop slashed across the old man's face. He did not flinch or raise his hands. He bowed. "I was in error."

"They will be filled before sundown, and new pits dug. Twice as many of them, with the male and female areas farther apart."

"As his Majesty commands, so it is."

Azak was staring straight ahead, over the crowd's heads. He had not spoken, or moved a muscle. The old man's tongue sneaked out to lick a trickle of blood.

Again Kar produced his astonishing roar. "His Majesty will now receive petitions, on any subject except taxes. All may speak freely, without fear. None but his Majesty will hear the words that are spoken."

With trembling hands, the headman pulled a dirty scrap of paper from his gown and held it up. The baby-faced prince took it. After a glance he let it fall, and a second slash turned the scarlet stripe into a cross. "I said no taxes!"

The old man bowed again and backed away.

"Any may speak!" Kar repeated, looking at the crowd.

A younger man took one step and then halted, losing his nerve.

"Approach!"

Then he came—legs stiff, head held high, and fists clenched.

His rags were barely decent covering. He sank down and touched his turban to the ground beside the hooves.

"Speak," Kar said softly.

The petitioner raised his head to address the horses' knees. "I am Zartha."

"You may speak without fear, Zartha."

Zartha licked his lips. "Two months ago an ox we—my brothers and me . . . our ox was struck by an arrow. The wound sickened and it died."

Kar stiffened. "Have you the arrow?"

The man scrambled to his feet. Head still down, he held up an arrowhead. The prince bent to take it, looked it over, and glanced to the sultan. There was an exchange of nods. Kar slipped the evidence into a pocket and produced a leather bag.

"Did you see who shot this arrow?"

The man nodded dumbly at the shadows on the dust.

"Would you know him?"

Another nod.

"He wore green?"

A pause, then another nod.

"You may be called to the palace to identify him. If a summons comes, do not be afraid. It is his Majesty's wish to punish the guilty, whoever they may be, as well as to recompense the victims. None is above his Majesty's justice, and none below. He gives you back your ox." Kar began tossing gold pieces down in the dust, five in all. The crowd *oooed* apreciatively, and the peasant fell on his knees to gather them up, crying blessings on the sultan.

"Any may speak!" Kar proclaimed again. A long pause . . .

The crowd rippled. A couple emerged, with a child walking between them, wrapped in a sheet. She could be no more than ten, too young to wear a veil, but the sheet concealed her hair and shadowed her face. Nevertheless, Inos decided she was terrified. The young father obviously was. The mother's face was invisible.

For a moment nothing happened, while Inos wondered if she would be able to contain her fury. She feared her veil might burst into flames if she looked at Azak. Then the parents opened the blanket, holding it out to the sides so the sultan could view the girl. They made her raise her arms and turn around.

Kar glanced inquiringly at Azak, who nodded. As the mother hastily wrapped up the girl again, Kar gestured. One of the family men slipped from his horse and came across. He made the surprised peasant bend over and then used his back as a writing desk, asking questions and making entries on a piece of parchment with a silverpoint. Then he handed the man the parchment.

"Bring her to the palace and show that letter," Kar commanded. "His Majesty will be munificent." Nodding steadily, the man put a hand on his wife's shoulder and began to pull her away, the child going with them. He was still nodding as he backed into the crowd.

"Next?"

Azak refused the next girl, and the next. But in all he bought four in that first village.

A couple of bowshots along the road, where olive trees were already giving way to pasture, Azak said, "Drop your veil."

Inos complied. "Why?"

He flashed white teeth in a contemptuous grimace. "Because you're beautiful when you're angry."

Angry? She was seething. "You bought those girls!"

"I agreed to take them into my household."

"You buy them like piglets!"

"I compensate the parents for the loss of their services."

"Slavery! You sell your own people into slavery? What sort of ruler . . ."

High on his giant stallion, he was smiling down at her, although there was a hint of something else on that arrogant mahogany face. Perhaps she had hurt his feelings. She hoped so.

"Inosolan, the parents have too many mouths to feed. My gold will benefit the whole village. The girls will be cleaned, clothed, and fed better than they have ever been. Trained, educated, and looked after, for three or four years—"

"Until they are ripe?"

He blinked, and his voice dropped half an octave. "Until they are ripe. Then they are free to go home."

"I don't—"

"They are escorted back to their parents and given the choice. Never, ever, has one preferred to return to her village. They always choose life in the palace."

"Well . . ." Those huts had been pigpens. Inos tried to imagine being faced with that decision. "So they return to the palace and the joys of your bed?"

A spasm like pain crossed his face. "I keep the prettiest, of course. That is what being sultan is all about. But most I give to princes I currently favor, or family men. As royal favors, they must be treated well.''

''Concubines! Toys!''

''Mothers of sultans!''

''Oh.'' Inos forgot what she had been about to say.

''Did your father have no mistresses? No kept women? No loyal subjects' wives?''

''None.'' She believed she was speaking the truth, but of course she would not have known, would she? She was glad she need not meet Azak's eyes when she did not choose to.

''None, never? Strange! But if he had made bastards, they would not have been eligible to inherit his throne, now would they?'' Azak chuckled mockingly. ''At least, that is how the Impire does things. But all my sons are equal, and all my future sons, also. Their age does not matter, nor their mother's father—prince or peasant. That is fairer, is it not? My mother was so brought. I will show you the village. My relatives lived there until quite recently.''

For a while there was only the thud of hooves. Inos was thinking of Vinisha and the others—witless, because they had no need for wits, but not unhappy. And she thought of that village.

A lady is never afraid to admit to a mistake, Kade always said. Inos assumed her most regal air. ''I should watch my tongue. I admit I would prefer raising babies in a palace to raising them in a hovel.''

''You might not raise them there. You might bear them and watch them die. Many more of them. And field work is hard on the fingernails.''

She glanced up ruefully, seeing the scorn. So much for a private chat! She almost preferred being ignored. ''Once again I must say that I am sorry.''

''You're not beautiful when you're sorry. You must learn that monarchs never apologize.'' He nudged Dread into a canter.

They visited seven villages that day, seven that had obviously been selected with care, for the royal procession took a winding route along the byways of Arakkaran. Yet this was not merely a pretense staged to impress Inos—Azak had done this before. In one village he inspected fencing he had ordered, and in another a new well. Kar tasted the water.

Olives, dates, citrus fruits, rice, horses, goats, shellfish . . . Inos saw a wide range of Arakkaran's agriculture, all of which was strange to her. Mostly it was a poor land, every crop scratched from the rocks by the fingernails of its people. The valleys were lush, but even there the peasants were thin and often diseased. The children . . . she did not like to look at the children. Almost every headman risked royal displeasure by mentioning taxes and then suffered for his temerity. One village had failed to obey an earlier royal command to repair the road. The family men executed the headman on the spot, while Inos fought nausea and horror behind her veil. Azak accepted twelve petitions and bought twenty-three girls.

After the fourth hamlet, the royal progress halted in an orange grove to dine on fresh oysters, jellied lamb in pastry, and many other treats. Inos sat on shaded grass with prince and sultan, while the family men stood guard at a distance. In the limp heat of noon the leaves hung drooped motionless on the trees. She thought that no place in all Pandemia could be less like her homeland of Krasnegar. And surely no ruler could be less like her father than Azak was. She had no appetite. Azak noted her distaste with evident amusement, then ignored her.

"The arrow," he said with his mouth full.

Kar smiled and produced the arrowhead.

Azak inspected it. "Hak?"

"Almost certainly."

Azak nodded and tossed the evidence over his shoulder.

That was too much for Inos. "What happened to the punishing-the-guilty procedure?" *Honest as a djinn.*

The red-brown eyes moved to study her. He stroked a finger along the fringe on his jaw—another petty habit that irked her. "Too late. Hakaraz ak'Azakar died last month."

She glanced at Kar and his inevitable boyish smile. "Snakebite," he said happily. She shivered at the ice in his eyes. They were discussing one of their brothers. Yesterday she had admired his collection of riding boots.

"A premature end to a most interesting career." Now Azak was taunting her. "But his archery was erratic. So were his loyalties."

After a few minutes of silent and desultory nibbling, Inos stoked up her courage and asked, "And what about the petitions you accepted?"

He shrugged. "I'll throw them in the tinder basket with the others. We monarchs are beset with petitions, are we not? I must get a dozen a day delivered to the palace. My women line shelves with them."

He spent his days in hunting and feasting. She tried raising one eyebrow, although she lacked his skill at the move. It amused him, but he quaffed wine from a drinking horn and did not comment.

It was the softly smiling Kar who spoke. "Queen Inosolan, he deals with every one of them. Every petition is answered within two days. He works half the night, exhausting whole teams of scribes. He never seems to—" The contents of the horn splashed in his face, silencing him.

Azak was scarlet with fury, menacing as a naked blade. "You are calling me a liar, your Highness?"

Kar made no attempt to wipe his dripping face. He continued to smile. "Of course not, Majesty. That would be a capital offense."

"Once more and you're pig feed!" Azak sprang bodily to his feet and yelled at the retainers to saddle up again. He went striding off. The food had been hardly touched, yet obviously the picnic was over. Kar gazed at Azak's retreating back, but Inos could not tell whether his continuing inscrutable smile implied brotherly affection or incipient murder.

If that episode had been staged for her benefit, it had been very well done.

4

The sun that beat so savagely on Zark had not yet begun to shift the morning mists in far-off Faerie. As first light gloomed in the east, Rap finished shaving and nudged Thinal.

"Now you," he said.

"You think I'm crazy?" The thief snorted. "In the dark? I'd cut myself to ribbons." But he sat up and stretched, growling.

The settled farmlands around Milflor had been much harder going for fugitives than the empty beaches farther north. Without Rap's farsight they would surely have blundered into guards or dogs, but he had persuaded the others that they must rest by day and trust him by night. The moon had helped, of course, but he had led the way along narrow trails, staying as much as possible within patches of woodland and scrub. Now there was no more good cover; they had reached a land of larger houses and dairy farms, signs that the city was close.

They had stolen a few hours' rest in a hayloft. Dawn was near and they must make themselves respectable, or relatively so. Somewhere Thinal had acquired a razor. With that he and Rap had already trimmed each other's hair. Little Chicken flatly refused to do anything about the straggly bristles round his mouth and Rap knew better than to suggest a haircut for him. No goblin would submit to that, and probably nothing less than an Imperial cohort could now impose it on this one. He had agreed to hide his face under a wide-brimmed straw hat. That would have to do, although he would be a conspicuous rarity in Faerie. Fortunately his beloved silk pants had failed to survive another day in shrubbery, and now he wore peasants' hessian like the others.

Their shabby assortment of clothes would attract no comment, having been acquired locally by the greatest burglary team in all Pandemia—Thinal the scrounger and Rap, the dog's best friend. There had been no further work for the third member of the group, the troll-killing strong-arm man.

Rap rose and went down the ladder to visit the bushes. He wondered where in his travels he had lost his conscience. At Raven totem, perhaps, when he had been driven by starvation to the larder? Or maybe it was still present and merely too ill-used to speak up; he hated this vagabond existence. He would have felt happier had Thinal confined his attentions to the rich in their grand plantation houses, but mostly he had preyed upon the humble. Those scrawny, overworked folk must be hard-put to feed even their own children without having to provide involuntary charity to a gang of robbers.

By the time he returned, Thinal had scraped some of the stubble from his face and seemed content to keep the rest. Shaving made his acne bleed.

"Ready?" he said, glancing around. "We can leave all this stuff. We'll buy better at the market."

"Not ready," Rap said. "I think we ought to have a word with Sagorn first."

Thinal considered that, his rodent eyes narrowing. "Not much point yet. Wait till we've got some money and decent clothes—that's what he'd tell us to do. Then we can see what he suggests." He leered. "Me, I'll go for a comfortable bed and a couple of girls, I think. Haven't had any of that since before you were born, laddie. You do realize I'm old enough to be your great-grandfather, don't you? No, Sagorn can wait. Let's go."

He sprang up and headed for the ladder. Rap followed uneasily. Trekking through woods and jungle was over. Ahead lay Milflor—and ships—but he distrusted this new cockiness in the imp as much as he distrusted the goblin's amused disdain. No matter what his birthdate had been, Thinal was physically no older than Rap and now he was taking a juvenile pride in his new accomplishments as a woodsman, and also relishing a return to his accustomed city environment. If overconfidence led him into making an error in the town like the one he had made with the troll, then even Little Chicken would not be able to produce a miracle rescue.

No, Rap's conscience was still there. It hadn't forgotten the troll.

5

As the sun was cowering low over the distant ranges, Azak led his troop northward along the coast from the dilapidated fishing village that had been its last stop. Inos was becoming worried, very worried. She had learned enough of the geography to know that the palace lay a long way from the sea. Obviously she was not going to be returned to the palace that evening. Azak never explained his plans and she would not inquire, but today's unusual interest in her company was beginning to seem very ominous. He had been paying her compliments, even if he had insulted her a few times, also. If he thought her beautiful when angry, then how angry—or frightened—did he plan to make her?

Kade would be alarmed when Inos failed to return, and also scandalized. Kade worried about appearances. Inos cared more about realities, and the realities of this situation were becoming disturbing.

The road had almost vanished, as the horses plodded wearily between sand dunes matted with coarse grass. The air was humid and salty. Nearby, but out of sight, waves fell on a beach with regular roars that were hypnotic after a long day's exertion. She ached from a long day in the saddle, her face burned from wind and sun.

He broke the long silence. "So I have shown you the sights, Queen Inosolan. What do you think of them?"

"I . . . I was thinking more of great buildings and scenery."

"Buildings? Scenery? A kingdom is not made of those. A kingdom is people! Now answer. And be honest."

Honest? "They are wretched—sick and overworked. Half starved, some of them." She waited for the earthquake.

"Exactly."

She blinked with astonishment. He was staring bleakly ahead, not looking at her.

"Are the taxes really so high?" she asked, marveling at her own courage.

"Obscenely high."

"Why don't you reduce them?"

"The taxes are needed to support the palace."

She had guessed that. "All those princes?"

"Parasites?" He sneered down at her. "Yes, princes are expensive and produce nothing. I should cut costs, you think?"

Heart in mouth, Inos said, "Drastically."

"Then I should be fortunate if the last thing I felt was merely Kar's fingers on my eyelid." He laughed at her expression. "I can't fight them all. I would not survive a week."

"Is there nothing you can do? They are your people."

"I know that, wench! Do you think I don't care? Yes, there is something I could do—if I can ever get the bitch sorceress out of my palace and be a free man again."

For a moment conversation became impossible as they urged their mounts up a steep dune. Inos caught a glimpse of water to the west, also, and her fear grew markedly.

"What would you do?" she asked, when she was able to reach his side again. "If you were rid of Rasha, what would you do?" Her neck was stiff with looking up at him so much.

"Make war."

Inos was both shocked and disappointed. She had thought better of him, somehow. "*War?* War never helps the people! Death and destruction and rape and . . ."

"War on Shuggaran—the next kingdom north. They can endure the death and so on. It is a bigger land, although less fair."

"Then they will smash you."

He shrugged. "It is possible, but my people would still be better off, I think. The two kingdoms could be ruled as one, easily. Shuggaran's royal family is even more bloated than mine. I would extirpate them. Then twice as many peasants support half as many princes. Taxes could be cut."

"They might extirpate you."

"If I lost, that would be their right. The peasants gain either way. Besides, the bazaars hum with talk of an Imperial campaign in Zark. That would mean my war would have to wait. Buildings, you said?"

He halted and sprang from his horse. Inos dismounted more circumspectly.

They had come to the end of a headland, with water spread out in three directions. To the north, dhows were slipping in through the harbor mouth, wafted by the evening breeze. East-ward, with perfect timing, a full moon was rising huge from the sea. To the west lay the sparkling waters of the bay, and beyond that the city of Arakkaran clambered up the hillside on steps and ledges, shadowed already. At the high edge of the plateau, the domes and spiky towers of the palace stood dark against the sunset and the jagged outline of the desert range.

For a moment sheer beauty left Inos speechless. Then she said, "Oh, Azak! It's gorgeous!"

"Wait until dawn. Then you will see the glory of my city."

"Where do we . . ."

Azak pointed down to an encampment of silken tents on the beach facing the harbor. A small boat was unloading people at a decrepit old jetty, but already a fire crackled and smoked on the sand and she could identify a goat on the spit. This had all been very carefully arranged. Even to the moon, perhaps.

"The small tent is yours, Inos." His eyes flickered in mock·ery and amusement. "Zana will take care of your needs."

"Zana is here?"

He chuckled then, a low and very masculine noise that she had not heard from him before. "You needn't worry about being royally raped."

"I wasn't—"

"You've been turning greener and greener for the last hour."

"We must make a striking couple, Red Face!"

He bellowed with laughter, and she felt herself blush, even as the knot of her anxiety fell loose. She ached, she was grubby and weary, and she felt wonderful.

"Azak, it's been a marvelous day!"

"And you hated most of it. Don't argue. I promised you a lesson in ruling, the seamier side of the business."

He was not so very many years older than she, but in expe-rience she was a child compared to him. She was a ruler in name but not in fact, and he in fact and not in name.

One of the family men bowed and took the reins. As the horses were led off down to the camp, Inos was left standing at Azak's side on the little hill. He turned to face the sea.

"I love this place. A pity it has no water."

His changes of mood baffled her, but overall he seemed to have mellowed since leaving the palace that morning. Was that a result of her civilizing conversation, or was it release from the constant peril of brothers and uncles? She stretched, aware that she also felt oddly content, despite her weariness. "I shall never forget this day. I am very grateful to you, Azak.'' She reached out a hand to him, but he began strolling seaward through the rough grass. She followed.

"I love the sea," he remarked pensively. "It never gives up." He stopped and stared down at the patient, mindless waves following one another to destruction. "The bathing is good here. Go ahead. I will send Zana with towels."

"Did you ever slide down sand dunes when you were a child?"

He peered at her oddly. "No, never."

"Then try it now! Come on!" She ran to the edge and launched herself down the shadowed slope on her seat, starting an avalanche of sand. There had been dunes near Krasnegar, but this sand was still so hot it almost burned through her jodhpurs. Stilt-legged birds on the beach ran and then took flight, low over the water.

She came to a halt when the angle lessened, her feet buried. In a moment Azak went sliding past. He stopped a little way lower and turned to grin at her, suddenly looking almost boyish.

"Yes, that's fun! I shall declare it a royal prerogative, and behead any commoner who tries it!"

She laughed—this was a much pleasanter Azak than the tyrant of the hunt. If the water was as hot as she suspected, a dip would be heavenly. He was right, this was a glorious spot. It was a great relief just to be out of the sun.

Azak had risen to his knees. Although he was lower than she, their eyes were level—the size of the lad! His face was curiously solemn, but Inos was not feeling solemn. She felt weary, but also glad the long day was over at last, and happy to be away from the eternal crowding of dozens of men; especially glad to be away from the confines of the palace. He must be feeling the same, of course, and more so. Here he need not fear the hidden archer or the poisoned flask.

She pulled off her headcloth and unfastened her hair, shaking it loose to fall heavy on her shoulders. She stretched and lay back against the slope, gazing up at pink wisps of cloud, running sand through her fingers, listening to the surf pounding on the beach below. "How many wives do you have, anyway?" she asked dreamily.

"None," Azak said, very softly. "I have many women in my household, and many men, also. I don't know how many. Not all the women are designated for the sort of personal service that bothers you so much. Cleaners, cooks, seamstresses . . . Dancers, singers, glovemakers.''

Inos snorted to indicate disbelief. "And when did you start . . . collecting?''

"At my coming of age, my thirteenth birthday. A boy's education is completed by a woman. She was much older than I, of course, but not too old, as I demonstrated.''

Maybe! That could have been faked, whether he knew about it or not. "But you never have queens regnant. What is a sultana?''

"The wife of a sultan. One day, when I am free of the odious sorceress, I shall marry—one of my women, or a royal daughter from elsewhere, to seal a treaty. She will be sultana and have charge of the palace. At the moment I have sisters to look after those things.''

"Only one wife?''

"Only one. And she may be spawn of prince or peasant, as I choose.''

"But you still keep all the others, just for fun.''

"And for sons.''

She sighed and dribbled more sand through her fingers.

"Inosolan!'' His voice was suddenly harsh. "You honor me greatly—but I can't!''

Can't what? Inos lifted her head to look at him. He had not moved. Then she read in his eyes what he was thinking. Horrified, she sat up and hugged her knees tightly, stammering as she sought words. Of course he had assumed . . .

They were completely alone on this warm sand, with nothing but distant fishing boats to overlook them, and certainly none of the palace staff would interrupt. She felt her face blaze hotter than the desert sands. Blatant provocation! "Come on!'' she had said—her idea, her invitation! She had led him here and then started babbling about wives and concubines. He was the ultimate arrogant male, so of course he would think she had meant—

Inos, what have you started?

The last ruddy blush of the sunset showed his face, yet the expression on it looked more like fury than passion.

"I thought women gossiped more,'' Azak said. "There is another curse on me. Everyone must know of it. Has no one told you?''

Inos swallowed and could find no words. She shook her head in frightened silence. *No more games!* she had vowed, and here she was, playing in the sand with a barbarian killer. She had forgotten politics, put them aside to relax, but Azak would never relax. Even procreation was politics to a royal stallion.

"I cannot touch a woman."

"What? But—"

"It is one of Rasha's torments. I would burn you like hot iron. A mare, a falcon, a bitch, any female animal, but not a woman."

The humiliation on his face was an agony, but he was keeping his eyes on hers, steady as nailheads. "I tried to have one of my women comb my hair. It scorched her fingers. From the oldest crone in the kingdom to my tiniest daughter, if her flesh touches mine, she will be blistered and burned."

With one exception, of course?

"Your Majesty! That's—I have never heard of anything so cruel."

"Nor I. But she will never break me!"

Aghast, Inos hugged her knees tighter, then hid her face on them. She was appalled at the sorceress' vindictiveness, but even more appalled at her own sense of relief, and at the narrowness of her escape. This was not the Impire, and she no longer had Kade hiding behind every bush. Idiot! Her heart was still pounding as she forced herself to look up and meet his eyes. "I assure you, that was not what I had in mind, your Majesty. But I deplore such evil sorcery. It is foul and wicked, and I despise the sorceress for it."

He frowned at her, as if puzzled.

The swift desert twilight was fading into night. She had finally achieved what she had been seeking for weeks, a private chat with Azak. She tried to collect her wits.

"Let us talk about Rasha now."

He shrugged. "Why not? Of course, she may be spying on us. Or she may wait until we return tomorrow and then just ask, but at least no one else can hear. Speak, Queen Inosolan!" He turned around and made himself comfortable, sitting slightly downhill from her and leaning back to face the sea, elbows against the slope.

She began to talk and he kept cutting her off, saying he knew that, as if every word she or Kade had spoken in the palace had been repeated to him, the whole Krasnegar story. But when she came to the meeting with Olybino, Azak fell silent, staring out at the waves, motionless as a tree until she had finished.

Even then, he seemed to speak to the sea and the huge bright moon. "I have never seen a goblin. Are they as bad as gnomes?"

"I don't know gnomes."

He stretched out and rolled over to lie on his belly and look up at her. "You seek another choice, but if you are forced to that one, will you marry a goblin to win back your kingdom?"

That question had haunted her for two nights now. "If it came to that, the choice would not likely be mine to make."

He grunted. "Good! Never answer hypothetical questions. What do you want me to do?"

"Help me!"

"Why?"

He had not asked *How!* Inos felt an upsurge of hope. This big, deadly young man might have a trick or two she had not thought of.

"Because: *My enemy's enemy is my friend.*"

"Not necessarily! Who are your enemies? Both Rasha and the warlock were willing to put you on your throne. It's not their objective you dislike, it's their price."

"No! They were not going to put me on my throne. They were willing to send me home, but not as a queen, not a real queen."

Azak bought troops of young girls and ordered them shipped to the palace like livestock. He would not view her problem as she did.

"True." He stirred sand with his finger, seemingly thinking. "And my enemies? Rasha, certainly. Should the warlock of the east enslave her and make her a—what was the word, votary?— then that might rid me of her. But the warden of the east can never be my friend, because he is occult preserver of the legions, and the Impire must be about due to invade us again. They are a generation behind their usual schedule. War growls in the long grass. I told you."

After a moment he added, "We do not share the same enemies, you and I."

She fought the tightening tentacles of his logic. "They are certainly not my friends, those two! They want to use me as a token, a coin!"

Azak leaned his chin on one hand and gazed up at her, studying her face in the moon's light, his own face shadowed. "In any market, the coins outnumber the traders. You object?"

"Of course I object! Rasha promised to help me, and now seeks to use me for her own ends." She would not add any remarks about helpless women, but she had never felt more helpless.

"Help usually has a price."

"I was hoping for advice, not aphorisms."

"They are more dependable. You want to escape? And go where? Back to your kingdom? Assuming you can elude the sorceress, it will take you at least a year to cross Pandemia, being realistic. And you will have to hire an army—and ships, also, as you say the land route is closed. Have you any money?"

Inos had already thought about this, the brute-force solution. "I have rich relatives within the Impire, but I know the Impire doesn't allow private armies. And who could I ever hire to fight an army of jotnar?"

Azak grunted thoughtfully. "Other jotnar? So you would head north to Nordland, to hire your mercenaries?"

And ten to one she would at once be raped, robbed, and find herself cooking fish in some thrall's hovel for the rest of her days. Jotnar would not follow a female leader anyway, and how would she get rid of them afterward?

"Nordland doesn't seem a very practical solution," she said.

"Fighting cholera with typhoid? No. So where do you go?"

She had expected answers, not questions, but she could see that he was clearing out the undergrowth. There might be nothing left when he had finished, of course.

"Hub?" she suggested.

Azak grunted again. "All roads lead to Hub! But the journey will take months. It will be very dangerous, a hard, long journey. You may finish up somewhere else, in much worse straits than you are now. You might yet wish you had settled for a green husband. They are green, aren't they?"

"Sort of. I know it would be long and hard. Is it possible?"

"The imperor will certainly marry you off to an imp in short order." He hadn't answered the question.

"Any imp would be better than a goblin! Well, almost any imp."

For a moment she thought a smile rippled Azak's ribbon of beard. He bent his head and began sifting the hot sand through his fingers. Seabirds cried; waves broke and tumbled. He seemed to have run out of questions.

"I thought I would appeal to the wardens," she said. "Rasha used magic against the Imperial troops in Krasnegar, and that's a violation of the Protocol."

"But East is the offended party, and East already knows about it. He doesn't need you to remind him of it. Or mention it to the others. He may prefer to keep them uninformed.''

When she was about to speak, Azak added, ''And she did it to rescue you. You will seem very ungrateful.''

Manners were unimportant in politics—he was taunting her. ''She's cast spells on you! That's more meddling in politics.''

She saw his eyes flash in the shadow as he glanced briefly up at her. ''But not your business.''

''If the Four are as split as Rasha says—''

''You can trust nothing the bitch said, nor the warlock either. Historically the wardens squabble like cats in a sack, but there is no way we can know what the current rivalries and alliances are.''

The conversation was not proving very helpful. ''So advise me! Is it possible for me to escape from Rasha?''

''It is always possible to try. Even sorceresses must sleep. At least this one does.'' He did not look at Inos as he said that, just trailed sand through fingers twice the size of hers. She felt a stir of hope.

''And you will aid me?''

''Why should I? It would annoy the harlot, and I suffer enough at her hands already.''

''Because I am the enemy of your enemy.''

''You can't harm her. It's a pretty problem, but immaterial to me. Why should I risk further hostility from the slut? I see no advantage in aiding you.''

In that case, Inos saw no advantage in further polite conversation. What would move Azak? Not conscience. Honor? This was politics, not a parlor game, so nerve was what was needed. She didn't feel very brave, but she had begun to feel angry.

''Further hostility?'' she snapped. ''How much hostility will you endure before you try to fight back? She's already gelded you, you say. What else do you want?''

His teeth flashed like daggers at that, but she rushed ahead regardless.

''So the Sultan of Arakkaran is gigolo for a dockside harlot? You called her that. She denies you your title—what new outrage will she think up next? You come when she whistles. You reward your women with smiles. How many sons are they bearing now, your Majesty? What will the other princes say when they stop bearing altogether, your Majesty? Or is that already obvious? You prance around on your fancy horses all day and whore for the sorceress all night. What sort of a sultan are you? What sort of a man, to endure such treatment without even trying to put an end to it? How can you—"

Azak rose to his knees. She stopped then, aghast at what she had said, wondering if he'd have her flogged.

Silence.

No one in the kingdom could speak to him like that. She felt her palms wet. Every nerve screamed at her to say "Sorry!" She didn't.

He looked down at her, his face in shadow; but when he spoke, his voice was unchanged. "If you can have your kingdom only by marrying a goblin, will you?"

The same hypothetical question again—and obviously this time she must not seek to escape it.

Answer no and she didn't care enough. Answer yes and she was a whore like him. She would never outwit this man. Her face was visible to him, awash in moonlight. She must speak the truth—what was the truth?

"You told me a kingdom is not buildings or scenery. If I can help my people by marrying a goblin, then I will do it."

"And if it helps your people for you to stay away forever?"

The words froze in her mouth, but she spoke them. "Then I stay away forever."

Azak reached down and hooked his fingers like claws in the silver sand. He stared at the backs of his hands. A wave fell. Another. Inos discovered she was holding her breath and couldn't any longer. Two more waves . . .

"In very old treaties," Azak said, without looking up, "there was always an item called the 'Appeal Clause.' It shows up in any treaty the Impire ever made with anyone, including Arakkaran or its allies of the day. Until about the Twelfth Dynasty. After that it seems to have been dropped. Forgotten, or just found inconvenient. Or unnecessary, maybe. But it's never been revoked that I know of. In that clause, the Impire promises to maintain the Right of Appeal."

He paused, but she did not ask, knowing it would come. This was the sort of expert advice she had been hoping for.

"Appeal by any state or ruler against illicit use of magic. You see, Emine's Protocol was supposedly designed to defend all peoples, all Pandemia. Not just the Impire. In theory, the Impire was going to do everyone a favor by suppressing the political use of magic. Even then, the Impire was the largest mundane power, so that was a very convenient altruism. But it did raise the question of whether the Four serve the Impire, or the Impire serves the Four. That's why for centuries the imperors have maintained that any ruler with a sorcery problem may appeal to the wardens. There isn't anyone else to appeal to, of course, since they've driven all lesser sorcerers into the bushes. Nowadays it may be nothing but a handy fiction; but if it still works, then you have an open-and-shut case.''

"I do?''

"Rasha kidnapped a queen. That's meddling in politics.''

Of course! Brilliant! Inos clapped her hands and almost wished she could spot a very warm kiss on this big djinn. Quite the best-educated barbarian she had ever met!

Except . . . "But of course we don't know what verdict they will come to,'' she said.

"No. You have no guarantee at all. But it is a little like Zartha's ox, this morning.'' He sensed her incomprehension. "I don't give a turd for a peasant's ox. My gold bought respect.''

"You mean the Four don't care for Krasnegar . . .''

"Arbitrary rule frightens people. Power tempered with justice is well loved.'' He shrugged. "It is a gamble, but I would much sooner trust the Four together, and in public, than any one of them alone, in private.''

Oh, he was a clever one, this sultan! Now that he had spelled it out, she understood the thinking. "Yes! Will you help me?''

"I shall do better.'' He held out an arm. The green cotton was silver in the moonlight. "Touch me.''

"What?''

"Gently, touch my sleeve. And be careful! Think of me as a hot stove.''

She tapped his arm cautiously with a fingertip.

"A little harder,'' he said, and pulled the cloth taut.

She tapped harder. Still nothing. She poked, and it was like poking a rock in there, and—*ouch*!

She tucked her finger in her mouth and stared at him. There was a faint scorch mark on his sleeve, although he seemed to have felt nothing. She would have a blister. Gods! It hurt.

"I was telling the truth.''

"I never said—''

"There is an old saying about the honesty of djinns. But you see you can trust me, at least in that way. You want to go to Hub. You have convinced me that I should go, also. I shall escort you, and we shall appeal to the Four together. We shall both demand justice.''

"You! What of your kingdom?''

"My kingdom?" he repeated harshly. "You said it yourself—the slut has gelded me. How long can a eunuch hold a kingdom in Zark?"

She had won! "You are joking!"

"I do not joke."

Won! Won! Won! "And what did I say to persuade you?"

He scrambled to his feet, a huge black shape among the wind-stroked dunes, dark against the moonlight. "That you would stay away if your duty required it. That hurt. Duties can usually be recognized by pain."

"And your duty?"

He laughed harshly. "To rescue my people from the rule of a woman, of course. Enjoy your swim now. I will send Zana."

Slave and sultan:
> With me along some Strip of Herbage strown
> That just divides the desert from the sown,
>   Where name of Slave and Sultan scarce is known,
> And pity Sultan Mahmud on his throne.
>
> Fitzgerald, *The Rubaiyat of Omar Khayyam*
> (§10, 1859)

❆ SIX ❆

Beset the road

1

A bath in warm surf was a new experience for Inos, but it soon impressed her as a facility much needed back home in Krasnegar, where the Winter Ocean stayed homicidal all year long. She had partied on beaches often enough in her youth, with friends—with Rap, especially—but the sea had been no more than something to look at. Just this once, she would admit that Zark held the advantage.

Occupied with learning how not to drown or be skinned against the sand, she could not dwell on the prospect of the coming escape, or what Kade would say, or how Azak thought he could arrange that miracle. Under the pumpkin moon, she romped and rolled like a kitten, barely conscious of time passing. Suddenly Zana's tall blackness stood on the beach, waiting for her, and she was exhausted and almost numb with the pounding.

"That was marvelous!" Inos said, toweling her tingling skin. "I wish I could carry the Spring Sea around in a bag, for use when needed."

Zana chuckled. "A large bag."

"Yes. But sea is much more fun to be in than on. I'm a rotten sailor." There were two ways from Arakkaran to the Impire—west to Qoble, or north to the Morning Sea and the Winnipango River. Which way would Azak choose? And Inos had let slip a careless remark in front of Zana—she must guard her tongue.

"I am sure your Majesty is a very capable traveler, well able to withstand the rigors of a long journey."

Inos had just wriggled into a clean robe. She sat down to wipe sand off her feet, and then Zana's odd comment registered. "Oh?"

The tall woman knelt to fumble in the bag she had brought. "I have some paper here, ma'am. You need to write to your aunt—that is, if you wish her to accompany you."

Drying ceased at the third toe. When in doubt, be stupid— that was one of Kade's rules, although she would never have admitted it.

"What?" Inos wished faces were easier to read in moonlight; Zana was smiling, but no more was visible; the dusky, wrinkled complexion was an enigma under the smile.

"You do wish your aunt to go with you to Hub? That was what I told the Big Man. He argued against it, but I said you would insist. Was I wrong?"

"No . . . No, of course not. I couldn't abandon her." Kade was a good sailor, and she had always yearned to visit Hub. "But . . . tonight?"

"Very soon. Cubslayer never wastes time."

Cubslayer? Inos tried to imagine a much younger Zana with a little brother, a very much younger little brother—precocious, ferocious, ungovernable. She had never heard the name before, but it sounded so genuine and so obviously appropriate that it somehow banished the small suspicions starting to sprout in her mind.

"I am the only man he trusts," Kar had boasted. He hadn't mentioned women. Zana was loyal. That was why she had been put in charge of the suspect royal visitors in the first place.

And Inos knew Azak was a man of instant decisions; his deadly archery alone proved that. Escape from the palace might be tricky, and here they were leagues from it already, a chance not to be missed. He might just haul her onto a passing ship with him and be gone before the sorceress could find out what was happening. And Kade was still back home in the palace . . . it was astonishing that Azak would ever agree to include Kade.

"What do I write?"

"Just that she must trust the bearer."

It was an added risk, obviously. Rasha might well be holding Kade as hostage for Inos's return and be keeping close watch on her, or might perhaps have cast some sort of spell to raise an alarm if she tried to leave, or . . . but how could one outwit a sorceress at all? Kade would be horrified, but she was much less inclined to put her trust in the sorceress since she had heard about the meeting with Olybino.

Inos leaned the paper on a knee and wrote, hoping the words would be legible.

"What now?" she asked, giving both feet a quick dust and then stuffing them into sandals.

"We carry on as if nothing had changed," Zana said, gathering up clothes and towels.

Hunch suddenly became certainty. "He was planning this all the time! That was why he wouldn't talk to me sooner?"

Zana straightened, jiggling her bundle into a comfortable position under her arm. She turned an unreadable gaze on Inos. "A wise sultan always has a variety of plans in store, and rarely tells anyone what they are. I suggest we go to the meal now, ma'am, and talk of other things."

Full moon hung over the Spring Sea, so bright that even the distant snowy peaks of the Agonistes glimmered. From the bustling encampment drifted smoke and mouth-watering scents and much laughter. Half of the people there were women, many of them sounding very young, all paired off with the brown-clad family men.

Neither Kar nor Azak was in sight. Inos, as befitted her rank, was served her meal in solitary magnificence on a rug under a canopy, although everyone else was sprawled on the sand at the edge of the firelight. Undoubtedly there were guards posted, but she could detect no activity more sinister than merrymaking and good humor.

Gradually eating gave way to singing and the uncanny twanging of citherns. Palace women would rarely have the chance for an outing such as this and they were making the most of it. Inos could not help wondering how many of them had been gifts from the sultan, girls snatched from poverty in childhood to stock the royal seraglio. It was, of course, none of her business.

Nor was it her business if the sultan chose to provide a holiday for his guards, and his disappearance was probably a tactful way of letting the company relax. He had unpredictable corners, did Azak. She was confident now that an escape from Arakkaran had been in his mind even before she spoke to him. Her arguments might have convinced him to put his plans into effect, or perhaps just to include her in them . . . or she might have had no influence on him at all. He might be already gone, and she was merely part of the camouflage. Time would tell.

She decided to follow his example and disappear. She withdrew into her tent, dismissing Zana and the other women who expected to attend her. Anything that she could possibly require had been brought and was already set up, including a soft and commodious bed.

She was exhausted by a wearying day, yet for a long while sleep evaded her. She lay and studied the centipede tracks on the tent roof, where moonlight peeked through needleholes. It was not the festive sounds from the shore that kept her awake, nor the distant boom of the surf beyond the headland. The flapping of a tent was a familiar lullaby.

Strangely, she did not even feel like gloating over her victory. If she had indeed won an ally, it was because in the end Azak had proved to be very vulnerable. Rasha had shattered his mystique as a sultan when she flaunted him before Inos as her plaything. Rasha had erred there, and she had certainly erred earlier in placing that fiendish second curse on him. More than anything else, that intolerable burden must be driving him to seek out the Four, even if he would not admit it. So Rasha had overreached herself, but Inos had learned of the second curse through sheer folly, not by any great triumph of wits. She was happy to believe that she had won, but she felt no need to celebrate yet.

The greater battle lay ahead. Her new ally must prove his worth by organizing their escape, and obviously Azak usually lost matches with the sorceress. The whole mad idea might vanish like a soap bubble before the hard edges of reality. Inos did not dwell much on that, either.

From time to time she would hear some particularly rousing chorus from the fireside, or an especially loud peal of laughter, but those disturbances were too filled with joy to be annoying, and in a way they were even reassuring. If what she had been told was true, then at least some of those women had come from the same poverty that had so shocked her that day. There could be happiness in Arakkaran, for some.

No, it was the faces of children that haunted her tent. She kept remembering the shameful poverty of the villages she had seen that day, and contrasting it with the luxury of the palace— like the luxury of silk sheets and soft bed she was enjoying at the moment.

Krasnegar was a humble place. In bad years there could be real hunger in Krasnegar, but then the king's household ate sparingly, also. She suspected that a famine in Arakkaran would fill the ditches with peasant corpses before it ever curtailed the princes' diet. As a native of the subarctic she had always believed that life would be easier in a warm climate. Obviously that was not the case, not for those so-forlorn children.

The fire died, the moon rose higher, the singing faded. Discourse became quieter and more intimate.

She had just drifted off to sleep when she jerked awake again, hearing a baby crying. A baby? Why would there be a baby? She had seen no children earlier, yet there could be absolutely no doubt that Azak himself had planned and approved every detail of this expedition. Why would he have ordered a baby? She had failed to think of even one logical reason before she was asleep again.

2

Although the sun had departed from Zark, it still beat down upon the sugarcane fields of Faerie, where Rap and his companions had been striding brazenly along a red-dirt track for what felt like a long and unmemorable lifetime. Now and then they passed scattered bands of peddlers, herders, and farmhands.

The view was restricted on both sides by high walls of greenery, but Rap could see that it contained nothing more dangerous than rats. He scanned the faces of the people, also, seeking some sign that the goblin had attracted attention, or that his own absurd tattoos had been noticed, but he detected nothing more than mild curiosity, soon to be forgotten in the press of the day's business. Once the three castaways took refuge on the verge with everyone else as a troop of cavalry went cantering by, and the legionaries paid them no more heed than they did the genuine peasants.

Most of the natives seemed to be imps, but Rap identified a few trolls and troll half-breeds, and once a troop of dwarves— short men, thick and broad, with rough, grayish skin. They carried picks and rolled as they walked. Rap had never seen dwarves before, but one brief glance was enough to convince him that they probably deserved their reputation for meanness.

Now it was almost noon; Milflor had been much farther away than Rap had expected. Swaggering along the dusty track, Thinal chattered disparagingly about the town, drawing on memories of Sagorn's visit long ago. Even though it was the largest settlement on Faerie, he said, it was tiny by mainland standards—a quaint, rambling little place sprawled aimlessly around a fine natural harbor. The beach was one of the finest in all Pandemia, so the shore was lined by great mansions belonging to rich aristocrats, most of them retired Imperial officials enjoying the fruits of a lifetime's corruption.

The harbor was famous for its beauty, he said, a bay sheltered by a high and rocky headland. The water there was deep even close to shore, making for good mooring. The proconsul's palace stood on the crest of the ridge. Then he chuckled.

"Now, just a minute!" Rap said. "What has the proconsul's palace got to do with us?"

Thinal shrugged. "You don't think we'd be welcome? Sagorn might be. And Andor certainly would. He'd be dancing with His Nibs' daughter before sundown. Sleeping with her by dawn, if she was worth it."

Rap caught a frowning glance from Little Chicken, walking on Thinal's far side. Obviously the goblin felt the same uneasiness. For a moment all three fell silent, being cautious as they overtook a shambling knot of elderly farm workers. A family of very small people went by in the opposite direction, hauling a cart: a man, two women, and about eight assorted children, all of them sour-faced and grubby. Thinal wrinkled his nose and said "Filthy gnomes!" with disgust, and quite loudly. The gnomes paid no attention, and soon the squeaking of their cart died away behind.

"I thought we were partners," Rap said. "Won't you tell us what exactly you're planning when we get to town?"

"Just a little comfort, Rap. Lift a purse or two. Get us decent clothes and a place to stay. That's all."

"I don't want to stay. I want a ship out of here."

Thinal smiled rather shiftily. "Not that easy, friend. You don't have a patron, either of you."

"Patron?"

"Protector. In Krasnegar you belonged to the king—"

"I served the king."

"You belonged to him, even if you didn't know it. Anyone'd tried to put fetters on you, Holindarn would have wanted to know why. Here—who cares?"

"So?"

"So you and the Chicken are a couple of likely-looking types, healthy and husky. Who's to complain if you finish up in a chain gang somewhere, planting rice or felling trees? That'll be the end of all your adventures."

"Then let's get out as soon as we can get a ship."

Walking eyes down, hands behind him, Thinal just smiled at the ruts.

"You're not planning to leave?" Rap demanded.

"I'll see—see what Sagorn decides. We might want to investigate Faerie a little. There could be valuable pickings here."

The imp turned a bland gaze on Rap then, and Rap was at a loss. He glanced again at the goblin and saw dark wariness. Little Chicken would not discuss the island's secrets, either; ever since the fairy child had died in his arms, that topic had been off-limits for all of them.

"Will you help me get back to the mainland, then?" Rap said, hating his need to beg. "Either buy a passage for me, or help me find a job as crewman. I don't mind working."

Thinal did. He scowled at the thought. "It's not quite that simple. The winds are shifty around here. And then there are the Nogids."

Rap wondered why he hadn't heard all this before, although he remembered Thinal had dropped some hints. "What's a nogid?"

"Islands. The Nogid Archipelago, between Faerie and the mainland. Sailing ships get becalmed in the Nogids."

"And?"

"And anthropophagi. Canoes. Fricassee of sailor. Cabin boy *au gratin* with a coconut in his mouth."

"They really do eat people? Why . . . I mean, what has that to do with me? You think I might get sold to a feed lot by way of trade?"

Thinal shook his head. "I mean most ships in these waters are galleys. Whether I pay gold for your passage or you work it, you end up chained to an oar. Even a free rower is chained to his oar."

"Why?"

"Tradition? Or because the captain wants to decide when he's worked off his contract?" Thinal shrugged, and for a moment seemed to revert more to his old friendliness. "I guess there's no such thing as a free sailor, Rap. Not around here. You might shake hands on a promise that you'd be released when you reached the mainland, but you'd still be just trusting the captain." The oily smile crept back. "Of course a servant of the famous Doctor Sagorn would be quite safe. He has friends in high places, so he'd be a good patron! You'd best be patient, Rap."

They had reached civilization. The thief was the expert now.

Sugarcane had given way to open fields, then those became muddy paddies and finally smallholdings of shacks and vegetable patches. At last the travelers topped a slight ridge, and Milflor ran down to the sea before them. Its renowned occult defenses, supposedly proof against monsters and headhunters, were revealed as no more than a decrepit stockade, half buried in weeds. Its gates hung awry on rusted hinges. The tumbledown gatehouse looked as if it were used only by vagrants; nor could Rap's farsight find any trace of magic shielding like the barrier around the castle at Krasnegar. He concluded that the magic defense was as fictitious as the dangers it was alleged to keep out, just one more puzzle in the overall mystery of Faerie, the mystery that so intrigued Thinal.

Inside the palisade, he saw trees and more trees, small buildings, shrubbery—and people. He caught one glimpse of distant blue water and ships sheltered by the high headland beyond. The cape was rocky in patches, but also bright with grass and flowers and trees, and the scattered buildings there seemed larger and more substantial than anything his vision or farsight detected on the mainland. But soon he found himself down among the streets of the town and was lost among the people.

Long ago Andor had tried to describe Milflor to him, while they sat in a dismal attic in subarctic Krasnegar. "Shabby as a miser's nightgown," he had called it. In the past few weeks Thinal had tried, also, interpreting the same set of memories in his own snide fashion. "A woodlot with dog kennels." But neither of them had prepared Rap for the reality. He had never seen a city, and his efforts to imagine Krasnegar grown large and lush had done him no good at all.

Milflor was certainly lush. There had been rain that morning; vibrant tropical greenery dripped and glistened everywhere, loading the air with heavy odors of blossoms and decay. Narrow streets, unpaved, unfenced, went weaving through the woods like animal tracks, and yet their mud steamed in hot sunlight, for these trees were like no trees Rap had ever imagined. They were not the solid, saturnine spruce of the taiga, nor yet the dense tangle of the jungle he had so recently left. Their canopies floated high overhead, transparent as lace, more like clouds of dust than foliage, letting sunlight fall through unhindered. Wind-stirred and dancing like gnats, their branches hardly darkened the sky. Palms Rap knew now, but Thinal babbled airily about acacias and eucalyptus and other strange names, although he was obviously unsure which was which.

The undergrowth, though, was a dark soup of shrubs and vines and flowers, half drowning the buildings. The houses were mostly small and no more substantial than the huts of the fairy village—timber and wicker and shingles. Rap saw crumbled ruins rotting away right next to new construction. If Milflor was old, it was also eternally being made new. And he felt as if some trick of the light, or a sweetness in the air, had bathed it all in pure and potent magic.

He had forgotten what crowds were. He had never been in a crowd of total strangers, of unfamiliar people thronging by in unfamiliar dress. They were imps, mostly, but draped in gowns or wraps of a brilliance that rivaled even the ever-present flowers. They jostled and jabbered all around him in unfamiliar accents, wielding mysterious burdens, driving donkey wagons or pulling carts, surrounded by laughing children, splattering mud.

Very likely he would have been overwhelmed by it all anyway, even had he not had farsight. Farsight in a crowd, in a strange town, was an overwhelming experience; it smothered him. He forgot to keep his head down to hide his tattoos; he forgot to care that the goblin might be noticed as alien. He was vaguely aware that there was something wrong—that his inner self was shouting warnings of something he should have noticed and been worrying about—but sheer overload mulched his mind. He saw the insides of the houses as well as the outsides; he saw people in the distance as clearly as he saw those close by; and he comprehended nothing.

He knew that Little Chicken was holding his arm and steering him through the milling hordes of people—thousands of them, it seemed, hurrying everywhere, in reds and blues and yellows, all gabbling busily. He was only vaguely aware that he and his companions had reached a marketplace: a muddy clearing cluttered with stalls and tables of wares, with people—lots of people.

Imps, and a scattering of others: dwarves and gnomes and a golden-skinned youth he guessed must be an elf, and a couple of barley-haired, blue-eyed jotnar—sailors, of course. And far away, on a street farther up the gentle hillside, two women stood deep in talk, holding babies on their hips, and they were fauns.

Like his mother. Like him. Here, for the first time in his life, he would not be a freak.

And the stalls held cloth and vegetables and shiny pots and painted pottery and straw sandals and even books and . . .

Farsight: people and sounds and colors and people and motion . . .

Then Little Chicken lifted Rap by the shoulders and shook him until his teeth rattled.

"What—"

They were out of the crowd now, some way along a weedy path that wound through thick shrubbery, down toward the seafront. Rap's attention had still been on the people. He had not been aware of leaving the marketplace.

"You all right?" Thinal demanded.

Rap picked up his wits from somewhere. "Yes . . . Huh?" He rubbed his neck and pouted at the goblin. "Did you have to do that?"

Little Chicken scowled back at him. "You were asleep. You wouldn't answer."

Rap said, "Oh!" and grabbed his mind before it went slithering right back into the bustle at the top of the slope. He must have been entranced for a long time, walking unawares right into the middle of town, for the market lay on a saddle where the hilly cape joined the mainland, at the nub of the wishbone-shaped harbor.

"Hold this!" Thinal tossed Rap a small leather bag that clinked. Its drawstring had been cut. "And this." He added a bundle of fabric.

"Wait!" Memory came flooding back, memory of inner warnings ignored, warnings of something badly wrong.

Thinal hauled his shirt over his head. "What?"

"Danger!" Frantically Rap scanned. What was it he had noticed and pushed away, out of mind? The little wooded slope was deserted. At the top of the hill was the crowd—and he hastily withdrew his farsight in case he mesmerized himself again. The muddy trail he stood on was a shortcut from the market down to the harborfront, emerging at the back of a row of scruffy, ugly buildings set on a wide and busy road. The far side of the road was the seafront, with small craft loading or unloading at little jetties. To his left lay the mainland, its shore a vista of silver beach and great mansions stretching out of sight. Off to the right lay the harbor proper, with real ships and the hilly cape topped by the—

"God of Fools!"

Thinal had dropped his pants and was holding out a hand for the garment he had given to Rap. "What?" he repeated, with little more interest.

"Magic!" Rap said. "Oh, Gods, why didn't I think? We've been landed, gutted, and cooked!" He waved a hand at the high parkland of the proconsul's palace grounds. "What's that up there? At the top?"

"The Gazebo. Local landmark. You can see it from all over."

"And it can see us! It's a sorcerer's tower!"

That was what had been scratching at his mind, wanting to be let in—the turrety little building on the highest crest of the headland. It was only two stories tall, likely no more than a single room on each level, ringed by a balcony and capped by a spiky roof. But he had been able to see it from everywhere in the town, and probably it would be visible for leagues in all directions. What really mattered was that he couldn't see the rest of the hill, not with farsight. Long practice had increased his range greatly, and he must have sensed the problem subconsciously as soon as he entered the town. Now that he was closer it was glaringly obvious. Much of the headland was a blank to his occult vision—missing, wiped, not there. Only the upper half of that little wooden watchtower was clear to him; it floated above the fog just as Inisso's chamber of puissance floated above Krasnegar.

And that was not the worst of it. He stumbled over his words as he tried to explain—

"For God's sake give me that gown!" Thinal yelled. He was dancing around in the nude, while Rap was waving the bundle to and fro to emphasize his warnings. Arms folded, Little Chicken was leaning against a mossy tree trunk and glowering sullenly at the argument.

"No!" Rap said, putting the robe behind his back. "You're going to call Sagorn aren't you and you mustn't because it isn't safe and don't you see—"

"What do you mean, mustn't?" Thinal put puny fists on bony hips and puffed up a scrawny chest.

"That's magic! No, you're not a sorcerer, but that's sorcerers' magic you're using. Don't you see? Magic can be heard! Bright Water told me. Every time I use my farsight I'm using magic. Every time I calm a watchdog, or you pilfer something, or Little Chi— Sorcerers can feel magic, or smell it, or something. And that's a sorcerer's tower up there! Why didn't we think? Of course there would be a sorcerer here in Faerie—right?''

Thinal grabbed for the gown, and Rap whirled it away. ''No!''

''Yes!'' The little thief was dancing with fury now. ''Evil take you! I can't run around like this all day. People'll come!''

Automatically, unable to help himself, Rap scanned—and saw. ''Soldiers!'' he wailed. ''In the market! *And down there, as well!*''

Two squads of legionaries were marching into the market from opposite directions. Sunlight flashed on sword and helmet, on cuirass and greave, while shoppers scampered out of the way. Another band approached on the dockfront road. The centurion's bellows came floating up over the roofs and through the trees.

''Give me that robe, young man!'' Sagorn said sternly. Rap blinked and obeyed. Little Chicken went scrambling up a tree to see over the bushes. The old man pulled the robe on and began buttoning. It was an expensive-looking garment, formal wear for a gentleman.

''Gather up Thinal's clothes,'' he said. ''We may need them later. Hand the money to the goblin. He looks more likely to be entrusted to defend it than you do. How many men?''

Rap told him—legionaries were lining up along the whole edge of the market, at least a full century. Seaward, the men had their swords out already and were pouring into the buildings, pushing through to find back doors facing the hillside, and where necessary clearing a path by hurling furniture and people aside like weeds.

Sagorn winced as he thrust his feet into Thinal's sandals. ''Is my hair all right? Very well, come.'' He set off down the trail, moving with the slow care of the elderly on the slippery.

''There's no way out down there!'' Rap said. He wondered what jail was going to be like. Theft and murder would bring the death penalty, most like, or at least a lifetime in irons. His legs trembled with the urge to start running.

The old man spoke without taking his attention off the path. ''I doubt that they are looking for me, lad. And I shall vouch for my servants—both of you. I can talk down a centurion, I promise you.''

''Not this time,'' Rap said. ''There's no one else on this hillside but us, no one at all.''

Sagorn stopped, carefully turned himself around, and glared.

"Will you stop using your farsight! You said yourself that it may attract attention!"

"Then stop using your brain!" Rap yelled. "You're occultly smart, aren't you? So every time you think, even—"

"Dolt! You are an idiot! How can I not think? Tell me what you saw."

"The path goes to an alley between two buildings, very narrow—single file. It's packed solid with legionaries. They're coming through some of the buildings, too, and they're lining up along the bottom of the slope."

The old man frowned, considering. "Then they have been directed to us, and your observation about magic was well founded. It may be necessary for us to split up and meet again later. There used to be a very fine inn called the Elves' Crystal. No, it may be gone by now. We'll meet at—"

"I'm not meeting anyone!" Rap said angrily. "I don't want to stay here one minute longer than I need. If I can get away, then I'm going!"

Jotunnish blue eyes flamed below the snowy brows. "Young fool! Go near a ship and you'll spend the rest of your life in fetters."

"I must get back to the mainland!"

"Why?"

"Inos!"

"Gods preserve us! When are you going to grow up, boy? Whatever was going to happen to Inos has happened long since. Weeks ago!"

Why couldn't they understand? "I'm still going to find her," Rap said, "if it takes the rest of my life. I'll tell her I'm sorry or I'll weep on her grave. And if not for her, then for me. So I'll not be ashamed any more."

"You have nothing to be asham— Oh, this is crazy! You do not belong in the world of royalty and politics and sorcery! Face facts, boy! You are never going to see Inos again. With your talent for animals your destiny is to find some kindly master who needs a good stockman; then you can marry a plump milkmaid and raise lots of wide-nosed babies."

Possibly, but Rap was nothing if not stubborn. "I am going to go to Zark and find Inos."

Sagorn threw up his hands. "What are the soldiers doing now?"

Rap made a quick mental scan, although he had not really ever stopped watching; he didn't seem able to turn off his farsight when there was need of it. "Lining up, top and bottom. They're almost ready, I think. They're going to flatten us like mash in a press, between two lines."

"Military exercise! Mere brute force, naturally." Sagorn's lantern jaw clenched, and his thin lips whitened. "Then I must leave, I think. Give me back those other clothes." He began unfastening his robe again.

Creak . . . Little Chicken had decided he needed a club. He had begun by snapping a tree trunk as thick as Rap's knee. It fell with a crash, flattening bushes far off. Sagorn shouted, "Stop that!" but the goblin ignored him, proceeding to break off a convenient length: *Crack!*

The old man threw down his robe, then lowered himself awkwardly and sat on it while he pulled on Thinal's shorts, which were much too small for him. A bugle blared in the marketplace.

"Here they come," Rap said. "And here I go."

"No!" Sagorn shouted, struggling back to his feet. "Wait! We'll meet at Emine's statue. Gods! A statue of Emine in plain view, and I still never realized—"

"No."

"Wait! Fool! Don't you see yet? If you really want to find your princess, there's only one way you'll ever do it. You know what's here in Faerie! If you didn't guess it before, then you must have done so when he killed the troll?"

Rap glanced at Little Chicken, who flashed him a tusky grin and twirled his giant's bludgeon around like a twig. Rap would have needed both hands even to lift it. Horrified, he looked back at the gaunt old man.

"Kill more children? Is that what you want me to do? Is that what you're planning to do?"

"Not necessarily children—I mean, not necessarily kill . . . But I must know!"

"You know where all the fairyfolk have gone!" Rap shouted. "And why. That's obvious! That's awful! I won't be part of that. I don't want to be a sorcerer anyway. That's certain!" He sensed movement and saw the two lines of men in leather and metal advancing abreast, one down, one up. But he also saw a squad of a dozen legionaries running down the path from the market, ahead of the main troop. "They're coming! They may have farsight, too!"

The goblin uttered a ferocious growl and went racing off up the path.

"Little Chicken!" Rap yelled. "You come back here!"

He received no answer and he could sense the goblin still running, at a fearsome pace.

"Trash, come back!" But it did no good. "That's it!" Rap said, giving up. " 'Bye, Doctor!"

Sagorn shouted, "Stop! Rap, it's your only hope of ever finding Inos!" Anything else he said was lost in the noise as Rap plowed away into the bushes.

3

The hillside was a tangle of shrubs and saplings, a few mature trees and some crumbling ruins. There were thorns and stinging things and ankle-breaking snags galore; the underlying loam was slick and wet. For a few moments Rap could spare no wits for anything more than finding a route without losing his balance on the steep slope or scratching his eyes out as he plunged through thickets, racing and leaping along the hillside in the faint hope that he could outflank the lines of legionaries advancing in line abreast from above and below. Then he had a path mapped out ahead and could spare a tendril of thought to check on the pursuit. If his farsight gave him away to a listening sorcerer, then so be it.

He heard distant shouts and saw that Little Chicken had gone all the way up the trail to meet the advance party descending. There seemed to be an almighty battle in progress already, with armored men hurtling bodily through the air.

For a moment Rap stopped, stricken. The goblin was being trash again, seeking to aid Rap's escape. How dare he! And now it was useless to go back and try to save him in his turn. Rap had no way of fighting armed men. Damned goblin! Whatever had happened to him when the fairy died, it surely had not made him sword-proof. How dare he be a martyr? He could be as elusive as a doe in undergrowth like this. If any of them had possessed even a hope of escaping, it had been Little Chicken.

Rap continued his own noisy, hectic flight.

And who had gone the other way? Thinal? Sagorn certainly would not have stayed around for the patrol to catch. Darad, maybe. That would be another mighty battle.

Like a fox gone to earth, Rap skittered in under a dense bush, hard against an ancient fragment of rotting timber wall. He panted the humid air like a dog and wiped his streaming forehead. Little Chicken was still at it. Even with occult strength, how could one unarmed man hold off a dozen or so legionaries?

And he had apparently already leveled half that many, for the shrubbery was hung with bodies. Over the mad beating of his own heart, Rap could hear the oaths and screams and the crashing of branches. Who ever said that goblins did not enjoy fighting?

A dozen? He scanned and saw that the soldiers had broken ranks, and were going to their comrades' aid. Uphill and downhill, armed men raced toward the racket. If that had been Little Chicken's purpose, he had succeeded. The way was not exactly clear, but now the lines were broken, and the bushes were full of running men. One more would not be heard.

The goblin had given his life for his master, then, and it would be folly to refuse the opportunity. It would also feel like cowardice to accept it, yet Rap could do nothing to help now. Cursing himself for a craven ingrate, he scrambled to his feet and went plunging down the slope.

Still the undergrowth was transparent to his farsight. He could find the best route with no difficulty, and in the long run a faun had a much better chance of evading notice in Faerie than a goblin ever would. *Coward!* He angled over to a narrow, muddy gully, the bed of an intermittent stream, and went slithering down it on his seat. It steepened; he tried to stop, caught a foot in a tangle of roots, went hurtling forward down a high bank, bounced off rock, and plunged into sudden darkness.

4

Inos was never at her best in boats. She had known enough to refuse breakfast, and the waves in the bay were harmless spawn of the mighty surf that thundered beyond the headlands, but the slimy little dhow reeked of fish and wallowed like a drunkard—or so it seemed to her wayward stomach.

She had always assumed that the tentlike garments of Zarkian women were hot and stuffy. She had been surprised to discover that the black chaddar she had been given was a relatively cool and comfortable garment, but it had not encountered soap in a long time, and neither had the half-naked fishermen who swarmed around her. They were a rough, unsettling crew, foulmouthed, hairy, and spangled with fish scales. They shouted illnatured jests about her and guffawed at them. She dared not reply, for she could not speak in their dialect. The captain was as bad as any, a bow-legged, squint-eyed boor.

Fortunately she need not look at the sailors, for her hood

restricted her side vision greatly. Her hands and face had been dyed with berry juice, but very little Inos showed above her veil. Her voice might betray her, and her green eyes—nothing else should.

A bloated meal sack rested heavily on her lap when she sat. Its ropes dug into her shoulders when she walked; but the worst of all her torments was Charak.

Charak in his swaddling clothes stank much worse than anything else. He yelled continuously, he writhed and squirmed. She cursed Azak a million times for Charak and an excessive quest for realism. She did not think Charak was a good idea at all, for he was more likely to draw attention to her by showing up her lack of expertise with babies than he was to provide disguise. He also seemed too young to be an older brother of the meal sack, although Zana must be a better judge of such things than Inos. The advantages of Charak were only that his foul stench tended to keep the sailors away and her constant dread of dropping the tiny monster kept her too busy to brood much.

She had no idea where Azak was. He had not been present when she had picked her away along the slippery boards of the ramshackle jetty to enter this unspeakable floating slum. She had seen no one of his height in her later views of the encampment, when the boat had brought her back again. The dhow had first sailed landward until it met with the fishing fleet, outward bound on the dawn breeze. It had then put about and hidden itself within the myriad of similar boats. Inos had assumed then that her destination was somewhere other than Arakkaran—somewhere north or south along the coast—but once the fleet had crossed the bar, her own craft had separated and circled back past the headland again.

By then the family men had been striking camp and embarking their horses in the little ferry that plied to and fro between the capes, for the dusty track through the dunes was apparently a common coastal highway, much used by the beggars and footpads and glib-spoken chapmen who preyed upon the honest laborers of the villages. To move the whole troop and their mounts would take many trips, and if Rasha thought to check on the sultan or his royal guest, she would have a long search before she could be sure they were not present. That, at least, must be the theory.

Now the dhow was heading in again toward the docks, tacking clumsily against the rising breeze and making poor way;

even a landlubber's eye could see it was not a weatherly craft.
Sternly ignoring the queasy twitchings within her, Inos kept her
eyes on Arakkaran itself, resplendent in the dawn's light and just
as glorious as Azak had promised. Built like Krasnegar on a
slope, it was many times larger, its hillside more stepped and
irregular, and its buildings were of marble and gold, not brick,
timber, and red tiles. In all of Krasnegar there were exactly six
trees, while jungle seemed to be breaking out everywhere in
Arakkaran, in any unused corner, on any angle too steep for
building. Nor could Inisso's spiky black castle ever compare
with the shining domes and minarets of Azak's palace sprawling
along the plateau's lip. Despite her discomfort, Inos had to admire the grandeur of Arakkaran.

At long last the wallowing dhow was closing in on the ship-
ping moored and anchored along the harborfront. Now the
squint-eyed captain bellowed at his rabble to lower sail and man
the sweeps. Grumbling, they set to honest labor. Lewd banter
was replaced by muttered curses and hard breathing.

With suspicious suddenness, Charak stopped yelling. Inos
held him up to look at. "Now what're you planning, you little
horror?" she whispered. His reply was a loud belch and a fountain of milk. Sweat broke out on her forehead and her insides
lurched. That was definitely the worst moment of the trip so far.

By the time Inos had restored her internal calm, Charak was
asleep on her shoulder, snoring, and the dhow had almost
reached the wharfs. She had missed her chance to admire the
many great vessels moored in the harbor. Some sightseeing trip
this was turning out to be!

Then the boat jostled against a high wall, whose ancient stones
were greasy and coated with brown weed. Hands steadied it,
but no lines were thrown. Clutching Charak so tightly that he
awoke and began yelling in an echo of her own terror, wobbling
off-balance because of the meal sack, Inos was roughly disem-
barked, like baggage, onto a slippery stone staircase. Even before she had properly found her footing, open water was showing
between her and the departing boat.

A few rusty spikes protruding from the slimy coating on the
wall showed where once there might have been a handrail. If
so, it had vanished long since and not been replaced. Unbal-
anced by the ridiculous padding she wore, clumsy in her long
gown, she hung on tightly to one of the sharp-prickled spikes
until the world steadied. Water surged and splashed just below
her. Charak went back to sleep.

Slowly and with great care, Inos climbed to the noisy road above. She peered back and forth, shocked and dismayed. Now what? Zana had explained nothing, saying only that she would be taken care of. Despite the early hour, crowds bustled: porters and sailors, mules and horses, wagons and even strings of camels, all wound back and forth between bales and crates and racks of nets. A hundred voices clamored in orders and oaths and the rhythmic chant of work gangs.

Inos felt absurdly unsafe, teetering on the edge of the seawall and in danger of being knocked off, yet to go forward was to risk being trampled under a caravan of camels. The meal sack was an absurdity—she must look as if she were in the eighteenth month of pregnancy at least, although perhaps nothing smaller would have shown under the accursed tent she wore. The hood restricted her vision horribly, and if she fell back one step she would drown. For her own sake, as well as that of the pestilential Charak, she must move to safety, yet if she left this spot she might miss whomever she was supposed to meet. Then she would be hopelessly lost, with no option but a walk to the palace and a humiliating surrender. She decided to take refuge beside a high rack of smelly nets, but before she could move a voice spoke the password: "God of Pilgrims!"

With a gasp of relief, Inos spun around and found herself facing a pair of long, gray ears. Beyond them, holding a bridle, stood a short, dirty, and ragged man she had never seen before. His weatherbeaten face wore a coating of mahogany stubble and an unfriendly scowl.

Inos and the donkey regarded each other with mutual disapproval. She dislodged Charak's grip and held him out for the man to hold. The scowl became a glare—in Zark babies were strictly women's problems. Wishing that she were at liberty to express her opinions, Inos somehow contrived to hoist herself up, sidesaddle, with baby and meal sack still in place. The man hit the little beast with a stick and set off along the road, tugging repeatedly at the rope.

In a few minutes she had managed to adjust her seating, adapting to the sway of the bony little back under the blanket. She began to take stock, peering around under her hood, being careful not to look at nearby faces, lest the owners glimpse her alien green eyes.

The ships were unlike any she had ever seen in Krasnegar, the crews more varied. Most common were the ruddy-hued djinns, but she saw swarthy imps and some diminutive men with grayish coloring, whom she thought must be gnomes; dwarves would be thicker and wider. Here and there, tall and flaxen and inevitable in any large harbor in Pandemia, were undoubted jotnar. She heard much shouting, both humor and invective, and just to have identified all the odors could have kept her busy for hours: fish and spices, the livestock and the people, hot coffee and the strong salt tang of the sea; plus many less agreeable things. Had her mind not been largely occupied with the baby and with not falling off the wretched donkey, she would probably have been enthralled.

Her guide began edging into and through the traffic, finally reaching the buildings that flanked the landward side of the dock. He stopped beside a grubby and tattered little coffee stall, tended by a woman as anonymously garbed as Inos herself. "God of Pilgrims?" she said, and held out her hands for Charak. Apparently Charak did not know her, and had come to trust Inos, for the last she heard of him was a long, despairing howl. Serves the little monster right!

Now her guide reversed direction, heading back the way they had come, still tugging the rope and periodically whacking the imperturbably ambling donkey. At a mysteriously dark doorway smelling strongly of spices, he handed the tether to a larger, bearded man and disappeared. The newcomer did not even glance at Inos. He set off at a slower pace, in the same direction.

Ten minutes later, a third man took his place. Slumped impassively on the donkey, Inos did not look at him. She wondered what her father would have said about all this.

Sudden insight whispered that she had never really known her father. At their last meeting he had been dying; at their farewell in the spring she had been a mere child. They had never spoken as adult to adult. A child could not comprehend a parent as a real person. So she had no way of knowing what her father would have thought and she never would have. She might try to behave in ways she believed would have pleased him, but she could never be truly certain. That was a crushing sorrow, and she wondered why she had not seen it before.

Another five minutes, and the third man stopped the donkey at the bottom of a public staircase that wound off up a narrow canyon between buildings. He leaned close to Inos and breathed fish at her. "Climb. Turn left at the minstrel."

With great relief, Inos slid from the saddle, wincing as the ropes bit into her shoulders. The meal sack had taken on a definite sag to the left. Triplets, maybe. Keeping her head down, she set off up the steps, staying close to the wall as a gang of boys came pelting down, waving their arms for balance and shouting noisily.

The alleyway bent; stairway became a steep slope, and then steps again, more gently pitched. Obviously all this deception had been planned in advance. Azak must not only have laid plans for his own escape, he must have been confident that Inos would want to accompany him. She wondered whether she should be flattered by that tribute to her courage or insulted that he thought so little of her brains, for all these precautions were merely emphasizing what a very long shot this escapade really was.

Hiding from a mundane was a fairly straightforward matter. Everyone knew how to do that, avoiding movements where they might be seen and sounds when they might be heard. Earshot and line of sight were easily comprehended; but no one knew how to avoid a sorceress, nor what the limits of her range might be. Her powers could well make all this subterfuge completely useless. Perhaps all she need do would be exclaim "Inosolan" to her looking glass and it might, perhaps, show the fugitive at once. All these changes of guide and appearance—baby and then no baby, donkey and no donkey—would make the task more difficult only if Rasha must somehow scan for her prey, or follow its trail. Obviously none of these accomplices was in on the plot; none would know any of the others, and each had been hired to perform one small task only. The organization was impressive. It might well be totally useless, and Rasha might well be screaming with laughter as she watched the mummery.

At first the walls of the alley held alcoves where artisans and merchants displayed their wares. Weavers wove and tailors stitched; goldsmiths tapped and potters threw; all of them at the same time chattering and arguing with the onlookers. Face averted, angry that she dared not linger, Inos pushed by the knots of haggling bystanders. One of the stalls was a bakery, and her stomach informed her there that it had repented and was ready for business again; she shuffled past with her mouth watering.

The steps grew steeper, the alley narrower. The little stores disappeared, and only forbiddingly massive doors broke the sweep of lime-washed masonry walls. All the windows were stoutly barred. Porters and veiled women, children in rags and laden donkeys—Inos was jostled repeatedly, and at times forced to stop and wait until the way had cleared. Krasnegar was steeper, but she had never carried a sack of meal up the hill there, and the ropes were cutting into her skin.

Even the ever-present Arakkaranian breeze could not penetrate the canyon; the air was stuffy and yesterday's heat still radiated from the walls. Krasnegar had many passageways such as this, but most of them were roofed, and none was so filthy or so thickly inhabited by insects. Every crevice in the walls and every crack between the cobbles seemed to form part of a separate subsystem of alleys for the use of ants and beetles.

From time to time the way divided or crossed over other ways, but always her instructions to climb gave her one obvious choice of route. Strange noises and smells drifted in from the side streets: the hammering of coppersmiths, the odor of boiling goat, or onions, the crowing of poultry, or the scent of the inevitable coffee. Dark, sinister archways led off into mysterious courtyards, which she had no desire to explore. And there were many little alcoves and nooks fitted with benches or seats where a line of men would be taking their ease and gossiping—never women. They sometimes exchanged loud comments on her size and shape.

She was going very slowly now, puffing hard, sweating; also cursing the chaffing of the damnable ropes. She had not expected to climb so far. She thought she must be drawing nigh to the palace, but the high buildings cut off any glimpse of it. The harbor, also, was invisible, and must be very far below her now. An absurd fear of failure was niggling at the back of her mind. She had been told to turn left at the minstrel, but suppose she had missed the minstrel in the crowd? Suppose he had taken his fee and gone elsewhere, or just grown tired of waiting for her?

Suppose—worse—that Rasha had detected the conspiracy and was now playing cat to Azak's mouse? All those mysterious, taciturn guides might have been agents of—or even guises of—the sorceress herself, and she might tease and torment Inos for hours, making her trek to and fro, up and down, until she collapsed from sheer exhaustion, or until the fiendish torment of the ropes cut off her arms and they fell to the ground at her feet.

Where an ancient building abutted an even older one, the angle of a doorway provided a small refuge, and there Inos stepped aside to rest while a string of panier-bearing mules minced by. As the clop of their feet died away, she heard a cithorn twanging faintly up ahead. Hoping that this signified the missing minstrel, she gave her sagging meal sack a surreptitious heave and stepped back into the throng to begin climbing again, feeling every muscle in her legs ache.

She had almost gone by another of the sinister dark archways when a familiar voice said, "God of Pilgrims."

The two men standing there were indistinct in the shadow and muffled in robes, but one was very tall. She stepped out of the crowd and smiled up at him before remembering that he could see little of her face.

"And may the God of Childbirth grant you safe labor," he added.

"And you also, Cubslayer. What minstrel?"

"Just another mirage to divert pursuit." Azak flashed one of his rare smiles, and it seemed less tinged than usual with mockery. "Come in and relax, then. Here you will be secure, and safe even from the power of the sorceress."

Beset the road:

> Oh Thou, who didst with pitfall and with gin
> Beset the Road I was to wander in,
>   Thou wilt not with Predestined Evil round
> Enmesh, and then impute my Fall to Sin!
>
> Fitzgerald, *The Rubaiyat of Omar Kayyam*
> (§80, 1879)

❰ SEVEN ❱

Dawn of nothing

1

Morning had come at last, and Rap was still alive, or at least he thought he probably was. He had been conscious a few times in the night, but more often not, which was better. His head felt as if it had split into two unequal halves; there was a lot of dried blood in his hair. His left ankle was swollen even bigger than the larger side of his head.

He had fallen down a steep slope at the bottom of the hill. There was a very narrow gap there, in back of a house, where the rock had been quarried away to make more room. It was cluttered with roots and branches and old rubbish. Overhead a patch of sky now showed through a chimney, a hole he must have made as he came down on his way to a pit that seemed to be part of an abandoned cesspool or tank of some sort, lined with rotted bricks. Whatever it might have held in its prime, it was now stuffed with mud and sodden leaves and Rap.

There was some stinking water, too, and around dawn he'd been desperate enough to drink from it. Walking was going to be the problem. He had never noticed how many bones there were in a man's ankle, and now he could count two more in his left one than he could in his right.

After throwing off the layers of debris that had followed him down and more or less buried him, Rap hauled himself to his feet. He whimpered aloud at the pain, leaned against the wall until his giddiness passed, and then fumbled in the muck to retrieve a missing sandal. Forcing his limbs to move against pain was much harder than he had expected; he cursed his own faint-heartedness. With maddening slowness, he clambered along the narrow canyon that separated the back of the building on one side from crumbly rock on the other. Both of them seemed to lean to the left, but that was just his farsight a little mixed up, that was all.

He reached a corner and a gap between two buildings, so narrow that he had to turn sideways to squeeze through. The planks were rough, but he was able to reach overhead and find handholds in them, and thus keep most of his weight off his ankle. Then he came to the road, and those acrobatics wouldn't take him any farther.

He should have brought along a stick or a branch, to use as a cane, and he had been too stupid to think of it.

He stood on one foot, wiping mud off himself as he contemplated the harborfront of Milflor. It was already bustling, but less busy than the market had been. The sun was up, although still hidden by the high ground of the cape, where the proconsul's palace lurked behind its occult shielding. He wished he had more control over his farsight, for it kept trying to snoop among the fishing boats at the jetties, or the taverns and merchants' establishments along the landward side of the road. It still gave everything a marked tilt to the left.

Soon he began to realize that there was something sadly wrong with his eyes, also, a foggy jumpiness. Partly they were full of tears because he was in pain, but there was more to it than that. Everywhere he looked he saw a glare of sunlight, as if the whole world was made of water, and reflecting. He let his fingers investigate the bump on his head. They came away red, so the gash was still oozing. Bad! Nothing would be more conspicuous than blood.

A road with only two directions to run was not a healthy place for a fugitive, but he couldn't run anyway. To his right was the palace and the sorcerer's tower, and the headland would be a dead end for him, so he should probably head left. If the cape was an arm and the mainland a body, then he was in the armpit, alongside the small-craft jetties. He'd find it easier to hide if he went left, landward, but the big ships were moored off to the right, just about at the giant's elbow, and directly below the sorcerer's tower, which Thinal had called the Gazebo. The only way out of Faerie was in one of those big ships. God of Pity, he was hungry! His headache was getting worse, and he suspected he was confused.

When his good leg began to complain that it couldn't hold him up all by itself forever, he decided to start by getting himself cleaned up. There was a whole ocean of water right across the road from him, and it must be warm, because he could see kids playing in it. Right!

He took a deep breath and lurched forward, intending to limp across to the waterfront itself. He must have made it because in a little while he discovered he was sitting on a stone bench there. Someone was hammering red-hot nails into his ankle all the time, though, and he was sweating hard enough to wash the mud off without any water at all. He did not remember arriving. Could a man walk in a faint?

The sun was above the palace ridge now, and already the sea was a richer color than he had ever seen it at Krasnegar; but the fishing boats looked much the same, as did the sea gulls—just as cheeky and noisy and graceful in flight. The smell of salt and weed and fish was not too different, but there were a lot more barrows and carts and wagons rattling and clanking along the road at his back.

Feeling homesick was not going to help at all.

The tide was in. The road stood about a span above the water, built of massive blocks of white stone. They looked old and worn, but of course the docks at Milflor could well be just as sorcerous in origin as Inisso's castle and causeway in Krasnegar. Fishing boats were tied to some slimy old wooden jetties.

Just to his right a stone staircase ran down to the sea. Five or six boys were playing there, jumping headfirst into the water, then running up the steps to do it again. It looked like good fun for rich kids; at their age Rap had been mucking out stables. That thought took his gaze to the white beach and big houses on the landward side of the bay. Children and some adults were splashing in the water there and playing in little sailboats.

This sea was not the Winter Ocean! Rap rose and hopped to the top of the stair. Leaning on the handrail, he worked his way down, step by step, to the water. The boys gave him startled looks, and soon afterward he realized that they had departed. Without removing his clothing he went down far enough to sit in water up to his neck, and it was marvelously refreshing, soothing his scrapes and scratches. He ducked his head, wincing at the sting of salt on his cut, but soon that stopped. Easing himself up and down on his arms while the little waves went by, he watched the barnacles and floating weed and wished his head would not throb quite so hard, and that his eyes would attend to their duties. His farsight still said that the sea had a tilt to the left.

He must have gone to sleep, because suddenly he was choking and thrashing, in danger of falling off the steps and drowning. Who would come to his rescue? Probably no one in Milflor would believe that a man couldn't swim.

He hauled himself up by the handrail and hopped back to the stone bench. Already it was hot as a griddle, so that he was glad his clothes were wet. He must rest his ankle for a while and wait until his eyes began behaving. His head pounded with every heartbeat, his vision flicked in harmony. But at least he seemed to have stopped bleeding; his tattoos were aimed safely seaward, away from the passersby.

He sat on the bench for quite a while, wondering when he would cook himself to death, when someone would come and investigate a solitary man being idle while everyone else was busy, and when he would die of starvation. Why, oh why, had he gone and broken his ankle?

For the first time in months he was truly alone, and the feeling was unexpectedly unpleasant. He had lived by himself for days on end when he was herding; why should solitude bother him now? Lonely lost boy had better start behaving like a man pretty soon!

He discovered he was mourning Little Chicken and told himself not to be crazy. The goblin had been dedicated to killing him in the nastiest ways possible, so his death should be good news, not bad. Perhaps Rap's sorrow was only guilt at having left him to fight alone, but that suicidal assault on armed men had been Little Chicken's own decision.

Or had it?

How many soldiers had the goblin dealt with before they, in turn, disposed of him? Why had those particular men broken ranks to come running down the path? Rap's scalp prickled as he considered the occult possibilities. Legionaries had ravaged the fairy village. The one surviving fairy had died in telling Little Chicken something, probably her name, and certainly a magic word—and for no apparent reason. The goblin's natural talent had been physical strength, which had been sorcerously magnified, and now a group of soldiers had rushed to their own destruction at his hands. Might those very men have been the perpetrators of the original crime? Could Faerie magic seek out its own vengeance like that?

Things on the water were very hard to see, and his farsight

was growing blurry, also. The head coming toward him had to be a seal, he decided. Then he squinted, shaded his eyes, and decided that it was a man swimming.

He had never watched swimming being done. It was obviously slower than walking and must be hard work, for when the swimmer reached the steps and clambered out, he was audibly gasping. After a moment he came plodding up, still stooped and puffing and wringing water out of his hair—pale blond hair hanging to his shoulders. He was short for a jotunn, but broad.

Although Rap had accepted that this was a warm climate where men might go around bare-chested even in a town, he was still shocked by the newcomer's scanty rag. That was indecent! Nor was it very practical, and when the man moved to sit on the other end of his bench Rap called out a warning. "Careful! The stone's hot!"

The man stopped and turned to stare at him over a silver mustache large enough to sweep out a stable. The rest of him had been put together from knotted rope, brown leather, and wet polar bear combings. His eyes were pale as an arctic sky, fog gray with only a hint of blueness—but they gleamed at the sight of Rap's scrapes. "Too hot for me, but not for you!"

"*No!* Sorry, sir! No, I didn't mean that at all, sir."

"Ah! You mean I'm being stupid?"

Rap had never expected to sweat any harder than he had been doing a few minutes earlier, especially not when feeling ice-cold, as he did now. "Not at all, sir. I should have seen that you have bare feet. I mean, that you know exactly what you're doing, sir. I meant well, sir, but I was wrong to presume to advise you—*sir!*"

The jotunn shrugged, disappointed. He sat down, deliberately leaning against the backrest and spreading his arms along it, carefully not flinching at the heat, while all the while keeping watch on Rap, as if inviting comment.

Even the homegrown jotnar at Krasnegar were dangerously touchy, even Rap's personal friends like Krath and Gith. He should have remembered that the nomadic sailor types were all homicidal maniacs, especially when fresh ashore after a voyage. Dockside taverns in Krasnegar spilled more blood than beer. Even to get up and leave now could be taken as an insult.

It would be nice to have Little Chicken handy.

Keeping his blurry eyes innocently pointed at the little boats sailing in the bay, Rap studied his new companion out of the corner of his mind. Jotnar turned pink in summer and shed skin in sheets; he had never seen one so bronzed, to about the same faunish shade as himself. To assume that a male jotunn was a sailor by trade was usually a safe bet, and quite certain in this case from the pictures tattooed on the man's arms and hands, all of which were either obscene or erotic, or both. He was regarding Rap with the open curiosity of a man who could choose to be nosy—hard and heavy. His knuckles were badly twisted by old breaks; his angular jotunnish face was ominously unmarked.

"What's that 'round your eyes, boy?"

"Goblin tattoos, sir."

"Make you look like a half-wit raccoon."

"Oh, I agree, sir! I didn't want them. I was unconscious."

The man sighed. "You haven't been fighting."

"No, sir. I fell."

The sailor groaned and looked away. For a while there was peaceful silence. Gradually Rap began to breathe more easily. Even when he was feeling his usual self, he had no interest in brawling as a sport.

Then the jotunn began studying him again. "You're not pure faun. That's a jotunn's jaw if I ever saw one."

Tell him it was none of his business? "My father was a jotunn, sir, my mother a faun."

"Rape, of course?"

"Probably. But he married her later, sir."

"Lucky girl." Resignedly the sailor clasped his hands behind his neck and turned his gaze on the harbor. Rap would have enjoyed being furious, but anger would be a dangerous luxury at the moment. Besides, this man might be of some help if he would ever accept that Rap did not want to fight.

So this time it was Rap who resumed the conversation. The jotunn had dried already and he glinted all over as if he were swathed in gossamer.

"My name's Rap, sir."

Elbows and arms pivoted like the wings of a banking gull. Faded eyes regarded him with bored contempt. "Who cares, halfman?"

"Sorry, sir."

A grunt. "But I'm Gathmor, first mate on *Stormdancer*."

"Sir . . . I'm seeking passage back to the mainland."

"Where on the mainland?"

"Zark, if possible, but anywhere will do."

The weatherbeaten skin around the sailor's eyes crinkled in amusement. "Then you'll walk to Zark?"

"Yes, sir."

"I hope they're not keeping your dinner warm?"

"Sir, I don't mind working. I'll row, if I have to."

"I bet you would! Nice try, though."

"I don't understand!"

"Excisemen can count, lad." He lowered his hands, as if about to rise.

"Sir? I still don't understand! I can't sign on as a sailor?"

Gathmor regarded him curiously. "You banged your head harder than I thought. Or else you haven't been here very long. There's a big—no, a huge—tax on exporting slaves from Faerie. Or importing them, for that matter. I use the word 'tax' loosely."

"I'm not a slave!"

"Of course not! Slavery's illegal within the Impire, we all know that! Terrible thing, slavery. Which is why you ran away, and why the excisemen know exactly how many we had in irons when we arrived and how many officers, and why they'll make sure we leave with no more and no less." He paused, as if asking if Rap was now satisfied.

"I was shipwrecked here!"

"What vessel?"

"Er . . . *Icedragon*."

"From?"

"Krasnegar."

"Master?"

"Kranderbad."

"Cargo?"

"Er . . ."

Gathmor laughed. "Nice try, halfman. You don't know a bight from a bowsprit. Go back to the taro patch, boy. It's safer." He rose and stretched like a sunwarmed cat.

"Sir? Exchange me? Throw out an older man and take me? Then the count would still be all right!"

Gathmor's smile faded into something blood-curdling. "And what do we say to his wife when we get home? You think she'd accept a mule in a man's place? Or what do we do when you manage to escape? You hinting we keep slaves, too?"

"No, sir! Not at all, sir!"

Gathmor looked disbelieving and stepped closer as if he had decided to crack a few bones on principle. Then he seemed to notice the purple eggplant that connected Rap's foot to the leg of his pants.

He frowned. "You ever done any rowing?"

"Not much, sir."

The sailor nodded. "It needs legs as well as arms. You'll get beaten for that, you know, damaging your master's property?"

Chuckling, he strutted to the edge of the dock and raised his arms. Then he lowered them and looked back. "I don't say I don't break laws, mongrel. I'm a jotunn and I've got standards to keep up. But I'm not such an idiot as to break them here. Not for a damaged half-breed." He hurled himself into the air, rolled up in a ball, and dropped out of sight. Rap heard no splash, but in a moment he saw the white head in the water, and brown arms thrusting against the sea as the sailor returned to his ship.

So that was that. Rap took a deep breath and tried to relax. And yet . . . and yet that sailor had seemed oddly familiar. Just at the end there . . . the way he walked? Rap wished he'd asked the man if he'd ever been to Krasnegar.

No, that was pure fancy. He was imagining it. His brains were all jangled by the bang on his head. Gathmor was just a very typical jotunn. Rap couldn't possibly have ever seen him before.

2

Zarkian etiquette frowned on women eating in the presence of men, so Inos sat facing the shrubbery, cross-legged on cushions on the grass. Free of her meal-sack burden, she wore a much cleaner and better quality chaddar, but she had defiantly left her hair uncovered and streaming loose. Honey cakes and sugared fruits, sweet coffee strong as horses, and pastries with heavenly centers . . . She was famished.

Behind her, Azak and the sheik sipped coffee and conversed in measured tones, loud enough for her to listen. Bees and hummingbirds flitted to and fro below a canopy of branches that the wind was moving purposefully around, making light and shadow dance. A fountain played in a corner below a tree laden with rose-pink blossom, and the scent of flowers was heady.

On one side the garden faded back to become a courtyard and then the interior of the house itself; the opposite side was bounded by a colonnade bearing flowered vines. Beyond that lay rooftops and a silver vista of the bay, shining in the sun. This haven of peace hidden amid the bustle of the city was one of the loveliest nooks Inos had ever seen. Even within the grandeur of the palace she had found nothing finer.

Azak had been recounting everything he knew about Krasnegar and Rasha's interference in its affairs. Evidently he and the sheik had talked before, but not at such length. Once or twice the old man interposed a gentle question, but mostly he listened in silence.

Then the story came to an end, and so did Inos's hunger. She gulped down a final glass of coffee and turned around to join the conversation, feeling equipped now to face the day.

"Have I left out anything?" Azak demanded, with a dark look that dared her to belittle his efforts.

"I don't think so," she said.

Both men sat cross-legged, as she did, on cushions. They were dressed for the desert. In place of royal finery, Azak wore a loose kibr of rather dirty, rough material, tied at the waist with a length of rope and large enough to giftwrap a camel. Inos noted with astonishment how far apart his knees were.

The old man was Sheik Elkarath ak'something ak'someone. He was short for a djinn but comfortably bulky in a robe of many colors, like clotted rainbows. His round, ruddy face was half hidden by a voluminous snowy beard and even bushier white mustache; he had the thickest, whitest eyebrows she had ever seen. Despite the presence of his sultan fleeing from a dangerous sorceress, Sheik Elkarath remained remarkably unperturbed. He was obviously a man of wealth and untroubled success, with fine gems glinting on his plump fingers and the hilt of a curved dagger tucked in his sash. His home was furnished with taste and riches, and Inos had been aware of many people busily employed there—she had been attended by two laughing granddaughters of remarkable beauty, and there had been efficient-looking young guards aplenty.

The old man acknowledged Inos with a faint indirect smile and then returned to studying his hands, fingering his rings. The morning sun was behind him, and his face was further shaded by a kaffiyeh so embroidered with gold and silver thread that it shone; the agal holding it in place bore four huge rubies. Azak's headdress, in contrast, resembled an old sack tied around by a strip of rag.

"The aunt is a complication," Elkarath remarked gently.

"A necessary one," Azak replied, with a reproachful glance at Inos.

Pause—the sheik was a slow-spoken man. "Of course. But

she provides another possible trail, and we did not have time to plan her escape as thoroughly.'' He moved a soft hand in a gesture of resignation.

"And the delay is dangerous,'' Azak agreed. "If the harlot has noticed our absence already, then she may follow. But the addition was unavoidable, as I said.''

The old man nodded without looking up. "We may yet turn events to our advantage, I think.''

Inos knew she ought to be suspicious of this unexpected— and so far unexplained—ally, but there was something very grandfatherly about him. His solid calmness was reassuring, and obviously Azak trusted him—Azak, who trusted nobody!

"On your side,'' the old man asked his hands, "those who helped are safely departed?''

"There is only one who could tell anything of substance,'' Azak said. "She has relatives in Thrugg. Since her mother's death she has continued to send support. She will be made welcome.''

Elkarath nodded gently again.

So Zana was only a half-sister, as Inos should have guessed from the great difference in age.

"What about Kar?'' she asked. "Does he know?''

A frown flashed across Azak's face and was gone. "He knows nothing. I told him I was following Atharaz.''

Inos waited to let the sheik ask, but he merely smiled understandingly. "Is that difficult?'' she inquired.

"It may be dangerous for Kar,'' Azak said, "but it is our main hope. My brothers will likely believe, and mayhap even the slut herself will. Sultan Atharaz was a mighty ruler of yesteryear, conqueror of half of Zark, great even among my predecessors. Early in his reign he vanished, inexplicably.''

After a moment's thought and irritation, Inos said, "He returned equally unexpectedly just after a successor had come forward and gained support?''

Azak's smile was as deadly as Kar's, even when it registered amusement. "Exactly. Since then the ploy has been used several times, frequently with success. Obviously it can turn against its user, but the ambitious will hesitate some time before volunteering to replace me.''

Silence fell. The two men stared at the grass, apparently lost in thought, neither seeming ready to inform Inos of all the things she wanted to know—where was Kade, why was this place safe, and whither the fugitives were bound.

"I trust," she said, "that my aunt's journey will be less strenuous than my own?"

"She will not be brought here," Azak said calmly. "Do not worry."

If he thought snubs would stop Inosolan asking questions, he had much to learn.

The sheik himself seemed as patient as a rock cultivating barnacles, but even Azak seemed unusually relaxed. She wondered which Azak was present now—the madcap horseman who rode over the roughest terrain at full suicidal gallop, or the cautious ruler who palmed a single fig rather than trust his subjects not to poison him. She wondered, also, if he ever visited his city without disguise, and she could not help but compare his style of kingship with her father's. Had anyone suggested to Holindarn that he needed guards—or even a sword—when he wandered about his realm, he would have hurled a bolt of royal scorn. She knew she did not understand Azak and might have involved herself in something worse than what she expected. Whatever that was, exactly.

"You had this expedition all planned before we had our talk last night?" she asked.

Azak frowned. "Not in detail. Sheik Elkarath made himself known to me some time ago and offered his services. I had toyed with the thought of going, but I was leaning toward sending Kar." An ironic smile twisted his face, and she noticed that he had not shaved. "The prospect of your company proved an irresistible persuasion."

Inos bowed her head in mocking acknowledgment of the compliment, thinking that she would not have dared entrust herself to Kar as protector—nor probably to Azak either, were he not defanged by the sorceress's curse.

"You told me outside," she asked him, "that here I should be secure from the sorceress?"

The big man scowled mightily. "I let my tongue run away like a woman's."

"Too late to call it back," she said. "What did you mean?"

Azak merely glanced at the sheik, who fingered his rings for a moment.

"Sorcery is a great evil," the old man said at last. "But it is merely the strongest form of occult power. There is also magic, which is a lesser form, and—"

"I know of the words of power. Four make a sorcerer, and three make a mage, and . . ." Inos caught a fiery glare from

Azak, telling her that she was not supposed to interrupt a sheik. "I beg your pardon, er . . . your Honor." What was the correct honorific for a sheik? There had been no sheiks around Kinvale. "Do please forgive my presumption and continue."

He frowned at his hands for a while, snowy brows hooding his eyes, but then he went on in a very soft voice. "If you already know of the words, then my task is simpler. You may not know that occult power is all about us. In my house in Ullacarn I have an actuary who is a genius with numbers. He can total a page of them at a single glance. His father served my father and was the finest doctor of sick camels in all Zark. Obviously their family cherishes a word of power."

As hers did! Inos had not told Azak of that and she did not think it had been mentioned during her shouting match with Rasha when she first arrived.

"In fact, I am certain of this," Elkarath said. He stretched out a hand, glittering in the sunlight. "This ring?" He pointed with a plump finger that shone just as bright.

Inos peered at the treasures. "Opal, is it not?" The stone was large, but it had a milky sheen, with little of the variegated fire for which opal was valued. The setting was of plain silver, and worn smooth. In a double handful of rubies and diamonds and sapphires, that seemed the least interesting gem by far. "It is magic?"

"Sorcerous!" the old man said dramatically. "It belonged to my great-grandfather. Where or how he acquired it I do not know."

"It detects sorcery?"

She was probably not supposed to have guessed that—Elkarath sighed crossly. "Yes, it does. When the actuary of whom I told you performs his wonders of ciphering, this stone will shine with green fire—and on the side closest to him."

"I thought the words of power could not be detected by magic?" Inos felt suddenly very uneasy. She wondered when— or how—she would provoke a green flame from this occult device, or whether she already had done so. Since she had yet to gain as much as one copper groat of benefit from the word her father had told her, it seemed unfair that it should constantly be throwing her into danger.

"Words can not be detected even by sorcery," Elkarath agreed, "so 'tis said. But their *use* can certainly be detected."

"Tell her of my grandfather, Greatness?" Azak suggested.

"My grandfather of blessed memory." He turned a blandly hypocritical gaze on Inos, as if daring her to comment.

"Blessed indeed." The sheik sighed. "An increaser of the Good, deeply mourned . . . I speak with all due respect, your Majesty."

"No offense. But should we not practice the relationships we agreed upon?"

"True, Lionslayer, then. He was a man of great powers. Your familiarity with the occult extends to comprehending the abilities of an adept?" The question appeared to be directed at Inos's knees, which was as close as the sheik had yet come to meeting her eye.

"An expert at anything?" Inos recalled Rasha saying that.

"So it seems. The late Sultan Zorazak was an adept. Oftentimes have I strolled past the palace of an evening and seen my ring flame yellow."

Azak chuckled coarsely. "Late in the evening, I presume?"

The sheik seemed to smile in his general direction. "Sometimes. His strengths were legendary. But even when he rode by on a horse, I could see the evidence of his adepthood."

"A flawless horseman," Azak agreed sadly.

"And Rasha?" Inos demanded.

Another exasperating pause told her that she was again misbehaving. The fountain tinkled, the leaves overhead rustled busily. Somewhere in the distance a child was crying. Inos persisted. "What color does Rasha turn your ring, Greatness?"

"Red," the old man said grumpily. "And very bright. Even here, so far from the palace, I can oftentimes tell when she is enchanting. You can understand my alarm when I first learned that there was sorcery loose in Arakkaran!"

"You said it was all around us."

"No!" the sheik snapped. "I said the occult was all around us, not sorcery. I had never detected a sorcerer before, although my father claimed to have done so. In Ullacarn my ring flashes often—there must be several mages there, and I know of an adept or two in the interior, as well as geniuses. Even here in Arakkaran, I estimate at least three geniuses."

Was this devious old rogue threatening her or wasn't he? Inos wasn't sure. He still hadn't looked at her, so he could not have noticed her uneasiness. She said, "Then why do you not start collecting them and become a sorcerer?"

"Why do you not become a whore and grow rich?"

She stammered out her apology, annoyed by the twinkle of

joy in Azak's red eyes. Apparently her words mollified Elkarath, or else he was content with having bested her, for he chuckled. Sunlight danced in the rubies on his headband.

"The theft would be not only immoral, but also difficult. A brief flash is not enough to locate a man exactly. When I said I knew of adepts in the interior, for example, I meant only that in certain villages I often see my ring shine yellow. Who the geniuses are in Arakkaran, I do not know. *There!* Did you see?"

"No, I didn't, your Greatness."

Azak frowned and shook his head, also.

"It was subtle," Elkarath said, "and likely distant, therefore, but a definite green flash. Downhill, toward the harbor." He poured himself another glass of coffee in celebration.

Downhill was not toward Inos, so she had not caused the signal, if there had been one. She decided she did not like this fusty old man and his stupid magic detector. It might endanger her, if her word of power ever started to do its job. It might alienate her from Azak, who would be happier not knowing about her supposed word. She had begun to have serious doubts about the sultan and his overly complex intriguing.

"So when you told me that here I would be safe from the sorceress, then all you meant was his Greatness's ring?"

Azak scowled and nodded. "I may have overstated the situation in my overweening joy at seeing you safely arrived, your Majesty."

Well! "But that's all?" Inos repeated. "A magic detector!"

What sort of idiocy had she got herself into? She wondered if Kade had successfully fled the palace. She might have already boarded some foul-smelling tub in the harbor. Had Rasha yet thought to inspect the spurious royal procession jogging northward from the bay?

Or was the sorceress even now rolling on the floor in merriment at the antics of these half-witted mundane conspirators?

"You don't also have a magic umbrella, do you, your Greatness?" Inos said. "Because I think that's what we need. I can see how your ring would help in a bazaar, or bargaining in the horse market. If it flashes for you every time your opponent opens his mouth, then you will be well advised to deal elsewhere. But that's not my—our—problem at the moment!" She caught herself starting to shout and forced some queenly dignity back into her voice. "At the moment we're attempting to escape, to hide from the sorceress. I fail to see how your ring can help at all. Suppose we get to the ship and set sail, and then your ring flashes red? That'll mean she's found us, won't it, and all the good it'll have done us will—''

"No ship," Azak said, pouring coffee from silver pot to crystal glass.

"No ship?"

"Too obvious. Too easy to search."

"Then how?" Inos could think of only one alternative, and she immediately didn't want to think about it.

"Camels, of course." Mockery tugged at the corners of Azak's mouth. "Not a dozen ships a day leave the harbor, half going north, half south. On the other hand, there are scores of camel trains and mule trains and wagons trekking around Arakkaran in a hundred different directions. We shall vanish into this web."

He was assuming that Rasha would need to inspect every traveler individually, but of course the alternative was to credit her with such power that nothing the fugitives could do would be any use at all. *Doing nothing achieves nothing.* That had been another of Rap's little mottoes.

Elkarath laughed softly. "I am a merchant. My caravan is even now being prepared. Every spring since long before you were born, child, I have made my annual journey to Ullacarn."

Spring? Summer was unpleasantly close. "Why not go in the winter?"

A sigh of patience. "Bulls come into season in winter. They become dangerous and unmanageable." If the sheik was smiling, she could not tell. The lack of eye contact was annoying her intensely. It wasn't just her—the old man never seemed to look directly at Azak, either.

"This was the opportunity his Greatness revealed to me," Azak said, as if explaining to a small, none-too-bright child.

Inos tried to imagine Kade balanced precariously high on the vertiginous hump of a camel. She groaned. "How long?"

The old man shrugged his pillowed shoulders. "If we effect our escape, well, three months, usually."

"Three months?" Bewildered, Inos stared at Azak. "You are willing to be gone for three months?"

"That should get us to Ullacarn." Azak was certainly amused. "The fastest road between two good ports is never by camel."

"I usually cross the Agonistes by Gaunt Pass," Elkarath said, "head north through the Central Desert to visit the emerald mines, and then south along the Progiste foothills. Sometimes it takes less time, sometimes more.''

"Hub is much farther, of course," Azak added.

They were mocking her, but she was thinking only of three months on a camel. Oh, poor Kade! Still, the desert on a camel could be no worse than the taiga on a horse—could it? And Rasha would never look for them in the desert unless she realized just how crazy they all were.

"As I said," the sheik added, having the same thought, "your aunt's presence may aid us. Knowing she is with us, the sorceress may look less keenly at camels."

Inos knew exactly how Kade would look at them. She would beam bravely and insist that she had always wanted to cross a continent on a camel. "Where is Ullacarn, exactly?" she asked in a small voice and saw Azak registering satisfaction, as if her ignorance were just what he had expected. The sheik was fingering his rings again.

"Almost due west, on the Sea of Sorrows."

The other side of Zark, then. "So what is at Ullacarn?"

"Nothing. From there we can sail."

"To where?"

"To Qoble," Azak said irritably. "That is in the Impire. Then by land to Hub, and the Four."

This was crazy! Three months on a camel, and then more months to Hub? The Krasnegar problem would be long solved by then. The wardens would dismiss her appeal as nothing but a historical curiosity. Maybe Kade's instincts had been right, and Rasha, whatever her failings, had been Inos's best hope. Three months!

It was too late to back out. Inos herself might just slink back to the palace and hope to escape punishment by pleading ignorance and the folly of youth, but Rasha would certainly find some spiteful torment to inflict on Azak for trying to deceive her, and the sheik might suffer even worse penalty for aiding him.

God of Madness!

Kade was always accusing her of being headstrong. What had she gotten herself into this time?

And then Inos caught a tiny flicker of a wink from Azak. It was so out of character that for a moment she thought she had been mistaken. But of course! He was doubling his tracks again. Elkarath was yet another blind alley, like the donkey.

"It will be an interesting experience," she said graciously.

A ruddy-skinned boy of about six came running in across the grass. He flashed a wide-eyed glance at Azak, ignored Inos, and fell on his knees before the sheik, bowing a head haloed in curls that flamed as if new-wrought in copper. Elkarath reached out and tousled them affectionately.

"Well, Hope of My House?"

The reply was so breathless as to be almost one long word. "Greatness-my-father-bids-me-tell-you-that-all-is-prepared!"

"Good!" Elkarath raised an elbow, and Azak moved to help the old man rise. "We shall be on our way."

The boy had sprung to his feet and was staring up at the tall sultan with awe. "You a real lionslayer?"

Azak put fists on hips and looked down sternly. "I am."

"Where's your sword, then?"

With a movement almost too fast to see, the big man snatched the front of the lad's robe and raised him at arm's length, so that their eyes were level. "Who dares question me?"

"Let me down!" The boy stopped squirming when he realized that he was going to wriggle himself out of his clothes; already his legs were visibly longer. He clutched at the big hand supporting him and grinned. "How long can you hold me up like this?"

"I can stand it as long as you can. Hours and hours."

"I'm going to be a lionslayer when I grow up! And kill brigands!"

"Grow up? Tall and strong like me?"

"Taller! Stronger!" But his breathing was becoming labored, and his face growing redder by the minute.

"This tall, maybe?" Azak effortlessly swung him overhead and hung him on a tree branch. He squealed, and his grandfather—or more likely great-grandfather—bellowed with laughter and asked him what he would do now.

Inos rose, marveling at this new, strangely playful Azak. How could anyone trust a man who changed roles so easily? How could she trust this Sheik Elkarath, a total stranger who never looked anyone in the eye? That curious shiftiness made him seem like an invisible man, as if she could not see him at all.

Months on a camel? Or not? She must just hope that Azak had indeed winked at her, that he did have another coil on his rope, a better plan than three months on a camel. She looked up to find him glowering at her, his arms folded, his face shadowed again by his kaffiyeh. The wind playing in the boughs overhead sent bright coins of sunlight dancing over him like a glory, and for a moment he seemed larger than human. Deadly. Cruel. Ruthless. And *honest as a djinn*. How could she have dreamed of trusting him? He could abandon her if she became inconvenient, or sell her off to a slaver.

She had no hold over him at all.

"Having second thoughts, your Majesty?" a soft voice asked.

Inos turned to look at the old sheik. He was plump, but it was only the contrast with Azak that had made him seem small. He was actually quite large, although stooped. For the first time she saw his eyes, red like a rooster's comb, shrouded in wrinkles, but as clear as the eyes of a child. Penetrating.

Inos raised her chin. "Of course not!" She had vowed to play politics from now on, and politics required taking risks.

And surely the risks were worthwhile in this case? This was the opportunity of a lifetime! She would experience the sort of wild escapade found only in the poets' romances—caravan to Ullacarn!

A woman of royal birth had no right ever to expect such an opportunity. A shiver of excitement ran through her, all the way to her toes and fingers. Adventure! Never since Yggingi's cohorts closed in around her had she felt truly free, and suddenly that oppressive aura of captivity fell away like breaking shell. Sensing escape at last, her heart began to pound with joy.

She grinned mightily at Azak. His scowl melted into a menacing smile. The big man smiled as he did everything else—deliberately, fearlessly, and very well. He must be feeling the same sense of release, even more strongly than she.

"I will show you the desert, lady!" he said. "And teach you to love it."

"You can try!"

They laughed simultaneously. How strange!

"Come then," the sheik said with a contented smile. "Let us depart." He gestured for Azak to precede him, and the sun flashed a dazzling rainbow of flames from his jeweled hand.

3

Like a wreck on a reef, Rap was still slumped on the bench overlooking Milflor harbor. He hoped that his ankle would start feeling better soon, or that he would find the manliness just to walk on it anyway. Or that he might think of something else to do. The sun was really cooking him now, and it wasn't near noon yet.

He had an infuriating hunch that he was overlooking some means of escape.

The bench would easily hold seven or eight people, and from time to time others had approached as if intending to sit.

After a glance at the tattered and battered young man sitting there, they had all just wandered on by.

Gathmor's lack of interest in him as either labor or merchandise had been alarming and unexpected. To have been thought worthy of a punch party was quite a compliment, though—he must have grown. If he had been in a fit state to accept the invitation and had endured the ensuing battering well enough, he might perhaps have been considered worth hiring.

Or enslaving. Everyone knew that jotnar traded in slaves. Why should that not be true in Faerie?

Father, where are you now that I need you?

He must find a way off the island soon. He could not survive in the town without Thinal, nor in the jungle without Little Chicken. He wondered if the Thinal gang had survived, and which of them was presently in being, but he had no intention of going in search of Emine's statue. He was going in search of Inos.

Except he didn't know how to swim, and now he couldn't even walk. Failure! He was a failure.

He was very hungry and very thirsty and the sun was cooking him. He stared glumly at the line of ships moored along the dock. None resembled in the slightest the fat little cogs that plied to and fro between Krasnegar and the Impire. He wanted to study all the various craft in detail, but his farsight wasn't working as well as usual. It made his head hurt more.

Gathmor's *Stormdancer* he should avoid. He would have to try all the others and hope to find one that needed an extra hand. He might be selling himself into slavery, but it seemed to be the only way he would ever reach the mainland. Staying here was going to result in slavery at best, with death a likely alternative.

What would a ship's captain say to a man who crawled up the gangplank on his hands and knees and asked to be hired?

How was he ever going to get to Zark to help Inos?

There had to be a way!

4

The courtyard was small and dusty. Camels were much bigger than Kadolan had realized, and she pressed back in a corner, half resigned to being knocked over and trampled before she left this place. High stone walls and a blazing sun made it very hot and bright; it was extremely full of camels. Their smell was overpowering, their continual bellowing intolerable.

Fiercely whiskered men in swishing robes were leading camels, loading camels, cursing and beating camels. The camels bellowed back at the men and displayed mouthfuls of large yellow teeth. When she had arrived, an hour or more ago, great heaps of merchandise had been scattered over the ground; now they had been attached somehow to the camels, making the beasts wider and even more threatening. Kadolan had been happy at first to sit in a shady nook and watch all this fascinating activity, for it was a most unusual experience, but now there was no shade left, and almost nothing to sit on or hide behind.

Except, of course, camels. Madness! Inosolan, dear Inosolan!

Midnight messages, disguises, secret underground passages!

Still, although she would not admit it except to herself, Kade was rather enjoying all the nonsense. Undoubtedly Queen Rasha must be behind it all, but if it amused her and amused Inos, there could be no harm in playing along with whatever they thought they were doing.

Having had a day to think the matter over, Kadolan had now decided that the idea of forcing Inosolan to marry a goblin was quite absurd. The imperor would never agree to such an abomination. The wardens, surely, were cultivated, civilized people who must know that goblins were vicious savages. They would never condemn an innocent girl to such a fate. Rasha herself had suffered at the hands of uncaring men. No, it had all been some sort of a bargaining ploy, obviously, not intended to be taken seriously.

Hrunnh!

Kadolan shied at the roar and looked up into the thick-lashed eyes of a very tall camel and into a mouth full of amber tusks. Feeling like a rowboat being molested by a galleon, she eased away along the wall. If the brute wanted the corner position, she would not argue.

The black bedsheet in which she had been wrapped was quite a comfortable garment. Although it made her feel conspicuous, in fact it must be having exactly the opposite effect, for all the women she could see were similarly garbed. But her ankles ached with all the standing, and the smell was making her nauseous. Moreover, her face and hands had been dyed with some sort of berry juice. It had left her with a nasty, sticky feeling, and it seemed to be attracting more than her share of the flies. There was no shortage of those.

"Aunt!"

Kadolan swung around and was surprised to see that the young woman beside her had green eyes, very unusual in . . . "Inos!"

The green eyes twinkled. "I fear you have made an error, ma'am. I am Mistress Hathark, the wife of Seventh Lionslayer."

"Oh? Well, if you say so, dear."

The newcomer peered around at the swirling mob of people and camels, having trouble because of the cloth hooding her face. Then, apparently reassured that no one was listening, she said quietly, "You are still my aunt, of course, but they are planning some other name for you. Did you have a pleasant journey?"

Nothing of Inosolan was visible except her eyes, but her voice gave her away. She was feeling guilty and wanted reassurance.

"A most interesting experience, dear."

"You always did want to visit Hub, didn't you?"

Hub? That seemed very unlikely. "Certainly. Is that our destination?"

Inosolan bent close. "We are going to appeal to the Four!" she whispered dramatically. The words were barely audible over the roaring of the camels.

"That will be nice, dear."

Green eyes registered relief. "I am sure a ride on a camel will be highly educational. You always did want a ride on a camel, didn't you?"

"An appetite easily sated, I am sure."

"Er, yes."

"Inos," Kadolan said gently, "you do not seriously believe that her Majesty is unaware of this escapade, do you?"

Her niece flinched. "What do you mean?"

"I mean that she is a sorceress, that's all."

"Oh!" Inosolan sighed with relief. "You didn't discuss it with her, or see her as you left, or . . . or anything?"

"No, dear. I followed instructions, and had a most curious journey through several very evil-smelling tunnels with some very unlikely-looking guides . . . But, no. I was just wondering how you could possibly expect to outwit anyone with Sultana Rasha's abilities. That's all.''

"Well, we have help. I think we've escaped—will escape. I'm tired of being a prisoner! I am going to go and *do* something. Going to recover my kingdom! Aha!''

A very tall man had emerged from behind a camel at Inosolan's side. He was almost as anonymous as she was, in dirty-looking robes. An enormous sword hung at his side.

"Aunt, may I present my husband? He is a lionslayer. I understand lionslayers have no names, only numbers. He is Seventh Lionslayer.''

"Fifth, now," Azak growled. "I am looking for Fourth. He has a slight squint, I believe.'' He stared all around, peering between the camels and over everyone else's head.

"What will you do with him when you find him?" Kadolan inquired uneasily.

The big man's red eyes fastened on her menacingly. "I shall persuade the poltroon to hasten at once to Sheik Elkarath and grovel before him, confessing the defects and shortcomings he has hitherto concealed.''

Nonplussed by that, Kadolan turned back to her niece. "Did you say 'husband', dear?''

A flush appeared around Inosolan's green eyes, under the berry-juice stain. "We shall be sharing a tent, of course, but I can explain—''

"No one," the sultan said loudly, "has ever complained that I snore!''

Inosolan glanced nervously at her aunt and sniggered. Kadolan sighed. Whatever nonsense they were planning, these youngsters were certainly convinced that they were outwitting the sorceress.

Then Azak said, "Ah!" triumphantly, and stalked off into the melee, shouldering smaller men aside.

"It's all right, Aunt," Inos said hastily. "Really, it is. I am quite safe with Azak! I'll explain as soon as we get a moment alone. He really did slay a lion, too—on his thirteenth birthday! So he tells me.''

"I'm sure he did.''

"You can trust me.''

"I'm sure I can, dear.''

"I haven't forgotten your eight-year-old Prince Whoever-he-is. I'm not making eyes at Azak, honestly I'm not!''

"No, dear, I'm sure you're not."

Obviously Inos had not yet noticed the way Azak looked at her.

Dawn of Nothing:
>   One Moment in Annihilation's Waste,
>   One Moment, of the Well of Life to taste,
>   The stars are setting and the Caravan
>   Starts for the Dawn of Nothing—Oh, make haste!
>   Fitzgerald, *The Rubaiyat of Omar Khayyam*
>   (§38, 1859)

⊄ EIGHT ⊅

Magic shadow shapes

1

Rap had sunk into a stupor. The sound of hooves on the flags roused him enough to glance behind him with farsight. Instantly he twisted around for a proper look at the procession advancing along the harbor road. The man in front was obviously a groom or a guide of some sort, and the four persons behind him were just as obviously rich visitors—a fat, balding man in front, an even fatter overdressed matron behind him, and then two overweight daughters.

They were riding hippogriffs.

A rush of memory sent his mind skittering back to a gloomy garret on icy winter nights in Krasnegar, with the debonair Andor suavely describing the great world to his wide-eyed young friend. In telling of Sagorn's visit to Faerie, claiming it as his own, he had mentioned his ride on a hippogriff. Of all the tall tales he had told in those yarn-spinning sessions, that had been the only one that Rap had wanted to disbelieve. He loved horses so much that he had been revolted by the idea of a half-horse monster. But obviously hippogriffs were real, and now he was seeing them with his own eyes.

And they were splendid. The one in front was black as midnight, its head and neck shaped like an eagle's, but as large as a horse's. Its beak was a fearsome scimitar, its golden gaze ferocious. The taloned forelegs could have torn a man in half, and they paced in strange silence, while the hooved rear feet clopped loudly on the cobbles. The great wings were folded

211

back, shrouding the riders' legs, and the feathers shone like jet. The second mount was a snowy gray; the other three were bays of various shades.

Entranced, Rap squinted, striving to squeeze the blurring out of his vision. As horses, these would have been beautiful creatures, and the daunting raptor heads made them magnificent. Unconsciously he reached out with his farsight and stroked the sable plumage of the lead mount. The hippogriff would feel nothing, but Rap could sense the texture of the feathers—hard, yet silken soft.

But . . . something was wrong.

He closed his eyes, and still his farsight said that there were wings there, and eagle beaks. The troop had drawn level with him in their stately progress, floating above their own inky shadows. The locals were going about their business unperturbed, accustomed to seeing these handsome wonders, but some visitors were conspicuously pointing and making appreciative noises. Some had pulled out sketchbooks.

Rap opened his eyes again and still he felt confused. These lovelies looked like hippogriffs. Obviously they rode like horses, placid, well-trained horses. All mares, he saw. They were not the ugly hybrids he had imagined. Sunlight rippled on their plumage and their coats. They had beauty and grace. Why, then, was he so upset?

The troop had gone by him before understanding came. He could not see inside a horse's mind exactly, but he had enough empathy to sense its emotions and understand its concerns. He could summon most horses, or send them away, or calm them. He could do the same with dogs and cattle—with almost anything on four legs. And they all felt different. Mules and jackasses did not think like horses, although more like them than sheep did. These hippogriffs had minds like horses. They thought like horses.

They thought they *were* horses.

And a drayman's ancient hack standing between its shafts thought they were horses, too. It was watching them quite placidly. It would not have reacted so calmly to a donkey.

Again Rap reached out, and this time not with farsight. He stroked the lead mount's horsey mind, as he might have patted its neck, or it might have nuzzled his hand. He said a silent *hello*.

The hippogriff swung its great raven head up to look for him. *Hello*, Rap said again. *I'm over here.*

Claws scratching, rear feet clattering, the hippogriff turned toward him, wanting to be friendly, just as a horse would. The groom on its back swore and tugged at the reins and kicked.

Rap said *hello* to all the hippogriffs.

The rich visitors were not as skilled as the groom. Their mounts veered toward Rap. The daughters screamed, and the hippogriffs flinched at the noise as horses would, rolling their eyes and twisting their ears . . . What ears?

They twisted their heads, too, as if the bits were hurting. How could bits hurt beaks like those?

But Rap was making trouble. The three bays were coming to visit him, ignoring their frantic riders. The man on the gray was disciplining it so crudely that it was fretting, rolling yellow eyes in its milk-white head, and starting to fight against his kicking and rein-jerking. Why did hippogriffs not flap their wings when they were upset like that? The spectators were starting to notice.

This was folly! Hastily Rap sent soothing farewells, adding his efforts to those of the furious guide. The hippogriffs calmed at once and set off along the road. Rap turned around and faced the harbor again. Peace returned to the waterfront. A fugitive was crazy to create such disturbances in his own vicinity, right under the eye of the Gazebo.

So the hippogriffs were another deception? Undoubtedly all the other monsters in the zoo would be false, too, a fake threat to keep visitors from straying too far from town, perhaps. How long had this been going on, for God's sake? More than just centuries, obviously—thousands of years! Emine and his Protocol had just regulated it, that was all, and perhaps one reason even then had been to save the fairy folk from being exterminated completely.

Idiot! There was his answer! He had been forgetting his mastery over animals, and there were horses going by all the time. All he needed to do was find an unattended horse and call it over to him. Then he could unharness it, if it came with a wagon, and ride off to hide in the jungle until his ankle healed. Easy! And he could steal a dog from somewhere, just as he had once taken Fleabag from the goblins. The dog could catch food for him! Why hadn't he seen that sooner?

"You're the one called Rap," said the woman. It was more a statement than a question.

"Yes, ma'am." Rap had not noticed her before, sitting where Gathmor had, on the far end of the bench, but she was much more welcome company. Even if her gown was a simple white thing, sleeveless and plain, it was obviously well made, and she wore silver sandals. Clearly she was a lady of wealth, as well as no small beauty. She was shading herself with a parasol decorated in white, red, green, and blue, but otherwise she bore no color at all, no gems or flowers or embroidery. Just red lips, black eyes, brown skin, white damask, and silver sandals.

It was a long, long time since a pretty girl had smiled at him.

His vision had cleared. The world was back in hard-edged focus. His head had stopped pounding, and the swelling on his ankle . . .

May the Good preserve me!

"You are feeling better?" Again, barely a question.

Neat white teeth.

"Yes, ma'am, thank you."

She frowned very slightly. Her face was a lovely thing, slender and delicate. She had a glorious complexion, far better than most imps'. Her dark hair was tied up in a tight bun. Quite obviously, she was a sorceress.

"You had a bad concussion, you know. And your ankle was broken. How on earth did you manage to walk this far?"

"I don't know, ma'am."

She shook her head reprovingly, but then she smiled again, a smile like a joyous carillon of bells. "Well, I want to hear the whole story."

"Starting where, ma'am?" She had the same sort of calm, inoffensive authority he'd seen in King Holindarn or his sister; it assumed a right to command so natural and unarguable that somehow the person being ordered around was not diminished by it. Inos had been starting to show some of the same manner when he had last met her. The sorceress must do her duty, which included giving orders; Rap's duty required him to obey them. They were equals, both just doing their duty.

"Start at the beginning, of course," she said. "No, you'll take that too literally—I'll try a few more questions first. You comfortable?"

He nodded sadly. He thought he had been happier before she cleared his head for him. Oh, what a mess he was in now! But he did feel good physically. He would sing and dance if that was what she wanted.

"I need to know about the imp," she said. "We've lost him, now he's stopped his pilfering. He's been using some other sort of power; very strong, but so brief that I can't locate it. Little Chicken I've met. He was badly shocked, but he'll be all right."

"Shocked, ma'am?"

"Would you like to be run through with a sword?"

"No, my lady. Please not!" And Rap was astonished at his own reaction. "I'm glad! I am really glad! I thought the soldiers had killed him."

She shrugged. "I arrived just before he ran out of blood. I was too late to save three of the legionaries, though."

Tragic, maybe, but there was something almost funny about one young goblin killing three armed Imperial soldiers and maiming however many others the sorceress had healed. "I'm glad to hear he survived, ma'am. I shouldn't be, because he hates me, but I'll be happy to see his big ugly face again."

"You will. Tell me about the imp."

"Thinal, my lady? That's a long story!" Rap leaned his elbows on his knees and scowled fiercely at the harbor as he tried to recall everything he knew about Thinal's gang. He'd begin with Sagorn coming to visit the king, which meant explaining about Krasnegar, and then Jalon . . . and Andor . . . and Darad . . .

Once he was started, he spoke very fast, faster than he ever had before, gabbling the words but never hesitating, pulling the story out of his memory in a smooth string, event after event in logical order, hardly having to think. He was vaguely grateful for the sunshade he was holding. It was similar to the lady's, but he had no idea where it had come from or when she had given it to him. He was even more grateful for the beaker of cold lemon cordial, although he did not remember getting that, either. Every few minutes he would pause and gulp some of it, and the beaker never seemed to run dry. He wondered in spare moments how it felt to do magic like that.

But he had little time for thinking of anything but his story. Almost before he stopped swallowing, his tongue would be racing off in full spate again, so fast that he wondered how she could comprehend a single word. She interrupted only once, though, asking for more details about the events in the fairy village.

Finished! He took a long draft and waited hopefully to hear if he had pleased her. The shadows had moved. His jaw ached.

And the lady did not look pleased. She was staring at her hands and biting her lip, her eyes shielded by long lashes. "You're a good man, Master Rap."

Astonished, Rap took another drink.

She blinked. "I would apologize, if it meant anything. I would make recompense if I could. I can only assure you that I would never have done this to you had I . . . had it not been necessary.''

"Done what, ma'am?"

"Put you in truth trance. I'll let it wear off slowly, so I don't give you a seizure."

Rap chuckled. "I should be worried, shouldn't I? You're a sorceress!"

She sighed. "Yes, I confess it. And you have occult powers yourself, don't you?"

You don't have to answer that, said a voice in his head. *Deny it. She can't tell if you lie about that.*

She had cured his ankle and the bump on his head. And he didn't like lying. Especially not to pretty ladies.

"Yes, ma'am."

Her eyes widened. "How many words?"

"Just one."

"One word and you have mastery over animals? And people?"

"No, just animals. And I have farsight."

"An occult genius, and in two manifestations?" She was surprised by something. "But words can't be detected with magic. The truth trance wouldn't have worked for that. Why did you tell me?"

"I'd already given myself away, hadn't I? You could hear it, or feel it, or something?"

"The mastery, not the farsight. Even the most powerful sorcerers have difficulty detecting the sights being used. As soon as you started meddling with the hippogriffs, though, we had you." She smiled quizzically, inviting comment.

"That's what they're for? Sorcerer traps?"

She nodded, amused. "I doubt if they ever caught a mere genius before, but mages and sorcerers can never resist the monsters. Even adepts give themselves away sometimes. I've never heard of one just admitting to it, though. Your honesty may get you into trouble."

"I'm not in trouble now?"

"Well, yes you are. By the way, I am Oothiana, his Imperial Majesty's trusty and faithful proconsul of Faerie."

Rap jumped up and bowed. Then he felt very foolish, standing there holding a parasol, so he sat down again. A proconsul was a very important person, a deputy of the imperor. She seemed much too young to hold such a post. Of course she was several years older than Inos, who was a queen, but that was different.

She raised her head and looked sadly at him with black eyes that took his breath away.

"Your story is fascinating, Master Rap. The trouble is, it doesn't make sense. You and Thinal followed the goblin through the magic casement—but magic casements don't do that. It might have been combined with a magic portal, I suppose, but a magic portal has to be specific, I think." A small frown marred her perfect brow. She was amazingly flawless. Rap could not find a single freckle or mole to spoil her perfection. "I suppose it may be possible. I'll ask. But you have certainly told me the truth as you know it, so I must assume that someone has planted a false-hood in your mind." She bit her lip again. "And I'm afraid I know someone who will try to get it out."

Rap was horrorstruck. "I haven't lied to you, my lady! I told you everything I know about Thinal and the sequentials."

Her sudden smile was a fair dawn after a stormy night. "I didn't ask you the right question, did I? Well, do you know how you came to Faerie?"

"Yes, ma'am. Bright Water sent me."

Color drained from Oothiana's face as from a flower struck by killer frost. After a minute she said, "Tell me what you know of Bright Water!"

"She's witch of the north, one of the wardens of the Four . . ."

Rap's tongue started to gallop again. This tale was shorter because she now knew much that he could leave out. He finished and took another swallow from that inexhaustible, ever-cool beaker.

The second story pleased the lady not at all. It seemed to worry her greatly. She laid the handle of her parasol across her lap and twirled it idly to and fro, using it as a toy instead of a sunshade, clearly not thinking of it at all.

"I have not handled this well," she muttered.

"My lady?"

"I never guessed one of the three would have the imperti-nence—the sheer, brazen audacity . . . How could I have known?"

She stopped and turned to look landward. Rap became aware that legionaries were coming, running along the harbor road, and the crowd was scattering to give them passage. He ought to be alarmed, he knew, but he stayed calm, either because of the lady's bewitchment, or just because he was with her and she was the imperor's deputy—so she said, anyway.

The soldiers ran in columns of two, all laden with full armor and bulky packs topped by mattocks and axes; with three javelins apiece, and swords and shields. That must be a terrible load for a man and a terrible pace, too, in this heat, and Rap could almost hear the sweat splashing off them as they pounded by on the far side of the broad street. One or two were staggering, eyes bulging in scarlet faces.

He turned to the lady, who was watching the procession with an expression of disgust.

"Punishment?"

"Partly. Is it fair? No, of course not. But two hundred men failing to arrest three juvenile vagrants must naturally be punished." She grimaced even more strongly and looked away. Gradually the sound of boots and clanking armor faded into the distance. Rap felt uneasy and puzzled.

"You arrived before dawn," Oothiana said, smiling again as if nothing had interrupted their talk. "That explains why none of us felt the ripples." She paused, and Rap had a strange feeling that she was not really speaking to him, that she was rehearsing excuses. What could possible frighten a sorceress who was also proconsul of an Imperial province?

Oothiana might be a very nice person when she wasn't governing or ensorceling. Maybe she wasn't as young or graceful as she seemed, in her simple white robe and silver sandals, but somehow he felt that much of her was genuine. Her manners certainly were. The Rasha sorceress had appeared far more beautiful, and *carnal*. She had almost driven him out of his mind. Consumed by love for her—all right, lust—he would have done anything to please her, but he'd never for a moment thought he'd *like* her.

"The first we knew of you," the lady said, "was the fairy death cry. Then there were a couple of those fast clicks. Those would have been the sequential spell in use, I see now, but they were too brief to track down. That must be how your group friend has stayed independent for so long. The spell must be a beautiful piece of work. When I finally did locate you, you looked fairly harmless. Three young smugglers been shipwrecked, I thought, but he was suspicious—he always is—and said just to watch and see what you did. You just came here, to Milflor."

"Who . . ." A young dwarf, of course! Rap failed to finish the question, not wanting to have his guess confirmed. O Gods!

Oothiana sighed. "We didn't know which one of you had been blessed by the fairy, but we picked up the thievery when you got close to town. That really was very funny to watch."

Rap held his breath, expecting to hear about trolls next. But apparently not.

"We never guessed that all three of you would turn out to have power! But we got the goblin, and now I have you. That only leaves the group, and he—they—can't evade us for long. An elderly scholar, or a handsome, apparently rich young playboy?"

"Or a minstrel, ma'am, but I don't think he's very likely, because the others don't trust his judgment. Or a giant jotunn warrior, but he'll need a doctor, because—"

"Rap," she said sadly, "do stop! You'll hate yourself terribly when you sober up. Let's go now." She rose and laid her parasol on the bench.

Sober? Rap had never felt more clear-headed in his life. And he had been trying to help! Feeling a little hurt, he stood up, also, laying his parasol beside hers, near the beaker of lemonade. After a moment he glanced back and saw that the bench was empty.

2

She was tall for an imp, but he was taller. He walked on her right, staying a handsbreadth back because that felt respectful, and all the time wondering if he was doing this because he wanted to or because she had made him want to, and what the difference was. What did the expression "changed his mind" ever really mean, anyway?

Oothiana seemed miraculously cool and fresh as she walked along the waterfront, where everyone else was slouching under the whip of the tropic sun. No one seemed to notice her go by, yet she was never crowded or jostled. Rap wondered if she wore a sort of low-grade sorcerous aura. Or something.

The column of loaded legionaries came running back, still in double time, but with a new centurion in command now. There did not seem to be as many of them as before, and more had the unsteady gait of men about to drop. The bystanders stared after them with expressions of contempt and bewilderment.

"What happens to the ones who fall down?" Rap asked brashly.

Oothiana kept her eyes on the cobbles. "That is the punishment. The first twenty to fall will be executed."

"What! That's barbaric! Weren't they just ordinary, mundane soldiers trying to do their best? Against magic?" What then would be the penalty for thieves, vagabonds, and murderers? "Dwarves enjoy cruelty, like goblins?" He was being foolish, but he couldn't have very much to lose.

She shook her head without looking up. "No. The punishment is incidental. What counts is the example."

Example? Somehow that coldblooded logic seemed to make the cruelty even more horrible, but obviously the proconsul did not approve either.

"I'm sorry," he muttered. "Not your idea, was it?"

She glanced sideways at him. "No. Now, I can tell you're bursting with questions. Go ahead and ask. I'll answer what I can."

"Thank you very much, ma'am. I just wondered . . . the men the goblin killed? Was that revenge? Magic justice?"

Oothiana looked puzzled. "How do you mean?"

"Were they the ones who killed the fairies in the village? Did Little Chicken's . . . er . . . power seek them out?"

"Oh, no! The words don't work that way. And the man who did that . . . He has been punished."

There was a strange intensity in that remark, and she quickly changed the subject. "You haven't asked what's in store for you."

"I think I can guess. It isn't the weather, is it?"

"What isn't?"

"Mother Unonini told me about the Four. Jotunn raiders, Imperial legions, dragons . . . but she said that West's prerogative was the weather. It isn't, is it?"

"No, it isn't weather. It's here, in Faerie. You know what it is. It's—"

The proconsul's attention was diverted by a wall exploding just ahead. Milflor taverns were flimsy, airy structures like the houses, and one of them now collapsed, emitting a rolling ball of four or five imps and two or three jotnar. The noise increased considerably as more revelers emerged from the ruins in search of room to brawl, waving furniture and leaping into the fray. The proconsul shrugged her lovely shoulders and detoured around them.

She walked in silence until Rap wondered if he had offended her, but then she said, "It's very evil, and completely unstoppable. West is always the most powerful of the Four, Master Rap. The Protocol says that when a warden dies, then the other three shall elect a successor, witch or warlock. Of course a very strong candidate may elect himself, as Zinixo did, but normally the vacant throne is filled by election. The exception is West. When the red throne becomes vacant, then the strongest of the three takes that one and leaves his former throne to a newcomer. Understand?"

"Yes, ma'am. That wasn't what happened this time?"

"No. Suddenly Ag-An was dead and Zinixo was warlock. Assassination's not rare for the other three, but it's only been done to West maybe six or seven times since Emine's day. West's strength comes from his prerogative, of course, although in this case he's also immensely powerful in his own right."

They were going by the ships now. As Thinal had said, most were galleys, but there were also a few barks and argosies, and larger, awkward lateen-rigged vessels—none of them types that ever came to Krasnegar. Rap would have enjoyed looking at them had he not been more concerned by his own approaching death. "In his own right, ma'am?"

Oothiana still did not look around. "Zinixo may well be the most powerful sorcerer since Is-an-ok, or even Thraine. Ag-An was no mean saint, yet he destroyed her and two guardian votaries single-handed. South and East didn't want Faerie to fall into the hands of an unknown, so they tried to take him out at once. He knocked them aside like puffballs."

Again conversation was interrupted. A dozen drunken, half-naked jotnar were staggering along the road in line abreast, bellowing out a bawdy song, waving clubs that looked like table legs, and forcing everyone else to back up. Rap expected Oothiana to summon troops, but she barely seemed to notice the disturbance. Just before the mob reached her, all the rioters suddenly turned hard left. Roaring happily, the line went lurching into a tavern. The crowd dispersed, grumbling, and the road was clear. She had not missed a step.

"By now, of course," the sorceress said, "the dwarf's unassailable. He'll hold the red throne for centuries. Only all the others acting together could kill him, and that would mean a pitched battle. He might even win it."

"West's prerogative is the supply of magic," Rap said, "so now he knows hundreds of words?"

"No. That isn't the way it works; four's the limit. But any sorcerer can be put under a loyalty spell by a stronger sorcerer. Then he's a votary, an aide. All warlocks and witches do it, but the others must hunt for people who already know words. West has a dependable supply. This is where they come from."

"One fairy, one word?"

She nodded.

"Oh, then you . . . Beg pardon, my lady."

She raised those glorious eyes to his, and he was astonished to see them glistening. "Yes, me. I want you to know, even if you can never understand completely. I can't help myself, Master Rap. I'm telling you all this because it doesn't matter and you deserve to know why you will suffer, but if talking might hurt my master's interests in any way, then I couldn't do it. I can't be disloyal in the slightest and I must obey any order he gives me; if he told me to kill myself, I would do it. I can't betray him."

"You don't like him, though?" Rap said.

"Dwarves," she said cautiously, "tend to be mean and suspicious and rapacious."

"Could he not make you like him?"

Oothiana walked a dozen paces in silence, and then her answer was very quiet. "Easily. Would that be kinder? You're going to hate me tomorrow, Rap. But he leaves my thoughts free because he values my advice, I think, or maybe just to see if I'm plotting something. He doesn't trust loyalty, whether it's occult or real. Your word is valuable, and my master told me to get it for him. So I must do as he says, even though I hate doing so."

"And Thinal's, when you catch them, and Little Chicken's."

"Especially Little Chicken's."

Three words? The warlock could force them to share, and have three mages, then perhaps kill two of them to have one stronger mage. Add one more word to have a slave sorcerer . . .

"So I become a slave?"

She bit her lip with pearly teeth. "It's worse than that! He's more likely to force your word out of you for somebody else. Even if he had use for a faun . . . Pardon my saying this, but you're not a very typical faun. You're too big."

Rap shivered, despite the heat. "But he could make me look like anything he wanted, couldn't he? An imp, a dwarf, an elf, even?"

"Yes, he could. But another sorcerer would see the spell on

you. That would be two spells, you see, and a glamour spell like that, an appearance spell, happens to be a conspicuous thing. A loyalty spell is much harder to detect. Unfortunately.''

Unfortunately! "So I tell my word and then I die?''

She spoke without looking at him. "It may not happen right away. Perhaps not for some time. But I have to take you to jail now, and I expect that's where you'll stay.''

Again they walked for a while in silence, the lady watching the ground, ignoring the watercarts and hucksters plying their wares to the ships. Now that his farsight had been restored, Rap had trouble ignoring the ships. The jotunn in him had always been interested in ships. One of the galleys must be Gathmor's *Stormdancer*. But he was going to die soon, here in Faerie, so ships did not matter now. Magic just possibly might.

"So a faun-jotunn cross won't be much use to him. How does he choose who gets elevated?''

She glanced at him oddly. "You think clearly, Master Rap. Yes, he has trouble, because there is always a faint chance he will create a sorcerer more powerful than himself. That's why I said you might live quite a while yet; while he makes up his mind.''

In a cell! "Little Chicken . . . Why did the fairy do that? I mean, why did she die?''

Oothiana hesitated. "I'm going to have to put a forbiddance on you, telling you all this. These are well-kept secrets you're learning!''

"That's all right, ma'am. I don't know why you're telling me all these things anyway. But I do appreciate it!'' he added hastily.

She flashed another of her sad little smiles. "Perhaps because I enjoy speaking to an honest man for a change.''

Rap turned his face away quickly. She did not seem to be joking, either.

"This way.'' She pointed, and headed across the road, which now branched, the left side going on along the waterfront and the moorings, the right angling up the hill. He could sense the shielding around the palace quite close by. On the skyline, still distinct, the roof and the upper level of the Gazebo formed a sinister all-seeing eye, bright in the rays of the sun setting over the mainland town.

"What the fairy told the goblin was her name. Alone of all the peoples of Pandemia, fairies seem to have no magic, but they are born knowing their names and die if they ever speak them.''

"But why?" Rap blurted. Then he felt very stupid. Ask her why the sky is blue, dummy! That was how the Gods had made the world.

Yet Oothiana did not seem to find the question stupid, "No one is certain. My master says—and he is a very powerful sorcerer, remember, so his wisdom is great—he suspects that a word is not truly a fairy's own name. What use is a name you can never use? He thinks they must be the names of elementals, a sort of guardian spirit . . ."

Ah! Now Rap sensed something intelligible in the insanity of magic.

"But he admits that even he is guessing," she concluded.

Straight ahead the road reached a high wall of pointed timbers and an imposing gateway topped by the imperor's four-pointed star. This palisade was in much better shape than the feeble ruin around the town and it was an occult barrier, also, blocking farsight completely. Beyond the archway were trees, flowers, and parkland that showed only to his eyes.

His chance to question might be coming to an end. He began planning his next query, but the proconsul forestalled him.

"Why would a fairy ever tell his secret name to anyone? Two reasons, Master Rap. One is that life can sometimes become the less pleasant alternative. Intense pain applied long enough will persuade anyone to do anything, and may move a man faster when applied to his dear ones. Apart from their names, fairies are as human as imps, or fauns, or jotnar—and they dislike watching their children suffer."

Rap remembered the bloodstains Little Chicken had found in the fairy hut. Whoever had done that had been punished—how? Why? He shivered. "And the second reason, my lady?"

"That is a great mystery. Rarely, a fairy will volunteer his name, or her name, to certain persons, like your goblin friend. What exactly did she ask him?"

"She asked all of us the same question—what our dream was."

At the gate guards were lining up, snapping to attention, drawing swords to greet the proconsul. Blades flashed bright enough to hurt the eye of the beholder.

"Most people don't know what they really want from life, Master Rap. We all think we know, but we often deceive ourselves in one way or another. We think we want to help a cause and secretly desire only power. We think we love, when what we feel is lust. We crave revenge and call it justice. Our self-deceptions are endless. Apparently the fairyfolk can always tell, and this is a curse upon them, for if a fairy meets someone who has a clear, driving, unswerving aim, then the fairy is driven, also—driven to tell his secret, occult name. You and the imp evidently do not have such an aim. You do not know what you are truly seeking. The goblin obviously does."

"He told her he wanted to kill me!"

"Then that is everything he wants from life. He would willingly die to achieve that one satisfaction, and the fairy recognized that. Whether she approved or disapproved would not matter; she could not escape her compulsion. She told him her name and so gave him a word of power to help him achieve his goal."

"But," Rap protested, "I told her my—"

"Then you lied. Unwittingly, I am sure, but either you do not want it enough, or you really want something else. The fairy would know your heart better than you. It is their only power, and their curse. Be silent a moment."

She stopped before she reached the honor guard now flanking the gateway. The commander advanced a step and saluted an empty patch of air several paces in front of her. He waited, then made a ritual reply, and waited again. Puzzled, Rap glanced at Oothiana. She was smiling mischievously as she watched the farcical performance. Apparently the legionaries saw the governor as being accompanied by a large escort. The one-sided ceremony continued for a few moments, but finally the imaginary force was given formal permission to proceed, and Oothiana began walking again. Her humble prisoner trailed alongside, being equally honored by the stiffly saluting soldiers. He wondered if he was riding in an invisible coach drawn by imaginary horses.

As he passed below the Imperial star, Rap lost his occult view of the town and harbor, and the palace grounds were revealed to his farsight. They surprised him—trees and folds in the hillside had been cleverly used to conceal many more buildings than he had suspected. Most were low wooden structures, largely open to the friendly climate. He identified stables and barracks nearby and grander mansions at higher levels. This was a garden palace, much more pleasant than Holinarn's bleak castle in Krasnegar, or the forbidding impish stronghold at Pondague, which he had glimpsed from afar while tracking Inos.

As they rounded a bend and drew out of sight of the be-

witched guards, Oothiana began to laugh. He turned to her in
surprise.

"I love doing that!" she said.

He smiled. Suddenly she was no great lady, but a pretty girl,
not so very much older than himself, sharing her mirth at the
juvenile prank she had just played. Not as beautiful as Inos, of
course, but fair enough, and human under the grandeur.

"After hiding my powers so long," she said, "I enjoy being
free to use them."

"Doing sorcery, you mean?"

"Yes, although that was only magic, and a small, illusion-
magic at that."

"I didn't know there was a difference."

"Oh, yes. Magic is what a mage does. It's temporary. A
sorcerer can also do sorcery, which is permanent, quite different. For instance—"

Rap's farsight picked up the newcomer at the same moment
as hers did. He wheeled around. The road was flanked here by
a grassy bank smothered in pale-blue flowers. On the top of it
stood a dwarf, who had certainly not been there a second earlier.

He had chosen a vantage point where he could look down on
them. On level ground he would not have reached to Rap's
shoulder, but he was thick and broad, with the oversize head
and hands of his race. His hair and beard were a metallic gray
shade, curled like turnings from a lathe, and his face had the
color and texture of rock.

But if dwarves aged like the races Rap knew, then this one
was in his sixties and therefore could not be Zinixo himself;
moreover a warlock would not wear such obviously shabby work
clothes and heavy boots.

"Raspnex?" Oothiana said coldly. "I thought you were
keeping watch."

"Change of orders." He gestured over his shoulder with an
oversize thumb. "He wants you. Now."

Oothiana stiffened and drew a nervous breath. "In the Gazebo?"

"In Hub. You have some explaining to do."

Instantly all expression left the lady's face. That had to be
magic, Rap thought.

"I—yes," she said calmly. "All right. This is one of the
intrud—"

"Not wanted. I'll take care of him."

Oothiana nodded, glanced at Rap as if about to say something, and just vanished. Rap jumped, then looked warily up at Raspnex, who was regarding him contemptuously.

"Never liked fauns. Stubborn lot. Roisterers and spend-thrifts."

Rap could not see how humility would improve his situation much. "Will you let me go if I promise to be boorish and nig-gardly, like a dwarf?"

Raspnex growled, an unpleasant grinding sound. "You told the lady your green friend wants to kill you, so I'd assume that—"

"You were spying?"

The older man scowled. "I was. Mind your manners, faun. You want to share a cell with him, or would you rather not?"

"Share," Rap said. "He wants to kill me in public. He won't hurt me without an audience."

"You pick odd buddies! Jail is along—"

"I'm hungry," Rap said.

The dwarf rubbed his beard, staring at Rap as if puzzled. Then he growled, "Come here, lad."

Rap walked over and climbed the bank. He stopped as soon as his eyes were level with the dwarf's—two beads of gray flint staring out from a face of pitted, weathered sandstone. Even the wrinkles around those eyes looked more like cracks.

"You know what's going to happen!" His voice was a sub-terranean rumble. "How come you're not more scared?"

Silly question. Rap would feel plenty scared if he let himself think about the matter. Fortunately, he hadn't had time yet to brood and screw himself up into a funk. "You're not dead till your heart stops," he said; one of his mother's little homilies. His heart was thumping pretty firmly right now.

Raspnex pouted. "Kinda fancy the proconsul?"

"Fine lady."

A faint nod. "Not just faun. What else are you?"

"Jotunn."

"Gods, what a horrible mixture! Explains that flash of temper we saw, though, doesn't it? Still, might work. A jotunn would've tried something brainless, and a faun would've just sulked. How are you for stubbornness, with those bloodlines?"

Rap had no trouble keeping his temper reined in when he knew he was being bated. The man had called him over to put him within punch-swinging range. Only idiots fell into traps that obvious.

The dwarf grinned suddenly, showing teeth like quartz pebbles. "Here," he said. He held out a sandwich of black bread and hot, greasy meat.

"Thank you, sir!" Rap grabbed the offering. As he bit into it, he noticed that some of it was already missing.

"Don't thank me; thank the skinny recruit with the buck teeth. What're you smirking about?"

Rap spoke with his mouth full. "Never thought I'd ever meet a better thief than Thinal."

Raspnex chuckled. "Jail's that way, faun. Be off with you!"

The jail was a long way north, at the end of the cape. Rap's feet knew the way and took him there, pacing unswervingly along the middle of the road, making confident choices at every branch or intersection. He remembered how Inos had been abducted by Rasha in the same manner.

Three times carriages veered around him in clouds of dust and oaths. Other pedestrians were rare, but once he came face to face with a full maniple marching toward him. Apparently his ensorceled behavior was not unknown in those parts, for where a free man would have been mindlessly trampled into the dirt, the centurion bellowed for the lines to open, and Rap proceeded along a corridor of oak-faced legionaries heading in the opposite direction. Not one of them met his eye.

His way led across grassy meadow, through groves of trees, and alongside formal gardens. Many of the buildings were shielded from his gaze, smaller shields within the greater shield around the whole complex. He identified the recruits' barracks, but not the particular buck-toothed lad who had lost his lunch. He saw workshops and a library and private houses. He admired flower beds and herb gardens.

He also saw a great many statues, some of them so ancient that they had weathered into shapeless pillars. They flanked the paths, being especially common at crossroads. He assumed that they represented former proconsuls or imperors or both, for almost all were male. Most were depicted in either uniform or antique costume, but many of the newer ones wore nothing at all, or only a helmet. He could think of few things sillier than a man brandishing a sword when he had no clothes on, but he saw some of those, also.

And at last he arrived at a patch of forest, an unkempt stretch of trees and undergrowth. His feet continued without hesitation along a winding dirt track through the middle of this. His eyes caught glimpses of many little huts hidden away in the bushes, but each one was enclosed in its own fence of occult shielding, so he could not tell who inhabited this strange settlement. He thought he could guess, though. The flimsy wickerwork structures were identical to the houses in the fairy village, and on the same miniature scale.

Finally his feet turned off along a narrow side path. He headed into a wall of shielding and broke through, and a few more steps released the compulsion on him. He stumbled to a halt a few paces from a cabin door. Lounging on a log in the shade, idly fanning away flies with a handful of fern fronds, sat Little Chicken.

His angular eyes widened, then he grinned.

"Welcome to prison, Flat Nose," he said.

3

She had escaped from jail—Inos clutched that thought as she would have clutched a rope while dangling over a precipice.

The caravan had departed before noon and struck out at once into unfamiliar terrain, skirting the hills she knew from Azak's hunting trips. She had thought she already knew what true desert was, but she had been mistaken.

The sun's light was a naked blade, its heat a bludgeon. The drab land lay dead and wrinkled as if it had been moist at the creation of the world and ever since been steadily shriveling and crumbling in that sadistic glare. A few goatherds and a scattering of miners were all who lived there; except of course for ants and millipedes and scorpions and poisonous snakes. And lots of flies. Lots and lots of flies.

Camels were noisy and smelly and untrustworthy. Their gait was better than the motion of a boat, perhaps, but similar enough to make her queasy. With no reins to hold, she felt like a useless passenger in a very uncomfortable chair floating high above the arid dirt. In a few days, when she had become more familiar with camels, and when there was no doubt that the fugitives had safely escaped from Rasha—then, Azak said, he would happily give his supposed wife a few lessons in the finer points of camel riding. Meanwhile, the nose rope of her mount would remain attached to the baggage animal in front, and if she needed anything she should just ask Fooni, and excuse-him-he-was-busy-now.

But they had escaped from Arakkaran. That one thought was

a lake of cool water in the barren mental landscape, a jewel
without equal, rain in a drought.

As the sun dipped to the dark sharp edges of the Agonistes,
the caravan came to an oasis. It was disappointing, not at all the
soothing romantic setting Inos had expected. There were no
buildings. The palms were few and scraggy, and the grass had
been grazed to the roots over the years by thousands of caravans
converging on the capital. There was a well for people and a
couple of muddy ponds for the livestock, but no shade or shelter
from a scorching wind that sprang up unexpectedly to blow dust
into eyes and teeth. The camels expressed their opinions very
loudly and unmistakably, and Inos agreed wholeheartedly.

Having been returned to ground level, with legs unexpectedly
wobbly, she learned that her first duty was to erect the tent in
which Azak and his supposed family would spend the night.
Azak, she discovered, was now Third Lionslayer and hunting
for Second, who had so far managed to avoid him.

The tent was erected, but Fooni did most of the work, while
mocking and berating Inos for her incompetence with invective
as shrill as a knife on glass.

Fooni was one of the sheik's great-granddaughters. She had
been attached to Inos as tutor and guide. Fooni was worse than
the flies. Having seen only her eyes and hands, Inos had no clear
idea of Fooni's age, but she could be no more that twelve. She
was tiny, shrill, impudent, and infuriatingly knowledgeable
about the nomadic life of a camel train. She treated Inos as a
moronic, benighted foreigner; nagged her, rode rings around
her on one of the baggage camels, and wasted no chance to
humiliate her. Inos spent the next half hour trying to locate
Fooni accurately on her list of Those Who Deserve to Die, and
eventually put her in fourth place, right after the dowager duchess of Kinvale.

But the tent was erected at last. It was emphatically not the
neatest of the many black tents that had sprouted among the
palms and it was the last to be completed. Inos was on the point
of heading off to fetch water when she noticed that the other
women were carrying their jars on their heads; she sent Fooni
instead.

Then she busied herself with laying out the bedding mats.
There was little room to spare, especially when she arranged a
safety zone around Azak's sleeping place. If any of the three

women accidentally touched him in the night—his hand or even his hair—she would be burned.

Having done what she could in the stuffy, flapping dimness, Inos emerged into the twilight. Kade sat on the entrance mat amid a swirl of white feathers.

"By the sacred balance, Aunt, what are you doing?"

"Plucking the fowl, dear."

Inos knelt down beside her on the rug, horrified and guilty. A royal princess plucking a miserable scrawny chicken? How could she have been so cruel as to subject the old woman to this? And her feelings were not helped by the twinkle of amusement in Kade's blue eyes. She was apparently smiling under her yashmak.

Inos gulped. "I didn't know . . . Where did you learn to do that?"

"In the palace kitchens, when I was small."

"Let me."

"No, it's quite a restful occupation. You can gut it for me, if you know how."

"I don't!"

"Doesn't matter," Kade said contentedly. "I do. It is great fun to try something one has not done for so long. It all comes back!"

Inos said. "Oh." And then words failed her. Dear Kade! She had obviously accepted this expedition and was making the best of it. Had Inos lost such an argument, she would have sulked for days.

Kade never sulked. "To be honest, dear, I was finding that opulent palace life a little *dull*. Travel is always very stimulating, is it not?"

"Yes. Very." Inos decided she would peel the onions and enjoy a good weep. She glanced around the bustling campground and there was no sign of the despicable Fooni. She was probably deep in gossip with other children, or women.

"I never realized," Kade said, "how beautiful the desert would be—in its own way, of course."

Beautiful? Inos looked again, more carefully. The sky was blood-red behind the peaks, the first stars were twinkling in the east, and all around the campground the little braziers were glowing in the dusk. The wind had dwindled until now it seemed almost cool on her face.

"I suppose it has a certain . . . unusual charm," she admitted. "But the best part is that I think we have escaped from the sorceress!"

"Too early to tell, dear." Kade held the runtish fowl at arm's length and squinted at it. "If she knows where we are, she can come and get us any time, I'm sure."

"You don't seem too worried by that prospect."

Kade sighed and picked at a few stray quills. "I am still inclined to trust Sultana Rasha, my dear. As for Hub—"

"What color pajamas," Inos snarled, "does a goblin wear? Sugar pink, to set off his green skin? Or arterial red in case he spills something on them?"

Kade tut-tutted dismissively, although she kept her attention on the scraggy little carcass. "I've told you, dear, I can't believe that they were serious about that. Certainly the imperor . . ."

Inos told her ears to stop listening. Kade had an unlimited ability to believe what she wanted to believe and she was determined not to admit that warlocks and imperors might ever do anything *ungentlemanly*, or a witch anything *unladylike*. Easy for her! She wasn't going to be bearing ugly little green babies.

Before Inos could find a logical argument to rebut Kade's impractical instincts, Azak came striding up with a swish of his long kibr. He sank down on his heels and stared at Inos.

"You survive, your Majesty?"

She thought he was being humorous, but she wasn't sure; his moods were too hard to read. "Certainly I survive. I wouldn't ache all over like this if I were dead."

He nodded in satisfaction and glanced at Kade, who was raptly holding the chicken over the brazier, singeing pinfeathers.

"We northern women are tough," Inos said.

"I knew that, or I would not have planned this."

Inos detected an odd note in his voice and wondered if she had at last managed to light a spark of admiration in the giant. Could tent erecting have succeeded where hawking and riding had failed? The idea brought a twinge of uneasiness, almost guilt. If anyone deserved admiration in this situation, it was Kade.

"Are you First Lionslayer yet?"

Azak grunted. "Second, still. First wishes to put the matter to the test. I do not anticipate any problems, but if he should be lucky enough to kill me, I am confident the sheik will see you safely to Ullacarn."

Kade looked around sharply, Inos dropped the onion and knife. "Kill you? . . ."

"Unlikely, as I said. I am undoubtedly the better man, and a minor flesh wound is normally adequate in these cases."

He was serious!

This was not the Impire.

And even in the Impire men fought duels.

Inos was so aghast that she could hardly find words. "What does it matter whether you are First or Second Lionslayer? Why—"

"It matters," he said flatly.

It mattered to *him*. Whether or not it mattered to anyone else was immaterial. Azak's life was his own to risk; Inos and her aunt were mere passengers on his expedition. He was not their paid guide or guard. He owed them nothing; they had no hold upon him.

Somehow this new outrage seemed to throw the whole insane situation into a different focus. Camels . . . desert . . . hiding from a sorceress . . .

"Azak! That's crazy! The whole thing is crazy! Surely everyone here knows who you really are, and—"

"Of course they know!" he snapped, his voice harsh enough to stop her protests dead in their tracks. "It will be the locals we must conceal you from."

"What locals?" She looked around at the empty land beyond the tents.

"Most nights we shall stop at more settled places than this—at mines, and goat farms. Elkarath is a trader, remember, not a tourist. As a djinn, I shall not be noticed, except for my stature and remarkable physical presence, and I can do nothing to diminish those. You have green eyes; your aunt's are blue. We do not want word of such freaks drifting back along the trade routes to Rasha. But the sheik's people are almost all his relatives, and reliable."

"Not the lionslayers, though. They're not his relatives!"

"Of course not. Most of them are mine. First is a nephew I banished only a few months ago. That is why he feels the call of honor, that one of us must bleed. Quite understandable. In his place I should feel the same, and I shall let him off as lightly as I can. But the lionslayers will not betray me. You can always trust the code of the lionslayers."

"I thought you despised lionslayers?"

Azak shook his head. In the fading light she could not make out his expression. "What leads you to think that?"

"Just something Kar said as we were leaving the palace."
That seemed like a long time ago.

"Kar may despise them. I neither know nor especially care
what Kar thinks about lionslayers, I pity them. Their fathers
ruled kingdoms; their sons will herd camels."

"Talking of kingdoms, how can you possibly risk being ab-
sent from yours for three months?"

"It will be longer," Azak said, but Inos thought she detected
an odd note in his voice, and she remembered his subtle wink
in Elkarath's garden. She also sensed a warning that made her
bristle. The only person within earshot was Kade.

What devious intrigue was boiling inside that deceitful djinn
mind? Surely he could not suspect Kade of being unfaithful?

He rose suddenly, looming against the stars. "I must go,
while there is still light enough for fighting.

"By the way," he added, "I don't like onions."

He stalked away before Inos could think of a suitable reply.
After a few minutes, she decided that there wasn't one.

4

Night came at last to Faerie.

Moonlight shone in through the wicker walls of the hut, and
Rap could not sleep.

He was not accustomed to a hammock, for one thing.

Little Chicken was snoring, for another.

There were bugs, for a million more.

He ought to be used to bugs by now.

He was going to die. The word his mother had told him was
worth more than his life; not that any man's life would be worth
very much to a warlock, probably.

He had always thought of jails as being cramped, dark places,
built of stone; smelly and cold, like the dungeons in Krasnegar.
In Holindarn's day those had been mainly used as storerooms,
and the palace children had played in them sometimes. At eleven
or so, Inos had enjoyed ordering people locked up, tortured,
and beheaded. As she would never let anyone else order such
things done to her, the rest of the gang had tired of that game
long before she did.

Proconsul Oothiana's jail was not like those nasty stone boxes
at all. The hut was airy and pleasant, and even reasonably clean.
Clear water flowed up magically in a stone bowl and trickled
away down a magical drain that served for a toilet.

There were many of these huts in the woods, and probably they were all much the same, all set in the same sort of grassy clearing. Quite probably these were the most pleasant dungeons in all Pandemia, with fresh air, room to exercise, and no ugly stone walls. Birdsong and sunlight.

The hut was enclosed in an invisible occult barrier. Merely by closing his eyes, Rap had been able to establish that the shielding cut off the tops of trees, so it was a dome like the dome that enclosed the whole palace compound, or the smaller shield over the castle at Krasnegar. Only someone with farsight would know that it was there.

But the magical cowl did more than block his farsight; it was also an aversion spell. Inisso's chamber of puissance had been protected by such a spell, but that one had been old and worn out. This one was irresistible. If he tried to walk away down the path, he felt a strong desire to turn back. If he persisted, he became giddy and nauseous. Inos had often accused him of being stubborn, but he wasn't stubborn enough to resist what that sorcery did to his mind. He just could not make his feet obey.

Simple!

A pleasant jail. At mealtimes imp slaves brought around baskets of food. Legionaries guarded them, and they were not affected by the spell.

Simple, but very effective.

He was going to die.

Unless the mosquitoes ate him first, he would be tortured until he told someone his word of power and then he would die, just like the fairies who had been abducted from the village.

And Inos would never know that he had even tried.

Buzzing of insects, and sea noises. Then the wind shifted in the treetops, and he heard a distant beat.

He sat up suddenly, tipping himself sprawling from the hammock to the dirt floor. He yelped. The goblin grunted, twisted, and went back to sleep.

Rap fumbled around to find his boots, then walked out into the moonlight. The night was warm and soft and restless.

Now that he was trying to hear it, it was quite audible, a rhythmic tattoo somewhere to the north of him, nearer the end of the headland. The fairy child had said, "I will clap for you to dance."

So at least some of the fairy captives were still alive, somewhere in this jail. The moon was shining, and they were danc-

ing. The beat was complex, and stirring, and joyous, and it
brought a hard knot to his throat. The fairies faced the same fate
as he did, but they were much more innocent. He was a thief,
an accessory to murder, and any respectable court of justice
would condemn him to death anyway. Their crime was to have
been born fairies.

In the faint, hopeless hope that the aversion spell did not work
at night, he headed for the path through the trees. In a few
minutes he felt strongly disinclined to go any farther. He
stopped, balked, a few paces from the occult shield that blocked
his farsight.

He was going to die.

So was the goblin, although he might not have realized that
yet. Possibly the forbiddance that Proconsul Oothiana had put
upon Rap would prevent him from warning Little Chicken of
his fate. He hadn't tried. There was no hurry. Warlock Zinixo
might take weeks or months to make up his mind, but eventually
he would come for all his captives, each in turn.

A pleasant jail. Night-flowering plants were putting out heavy,
drowsy scents. Bugs whined nearby, and the sea rumbled far
away. Somewhere in middle distance the beat of the fairy dance
rose and fell as the warm wind toyed with it. If he were Zinixo,
Rap decided, then he would definitely harvest the faun and the
goblin before slaughtering any of the fairies.

With a sudden chilling insight, he realized that this was not
a prison at all, it was a farm. The fairy inmates were livestock,
and this jungle jail had been designed to give them familiar
surroundings. There might be hundreds of them living here,
generation after generation, bred to die. Oothiana had hinted—
very evil, she had said. Completely unstoppable.

He'd tried to escape, of course, but the aversion spell was
implacable. The twists in the path had prevented him from working up any real speed, and no matter how hard he had tried, he
had always flailed to a stop before he reached the barricade, then
come scrambling back from it in panic and revulsion.

He'd persuaded Little Chicken to make the attempt, too. The
goblin did not even need a long runway to build up speed. His
occult strength let him take off from a crouch like an arrow
leaving a bow; but it also enabled him to stop dead in his tracks
when he wanted to, and of course the aversion spell made him
want to. The advantage of his great speed had been completely
canceled out. The path was gouged where he had dug in his

heels, and he had come no nearer the invisible barricade than Rap had.

But possibly his heart had not been in it. He had not seemed very convinced by Rap's explanations, preferring to believe his own conclusion that the magic merely stopped him from going more than a certain distance from the hut. He thought in terms of a tether, not a fence. That was very logical, Rap supposed, if you didn't have farsight. It might even be true, and the aversion spell might be quite unrelated to the shielding. It might just increase in power indefinitely as the distance from the hut increased. He couldn't prove matters either way, because he couldn't tell if the aversion spell extended outside the shielding . . .

Oh, yes he could!

With a yelp of triumph, Rap went racing back to the hut to waken the goblin.

Rap's mother had firmly maintained that all cats were gray in the dark. Goblins in moonlight, likewise, lost any hint of being green. But they could still look dangerously surly at having been roused from a sound sleep. What dreams a goblin might enjoy did not bear thinking about.

Little Chicken stood on the path, scratching, slapping bugs, and showing his teeth in a fearsome scowl. His angular eyes glinted crossly as he listened to Rap's proposal. He nodded agreement. "Easy."

"You'll do it?"

"No. Then you leave the island? Leave me? You think again, Flat Nose. Find better idea."

He turned on his heel, intent on returning to his hammock. Rap grabbed his shoulder. Little Chicken spun around, knocking Rap's arm away with a blow so hard that for a moment Rap thought the bones were broken.

Never let him save your life . . .

Facing a hate-filled glare, he wondered if he was about to die at once. The goblin had not mentioned the subject of trash since Rap had come to the jail. He had spoken very little, spending most of the afternoon just eyeing Rap like a cat eyeing a bird. He might now consider that his diversionary attack on the soldiers had relieved him of any further obligation to his former master. In that case, Little Chicken was now free to pursue his life's ambition. The only thing that could be restraining him was the flimsy hope that he might one day drag his victim back to

Raven Totem to enjoy the fun in relaxed family surroundings. If he ever discarded that hope, then he could start work anytime. Like now.

"I'll get you out, too!" Rap protested, gingerly rubbing his bruise.

Even the silvery trail of moonlight was enough to show the goblin's skepticism. "How?"

"I'll go and get a horse and a rope. I know where the stables are."

Little Chicken scowled. "Two horses, maybe?"

He thought he could outwrestle a horse? He might be right, although he knew little about horses.

"Isn't room on the path for two," Rap said. "I'll toss the rope in to you. You tie it around yourself and turn your back. When the horse moves, you won't have time to undo the knots."

Giant goblin teeth showed in a sneer. "Break rope!"

"I'll yank you out before you have time to break the rope! What's the matter, you scared?"

"Don't trust you." Again he moved as if headed for bed.

"I'm sorry," Rap said. "I thought we were friends and buddies right now, or I wouldn't have asked to be put in your cage. You won't trust my word that I'll come back for you?"

The goblin was still standing there, his back turned. "No."

"I'll have a lot more chance of escaping from the island if you're still helping me. You must see that!"

Silence. Obviously Little Chicken was tempted.

"I'm going to try to stow away on a ship. If I can reach the mainland, then I'll head for Zark, to find Inos. But you might be able to knock me on the head and carry me off to the northlands. You never know your luck. You certainly can't do that here in Faerie."

Slowly the goblin turned around. He stared hard at Rap. "You promise to come back with horse and get me out?"

"I swear."

Little Chicken grunted. "Suppose I try what you want. Suppose you break both legs, and the spell isn't thin, like you said. Suppose you land *in* it, not *through* it?"

"Then I'll probably go insane. You'll be able to listen to my screams all night long."

"Real men don't scream!" The goblin stepped forward and grasped the back of Rap's belt. "Feet first, faceup?"

"Good a way as any," Rap said, and was immediately hoisted into the air. Fingers like ropes tightened around his left ankle.

He held himself rigid. He watched treetops rush by against the moon-washed sky. Little Chicken hurtled along the path, bearing Rap overhead like a javelin. When the aversion spell stopped him, he threw, and Rap went soaring onward, feet first.

He felt a spasm of unspeakable horror, but he was through the magic before he could even cry out.

He did not break his legs, although he did twist an ankle, the same one he had injured before. He also collected an assortment of scrapes and bruises while rolling to a stop in a bush. He rose, dusted himself off, and tried a few steps to make sure he could walk. Then he looked back at the goblin, who had retreated away from the barrier.

"Thanks!" Rap said. "Guess it worked. I'll be back, I promise."

One way or the other . . .

Limping as fast as he could bear, he headed for the stables he had seen near the main gate. Proconsul Oothiana, the dwarf Raspnex, the warlock himself . . . and there might be many other sorcerers around the palace grounds, Zinixo's votaries.

He shunned the paths, cutting across-country, staying close to patches of woodland whenever possible, and also close to the many shielded buildings because what blocked his farsight must block sorcerers' farsight, too. The wind was rising, and clouds scudded through the moonlit sky. Far off to his right lay the town of Milflor, its dying cooking fires a scattering of fallen stars. To his left was the hogback of the headland. Beyond that lay the ocean, and the mainland, and Zark. And Inos.

He was only one man, moving in darkness in a very large area. He thought he would reach the stables safely, but they might well be guarded, and to steal one horse in the middle of the night would panic all the others unless he used mastery. Mastery might be detected if there was another sorcerer awake somewhere. Even if he could pull off the horsethievery, he would then have to cross the palace grounds again, back to the jail. Only when he had done all that would he be able to make tracks for the harbor.

Common sense said he should forget the goblin and head straight for the docks. He resisted the temptation. He planned to live to an extreme old age, and that meant he must live with his conscience for a long time yet. He had promised to return.

It was a very long shot, and yet he was beginning to feel hopeful again. A word of power made its owner lucky, Sagorn had said. His luck was holding so far, for he was almost at the stables. He came around the corner of a shielded building, heard a voice, and dropped flat in the grass.

Farsight found no one to explain the voice, but it did tell him that there was a local circle of shielding a short way in front of the building. The sound seemed to be coming from there, at the edge of one of the major roads. After a moment, when there was no outcry, he raised his head cautiously and took a look. As he suspected, the speaker was Proconsul Oothiana, her white robe glimmering in the moonlight.

She was standing on a grass verge between the pavement and an ornamental flower bed. She had her back to him, and she was speaking in low, rapid tones to a man. All Rap could see of the man was that he was tall, and wearing a military helmet, and holding a spear.

Oothiana could not detect Rap with farsight while she was inside that shielding. He certainly ought to vanish before she emerged, but . . .

But why would these two hold their conversation out here in the middle of the night, and why had the sorceress cast an occult shield around them? It overlapped half the width of the roadway, but it enclosed nothing except the two people.

A word of power made its owner lucky. Was this curious opportunity somehow important?

The moon sailed majestically into a cloud, the parkland sank into darkness. Faunish common sense went down to abject defeat before a harebrained nosiness that would have shamed an imp—Rap began to wriggle forward through the dewy grass. He aimed for some of the shrubbery on his side of the road, across from the sorceress. When he reached it, he rose on hands and knees in the dark and crawled around until he was as close as he could get to the strange conversation. He lay down and watched, straining his ears to catch the words.

She was talking about him! Describing how she had caught him. He had not expected that. It made him realize that he was eavesdropping on a private conversation. He felt even worse when she made some nonsensical comments about his manners and his courage. And then the moon found a gap in the clouds, the darkness lifted, and Rap's hair rose on his scalp. Proconsul Oothiana was speaking to a statue.

It represented a warrior leaning on a spear, and the helmet Rap had noticed earlier was all it was wearing. One arm was raised high to clutch the spear; its head was bowed, its shoulders drooped in a stance of weariness and defeat. That was curious, because all the others Rap had bothered to look at had depicted arrogance and triumph. They had all been set on high stone pedestals, while this one stood on a low plinth, no higher than a herring box; and only this one had occult shielding around it.

Why should a sorceress be telling a statue about Rap? Andor had mentioned talking statues that would predict the future, just as magic casements and preflecting pools did.

Then the lady got to the part about Bright Water. Somebody whistled in astonishment, and scorpions danced on Rap's skin.

"I bet that upset the mole!" said a deep male voice.

"He was almost too furious to be scared, I think!"

"That would be historic!"

"He thinks she's in league with the other two, ganging up on him."

"Ha!" the statue said. "Our esteemed master thinks *everyone* is ganging up on him."

"But why would she have sent them to Faerie? That's trespass!"

"I don't know." The statue straightened, suddenly tall, rubbing its back with its free hand as if it ached.

Rap dropped his face into the grass. Oothiana still had her back to him, but the statue was staring over her head in his direction—assuming that talking statues could see, of course.

"Can't you think of anything?" Oothiana cried. "If you can come up with some good ideas, then he'll realize that you're valuable to him—"

"Goose droppings! I'm more valuable to him here. You know that! Why doesn't he just ask her?"

"That's what I suggested," the sorceress said sadly. "I think he will. But it gets him involved in the Krasnegar thing, you see? And now he wants the girl."

Rap's head lifted of its own accord. What girl?

"What girl?" the statue asked. It had slumped back into its former slouch, but perhaps it was just looking down at the sorceress. If it was supposed to represent an imp, it was a little larger than life size, and it stood on a plinth. Oothiana was on the ground, and lower.

"The princess, or queen. Inosolan."

"I thought East promised to produce her for the imperor?"

"But he hasn't. Not yet. And now it seems that whoever stole her away wasn't one of his votaries!"

"Whose, then?"

"Don't now. Maybe no one's. The faun says she was a djinn, named Rasha."

"Mm?" the statue said. "A wild card? Well, why does the dwarf want her, this Inosolan?"

"Who knows? Just because the others do, maybe. She seems to be important."

The statue grunted. "Can he find her?"

"I don't know! That's what I have to do next . . . Oh, Gods— the time! I must go, love! I have to find out if the faun knows where this Rasha woman took her."

Again insects crawled on Rap's skin. He had told the lady about Rasha and he'd said she was a djinn, but perhaps he hadn't mentioned Arakkaran. He laid his head down on the damp, earth-scented grass and shivered. If Oothiana went looking for him and discovered his absence, then the chase would be on at once. Now he dare not go back to rescue Little Chicken. For Inos's sake, he *must* escape now, or else kill himself before they caught him.

Silence.

The moon was sliding behind another cloud. He sneaked a quick look as the light faded. Oothiana had stepped up on the plinth and was embracing the statue, kissing it. Its free arm was around her, holding her tight.

The kiss ended. She whispered something. The statue responded, equally quietly. Endearments. "I must go, my love," she said, and her voice cracked.

Rap started easing backward, planning to leave, but Oothiana jumped down to the ground then, and he froze. She set off at once, heading toward the building. When she left the circle of shielding she could have detected him with farsight, but either his stillness escaped her notice or she was too intent on her own troubles. As she vanished into the doorway, he relaxed and wiped his streaming forehead on the grass. Whew!

He began to move again.

The statue said, "You! Faun! Come here."

5

"Always did have good night vision," the statue said in a satisfied tone.

Standing within the shielding, Rap had farsight now to confirm what his eyes had been refusing to believe. Furthermore, the moon had come out again. The statue was only partly a statue. Feet and legs of solid marble supported a torso of . . . *meat*, a living man. His right hand, the one held high to grip the spear, was stone also, almost to the elbow. That was what was holding him upright. His left arm seemed unaffected. So far.

"I'm Rap," Rap said hoarsely, mostly to see if he was capable of speaking without throwing up.

"Yodello, legate of the army in Faerie, retired."

He had been a burly, well-built man, big for an imp. Even now, with pain and horror shining out of half-mad eyes, he retained some trace of his former authority.

"How'd you get out, prisoner?"

Rap started to back away, and his feet froze as firmly as Yodello's. His mouth spoke without his wanting it to. "I was caged with the goblin. He has a word of power, and it's made him inhumanly strong. He threw me through the aversion spell."

Yodello chortled harshly. "And how did he know to try that? And what do you know about aversion spells?"

"I have a word, also. I have farsight, so I could see the shielding, and I met an aversion spell in Inisso's castle."

"In Krasnegar?"

"Yes, sir."

"A faun in the far north? And do you know where this Inosolan is?"

Rap tried to bite his tongue, but again his mouth seemed to have a mind of its own. "The sorceress said she was from somewhere called Arakkaran. You're a mage!" Rap added quickly. That was why he also was rooted to the spot.

"My, my! You know a lot! For a mere genius, that is."

"You killed the fairies. Three of them. The lady told me that the man who did that was being punished." But Rap found it hard to believe that even three murders justified this ghastly death, a creeping petrification. How long had this wretch endured his public torment?

"Not punished by her!" said the half-man.

"Please, sir, let me go? I have to escape, to save Inos! I must find a ship to hide in." Surely this Yodello could never be on Zinixo's side?

The soldier shook his head, and moonlight flashed from his bronze helmet. "They'd search all the ships with a looking glass. If you go somewhere else, you might manage to elude Oothie for a while, but the dwarf could track you like a bloodhound, if he was upset enough to come after you himself. Or his uncle might, even. He has others. No one escapes from a sorcerer, Master Rap.''

And Little Chicken had been present in the chamber when Rasha appeared. He, too, had heard the name of Arakkaran. Rap sank down on the grass in despair. His ankle throbbed painfully, but worse was the sudden horror eating into his heart like an arctic chill. Inos! For a moment there was silence, then he said, ''You're a mage? You could help me.''

''You could help me.''

''Me?'' Rap peered up at the man's face, silver in the moonlight. He wasn't sure if the soldier was joking, or mocking him, or had just been driven mad by his ordeal. It must be at least a month, maybe two, since the attack on the fairy village. Had Yodello been suffering here all that time? Every day his former subordinates would go marching past. Someone must have to feed him, clean him.

''How can I possibly help you?''

''Scratch my left ankle. It's driving me crazy.''

''Very funny,'' Rap said. ''If I can do anything to help, I will, but if I can't, then I'd like to go now.''

''But I never have anyone to talk to! You can keep me company for a while. Talk to me. Kill me.''

''What?''

''Yes!'' The soldier sighed and rubbed his ribs with his elbow, as if he had an itch there. ''You can, of course. That's how you can help me, see? There's a shed around the back. You go find a shovel. They might even have an ax. Then you can cut my throat. You can put me out of my misery.''

''I couldn't do that,'' Rap said with a very dry mouth.

''Sure you could!'' Yodello sounded jovial, fatherly. He might have been encouraging a nervous recruit. ''Very good opportunity for you. A man never knows what he is until he's killed someone. Ready?''

''No!'' Rap slithered backward on the grass. He felt the edge of the roadway under one elbow. Behead a man with a shovel?

''But you answered my call, Master Rap! You came within the shield. Then I had you. I'm a mage. Not as much a mage as I was, but I can still control a boy with only one word of power.''

''Once I'm outside the shielding again you can't!'' Rap protested. What an idiot he had been! He should have run away when Yodello summoned him, but he'd thought the statue might shout loud enough to bring the lady back.

''Oh, but I can!'' Yodello smiled grimly and dropped his

voice to a confidential whisper. "Stand up, Master Rap. Right. Now, Master Rap, you're going to go over to where you were eavesdropping and then come back here."

Rap's legs spun him around so suddenly that he almost lost his balance. Without even favoring his sore ankle, he raced across the road, turned, and raced back again. Then he stood and scowled up at the soldier in baffled humiliation.

Yodello was smiling happily. "See? I can make you do anything. It's only magic, but it would last long enough for you to go and bring a shovel to kill me with."

"But you're not going to," Rap said. "You're Zinixo's votary, aren't you? You're bound to serve him, and he wouldn't want you to die soon, because he enjoys watching you suffer. So you can't make me kill you."

"Not bad. Good guess. Sit down. Let's talk."

Rap sat, not sure whether he had a choice in the matter or not. He didn't want to talk, but he wouldn't mind listening. "I thought magic was temporary?" Oothiana had said that.

"Sir."

"Sir! Beg pardon. Sir."

Yodello stretched painfully and rubbed his back again. Then he reached up to swat a bug on the living part of his raised arm. How could a mosquito possibly find any blood in an arm that had been held up like that for weeks? The mosquitoes must be a large part of the torture. His meat parts were speckled like sandpaper.

"Yes, magic is temporary. I put a compulsion on you to make you go out and come back, but if I sent you into town and back, it might wear off before you returned. Lot o' times it makes no difference. I could turn your head into an anvil. It would be a temporary anvil, but you'd be permanently dead."

Andor's mastery had worn off with time, Rap recalled.

The moon soared into silver-hemmed cloud again, and the light faded. Yodello slumped lower, hanging by his grip on the spear, his head sagging. He had closed his eyes, as if half asleep.

"Why won't you help me escape from the warlock?" Rap whispered.

The soldier whispered back. "Same reason I can't make you kill me. Same reason I'm going to send you back to your cell. Loyalty."

He wanted Rap to kill him, though, and it would certainly be an act of mercy. Was Rap man enough to do it, not because of a compulsion, but just out of pity?

"I'll try," he said suddenly. "I can't promise, but I'll go and see what they have in the shed, and . . ."

The tribune spoke to his own feet, not raising his head. "Thanks, lad, but it's no go. Even if you found a sword, I'd have to stop you. Out of loyalty. A mage is never a match for any sorcerer. 'Specially the dwarf. He's a giant!" Yodello chuckled softly.

"Think I'm mad," he added, "don't you?"

"Yes, sir."

"Doesn't matter whether I am or not. In a week or so it'll get to my plumbing. Then I burst, I suppose. I'm looking forward to it. I just wish he cared more."

Rap waited a puzzled moment and then said, "Wish who cared, sir?"

"The dwarf!" the statue said angrily. "If he would just come and gloat, then I could defy him. I could show courage. I'm not afraid to die!" He thumped his free fist against a stone thigh. His voice rose. "I'm a soldier! I'll die bravely! But he won't give me the satisfaction. He never comes. He gave the orders, so here I am, on view. I'm washed, fed, and shaved. It's all done as he said, every day. Every day the stone creeps higher up my legs. The centuries march by here every day and see, but he never does. He doesn't care! Whether I'm brave or not doesn't matter at all. He's probably forgotten all about me. I'm an example, that's all. A human poster." His voice trailed away in despair.

Rap thought of the legionaries he'd seen running. Oothiana had called them examples. "Why an example? Why all this? Because you killed the fairies?"

"Because I tried to steal from a dwarf," Yodello said dully.

Dwarves' parsimony was legendary. Ask a man where he acquired something and, if he didn't want to tell, he'd say, *I stole it from a dwarf.*

"Inos?" Rap whispered. "What will he do with Inos if he finds her?"

"Anything he fancies. He's a warlock." The imp opened his eyes, opened them very wide, and stared down at Rap. "Let this be a lesson for you, faun!"

"Sir?" Rap felt his flesh creep as he tried to meet that tortured, crazy gaze.

"Never tell people about your power, your word! It will get you into trouble."

Rap couldn't see how he could possibly be in much worse

trouble than he was in already. Then he saw the silent scream in Yodello's sunken eyes and realized that he could be in *much* worse trouble. And mostly he'd gotten into this mess by refusing to learn more words, by refusing to become a mage and help Inos.

"Oothie was a brainless bitch," Yodello said, but softly. He raised his head, peered out into the scented dark of the Faerie night, and seemed to speak to ghosts. "I love her madly, always. She was never much of a sorceress, though. Got her words from Urlocksea, great-grandfather, not from fairies. Nice old fellow. Didn't do much with his power except some healing, but Pian'doth found him anyway. Pian' was East. When he died, the old guy got away before Olybino took over the gold palace. Died, too, soon after. Gave his words to Oothie. Warned her never to use them."

The soldier seemed to have forgotten Rap altogether and to be talking for his own sake. He must have been a remarkable man once. Mutilated, naked, close to a terrible death, he still wore some shreds of dignity. Splinters of authority still glimmered through his madness.

"She didn't do much. Fast promotion for her husband, easy labor for the second child, a few things like that. Tried to resist the little worm when he took a fancy to her—stupid bitch! As if I'd have cared! That was what gave her away. He had her anyway, of course. Didn't even make her his votary till morning . . . got to be warlock . . . made her proconsul . . ."

Rap was struck by a sudden mad idea, a way both he and Yodello might escape. Dare he suggest it? Really, what did he have to lose?

The imp's voice grew louder. "But in the case of Faerie, it's different, you see. The imperor appoints whomever West wants. The runt thought it'd be fun to make Emshandar send in Oothie's name."

"You know three words!" Rap said, in a rush, "and I know one, so if I tell you mine, then you'll be a sorcerer! You can break free of the loyalty spell and turn your legs back—couldn't you? And maybe rescue Oothiana?"

Chin high, the soldier spoke to a point above Rap's head. "A female proconsul! Senators all had miscarriages over that, but they don't argue with warlocks."

"If you promise to help me," Rap said hoarsely, "I'll make you a full sorcerer. So we can both escape."

"New proconsul appoints his own officers. Oothie picked the

best soldier she knew as tribune.'' The statue sighed. ''And I *was* the best, too! But she made me loyal to her, instead of the dwarf.''

Rap began to feel desperate. ''Or you tell me your three words, and I promise I'll do everything I can for you and your lady.''

''It was an honest mistake. She meant no disloyalty. She *couldn't* have meant to be disloyal. She was his votary.''

Rap jumped up. On level footing, he would have been about the same height as the imp. Yet he still couldn't meet those proud, sad eyes, for now they were looking past his head. He moved; they shifted. They gleamed, moonlight reflecting from haunted caves.

''You can save her, sir! Save yourself, too, maybe! Let me tell you my word of power.''

''You should have thought of that sooner,'' said a new voice, a gravelly bass. Rap spun around.

Arms akimbo, Raspnex stood on the road just outside the shielding like a stone pillar. He still wore the same disreputable work clothes, but now he had added a shapeless woolen cap. His iron-gray beard was bunched up in a dangerous scowl.

''Wouldn't have worked, anyway,'' Yodello remarked sadly. ''I'm loyal to him now. Aren't I?''

Raspnex ignored him, addressing Rap. ''Nice try, faun! I'll settle the score later, never fear.''

''I suffer loyally,'' Yodello said, seemingly to the night itself. ''I am a very good example.''

''I didn't deliberately try to deceive you, sir,'' Rap told the dwarf. ''I didn't think of—''

''I know. You couldn't have fooled me. But I'll settle, anyway.'' Raspnex glowered. Perhaps he was afraid of being made an example, too.

''About a week until I burst,'' Yodello announced cheerfully. ''Remember to come and watch that.''

''Arakkaran, faun?''

''Yes,'' said Rap's mouth.

Raspnex nodded, satisfied. ''What the goblin said.''

''She may not still be there!'' Rap said hopefully.

The dwarf shrugged his giant shoulders. ''We'll see. Come along now. The boss wants you. He hates to be kept waiting.''

''Come early and get ahead of the crowds,'' Yodello said.

6

Ekka was talking about spiders' webs. She kept on talking about spiders' webs. She would not stop talking about spiders' webs, and yet Kadolan could not hear a word she was saying because she was whispering. Whispering was not ladylike. It was very annoying. She decided she must tell Ekka that she should either speak up clearly, or else she should keep quiet and let Kadolan go back to . . . *sleep*?

She was very stiff. Her back felt as if it had been tenderized with a meat mallet. Even her knees. Bells jingling in the distance. There was no light in the tent. *Tent?*

It wasn't Ekka. It was Inosolan who was doing all the whispering. Shaking Kadolan's shoulder.

"Mmph?"

"Don't waken the girl, Aunt!"

"What g—"

"Shh!"

There was someone else moving. Gods! A man! The sultan, of course. Kadolan certainly did not want to jostle *him*, not after seeing the blister on Inosolan's finger.

Inosolan had her lips to Kadolan's ear. "Get dressed quickly. It's almost dawn. We're leaving."

"Leav—"

"*Shh!*"

Kadolan struggled to sit up. She felt impossibly stiff, and very grateful that the other two could not see her. This was what came from only one-half of a day on a camel. She must have a whole day ahead of her now. There were weeks and weeks of it to come. She was too old for this. Her eyes felt full of sand. She shivered, and not just from sleepiness; the air was nippy.

"Watch out for the girl!" Inosolan whispered again.

"I don't know where she is!" Kadolan whispered back. Fooni had been sleeping somewhere on her left, but that was not much help in pitch darkness after hours of sleeping. She could have rolled anywhere. "What is that revolting noise?"

"Camels!" Inosolan said.

Did they never stop bellowing? If the Fooni child could sleep through that racket, then Kadolan could practice a trumpet fanfare without disturbing her. If the camels came any closer, they would step on the tent. That would do it! They smelled close but that was probably just the tent itself. Everything smelled of camel.

Azak pushed back a corner of the flap, and a slightly lesser darkness surged in.

"There she is," Inosolan whispered.

Things were beginning to make more sense, as Kade's old brains awoke, taking their time. She didn't like some of the implications.

"Why mustn't we waken her?"

Inosolan made an exasperated sound. She was on her knees, brushing out her hair, which was crackling and sparking in the cold dryness. Azak was a featureless enormity, an undefined impression of size. He must be kneeling, also, for the tent was much too low to let him stand, and he sounded as if he were busy. Stuffing things in bags, maybe?

"We're going to sneak away before dawn!" Inosolan whispered.

Kadolan thought *Oh-oh!* and felt a twinge of a sinking feeling. She was quite convinced in her own mind that this whole mad escapade had been organized by the sorceress. Or, if Rasha had not planned it, she must be aware of it and be tolerating it for her own reasons. Kadolan wasn't sure why she thought that, but she did; and she in turn had been willing to humor Inosolan and Azak by pretending that it was a serious attempt to escape from Arakkaran.

"Why?"

Inosolan made another cross noise. "Just in case Master Elkarath is not what he seems."

"But what could he be?"

This time it was Azak who answered, deep and urgent. "His timing was very suspicious, ma'am. He furtively sent me word just two days after you and your niece arrived, claiming that he had often transported messages, or even messengers, for my grandsire, and that he would be happy to perform such services for myself. There was no way to confirm his tale, although it is plausible."

At least he had given Kadolan the courtesy of a civil answer.

"But what else could he be?" she asked. "What evil could he be plotting, with you to guard us, Sire—I mean Lionslayer?"

"He could be an agent of the harlot."

"Do hurry, Aunt!" Inosolan whispered urgently.

"I've been telling Inos that." Kadolan did not budge, except to rub her back plaintively. The camel roarings and jinglings seemed to be coming closer. They would surely waken the Fooni girl soon. "I admit I don't understand why Rasha should indulge in such a devious silly game, but—"

"To hide your niece from the warlock."

Oh, dear! That made excellent sense. Inosolan was a valuable political property, apparently, and Warlock Olybino might very well attempt to steal her away from the sultana if he thought the asking price too high. So Rasha had hidden her treasure away in the desert until the deal had been made; then it would be safe to come and get her. Kadolan felt relieved at finding so logical a confirmation of her instincts.

"Then why do you . . ." But the answer was obvious. Azak wanted to leave because he could not bear to remain within reach of the sorceress, if he still was. It was another of these double or triple or quadruple gambits, like the enormously complicated ways he had used to extract Kadolan herself from the palace and smuggle Inosolan to Elkarath's house from the state procession.

If Elkarath was Rasha's agent, then this would be the real escape from her power. If he was genuine, then he became merely another false trail.

"We are going to double back to the coast," Azak whispered.

"He has a boat waiting," Inosolan added impatiently, "at some little fishing village. We can sail north to Shuggaran and catch a ship. You can forget about three months on a camel, Aunt! In three months we should be in Hub. Now, does that appeal or not?"

Well, yes, that was certainly tempting.

Before Kadolan could make up her mind, a voice called faintly outside the tent, barely audible over the rumpus the camels were making, *"Queen Inosolan?"*

They all heard it. They all froze, staring at the triangle of light that marked a corner of the doorway; dawn was close now. Dribbles of icy water ran down Kadolan's back as she remembered the meeting in the forest, when Master Rap had appeared so mysteriously out of the shadows. He had called to Inosolan like that.

"What was *that*?" Azak demanded in louder tones than before.

"It sounded like somebody calling me!" Inosolan's voice trembled. "A long way off."

"Queen Inosolan!" Closer this time. No mistake this time.

It was not a man's voice, though.

And Master Rap was dead, anyway, killed by the imps.

Inosolan uttered a strangled sort of gulp. "Nobody here knows me by that name!" she whispered.

Kadolan guessed what was about to happen and grabbed for her niece's shoulder. Inosolan was always so impulsive!

She was too late. Inosolan went scrambling on hands and knees over the litter of bedding. For a moment her shape obscured the hint of gray glow of the entrance, and then she was outside.

Nothing particular happened. Kadolan relaxed. It had perhaps been an illusion. A herdboy singing, or some such.

Azak was more visible than before, and he had indeed been stuffing things into a sack and was now roping it, with swift, jerky movements. "Are you ready, mistress?"

Kadolan sprang to wakefulness. She was far from ready, but she certainly did not intend to be left behind. She was too old for this, she thought, rummaging to find her shoes, but a swift ride to the coast and then a sea voyage was a far more pleasing prospect than a camel ride to Ullacarn, wherever that was.

Hub, the city of the Gods! Who would choose to remain in this ugly desert when offered a journey to Hub?

Dragging a bundle, Azak crawled over to the doorway, making the tent darker. Kadolan decided she would have to forget about brushing her hair, just this once.

And then Inos screamed.

7

"He's a brave man!" Rap shouted, leaning into the wind. The seaward side of the headland was much steeper than the harbor side. A steady thunder of surf came drifting up from the darkness below. The air was cool and salty.

"Who is?" Raspnex was trudging solidly through the night, with one hand clasping his cap firmly on his head.

"Tribune Yodello."

The dwarf grunted. "Hasn't got much choice, has he?" he said indifferently.

But Yodello had very nearly succeeded in stealing from a dwarf, and a warlock dwarf at that. He had learned three words in the fairy village. It was a reasonable assumption that either the proconsul or the warlock had stopped him while he was trying to collect a fourth.

"How does a man get around a loyalty spell?"

That question earned no answer but an angry glare. Rap himself had evaded capture for half a day and then broken out of jail. Both times he had been more lucky than clever, but obviously sorcery and magic had limitations that could be exploited if one knew how. He wished he knew how.

The journey to the crest of the ridge had taken almost no time, so Raspnex must have used power. The Gazebo itself loomed dead ahead, larger than Rap had expected, overtopping the trees around it. It was a circular wooden structure, two levels surmounted by a conical roof. Lights were wavering strangely in the upper story, but that was cut off from his farsight by an opaque ceiling. The lower room seemed to be used mainly as storage: furniture and rolls of matting, metal tools and stone statuary, boxes of shells and glass cases full of butterflies, and much more that he had no time to make out, the accumulated junk of generations.

A line of armed legionaries encircled the building, all standing stiffly to attention in the salty wind. The centurion saluted the dwarf, who stumped by him without a word or glance.

"What need has a warlock for mundane guards?" Rap shouted.

"Curb your tongue, faun, or I'll tie a knot in it."

A wooden stair wound up the outside to connect with a wide observation gallery, silhouetted against the weirdly dancing light. Rap followed the thump of the dwarf's boots up the steps, watching the occult barrier approach as he had done in Inisso's Tower in Krasnegar. Then his head broke through, and the rest of the palace had gone.

The upper level was one large room, whose walls were merely widely spaced wooden panels; they held up the roof but made no clear distinction between the interior floor and the deck of the surrounding gallery. The wind blustered through unhindered. Sleeping bats hung within the high cone of the roof, and the rafters were heaped with ancient birds' nests. Faded rugs and wicker furniture lay scattered around in no particular pattern, together with some other buzzing, twitching things that Rap preferred not to inspect.

The wavering light came from overhead lanterns on long chains, swinging wildly in the gale. Even very ordinary-seeming chairs were gifted with many sinister shadows, writhing like black spiders in the golden glow on the floor. Tree branches outside seemed to fade in and out of the night.

Raspnex headed for Oothiana, who stood before one of the larger wall panels, apparently examining a picture. She had unfastened her hair, and it surged and rippled in the wind, like a black flag. So did her white gown. Rap tried not to stare at that as he followed the dwarf across to her. He was foolish to be so scrupulous, really, for no one's clothes held secrets from his farsight; yet he found those delicate curves sketched out in white fabric far more enticing and disturbing than crude certainty could ever be. He was learning how to control his power when he needed to, by diverting it to other things and away from places he should not pry, but that wasn't always easy.

Little Chicken stood at the proconsul's side, bare-chested, arms crossed, and greener in the dim gold light than Rap had ever seen him. He was probably enjoying the cold. His angular eyes narrowed when he saw Rap, his lip curled in silent contempt.

"Any luck?" Raspnex demanded.

Oothiana turned. She looked weary. "Some. The palace is shielded." She glanced at Rap, but her face gave away nothing.

The thing she had been studying was not a picture but a large mirror in an intricate silver frame. It had a dark, oily look to it that Rap disliked, but it seemed no more sinister than some of the other odd things, such as the potted plant that kept making finger-snapping noises, or the fairy statue that farsight said wasn't there at all.

Raspnex pulled off his ugly cap and stuffed it inside his flannel shirt. He rolled down his sleeves, meanwhile glancing thoughtfully around the room. Rap wondered what he was studying.

"Votaries don't put up shielding, usually," the dwarf said.

"Of course not."

No love lost there.

Rap bowed to her. "Your Highness."

Her face remained expressionless. "I'm only an excellency, Master Rap."

"Beg pardon, your Excellency." He bowed again. "May I congratulate your Excellency on the quality of your jail?"

This time he earned a faint smile. "Are you an expert?"

"I have seen enough jails that I never need see another." Rap bowed again.

"But you tried to leave."

"I hope you understand that I meant no discourtesy, ma'am."

She turned away from him and glanced around the room.

He shrugged. Well, he had tried. At least she knew now that he bore her no grudge, and he thought she would care about that.

"I'll tell him we're ready," Raspnex said. He marched across to another section of wall, which surprisingly contained a completely unnecessary door. It was massive, embellished with intricate carvings and inset with golden hieroglyphics. The dwarf pulled it open, walked through, and thumped it heavily behind him.

He did not appear on the balcony beyond.

Feeling an unpleasant shiver run down his back, Rap said, "Huh?"

"Magic portal." Oothiana took a deep breath. "Leads to Hub. Rap, all I can tell you is to be polite, very polite. He takes offense easily. Come."

She walked over to a couch and sat down. Something about the way she did it prompted Rap to go and sit beside her, surprised by his own presumption. It was ages since he had sat close to a beautiful woman. He could not remember doing so since he had held hands with Inos, the night Jalon had sung in the castle hall, back home in Krasnegar. There must have been others in the early winter, when he had been factor's clerk eating in the castle commons. He could not recall them, though. Only Inos, long ago.

In a manner suggestive of a cat staking out a mousehole, Little Chicken selected a chair close to Rap. He leaned back, smiling hungrily. Rap ignored him and inspected the room again, wondering what the two sorcerers had been studying so oddly. His farsight was starting to pick up odd shimmers that his eyes could not explain.

"Dwarfs don't like luxury," Oothiana said.

"What? I mean, I beg your—"

"Warlock Zinixo can have anything he wants. He can make sand into gold, or sugar lumps into diamonds. But he grew up with shabby, old things, like most dwarves do. It's just their way. He's not comfortable with . . . with comfort. He likes dead leaves around."

She must have thought Rap was inspecting the furniture, which was lumpish but comfy. Only now did he notice spots where the wicker was worn and stuffing protruded from cushions; it had all seemed fine to him. And of course there were low heaps of dead leaves in every cranny; this place was more outdoors than in. Bird droppings aplenty, too.

"There were no dead leaves where I grew up, no leaves at all." He started to smile at her, but she was close, and he found himself too much aware of her smooth round breasts. Angry, he looked away and struggled to keep his farsight under control.

Oothiana did not seem to mind. "And not much else but leaves where you grew up, Master Goblin? Or pine needles, I suppose?"

"Who's coming?" asked Little Chicken, looking surly.

"Warlock Zinixo, warden of the west. Address him as 'your Omnipotence.' Don't lip him, or he'll make your guts rot."

The goblin's eyes widened, becoming more triangular in the process.

Rap's nerves were too taut to stand the ensuing silence. "I met Legate Yodello, ma'am," he said, blurting out the words and regretting them at once.

Oothiana seemed to glance around the room again, inspecting . . .

He gulped. "I'm sorry. I mean, I don't think he deserves—that."

She regarded him coldly. "He was the one who killed the fairies."

Rap nodded. "But I think he did it for . . . for a good reason, ma'am."

"What reason could justify torture and murder?"

"I—I don't know," Rap said miserably.

"He did it for me, is what you mean. Yes, he did." She sighed and looked away. "And maybe he wanted to save the other fairyfolk. He says he did, and I believe him." She paused, picking at the fabric of her dress where it curved over her knee. "You've guessed what happened? The warlock had been hunting for wild fairies. They're very rare now, but eventually he discovered that village. He ordered me to have the inhabitants brought in. I told the legate, of course. Except I didn't—didn't give him quite the right orders. That was my second mistake. I hadn't put the right loyalty spell on him when I appointed him, and I didn't tell him to do the job himself. I told him to send someone to do it."

After a moment, Rap said, "How did that matter?"

"He obeyed my exact orders, of course. He had no choice there. He sent his best maniple and put his best centurion in charge. But then he went along himself. He was just able to avoid my intent without actually disobeying my words. Somehow he convinced himself that he was acting in my best interests. It was an astonishing feat—he circumvented a binding spell. He couldn't give any contrary orders, but the centurion was only

bound by an oath, not by sorcery, and he wasn't going to interfere with anything a legate wanted to do. So Yodello tried to
win four words for himself. He thought the fastest way would
be to flog children to make their parents tell. He got three before
the warlock arrived.''

Silence fell, while she continued to worry the threads of her
gown. Rap had found three bodies; the parents, dead from telling their secret names. No children had died, therefore, at least
not then.

''Arrived mad?''

''Very, very mad.'' As if realizing how she was fidgeting,
Oothiana pulled her hand away from her knee and folded her
arms.

''It was a stupid plan anyway!'' she snapped. ''Even if he
had learned four words and become a full sorcerer, he would
never have been able to defy the warlock. Sorcerers as strong as
the dwarf are historical freaks. Oh, Yodello might have managed
to break free of my binding, but he'd never have broken the one
on me. And he'd have had to face the warlock eventually. It was
a crazy dream.''

It had been the sort of mad risk a man might take for the
woman he loved, and for his children. Rap decided he could
almost forgive the crime Little Chicken had uncovered in that
jungle hamlet. Almost. What was being done to Yodello himself
could never be forgiven.

Again the sorceress glanced around the room. Why were there
mundane legionaries guarding this building? *Who else was in
here?* Invisible guards?

The magic portal opened a crack, slashing a sliver of brighter
light across a rug so threadbare that boards showed through it
in spots. Rap's heartbeat speeded up disgracefully. For a moment nothing more happened. Then the door swung wide, revealing a brief glimpse of a book-lined chamber with a fire
crackling in a grate. A blast of air swirled through, and the door
slammed shut by itself.

Silence again . . . except that the tension had just doubled,
or tripled. The warlock was now present, and Rap no longer
doubted that there were more bodyguards around than he could
see.

Little Chicken looked puzzled. Oothiana was tense, staring
straight ahead. The wind stirred the trees with a dry, insectile
sound.

Then a voice spoke out of the air beside Little Chicken, and he jumped. It was the deepest voice Rap had ever heard, even deeper than Raspnex's.

"Goblin! Tell me what you know about Bright Water."

Little Chicken's eyes stretched wide, and he glanced all about and then licked his lips. Even his tongue seemed an odd color in this light. "Nothing," he said shakily, "your Omnipotence. Not seen her. Not heard of her, until Flat—the faun—told me about her."

"Tally your ancestors."

The goblin stammered, then rattled off his forebears for a dozen generations.

Silence fell again, but Rap was not surprised when the voice addressed him next, from somewhere just in front of him.

"How did you escape, faun?"

Rap explained.

There was no answer, no further question. Oothiana was still as a statue, not revealing the warlock's position with her eyes.

Why should the most powerful sorcerer in the world bother to play such tricks?

Then the sepulchral voice spoke again, from farther away.

"In the morning we'll give the goblin three fairies. Have you picked out three older men, as I ordered?"

"Yes, your Omnipotence," Oothiana said.

The unseen warlock grunted. "Good. I'm tired of having them die without speaking. Too many suicides, too. It's inefficient. That woman I was burning—has she recovered her wits yet?"

"Not yet, Omnipotence."

"Exactly! It's too slow. This way we'll get three words quickly."

There was no hint of regret in the voice, and yet the implications were enough to freeze Rap's blood. Little Chicken had his mouth open and eyes wide, stunned by the idea of a woman being tortured.

"So you'll have a goblin sorcerer!" Rap shouted. "What do you do then? You planning to torture words out of a goblin?"

Oothiana started, shooting him a look of warning.

Suddenly the warlock became visible. He had the same heavy build as his uncle, but his clothes were even shabbier—moth-eaten, and frayed at the knees. He was young and his shortness made him seem younger, yet his hair was as gray as the older dwarf's; his colorless, unbearded face looked like stone freshly quarried. He stood in front of Rap, studying him with a look of cold dislike, nibbling at a hangnail. By repute, he was the most powerful sorcerer in the world. He could have been a farmhand, or a gardener's boy.

He took his finger from his mouth. "No. I don't plan to torture anything out of a goblin. I shall bribe him." He grinned teeth like white pebbles. "We both know what he wants, don't we? And I can keep you alive as long as I want while he satisfies his ambitions."

Little Chicken had apparently worked out what was involved. He grinned at Rap, also, gloating.

Rap failed to restrain a shudder. "Then he'll kill you, too!" he told the goblin.

Little Chicken laughed gleefully. "Don't care!"

"There!" said Zinixo. "That's all arranged, then." He spun on his heel and began pacing the room, gnawing his hangnail and thumping the dusty floor with heavy boots. Goblins, fauns, legionaries, fairies, legates—this dwarf's indifference to other people was even nastier than Little Chicken's deliberate cruelty. At least Little Chicken regarded agony as an honor and had been prepared to endure it himself when Rap bested him. Obviously Zinixo's world held no one of importance except Zinixo.

After a moment, Oothiana said, "I found Arakkaran, Omnipotence. There's shielding around the palace."

Zinixo ignored her. Little Chicken was still beaming happily. Rap wondered how many invisible guards were present in the room, and what he would have to endure to satisfy the goblin, and why the magic casement had not done a better job of prophecy.

The warlock stopped his pacing. He put his back against a wall panel and let his gaze jerk to and fro around the room. "What's keeping them? This isn't some sort of trap, is it?"

"I'm sure it isn't, your Omnipotence," Oothiana said soothingly.

"They're ganging up on me!" His voice was an octave higher already, and rising.

"No, Sire! I expect—"

The dwarf jumped and spun around as the door flew open, but it was only Raspnex returning. He bore a long roll of fabric like a blanket draped slackly over his shoulder. He closed the door firmly.

"Well?" the warlock yelled. "Out with it, Uncle!"

"She's coming."

"Ah!" Zinixo looked around. "Ready? If she tries anything, strike at once! Blast the whole building if you have to."

Oothiana and Raspnex nodded obediently. Perhaps the unseen others nodded, also.

"Let her come." Zinixo wiped a sleeve over his forehead; he flexed his thick shoulders as if readying himself for a tussle.

Raspnex threw down his bundle in the middle of the room and kicked it. It unrolled and became a small oblong rug; an oddly shiny one, glittering in the dim golden glow of the lamps.

Both dwarves backed away a few paces. For a moment no one spoke, and Rap sensed tension coming to a boil. Oothiana was kneading her hands together and the warlock chewing fingernails again. The older man had crossed his arms, but he was wary, also. He remained standing.

For a few moments the only sounds were the distant surf, grinding the coast with ageless hunger, and leaves skittering thinly in the wind. Rap was becoming inured to magic; the most incredible sorceries now seemed quite commonplace to him, and he was not at all surprised when a faint shimmer appeared above the little carpet and quickly solidified into a tiny woman.

Had he not been expecting Bright Water, though, he might not have recognized her. On the two occasions he had met her before, her garb had been a goblin woman's long buckskin gown, but now she wore a frilly white dress, short and sleeveless. It glittered in a thousand dewy rainbow twinkles of sequins or perhaps gems, but it was also rumpled and soiled. Below the brief, flared skirt, her bare legs were fleshless as a crab's, ending in incongruous boots. Her dusky arms and shoulders were scraggy and gnarled, her chest flat and leathery. In absurd contrast to her goblin-khaki skin, her hair shone a brilliant auburn, lush and youthful. It had been piled high on her head and pinned there with combs of ivory—and apparently some time ago, for the coiffure was falling apart, and stray wisps and tresses tumbled loose. The effect was ludicrous, as if a crone had turned herself into an adolescent to go to a ball and then changed only partway back. Judging by the hair and the dress, the ball had been over for days.

Strangest of all, a pale-pink flame burned upon the hag's humped left shoulder. It flickered, changed color a few times, and congealed into the shape of a small, crouching animal. But it was still glowing and Rap's farsight could detect only a vague, fuzzy presence and an odd sense of something alive.

"Well!" the warlock shouted. "And what is the witch of the north doing with a dragon?"

Bright Water wheeled around to look for him. The light on her shoulder brightened and seemed to grip harder, as if afraid it might fall off.

"A gift!" she shrilled. "Isn't she lovely? Precious, I call her, a present from Lith'rian."

The uncanny sense of madness unsettled Rap. Zinixo, however, merely thumped his fists onto his hips and leaned forward, the better to scowl at her.

"How sweet! I never heard of South giving away dragons to anyone. Did this exceptional gift seal some secret agreement?"

"Oh, no!" The old woman cackled. "No, no, no! He knows I like them, that's all. I've had fire chicks before, well before your time, sonny. Just hatchlings. Can't keep them very long, you know! Haven't got big enough shoulders!"

She shrieked another cackle of amusement and reached up to stroke the luminescence as if it were a kitten. It turned a warm blue—and Rap felt a strange *purr*. That wasn't farsight; that was his empathy for animals. Apparently the flame was alive, or enough alive that he could hear its feelings, but the sensation was bitter and alien, like a metallic taste in his mind. He shut it out.

But he could not shut out the stories he had heard about dragons and metal, and there must be metal around this bizarre summer house. Nails, lamps . . . he glanced up at the wind-stirred lanterns, and they certainly looked as if they were made of gold, or at least trimmed with it. Gold was worst of all; all the tales warned about the terrible things that happened when dragons found gold.

"Now!" The witch turned around, peering. "Haven't been here since the days of Ho-Ilth. Not much change. Same furniture, by the look of it. We ate mangoes on that sofa and threw passion spells at each other. Where did you . . . Ah! Death Bird! Are you all right, my sweet?"

Clumping in her boots, she marched straight off the mat, heading for Little Chicken, who was sprawled back in his chair, eyes and mouth wide with disbelief.

Zinixo twitched, as if startled.

The witch wheeled with incredible agility, the fire chick on her shoulder flashing momentarily orange. *"Stop that!"* she snapped. "That's no way to treat guests!"

Pause. The warlock had bared teeth like rows of tombstones.

He was rigid as a granite boulder, and his youthful face gleamed wetly in the glow of the swinging lamps. His cheeks were chalky.

Then he forced his grimace into a cynical and dangerous smile. He made a small bow, without taking his eyes off the old woman. "Of course, Grandmother. But don't do anything rash."

"Course not!" Bright Water said. "That's—" The baby dragon flared green and flew up off her shoulder in an erratic, wobbling flight. "Oh! Be careful, my Precious!"

The dragon chick fluttered around the room at head height as if exploring. Eventually it came to hover suspiciously above Rap. There was very little substance to it, but he thought perhaps he could see a dragon shape there more often than anything else. At times it was a star, or a bird, or a butterfly, and often just a blur of light.

The witch put two fingers in her mouth and whistled shrilly. Precious changed to a nervous yellow shade and zigzagged back to her shoulder. Cooing, she stroked it until it was blue again. Strangely, the incomprehensible tension somehow faded then. Oothiana and Raspnex exchanged puzzled glances.

And the witch seemed to notice Raspnex for the first time.

"What was I about to say?" she inquired stiffly.

The dwarf blinked and shrugged.

"Well, then!" she snapped. "Haven't we met somewhere recently, young man?"

"We spoke about five minutes ago in the glass."

"Oh?" She looked vaguely around the room and frowned at Oothiana. "Aren't you Urmoontra, what's-his-name's wife?"

"Her great-granddaughter, your Omnipotence."

"Oh, Gods and mortals!" Bright Water shook her head sadly, causing another rope of hair to fall loose. "It is getting late, isn't it? Bedtime, everybody." She leered uncertainly in the direction of a potted palm, then curtsied. "Evening, Senator."

There might be an invisible senator there, of course. Nothing was impossible in this madhouse.

Finally the witch discovered Zinixo. "And you, lad?"

"You know who I am, you stinking offal bucket! Stop the play-acting." He stamped around her to reach Little Chicken, whom he indicated with a downward-jabbing finger. "Tell us what your interest is in this."

Bright Water blinked at the prisoner for a moment or two. Then she beamed, displaying a mouthful of huge goblin teeth, whose shiny perfection was not in keeping with her otherwise decrepit appearance. "Death Bird! Knew I'd put him somewhere safe. Couldn't remember where. Isn't the resemblance wonderful?''

"What resemblance?" Zinixo was taut as a harp string, wary as a stalking cat, and growing madder by the minute.

"Blood Fan. My oldest brother, you know. When he was this age?"

"The oaf's related to you, then? He doesn't know it."

The witch chuckled hoarsely, for what seemed like too long. Crazy, but not necessarily stupid—Rap had seen old Hononin act dim-witted often enough, usually when Foronod had gone barging into the stables to demand something the hostler had not wanted to grant. Almost always the factor had been driven to losing his temper and therefore the argument. This seemed like the same technique. If the witch made Zinixo much angrier, he might be capable of any sort of folly.

"He wouldn't know," Bright Water crooned. "Blood Fan was a sly lad, eh? A very quiet crawler when the fires were banked. Not a wife in the lodge didn't feign sleep for him at least once. They caught him eventually and he put on a wonderful show. Almost three days. You're very like him," she added to Little Chicken, who was frowning as he tried to follow the outlandish conversation going on over his head. "Ho-Ilth liked mangoes, and what good did they ever do him, eh? Blood Fan fathered Gut Thrust on Petal Bed, and Gut Thrust—"

"And is that all?" the warlock shouted furiously, his anger booming like a mountain thunderstorm. "Is that the only reason you're interested in him? That he's some distant bastard descendant of yours?"

The ancient goblin drew herself up stiffly and tried to look down her long nose at the dwarf. She failed, because she was even shorter than he was, except for her tangle of red hair and ivory combs. "Course not. Fill your guts with hot coals. Do you mean you haven't foreseen him?"

Zinixo seemed taken aback at the question. "No," he admitted. "He's got a destiny?"

"Oh, yes!"

The warlock shot Oothiana a meaningful look. "You're no good at this, are you?"

"Not much, Omnipotence."

He nodded, then spun around to face Little Chicken. The goblin's eyes rolled up, and he slumped in his chair, unconscious. His face turned a pale-lime color.

Looking intrigued, Raspnex moved in, also, so that the goblin was surrounded by three sorcerers, all staring down at him fixedly.

Oothiana leaned back on the couch.

"My lady?" Rap whispered uneasily.

She did not turn to him. She was watching the room intently—especially the magic rug—and he wondered if she had been left on guard while the dwarves' attention was on other things. "It's very difficult," she said softly. "Like trying to follow a river through a swamp. There are always so many channels. Sometimes they join up again, sometimes not. Even the thoughts of people nearby can affect a man's future. It gives me a terrible headache."

"So all you can see are possibilities?"

"The Gods decree destinies for some mortals. Most of us are only given chances." She smiled absently. "Of course someone like a quarry slave wouldn't have many, would he? Any fool could foresee his future—more life unchanging, then death. A sailor, now, or a jotunn raider, he'd usually have so many they'd be almost impossible to unravel. But the rest of us . . ." She fell silent.

Inisso's magic casement had forecast several fates for Rap—being roasted by dragons, being hacked to bits by Kalkor, being filleted by Little Chicken. Perhaps those had been alternatives that depended upon who did what first. That might explain why he had seemed doomed to die three times. If he could choose one of those deaths, though, it would never be the third.

"Can you foresee your own destiny, then?" he whispered.

She shook her head, watching the others, but in a moment she added, "Very hard. Your own reactions change the images. That's one reason sorcerers make magic casements, or preflecting pools."

"I can kill him," Zinixo muttered. In the dim golden glow of the whirling lanterns, his rough-skinned face was again shining with sweat. Raspnex's was worse. The little goblin woman was scratching at her scalp with all ten fingers, making the precarious hairdo rock. The dragon had shrunk to a tiny wisp of yellow light, pulsating on her shoulder.

"That's always a choice," she croaked. "Not always wise, though. *Time with all his banners rolling* . . . See the faun?"

"No."

"Push ahead. Back in the north. Snow! See now? All roads lead to the faun."

"Almost all."

"Pah!" The witch spoke as if her throat hurt. "Almost all, then. Never seen a clearer destiny."

It was all gibberish to Rap, but he thought of the swamp that Oothiana had mentioned and the many river channels emptying into a large lake within it. That might fit. And the mention of him sounded like the casement's third prophecy. At least there had been no word of Inos yet, in all this insanity.

"So?" The hiss might have come from either of the dwarves.

"So what's beyond, eh?" the old woman whispered.

Without warning the little grouping broke up. Raspnex staggered aside, knuckling his eyes and gasping as if he had been running. Zinixo threw back his head and bellowed with heavy laughter like falling rocks. The witch bent down, took Little Chicken's face in both hands, and kissed him. His eyes flew open.

"Got it!" the warlock shouted.

"You see now?" Bright Water scrambled onto Little Chicken's lap, stroking his hairy cheek with a hand like dead roots. The dragon swelled and burned in pale mauve. Apparently not liking the younger goblin so close, it crawled around the back of her neck, balancing on her hump, and settled on her other shoulder.

"Oh, yes!" Zinixo favored Oothiana with a huge, childish smile. His change of mood was astonishing. "The goblin butchers the faun—no doubt about that. And then—" He laughed again, looking at his uncle, who was grinning a dwarf's pebbly grin.

"Then," the older man said, "we see something new, *your Majesty!*" He bowed, and both sorcerers howled with mirth.

Little Chicken's eyes grew to very large triangles indeed. Again, he was fondly kissed by the old woman perched in his lap.

"That's right, my darling. A goblin king!"

"Kill Flat Nose?"

She nodded vigorously, beaming. "Oh, yes! Back at Raven Totem."

"Long pain?"

"Very long, by the looks of it. Give good show."

Little Chicken sighed happily and smiled at Rap. "Is good, Flat Nose." He was speaking goblin again.

"A goblin king!" The witch sighed on his lap.

So that was it! Rap felt horror boil up in him like vomit. The imperor didn't want Kalkor as king of Krasnegar, and the thanes wouldn't let it fall to the Impire, but the two sides might still agree on a compromise. Neither imp nor jotunn, so a goblin, of course! Marry Inos to Little Chicken and then everybody would be happy.

Zinixo frowned. "Let us talk business, then. You want this goblin prince of yours back."

The witch patted Little Chicken's cheek. "Death Bird is my darling, my darling."

"But you gave him to me. You dropped him here, in my territory. I can kill him yet—we saw that."

The old woman pouted and threw a skinny arm around Little Chicken's head, clutching it protectively to where she once had a bosom. "Not my sweeting! No, we save him, to be a king."

The expression on Little Chicken's face suggested that he was not enjoying this.

Zinixo smiled grimly. "And you want him loaded up with more words, of course?"

"More? Eh? No, no words!" Bright Water looked startled.

"He stole one from a fairy!"

The witch's eyes flickered toward Rap, then back to Little Chicken . . . Rap . . . "Eh? Death Bird got the word?" She giggled faintly.

She was surprised by something. Then she recovered, shaking her head so that even more hair fell loose. "No, no, no!" She released her victim and scrambled down off his lap. "You didn't foresee properly! Words don't help. Give him words, and he doesn't become a king!"

"Then why send him here?" The dwarf looked puzzled and angry.

She shrugged her knobby shoulders and cackled. "Had to move him somewhere. Safe, far away! Thought things might get nasty in the north. Olybino."

Zinixo folded his arms. "What are you offering, witch? What's he worth?"

"Ah! *Patient is the heron in silver waters wading!*" The old woman raised one arm high overhead, spun around in a pirouette, and then staggered off-balance with a clamor of boots on planks. Regaining her balance, she bowed to a patch of empty air. "Begging your pardon, ma'am!" Then she peered around slyly at the dwarf. "What's your price?"

"The elf's balls on a fork."

She cackled shrilly. "Naughty! You boys are all the same! He wants to tie yours to an anchor."

The dwarf scowled, unamused. He folded his arms. "What did you pay him for the fire chick?"

"Me? Nothing!" The hag stuck her long goblin nose in the air as if taking offense.

Rap sneaked a glance at Oothiana, who was frowning and twisting her fingers together. He decided that Bright Water had now succeeded in confusing everybody, perhaps including herself. He believed almost nothing he had heard so far, except that the dwarf and the elf detested each other, and he had known that before.

Was the witch truly as crazy as she acted? He had an absurd conviction that Bright Water had been lurking in his shadow ever since he first met her in Raven Totem. She professed to be only interested in Little Chicken, but whenever she had materialized before, it had always been to Rap. What were her real motives? Why should she care about Krasnegar, or who ruled it? And now he had developed a weird certainty that she had known about the fairy child and had expected Rap to learn the word, not Little Chicken. Obviously his imagination was becoming infected by the prevailing insanity.

And Bright Water had claimed that she could not foresee Rap's future. He hoped she did not mention that now, because the warlock would certainly take the information as a challenge, and if his foresight also failed, then he might feel threatened. Apparently almost anything made him feel threatened, in spite of his great powers.

"You're a liar!" Zinixo decided. "You bought that dragon with something." A molten hue in his cheeks suggested he was flushing.

The witch tossed her head, shaking loose more strands of copper hair. "I gave him the girl," she admitted.

Rap opened his mouth, and invisible lips whispered, "Shh!" in his ear. "Listen!" It was Oothiana's voice, but she had not moved and she seemed to be concentrating entirely on the argument in progress.

"The Krasnegar girl?" Zinixo demanded. "Inosolan? Why?"

"Why did I?" Bright Water said airily. "Because he offered me Precious." She stroked the flame on her shoulder, and it purred and burned up violet. "Dum-de-dum-dum . . . Why'd he? No idea. Never ask 'why' of an elf, sonny. Elves' explanations are the commonest cause of suicide among the young."

"You're in league with him against me!"

The old hag sneered. "Flammery! He's in cahoots with East. If I join them against you, sonny, you're mole pie."

The dwarf almost screamed. "Oh, am I? Well, we'll see about that!"

"You listen to me, boy! Leave Yellow-belly's organs in place for now. Would you settle for the imp's guts instead?"

A chair slid across the floor as if moved by the wind and came to rest behind the warlock. He sat down, crossed his stumpy legs, and scowled up at Bright Water with a sudden show of calm. "Cut the chaff. I've got your darling Death Bird, or whatever you call him. He could be very useful to me. You want him back, then make an offer."

Bright Water shook her head pityingly. She turned away, and Rap expected her to step on the magic mat and disappear, but she paused and seemed to have second thoughts.

"Isn't easy being a warlock," she said, sneering at the night, or perhaps at one of the unseen watchers. "He's discovered that by now. He thought he'd feel safer, but he doesn't, does he? Now he's public knowledge, and they're all out to get him. So he needs votaries to defend him. Thought that being West would be easy, because he could make lots of votaries. But it isn't easy. Never knows when he may raise a monster!"

Zinixo gritted his teeth. "Go on. It's late, I'm tired."

"Early, early, early!" Bright Water whirled around in one of her absurd pirouettes and ended facing toward Oothiana. "Much safer to steal your opponents' helpers than make new ones of your own, eh?" She waggled a finger. "Isn't it? Men never see that."

Oothiana said, "Ma'am?" in a puzzled voice.

The dwarf's pebble eyes seemed to shine a little brighter.

The witch sighed. "You remember at the end of the meeting, the imperor decided to pull his men from Krasnegar?"

Rap stiffened. If the Council of Four had met with the imperor to discuss Krasnegar, that was important news. There might be word of Inos coming next.

Oothiana shot a baffled glance at the warlock, then said, "I wasn't there, ma'am."

In the background, Zinixo was looking skeptical. "Warlock Olybino agreed to send the orders. Witch Bright Water promised to hold Kalkor and the Nordlanders off for at least two more weeks, to give the imps time. But does she remember that?"

The old woman giggled shrilly, a mad sound. "Don't need

to remember,'' she told Oothiana in a whisper. ''Kalkor's at the other end of the world.''

''What? But you said . . .'' The young dwarf rubbed his chin. ''No, you didn't, did you? Just hinted.''

Raspnex grinned, as if he was finding the witch's performance amusing.

She bared her big, perfect teeth at Rap, switching her attention to him, still whispering. ''Kalkor's down south, on a raping holiday around Qoble. And I didn't say I'd hold back the goblins! They're going to pave the road with impish hides, all the way to Pondague. Oh, pity the poor prisoners!''

Rap shuddered. The witch was drooling, and Little Chicken was leering, doubtless remembering his own revenge on Yggingi. The goblins' traditions of peace had been discarded.

Zinixo was obviously intrigued. ''So Olybino will try to cover the troops' retreat? So he'll want to send votaries up there!''

''So I refuse my gracious permission!'' Bright Water danced a few steps in front of Rap. ''So he'll do it anyway! You're not a dwarf! Where'd he go?'' She spun around to locate Zinixo. ''So do you want them?''

The warlock glanced at his uncle, who grinned and nodded, then at Oothiana.

She shook her head. ''He'll make them legionaries. Then you can't touch them.''

''But you can mark them!'' the old witch shouted. ''Every time they deflect an arrow or avoid an ambush, you'll know them. When they get back to Hub, they'll be off duty, and you can take 'em then, whenever you want. You'll have Olybino gutted and smoked. Fanfares and flying horsedung!''

''Why don't you do this?'' Zinixo asked, with his usual dark suspicion.

She pouted and stalked across to Little Chicken. ''I was going to. You said you wanted an offer. I need my darling.'' She stroked the goblin's hair. Infected by either jealousy or her distress, the baby dragon surged away, off her shoulder. Again it headed for Rap, then changed course and whirled up in a spiral toward the wildly swinging lanterns.

Gold! If a full-grown dragon could devastate a county on one taste of gold, then even the tiny fire chick might destroy the Gazebo. Without thinking, Rap hurled a summons at it, calling it away from the metal. He had never had any success using his mastery on birds, only on four-legged things. It worked best on horses, almost as well on dogs, cats less. But apparently a dragon was a four-legged creature of a sort, because he felt a response, and the lambent flicker reversed direction, coming toward him.

Something that felt like an invisible leather belt slashed across his face, hard enough to wrench his neck. He yelped in pain and surprise. Another sickening blow lashed him on the other cheek, throwing him across Oothiana's lap.

"Idiot!" she whispered, helping him up.

Dazed and trying not to whimper, he raised a hand to a face that felt as if he had just shaved with boiling water. Bright Water was glaring very angrily at him, and the dragon chick had settled again on her shoulder.

"You stay away from my Precious, half-breed! If Death Bird didn't need you, I'd fill your belly with worms and rot your bones and—"

"Leave him!" Zinixo growled. "You want your goblin king. You let me put Raspnex up there to watch the rout? How do I know you're not just trapping my votary to aid East and South?"

She cackled shrilly again and spun around to find Raspnex. "Foresee him!"

This time the inspection was brief. Zinixo merely stared at his uncle for a minute and then chuckled heavily, his laughter as deep as the surf on the coast below. "Yes, you come back. As long as you stay away from the women, you do."

"Green doesn't appeal much," Raspnex said.

The witch waggled a lumpy finger at him. "Watch your tongue, dwarf! Let's see a goblin."

The sorcerer shrugged. He began pulling off his shirt, and seemed to melt as he did so. His grayness faded to khaki, his curly hair grew long and straight, solidifying and crawling down his chest in a greasy cue. His head shrank, his legs grew. Nose and ears became longer and pointed. In a few moments he was a middle-aged goblin in a leather loincloth. He smiled, showing that his dwarvish rock-crusher teeth had become more pointed. A whiff of rancid goblin scent wrinkled every nose in the Gazebo.

"Oh, handsome!" the crone shrilled. "And steady! Take a good eye to see that!" She pointed a finger, and arabesques of tattoo appeared on the former dwarf's face. "Long Runner of the Wolves!"

Zinixo stood up. "Stand over there, Long Runner. Downwind! One thing more, Witch." He scowled at Little Chicken. "He took a word that belongs to me!"

Yodello: *I stole it from a dwarf.*

"Phoo! There's a third one; the sequentials know a word. Take theirs in exchange."

For a moment longer the warlock hesitated. Then he nodded. "It's a deal. Go, Uncle. Here's a chance to redeem yourself. You want to take the goblin with you, *your Omnipotence*, or shall I have it delivered?"

Bright Water shrugged her bony shoulders, and the dragon wobbled. Wind blew straggles of copper hair across her face. "No. Just send them back to the mainland. With a destiny like that, he'll find it."

Humming, she clumped over to the magic carpet.

"Not *them*," Zinixo said. *"Him!"*

Rap felt a sudden twinge of hope.

Bright Water turned and scowled. "Need the faun! Death Bird butchers the faun! Doesn't work else. You saw!"

The warlock shook his oversized head, leering triumphantly. "You bought one! I keep the other."

"He's no use to you!"

"He won't be any use to you if I kill him. And I will! Now!"

"No!"

"Yes. I'll count to three!" The dwarf pointed at Rap. "One!"

Oothiana jumped from the couch and moved quickly to a safe distance. Rap's throat tightened so he could hardly breathe. Zinixo was capable of destroying him without a second thought.

"What else d'you want?" Bright Water demanded angrily. For the first time she seemed to be at a loss.

"You've got your king. I'll take the queen."

"Why? What do you want of her?"

The dwarf snarled. "I'll decide that later. She's valuable, that's enough for now. Two!"

Oothiana was staring in horror, hands at her mouth. Rap tried to move, and some invisible power locked him to the couch. And why should he struggle? This would be a much faster death than being handed over to the goblin witch and her beloved Death Bird.

"Haven't got her," Bright Water said sulkily.

"But you know where she is!"

The witch nodded with obvious reluctance.

"Tell!" snapped the warlock—but he did not complete his deadly counting.

"The Rasha woman took her. Tried to sell her to Olybino. East didn't like the price."

Zinixo hissed and hunched his head down, as if facing an attack. "What was that price?"

"Your guess is as good a bag of nuts as any." Bright Water's mad confidence seemed to be returning. "But neither has her now, so you can relax, sonny."

The warlock did not look as if he would ever relax, but he had released the invisible bands around Rap, and Oothiana was looking less frightened. The wind blew cool on Rap's sweat-soaked hair.

The witch stroked her fire chick, turning it mauve again. Rap heard its strange purring noise inside his head.

"The elf wanted her, and I told him where she was."

"So?"

"She was in Zark, in Arakkaran. Lith'rian just happened to have a votary in the town, and he got the child away before Olybino did."

"What's South doing with a votary in East's sector?" Zinixo growled, looking puzzled and even more suspicious than before.

"Who knows? You mean you don't have any tucked away in odd places? Dear Gods, the kid's more honest than he looks! Anyway, this one's only a mage, but he charmed her into going off with him somehow. She's out in the desert—heading for South's sector, I expect. East doesn't know where she is, so he can't produce her for the imperor, as he said he would."

"What's South up to?" The dwarf's expression had turned murderous again, at this talk of the elf.

Rap was wondering the same. He cared nothing for the fate of the impish troops in Krasnegar, nor what the goblins might do to harry them when they left; but he did care about Inos. If the warlock of the south was as bad as these other two wardens, then she must be in horrible danger. He had hated the thought of her being in the power of the sorceress Rasha, but now he thought the wardens were even worse. They were going to marry her off to a goblin, and it sounded as if the imperor had agreed.

"I warned you," Bright Water sneered. "Never ask 'why' of elves, lad. They think like drunk moths. But East thinks he has Kalkor to worry about, the goblins have burned Pondague and are raiding over the pass, and now he can't deliver up a girl the imperor wants to meet. Poor ninny's as red as a djinn."

Zinixo chewed a fingernail. His suspicion seemed to darken the night. "Show me!" he said.

Bright Water shrugged, almost dislodging the fire chick. She glanced around the room, then went into her weird dance again, waltzing over the magic carpet, and eventually arriving in front of the big oval mirror on the wall. She pouted at it for a moment, stroking her fire chick, which turned a ghostly rose shade.

"Must be almost dawn in Zark," she muttered. "They may have struck camp already." The glass shimmered and changed. Rap discovered that he was digging his nails into his palms—this was nastily reminiscent of the magic casement in Krasnegar, which had caused so much trouble.

Soon he heard a strange noise, unlike anything he had ever heard before. It was faint, but it came from the mirror, a monstrous bellowing, distant and muffled, as if filtered through a thick window. Everyone in the Gazebo was watching whatever it was that the witch was doing.

Without warning, a hairy animal face appeared in the frame. It bared giant teeth and roared.

Zinixo leaped to his feet. "What the Evil?"

"It's a camel!" Oothiana shouted, and Bright Water cackled shrilly. The monster faded back into darkness. Now a pearly light flowed from the glass, as if it were a window to somewhere brighter than the darkness that still enshrouded the Gazebo. Bright Water's shadow lay long on the floor; the lamps seemed to have dimmed.

Then a new scene appeared, a row of dark shapes under trees. Rap recognized the trees. They were palms, and Thinal had said that there were palms in Zark. He wiped his forehead and glanced at Little Chicken, who was scowling, and at Oothiana, obviously fascinated. Zinixo was still gnawing his finger. At the far side of the room, the fake goblin Raspnex was being inscrutable, thick greenish arms folded over his barrel chest.

The view crept closer to the dark shapes, and they became more distinct, a line of black tents.

"This one, I think," the witch said. She might be crazy, but her sorcery was impressive. The tent that now dominated the view was much like all the others, except that it seemed to be flapping more, as if its ropes were loose, and its door flap hung awry. "Let's see, shall we? *Queen Inosolan!*" Everyone jumped at her shout.

Rap eased forward to the edge of the couch. Nobody noticed.

For a moment only the wind and the sea spoke, and the muffled monster howls from the glass. He held his breath. Inos? Alive and well? He could hear his heart pounding. Again the witch called out *"Queen Inosolan!"*

The flap moved. Someone scrambled out on hands and knees,

then stood up, a dark-shrouded figure with long bright hair. She peered around as if to locate the voice. Even in the predawn gloom, Rap knew her. Tears prickled under his eyelids.

"There she is!" Bright Water remarked triumphantly, stepping aside so that everyone could have a clear view.

They were going to marry Inos off to Little Chicken!

"Oh, that's very nice!" Zinixo said. "Tender and succulent! She shall be my guest until the Four have arranged a marriage for her."

No! No! Rap lurched to his feet, ignoring a gesture from Oothiana. He bounded across the room to the looking glass.

"Inos!" he shouted. "It's me! Rap!"

Inos looked around, puzzled. The glass was muffling his voice. Then she seemed to see him. Her mouth opened, and he heard a faint scream.

Clutching the ornate frame with both hands, he yelled as loud as he could. "Inos! It's a trap! Run away, Inos! Don't stay with them!"

He had hardly time to register another shape that came bursting out of the tent. It charged straight at him with sword flashing in the dawn. Yet an image in a mirror could not hurt him.

Magic could. Before he could utter another word he was hurled away by an invisible impact as heavy as a charging bull.

He crashed full length to the floor, far from the looking glass.

Magic shadow shapes:
>   We are no other than a moving row
>   Of Magic Shadow-shapes that come and go
>   Round with the Sun-illumined Lantern held
>   In Midnight by the Master of the Show.
>   Fitzgerald, *The Rubaiyat of Omar Khayyam*
>   (§68, 1879)

❰ NINE ❱

Dead yesterday

1

The stones dug sharply into Inos's hands and hip. She was
sprawled on the cold ground with Kade's comforting arms around
her; shaking uncontrollably, not trusting herself to speak.

"I saw it, also!" Azak loomed protectively over them, still
holding his scimitar and glowering around at the dawn. Fooni
had come out, rubbing sleep from her eyes, bewildered but mer-
cifully silent. Other people were emerging from other tents,
alerted by Inos's scream. The camels kept up their awful bawling
in the background, and the peaks of the Agonistes glowed pink
to the west.

"A *wraith*?" Kade repeated.

"I know not what else," Azak snarled. "Not that I have ever
seen one before. You knew him?" he demanded of Inos.

She nodded miserably.

Rap, oh Rap! It had sounded like Rap. It had looked like
Rap, a faint transparent image in a blur of darkness. She had
even made out his ever-tangled hair and the stupid tattoos on his
face.

But why Rap? She had never thought of Rap as being wicked.
Clumsy, maybe. Stubborn. Apt to do damage without meaning
to, but never *wicked*. Ygginggi had been an evil man. Andor,
too, perhaps. Ekka had certainly schemed most foully. But Inos
would never have imagined that there had been more evil than
good in *Rap*. When the Gods had weighed his soul, then surely
the balance would have been good, and gone to join the Good

275

and become part of it forever, as the sacred texts said. Only a great sinner left a residue of evil that the Evil itself rejected and left behind to haunt the world as a wraith. Not Rap! If Rap had been judged so evil, than what hope was there for her, for her dead father, for anyone?

The others were approaching warily, starting to ask questions. Then the men noticed uncovered female faces and turned back. The women drew closer, jabbering.

" 'Twas nothing!'' Azak insisted, whirling on them fiercely. "Merely a bad dream." When they retreated in haste, he seemed to realize that he was still brandishing his sword; he sheathed it.

Kade tried to lift, and Inos let herself be helped to her feet. She fought to control her trembling limbs. "I'm fine!'' she said.

"Inos?'' Kade whispered, blue eyes wide. "Who was it?''

"It was Rap.''

"Rap? Oh, no!'' But probably Kade was relieved that Inos had not seen her father.

"Who was this Rap?'' Azak demanded.

Inos just shook her head.

Kade explained. "A servant in her father's house. A groom. He was slain by the imps, we thought.''

"He must have died somehow. There are no footprints where I saw him. My blade passed right through the vision.'' Azak also was showing the whites of his eyes. He must be more troubled than he would admit. He rounded on little Fooni and roared at her to make coffee. Fooni fled. Kade helped Inos toward the tent, and suddenly her legs steadied.

"I'm all right,'' she insisted. "I can walk.''

Azak lifted the flap, and they all went inside, away from prying eyes. Inos sprawled loosely down on her bedding and shivered. Kade drew a blanket over her shoulders for her.

"It spoke,'' Azak said. "What did this apparition say to you?''

"It . . . he . . . it said something about me being in a trap. It said to flee, to run away.''

The big man grunted. He adjusted his sword and sat down cross-legged. "Which is exactly what we were about to do.''

"We can't now,'' Inos whispered, thinking of the crowd that had appeared. She huddled the blanket tighter.

"Not today, anyway. Tomorrow we shall be farther inland, away from the boat. And it may not wait for us.'' He scratched at his stubbled face and scowled.

"Wraiths are the embodiment of Evil!" Kade protested. "Whatever it said we must ignore! It would be the height of folly to take the advice of a wraith!"

Inos looked at Azak and they nodded simultaneously.

"We must not trust it!" he said.

Yet it had seemed so much like Rap! It had sounded so much like Rap, Rap very agitated about something. She had never thought of Rap as especially clever. Dogged. Well meaning. Earnest. And had Rap spoken as emphatically as that, he would have had good reason. He had never played silly practical jokes, like Lin or Verantor.

She discovered that her instincts were telling her to trust what the eerie vision had said. *Run away!* But Kade was being sensible. To take the advice of a ghost would be insanely foolish. Its motives would always be evil.

Rap had helped the goblin kill the proconsul. Had that been the wickedness that had tipped the balance? Oh, Rap!

Azak was staring. What must he be thinking of her?

"I'm a fool," she said. "I should not have cried out like that. It was just so sudden, so unexpected."

"Perfectly natural."

Perfectly natural for sheltered palace flowers, but that was not how she wished to be judged.

"No, it was unforgivable. I am ashamed."

"Queen Inosolan," Azak said softly, his dark gaze unwavering, "you reacted by shouting for help. Why not? You faced an unexpected danger. You were alone and unarmed. I reacted by charging like a mad bull. That was not rational or forgivable, for I had not taken time to assess the nature of the enemy. And if you fear that I may think the less of you because of what has just happened, then please set your mind completely at rest. Ever since I watched you ride my most ungovernable horse, my lady, I have never doubted your courage, nor shall I ever doubt it. You taught me that a woman could be brave like few men I know, and that was a wonder beyond all my experience and outside the lore of the ancients."

Huh? Inos gaped. She had never expected to provoke a speech like that from the giant. In fact, she was astonished to discover he was capable of it. She had just found another unexpected facet of his character.

Before she could frame a reply worthy of her Kinvale training, the tent door was darkened by a large bulk. "First Lionslayer, may I enter?"

Azak flashed the women a glance of warning. "Enter and be welcome to my humble abode, Greatness."

Sheik Elkarath stooped and came in, wheezing softly, massive enough to make the tent seem crowded. He had discarded his many-colored garments before leaving the city and now wore a simple white robe. He sank to his knees, not looking at faces. "May all the Gods respect this house," he muttered formally to the matting.

Azak gave a ritual response, offering food and water.

"You have troubles, Lionslayer?" The sheik fingered his rings and still did not raise his eyes.

Azak hesitated, then told the story. Swift sunrise brightened the tent. Inos cowered inside her blanket, still trying to control her shivers.

Thinking of Rap.

"And her Majesty knew the man," Azak concluded. The only item he had not mentioned was that the sheik's chief guard had been planning to desert and take his companions with him. But there were bundles lying around, and a wily old trader might well be wondering why someone had been packing at so early an hour.

"Majesty?" he murmured, with a glance in the general direction of Inos.

"One of her late father's stablehands," Kade explained. "Slain by the imps who pursued us."

The old man thoughtfully stroked his snowy beard with plump fingers that splattered rainbows. "And what did it say to you?"

Inos found her tongue and repeated the wraith's words as well as she could recall them.

"Ah!" Elkarath nodded. The sunlight flashed crimson from the rubies on his headband, and some jewel among his rings streaked orange fire. "Did the sorceress ever meet this man?"

"Yes!" Inos said excitedly. "Yes, he was in the chamber when she came. It was she who showed me later that he had been killed!"

He chuckled. "Then she is playing tricks on you! Do you see?"

"Of course!" Relief surged through Inos like spring sunshine melting winter snow. "It was a sending from Rasha!" She looked to Azak, who grinned with a ferocious joy.

"Indeed!" he exclaimed. "This is most logical! Mayhap the harlot cannot find us herself, but is capable of sending evil spirits after us. They might take any form! Who knows the limita-

tions of her power? I do think you have solved the mystery,
Greatness!''

"I agree!'' Inos said. ''Aunt?''

Kade nodded, although she still seemed doubtful.

''Then I take it that you will not obey the commands of this
abomination?'' Elkarath inquired softly.

''Of course not!'' Inos said. ''Your wisdom has solved the
mystery, your Greatness. We are relieved, and much in your
debt.''

''Let us hope that by nightfall we shall be out of her range,
then.''

The others exchanged smiles of agreement and relief. The
sinister chill of the evil undead had been banished and replaced
by indignation at the sorceress's spite. Feeling much warmer
now and rather foolish under her blanket, Inos threw it off and
laughed. How stupid to be frightened by an apparition so insub-
stantial that Azak's sword had passed right through it!

Rap must still be dead, but she need not worry that he had
become a wraith. After all, death came to everyone. Rap's end
had been tragic, but she was beginning to accept it, and her
father's, also. They would both have gone to join the Good, and
she would not let Rasha persuade her otherwise.

Elkarath chuckled and started to rise. Azak jumped up to help
him. Even Kade was smiling.

There could be no thought now of leaving the sheik's caravan.
Ahead lay the desert and adventure and the road to Ullacarn.

The emergency was over.

2

For some minutes, Rap just lay and tried to collect his spilled
wits. The impact with the floor had left him winded and shaken,
hurting at every protruding bone: knees, elbows, and hips. There
had been a man in her tent. Two hard landings in one night were
two too many. Counting the one the night before would make
three, but a convenient sorcery had cured the effects of the first
one. Even so, he ought to take better care of himself. Wouldn't
always have sorcery around to help. His face still throbbed from
Bright Water's first attack, and it was resting on a threadbare
rug stinking of age and dust; his nose was dribbling blood on
it. A man in her tent?

There were dead leaves all around him. A moment ago they
had been casting shadows across the tattered landscape of car-

pet. Now they weren't. That meant that the magic mirror was no longer showing Zark; no more dawn sunshine and palms and sand and tents and Inos. He couldn't hear the camels, either.

No need to hurry, then. There had been a man in her tent. Bright Water was speaking. Then the dwarf. They both laughed. Zinixo must be feeling extremely sure of himself if he could laugh. Perhaps they were laughing at him, idiot stableboy spread out bleeding on the floor. What ever happened to the bold young hero who was going to go to Zark and find Inos because he'd told her he was coming and he wanted to keep his word? A few hard knocks and he shattered like a crystal goblet.

He raised his head, and it didn't fall off. It was none of his business if Inos had been sharing a tent with a man. The witch was babbling something to Oothiana, calling her by the wrong name. Then she spun around, warbling one of her fragments of song, and somehow arrived on the shiny magic mat. There might be a moral there: Bright Water goes round and round but she gets where she wants to be. With the dragon glowing amber, witch and fire chick faded away and vanished.

Had she bought him from the dwarf or not? Had Zinixo bought Inos? Would Inos heed Rap's pathetic warning? It had been all he could do, to shout to her like that. He hoped she had understood.

He pushed himself up, but didn't quite make it to a sitting position. He leaned on his arms instead and blinked to get his eyes working. It couldn't be any more than a month since Inos left Krasnegar, and probably not as much. His head ached.

"Right, Uncle," the warlock said. "Go and get 'em!"

The fake goblin stalked over to the magic portal. Rap caught a rank whiff of rancid grease as he went by. Of course Inos had always been popular and could probably make new friends very easily, but a month wasn't very long to make really close friends. Intimate friends.

"Tell me exactly what I must do, Omnipotence," Raspnex said.

"Being cautious, Uncle?"

"Nephew, you make anyone cautious."

The boy laughed, but his mirth had a mean ring to it. "Go north and stay close to the imps when they leave Krasnegar. If you detect power, mark who's using it. Don't reveal yourself. Serve my interests as you see them."

"To the death, of course?"

"Of course. Take the welcome mat with you."

The older dwarf shrugged and headed over to stand on the shiny rug. He shut his eyes, as if he were concentrating hard.

Rap struggled to his knees. The witch had shouted, Inos had come out of the tent, Rap had frightened her, she had screamed, and the man had come out. Big. Young. Can use a sword. Same tent.

Raspnex and magic carpet faded away together.

The warlock yelled in triumph and did a little dance like Bright Water's, his boots thumping loud on the planks. He held out a hand to Oothiana and spun her around roughly.

"Oh, I shall have East where I want him! He'll be ordering his legions about in a shrill soprano from now on!"

Rap scrambled to his feet and reeled out of the way as the two sorcerers went whirling by. Inos's tent had been quite large, hadn't it? Too big for just two people, maybe. There might have been other people in there, as well. Her aunt, perhaps.

Zinixo stopped dancing. He gripped Oothiana's face in both hands and pulled it down to kiss. Then he released her and spun around to face the oval glass, which had become a mirror again.

"Now, the girl!"

Alarms rang in Rap's aching head. This vile little monster was not going to get his hands on Inos! Except that there was no one who could stop him. Not Rap. Not that big man with the sword. He must have been a guard, and there would have been other people in that tent, as well. Queens did not travel alone in the desert.

But before Rap could force his muddled brains to work, someone or something did stop the warlock. He turned back to scowl at Oothiana. "You agree?" he demanded, although she had said nothing.

She shook her head.

Apparently the dwarf valued her judgment. He pouted up at her and said, "Explain!"

"The witch said that South had stolen her away from East—"

"From the sorceress, she said."

"Well, before East could steal her from the sorceress, South did. And in East's sector. Why?"

"They're allies, you mean?"

"Yes, Omnipotence. And that so-convenient votary? It doesn't ring true, even for an elf."

"You think North was lying?" His stony face darkened.

The proconsul nodded. She seemed to have relaxed her magic,

because she was looking drained and exhausted. Haggard, even. "She made friends with you tonight, but she may be trying to make trouble for you, too. If you snatch the girl from East's sector, he isn't going to like it."

Zinixo guffawed. "But I'm going to have him staked out on the anthill! And he tried to kill me," he added angrily. Getting no response, he said, "Tell me what you think!"

The sorceress ran fingers through her hair, pushing it back. She took a minute to gather her thoughts. Rap's head was clearing, too. Bright Water had apparently gained what she wanted, Little Chicken, and she had given up nothing of her own, merely a chance to spy on Warlock Olybino. She could spy on him herself at the same time, with her own votaries, so she hadn't lost anything very much, and the dwarf didn't seem to have thought of that. Had Oothiana?

"You've done North a favor," she said, "for what it's worth. The elf's your big trouble. He always will be. I think you should woo East. You're going to know his votaries, or some of them. He's the weakest of the four of you, isn't he?" When the warlock nodded, she said, "Well, then he would value an alliance with you, because you're stronger than either of the others. Don't make him mad. Woo him!"

"Isolate South!" The dwarf showed his teeth. "Very good! And we still don't really know what the yellow whoreson was doing when he gave North that dragon. Tell East where the girl is, you think?"

"No, Sire. No yet, anyway. He's promised her to the imperor, so he must be hunting for her. But wait and see what happens. Find out who does control her. If South really does steal her away from East's sector, then their alliance will surely be over! Play a waiting game. Knowledge is power."

Zinixo thought about it, then nodded reluctantly. "All right. We'll wait and see." Abruptly he headed for the magic portal.

"Master!" Oothiana said. "What do I do with the prisoners?"

Faun and goblin caught each other's eyes. They, also, were interested in the answer to that question.

The warlock scowled at Little Chicken, then at Rap. "We have to send them back to the mainland."

"Buy passage for them, then?"

He shook his big head vehemently. "Why waste money? They're healthy-looking types. Send them down to the docks in the morning and sell them to a galley master. Be sure you get at least ten gold imperials for each of them. What happens after is their problem.''

And with that, Warlock Zinixo hauled open the magic portal and went back to Hub. The door slammed behind him.

The others all relaxed with audible sighs.

A load of weariness fell on Rap like an avalanche. It had been a very hard night!

So he was going to be a galley slave after all?

Back to the mainland. Then what? A lifetime chained to an oar? Or Raven Totem and a terrible death? Or Zark and Inos?

There had been a man in her tent.

3

For once the cool sea breeze had failed in Milflor. Muggy air stuffed throats like wool and although the sun was barely above the spiky roof of the Gazebo, it was brutally roasting the docks already. Noontime was going to be hell. Sailors and slaves, merchants and porters—all dragged their feet as they slouched about their business. All cursed and sweated and wiped and panted. Even the sea gulls seemed to have deserted their usual hunting grounds. No one was moving fast.

Rap certainly wasn't. Fettered at ankle and wrist and neck, all chained together so that he was doubled over, he walked with his hands between his knees. He was very close to being naked. The sun scorched his bare back, flagstones broiled his bare feet, and the anklets took more skin with every step. He would not have Oothiana around to mend him any more. She had repaired his bruises when she put him back in the jail, and that had not been very long before dawn. She had also put a compulsion on him so he could make no more escape attempts, but he could hardly blame her for doing that. He had liked Oothiana. She deserved better than to be slave and plaything for the warlock.

And she had talked Zinixo out of kidnapping Inos.

At last Rap had a chance to inspect the ships tied up in Milflor. He had shuffled half the length of the docks and would likely have to shuffle all the way to the end, and then partway back. If he went too fast he lost more skin; if he went too slow he got hit with a sword, and even the flat of a sword could hurt.

He was doing better than Little Chicken, though. The legionaries had comrades to commemorate, and they knew of only one goblin in Faerie. Every few minutes their victim would be pushed too hard, or just tripped up, and would crash to the roadway in a wild jangle of chains. Then two men would kick him until he scrambled up again. The dull-faced young tesserary was not merely encouraging his men in this entertainment, he was taking his turn with the others. Rap's heart jumped into his mouth every time, for if Little Chicken lost his temper, he would tear those chains off like spiderwebs and hold another massacre. Fortunately he was very eager to be put on a ship and was therefore willing to endure the indignity. The physical pain he would be accepting as an honor.

There were galleys and there were sailing ships. The latter were impressive, for the tide was in and their freeboard put their decks high above the roadway. Some were large as floating castles, grander than anything Rap had ever seen in Krasnegar—vast ornamental wooden palaces, colorful, intricate, and strange. Their luxury cabins would have honored monarchs. In most of them the lesser passengers' deck was an overcrowded slum, while the crew's quarters below them were a prospect to nauseate maggots.

But the galleys interested him more at the moment. They were much smaller; narrow and low, and generally cleaner, because galleys were entirely reserved to the rich. A galley needed an enormous crew for its size, all of whom would have good appetites. Galleys could carry very little paying cargo, but they were the safest vessels in the doldrums of the Nogids.

Most of the galleys he saw were little more than open boats with a row of cramped passenger cabins standing along the centerline. They looked top-heavy and would be unmanageable in any sort of crosswind. The rowers must sleep on their benches, or on bare planks.

Letting his farsight roam the harbor was much more entertaining than staring down at the flags or his own dusty, blood-streaked feet, or Little Chicken's, or the soldiers' boots. Whatever the future held, he would not regret leaving the baleful land of Faerie. Even slavery could be accepted for a while, if it moved him closer to Inos.

There had been a man in her tent. He had thought about that when he should have been catching some sleep in the fag end of the night. He had concluded that there were so many possible explanations for what he might possibly have seen that he must just forget the whole incident. It was none of his business anyway. Inos was his queen, and he was merely her loyal subject, nothing more. Even if she chose to create a public scandal, it would be none of his business. He could not imagine Inos creating a public scandal—not, at least, that sort of public scandal—but she was certainly entitled to do so if she chose.

The big man with the sword might even have been the mage Bright Water had mentioned, assuming that the witch had spoken any truth at all. Inos could no more keep a mage out of her tent than Lady Oothiana could refuse to serve the disgusting warlock.

Forget about the man in the tent.

Rap had escaped from goblins, from imps, and now from a warlock. That was the most surprising escape of all. And why should sailors be any different? Once on the mainland, he would escape again and start walking.

There was no such thing as slavery in the Impire. The legionaries were seeking a ship's captain willing to transport two convicts back to the mainland. It was an interesting fable, but in practice the sailors inspected the alleged convicts as carefully as old Hononin scrutinized a horse—poking, pinching, peering in their mouths and eyes, lifting their slaves' loincloths to check for disease or mutilation. The ship's destination was irrelevant and never mentioned. These convicts would sail to the ends of their lives, or until they reached a land where marketing of people was less overregulated.

The bidding was a farce. How much to ship them, then? the bored tesserary would ask. The sailor would name a price. The soldier would automatically tell him it was too low, he must charge more.

He would write down the final offer, and then move on to the next berth to offer his wares again. In time the parade would return to the highest bidder. It was going to take all day, likely.

But suddenly Rap's chin was grabbed in a horny hand and twisted up until he was staring into pallid blue eyes above a silver floor-brush mustache.

"You heal quickly, halfman." Gathmor was wearing more than he had done the previous day, but he was still bare-chested, crude and dangerous as a white bear.

"I had help, thir." Of necessity, Rap spoke through clenched teeth.

"Still want to be a rower?"

"Yeth, thir."

"How many fingers am I holding out on my other hand?"

The jotunn's voice was low, his other hand was behind his

back, but when Rap hesitated, his thumb found the pressure point below Rap's ear and squeezed mercilessly.

"Three, thir," Rap said as tears of pain sprang unbidden into his eyes.

"Now?"

"Two, thir." He was released.

"What was all that about?" the tesserary asked, not caring much.

"That goblin really mess up half a century coupla days ago?"

Rap could not see the speakers' faces, but he heard the change in tone. "Where did you hear that lie, sailor?"

"Saloon gossip. Did he?"

"There was a riot."

"I heard otherwise. How much for them both?"

"You bid on a contract to—"

"Come with me." The jotunn led the tesserary aside for serious talk. Gathmor's eyes would have told him that Rap's injuries had been cured by sorcery, but how had he learned that Rap had farsight? A sailor with occult farsight would be invaluable. And he seemingly knew that this goblin could outrow anyone—if he chose to, of course. Gathmor was seemingly remarkably well informed.

Rap edged his feet around and twisted his head sideways to see how the bribery was coming along. Another man was blocking his view. He was dashingly dressed in the loose clothes that the rich affected in such warm climes, but they were superbly cut and were being worn with supreme élan. A broad-brimmed hat shadowed his handsome bronzed face, a rapier dangled rakishly at his hip. He flashed Rap a smile of snow-white teeth.

In the first surge of his fury, Rap tried to straighten. He paid for his error with more skin from wrists and ankles. Had he not been chained, he would have attacked, for this was the monster who had used foul occult mastery to deceive Inos. Hatred made Rap tremble. He could imagine nothing in the world more pleasurable than grinding that pretty face into the street.

His second emotion was a stab of fear. Where there was Andor, there could be Darad.

"Hello again, Rap."

"What'd you want?"

Andor's smile became tinged with sadness, or possibly pity. "Thinal thinks you're lying, Rap."

"What?"

"Thinal's very good at detecting lies, you know. Best of the lot of us. He thought you were lying when you said you didn't know your word of power. Not nice to lie to your friends, Rap!''

So Andor was still after Rap's word, and if Rap was now capable of telling it, then Darad could be called to encourage the telling and arrange the unfortunate consequences.

Andor watched Rap's reaction, and his smile grew even wider. "Rowing is fine exercise! Better even than running, I'm told.''

"But you won't be trying it.''

"Er, no.'' Andor sighed regretfully. "I'm often told that my hands are one of my best features. But I'll be in Cabin One. Do drop in for a chat sometime. Ah . . . Looks like your fare has been paid. Well, see you on board, old buddy. *Bon voyage!*''

4

Andor led the way along the quay. Rap followed, with Little Chicken hobbling behind him, and the sailor bringing up the rear; having just paid out much good gold for two healthy thralls, Gathmor was taking no chances on losing them before they even reached *Stormdancer*.

A thrall with farsight, an occult slave . . . to sailors, Rap was beyond price. Shuffling along in his awkward trussed posture, he lamented the irony of his new situation. Minutes ago he had been congratulating himself on escaping from Faerie. Faerie was a good place to escape out of, but what had he escaped into?

What chance would he ever have of escaping from sailors who knew of his occult talent? A pilot who could see in fog, in the dark? The crew would guard him like a chest of rubies, the most precious thing aboard.

So the sailors wanted his talent, but Andor was still after his word of power. Perhaps Rap had been unfair in his attitude to Thinal, for whatever his suspicions, the little alleyrat had at least refrained from calling Darad. Andor was not so picky. The gentleman had fewer scruples than the thief.

And Little Chicken wanted his hide. Having been hailed as a king by a coven of sorcerers, the goblin saw himself as nobody's trash now. Now he was the worst danger of all. Given a fraction of a chance, he was going to toss Rap over his shoulder and lay course for the taiga, for Raven Totem and his destiny.

Bystanders on the Milflor dock saw a gentleman and a sailor escorting two convicts, and they paid slim heed. What Rap saw was three jailers escorting him. He wondered which one was going to get him.

He wondered if they might all kill one another off and leave him free to go.

Of it they might end up with one-third apiece.

Then he was following Andor down the plank to *Stormdancer*'s deck and a future as a galley slave.

Dead yesterday:
> Ah, fill the Cup:—what boots it to repeat
> How time is slipping underneath our Feet:
>   Unborn Tomorrow, and dead Yesterday,
> Why fret about them if Today be sweet!
>
>   Fitzgerald, *Rubaiyat of Omar Khayyam*
>   (§37, 1859)

⫷ TEN ⫸

Water willy-nilly

1

The helmsman's deck aft was very tiny and presently crowded. Still clattering chains, Rap was handed over to Kani, a wiry young fellow with the hopelessly battered face of a jotunn who couldn't fight well. That was not his only surprising quality. His sea-blue eyes twinkling happily through a straggling mop of silver-blond hair, his lopsided, gap-toothed grin was half hidden by a matching mustache, and yet he chattered like a purebred imp.

He began by shaking Rap's hand crushingly—a noisy and awkward procedure because of the chains—and thereafter he just kept talking. Wind's from the west, unusual, he said as he set to work removing Rap's fetters, be underway in an hour. What's that round your eyes? he asked. Makes you look like a raccoon. Ever done any rowing? Is that other one really a goblin? Heard of them, never seen one. Are you left-handed or right-handed? Can't row bare-assed like that, get you some decent gear. Grab some chow from that basket if you're hungry and come along and meet the lads. And as soon as Rap was unshackled, Kani led the way into the chaos of a hot, dim, and very crowded tunnel.

On one hand the walls and doors of the passengers' cabins stood taller than a man. On the other, shade awnings slanted steeply down to the ship's side, ending barely high enough to clear the heads of men sitting there. More air and light could have struggled in from both ends of this awkward gut, had not it been so completely packed with bodies: men on benches, men on the baggage between the benches, men sitting or kneeling in the gangway, men walking and standing and passing bundles and bags around. In all there were at least forty sailors scrambling about in the narrow space, and it was dark and hot and unpleasant, filled with odors of men and ancient spills of every fluid the human body could produce.

Bewildered by the friendly reception, Rap followed Kani as best he could, banging knees and elbows, stubbing toes, squeezing past people, and clambering over oars and benches and stacks of supplies, all of which were being crammed into completely inadequate storage below the seats. And Kani was continually introducing him, so he must cling greedily to his treasure of victuals with his left arm, while at the same time trying to smile convincingly as his right hand was deliberately juiced by the boisterous grips of professional oarsmen.

At times he found himself squashed breathless inside a pack of six or seven sweaty sailors while someone or something important went by. One of these close encounters put him nose to nose with Kani, who peered through his dangling flaxen thatch and exclaimed, "You've got gray eyes! Never saw a faun with gray eyes."

"I'm half jotunn."

"*Hey!* Why didn't you say so? Rape, of course? But that's terrific! Was wondering why Number One would buy a faun, even a large economy size. Guys, Rap's got jotunn blood in him!"

Rap was then congratulated all around on being part jotunn, his back slapped bruisingly, and his hand pumped again, more vigorously and agonizingly than ever. Gradually he made sense out of Kani's disorganized chatter. Although *Stormdancer*'s home port was Durthing, on the Imperial island of Kith, all of her officers were jotnar, as were all the rowers except for two imps, one djinn, and a few assorted half-breeds.

"I'm pure jotunn, of course," Kani said, his eyes daring Rap to contest the point or belittle its importance, "but it's no secret that I've never seen Nordland."

"Nor your father, nor his before him," remarked another voice. Kani wheeled, and eyed the speaker. He was a sour-faced jotunn rating named Crunterp, much larger than Kani. Too large, evidently, because Kani did not take offense. He said, "Um."

Crunterp smirked and went back to coiling a rope.

"O'course jotnar prefer jotnar," Kani said, squeezing by him.

"Only natural. But you being half jotunn helps, and Number One runs a fair ship. Pull your weight and the worst you'll get is wisecracks and a bit o' jostling to keep you humble. No real hardship."

An inexplicable lump had settled in Rap's throat. Apparently life on *Stormdancer* would not be the living hell he had been expecting. In fact it might turn out to be dangerously enjoyable. For far too long, he had been deprived of friendly company. Goblins didn't count, and even before he'd acquired his green shadow, he'd been shunned as a seer in Krasnegar. Just to be smiled at and smile back was a forgotten treat. Let them batter his shoulders and crush his fingers! He'd grown up around jotnar and knew their rough ways. He knew their good points, too.

After much further heaving and pushing, Kani brought Rap to his assigned bench, almost all of it already occupied by his assigned benchmate, a dog-faced rolypoly giant who apparently answered to the name of Ballast.

"Ballast," Kani said solemnly, "is one-quarter troll and three-quarters jotunn, and therefore mostly troll."

The big man exploded in bellows of laughter that seemed to rock the ship, while Kani's eye said plainly that the joke was old and threadbare. Probably it always won the same reaction from the big man, for if Ballast had twice normal bulk, he seemed to combine it with little more than half normal brains. But he was the first man on board to shake Rap's hand without deliberately squeezing it. Alone among the half-naked crew, he was fully dressed, even his arms being draped in long sleeves. Rap decided that he liked this good-natured colossus and hoped that it was only his clothes that smelled so bad. He would obviously be capable of doing much more than his fair share of the rowing.

Feeling happier by the minute, Rap perched on the tiny corner of bench left to him and began to tear at the loaf and cheese he had been clutching so fondly.

"Here, put your chains on," Kani said and knelt to shackle Rap's ankles. When he stood up, he grinned and remarked, "Don't forget to unfasten 'em if you need go to the heads. You'll break your neck otherwise. Want anything, just ask Ballast." And he went wriggling off through the mad chaos of bodies and baggage.

What Rap wanted right away was an explanation of the chains, but he quickly discovered that Ballast was not the man to ask. He turned instead to Ogi, who was one of the two purebred imps—short, swarthy, and almost as wide as a dwarf. Ogi shared the next bench forward with a jotunn named Verg.

He chuckled at the question and rattled the chain on his own ankle. "A sailor's always chained to his ship. An old jotunn tradition!"

"Not in the north, it isn't," Rap said.

Another chuckle. "There's no slavery in the Impire, right? That's the legal legend, right? We're all free men on this ship—or we were until you got here. 'Cept for a couple of rookies, we're all partners; every man has a share. But there are bought sailors on the Summer Seas, lad. You and your friend aren't the only thralls around. So there's the tradition—all the hands are chained, always. I've heard some farm workers have similar customs, except it's more of a religious rite with them, symbolizing brotherhood of the soil, or something. We tend to observe ours in Imperial ports, and not elsewhere. Un'erstand now?"

So Rap was a real slave wearing fake chains. He found that quite ironic—and very realistic. He wasn't going to do much escaping with seventy or eighty sailors watching him. Not when they all owned a piece of him.

A couple of hours after he boarded, lines were cast off, and the oars run out, but no green hand would be allowed to row while the vessel was still in harbor. Ballast rowed while Rap sat in the gangway and gutted fish.

Only one man was needed on each oar, usually, and in this case it was not for long. As soon as the ship had crossed the bar, the sail was hoisted. There had been no wind in the town and there was little enough even out to sea, but what there was could still move a ship about as fast as rowers could. And always it had to be one or the other; under sail the ship heeled over, making rowing impossible.

Sliding smoothly over the swell, *Stormdancer* set course for the horizon within a convoy of fourteen.

The awnings were taken down and the chains were thrown off, with no regrets. Sunlight and a fresh breeze made Rap feel even better than before, confident that he had enough jotunn in him that he need never fear seasickness. By then, too, he had realized that neither his faunish appearance nor his slave status was going to matter at all on *Stormdancer*. His inexperience would, and everyone was going to work very hard at curing him of that, but otherwise he was being accepted as just another new hand. That discovery was so unexpected and so exhilarating that he felt drunk.

Soon after departure, young Kani's demolished face appeared again, complete with grin. He had been sent to give some lessons, he said, and he thereupon conducted Rap all over the ship, from stem to stern and up the mast, also, naming and explaining. Use the wrong name for anything after this, he warned, and Rap would feel the mate's fist.

The master was the Old Man, and a truly old man, Gnurr. He left most of the work to Gathmor, who was Number One, and this Number One could lick any man aboard and was willing to prove it at any time. Kani obviously admired his talent greatly, but he did add in passing that Gathmor was a fine mariner, as well.

The tour ended on the catwalk that ran along the top of the line of cabins, and this seemed to be the only clear space on the ship. An elderly couple sat on chairs at the forward end, frowning at the intruders.

"Passengers' deck," Kani said. "Don't come up here without orders. Now, any questions?" He leaned back against the flimsy rail.

"Why did we come up here now?" Rap asked.

"Time to start your exercises. Hey, Verg! Pass up an oar, lad."

An oar was three spans long and loaded at the handle end with a counterweight of solid lead. Kani dropped it at Rap's feet.

"What do I do with this?"

"Lift it overhead and then lay down. That's all."

"For how long?" Rap asked unhappily.

Kani considered, smirking under his windswept mustache. "Two months and you might risk some arm wrestling. Four months you could try a fight or two. Six months and you may be an oarsman. Now there's something I didn't mention—no fighting on board! Save it up for shore, or settle with arm wrestling."

Rap had heard of the rule; it was why newly docked jotnar were notoriously homicidal. "I'll try to restrain myself."

"Except Gathmor, o'course. He's got to be able to maintain discipline."

Rap could not imagine himself ever deliberately provoking Gathmor to a fight, afloat or ashore. "Is the culprit allowed to defend himself?"

Kani chuckled. "Against Gathmor? Defend yourself all you want. It won't make any difference."

About to pick up the oar, Rap hesitated. He decided that he liked Kani, except that he was so reminiscent of any one of a dozen or so jotnar back in Krasnegar that he was making Rap homesick. "The goblin?"

"I 'spect he'll be next. No more questions? Then get moving." Kani turned away.

"You mentioned arm wrestling?"

Kani turned back, alert. "Ship's sport."

"Any side bets?" Rap knew what the answer would be even before the sailor nodded. "Then go lay all the money you can that anyone you like can't beat the goblin."

Kani moved a pace closer. Foam-white lashes drooped menacingly over eyes as blue and deadly as the sea. "I would be very, very upset if I lost a bet like that, Rap," he murmured.

"You won't. It's free coin, but you'll need to do it before you exercise him." Rap stooped to pick up the oar.

A jotunn's favorite sport was brawling, always. Whether wenching or gambling came second depended strictly on the opportunities. Rap had just made a friend.

2

Stormdancer had set sail from Milflor in a convoy of fourteen. By the next morning only eight were still in sight, and the mountains of Faerie had vanished over the edge of the sea. The wind was fitful and continued to veer too much southerly for the crew's comfort, but it was strong enough to prohibit rowing.

The galley was little more than a large boat, and tiny for her complement of eighty. She mounted a square sail on her single mast, but her superstructure and shallow draft made her unweatherly, and under sail she could do nothing but run before the wind. In a calm the rowers would be sheltered by awnings, but those were taken down when the wind blew. The spaces below the benches were crammed with baggage, the benches themselves laden with men, either working or sleeping. The only clear places aboard were tiny decks at stem and stern, and the cabin roof that was reserved for passengers.

Little Chicken soon demonstrated that exercises were wasted on him, so Rap had to suffer up there alone each day with the oar. He would not have believed that anything could have hurt more than his run through the forest with the goblin, but now he was far from sure. He ached from fingers to toes. His hands were raw with blisters, although every man aboard had blisters and always would.

On the second day, while he was slumped in a heap on the boards, enjoying a few minutes' blessed break, he found himself staring at a pair of expensive shoes. He looked up just as Andor crouched down and smiled winningly.

"Hello," he said.

"Go swim," Rap panted.

His remark earned an expression of pained reproof. "I got you off Faerie, didn't I? That was what you wanted?"

Rap ached all over. He was shivering as the sea breeze chilled his sweat. The last thing he wanted was a talk with Andor. "I'd have managed without you."

"But not on this ship. It's a good one, Rap. Lots are worse. Gathmor has a good reputation—I checked. Believe me, I checked very carefully!"

Rap scowled at the too-handsome face. "Why're you leaving? I thought Sagorn wanted to stay?"

Andor snorted. "Crazy old man! Faerie's obviously swarming with magic. Far too dangerous for us!"

"Including me, or just you and the others?"

"All of us! Sagorn's a nitwit in some ways. He'll do anything to gain more learning, but he'd achieve nothing in Faerie except to get us all caught. I saw you talking with Gathmor on the bench. I want to know what happened afterward. Who healed your injuries?"

Already Rap could feel the mastery working on him, softening his resentment, whispering that Andor was a useful friend, that he could be trusted.

"Go away! I don't want to talk to you."

"But you should! We can help each other. Listen, Rap. It wasn't me that sold you to the goblins. It was Darad. I didn't want to call him. I had no choice."

"You set that up—"

Andor looked hurt. "No! If I'd planned to loose Darad on you, I could have done it as soon as we left Krasnegar, couldn't I? God of Villains, I could have done it any time. I had months when I could have trapped you—in your room, or the guards' gym, or the stables. I really hoped we'd get through the forest without trouble. And if we did meet with the goblins, I honestly thought you'd agree to share, then." He sighed. "Yes, I was after your word of power, but I'd have shared mine, also. Believe me!''

Rap knew he could never look Andor in the eye and lie to him. He stared at the hateful oar lying on the deck between them. "I don't know any word of power!"

"Thinal thinks you do."

"He's wrong."

Andor sighed. "I told you, Thinal's the best of all of us at detecting lies. He decided that you do know your word of power. That's good enough for me. Maybe you didn't once, but you do now."

Rap did not answer. He was shivering and starting to stiffen up, and any minute now Gathmor would be shouting at him to get back to work. Below him the sailors were noisily arguing, cleaning, tidying, repairing, or just sprawled on benches, snoring.

"Sagorn hoped to find more words in Faerie," Andor said. "Me, I'm a gambler."

Now Rap did look up to meet that soulful, earnest gaze. "Gambler?"

Andor smiled triumphantly. "You're a man of destiny, my friend. I don't know what that destiny is, but magic seems to collect around you in a way I've never met before; that none of us have met before. A witch? A sorceress? How about a warlock, maybe? In Faerie?"

"Go away!" Rap shouted, tearing loose from those hypnotic dark eyes. He stared instead at Andor's silver-buckled shoes; he heard a hateful chuckle.

"Can't go very far at the moment. But we'll see when we get to Kith. You and I will have a talk then. I'll have to think of some way to get you off this tub, as I did help to get you on. We might encourage our green friend to take up a maritime career permanently, though?"

"That won't be easy."

"Perhaps not. But I do think Sagorn was wrong. I think our best bet is to stay close to our friend Rap. That way we'll meet lots of sorcerers, I suspect. And maybe one of them will be willing to lift our curse."

"Rap!" Gathmor's voice roared from below. "Get busy!"

Rap rose stiffly and stooped to grasp the accursed oar.

Andor stood up, also. "That would be easy work for an adept."

Rap heaved the oar overhead, scowled at his companion, and

lowered it back to the deck again. He managed not to whimper at the pain.

"Come to my cabin later," Andor said. "I'll tell you my word first. I promise that! Mine first, then you tell me yours."

Again Rap raised the oar, keeping time with the roll of the ship, but this time he closed his eyes. Down . . .

"I'll tell you mine first, Rap, if you'll promise to share."

Up . . . And then call Darad, later?

"You're an honest man, Rap. I'll trust you."

Down . . .

"Even if you won't trust me, I'll trust you."

Up . . .

Gods, but it was tempting! Andor had been a good friend to him in Krasnegar, when no one else would speak to him. An adept would handle this damnable oar easily.

Down . . .

Eventually Andor tired of the game and went away.

Up . . .

Blinking sweat from his eyes, Rap watched him go.

Down . . .

Had Andor stayed another ten seconds, likely he would have won.

Up . . .

Rap could no more resist Andor than he could fight Darad.

Down . . .

3

Year in and year out, *Stormdancer* shuttled back and forth to Faerie. By playing off the prevailing wind—such as it was— against the prevailing current, on four trips out of five a skilled mariner like Gnurr or Gathmor could manage the run from Milflor to Kith with very little need for oars. But on Rap's second night aboard, a gale sprang up out of the south-southeast, a very rare event. For four days Gnurr held her head as much to the east and north as he could, but no one liked the resulting course, or where it led. Rowing was impossible in that weather. The crew became crabby; the passengers vanished into the hell of seasickness.

Every day Rap endured longer periods of lonely torment with the oar. As his strength increased, so Gathmor raised his demands, and Rap was amused to find himself savoring nostalgic memories of old Sergeant Thosolin and his petty testings. He was pestered no more by Andor, for Andor was an imp, and imps were poor sailors. Rap had the passengers' deck to himself as he swung his oar up and down in a mindless fog.

Even Little Chicken rarely bothered him. The goblin, of course, had soon become arm-wrestling champion of the ship, unwittingly earning Kani a year's wages on his first two bouts. No one had been willing to bet on the third. The sailors quickly accepted him as just another nonjotunn curiosity. They assumed that his unnatural strength was a racial trait and joked about raiding the northlands to collect more like him.

Stormdancer carried seven passengers: Andor the gentleman tourist, an elderly bishop and his wife, a young Imperial playboy who had been visiting his retired parents, a horse-faced, desiccated matron who wrote popular romances and was planning one about Faerie, and a viscount of middle years, honeymooning with a much younger wife. Obviously they must all be wealthy, or they could not have afforded the fare. Obviously they were all either brave or foolish, also, for the crossing from Faerie was never a sure thing. As the days passed, one by one they found their sea legs and emerged again from their cabins.

Night by night the convoy scattered. By the fifth day the last two sails had gone and thereafter *Stormdancer* was alone under the blue dome of heaven. On the sixth day the wind suddenly failed, having done all the damage it could. Thereafter Rap made muscles and blisters with real rowing. Real rowing was much worse than exercising, and he was grateful for the extra strength he had gained already.

Day by day he settled into the routine life of a sailor. When not rowing, he scrubbed and peeled and baited as he was told. He emptied the passenger's slop buckets, he cleaned fish, he polished and mopped. Such simple labor he could handle as well as any man alive, always doing the best he could, because that was his way. As he completed each task he was rewarded with another. He received neither punishment nor praise and looked for neither; he was more than happy to be accepted as just another hand. Somewhere between Hononin's stables and *Stormdancer*, a boy had become a man. That discovery was enormously welcome, and Rap was determined to do anything at all to live up to his new status.

He listened to the sailors' talk; he asked questions; they were happy to answer. They borrowed the master's charts and spread them out and showed him. The simplest route to Hub was to sail northward through Westerwater to the great Ambly River, which was navigable all the way to Cenmere. But the winds and currents were treacherous that way. Many a fine ship had been hurled onto the lee shores, or swept into the maw of the Nogids. There were always pirates, and the Imperial navy did not patrol much in Westerwater.

Safer by far was a course to the south of the archipelago, usually to Kith, the Impire's island stronghold in the Summer Seas. The currents were strong, though, and the winds were fickle. Sailing ships becalmed often turned up years later as desiccated husks being battered by the surf against the rock-bound coast of Zark. Galleys were safer, but they faced dangers, also, and the gale had left Gathmor unsure of *Stormdancer*'s position. In that situation, in the Summer Seas, the only solution was to head north and make landfall.

Day after day the air remained as calm as rock, the sea flat as well water. Men's muscles urged the ship onward, northward, against the southerly current. The more experienced men grew thoughtful. This might not turn out to be one of their better trips, they muttered. Thirst became a large part of Rap's life. Even the passengers complained at the scanty water ration, and they were not rowing.

Two men to an oar . . . but only in emergencies would both men row at once. The other would rest as well as he could, curled up on the baggage under the bench, or be off somewhere else doing work for Gathmor. Rap soon learned to sleep on any surface, in any position, lulled by exhaustion and the surge of the ship, by the hiss of water beyond the hull, by the rhythmic creak of oar against thole pin, and the pulsing susurrus of many men breathing in unison.

And when it was his turn to row, then stroke merged into stroke, watch into watch, day into night, and all into a fog of pain and burning thirst. A sip of water became a lifelong ambition, one moment's rest a dream of paradise.

Whispers told of ships that had died of thirst, of floating coffins filled with skeletons, drifting for years upon the Summer Seas, but after a while even the whispering stopped. No one had breath or spit to waste.

Especially not the green hand. At first Ballast did far more rowing than his share. Inevitably Rap flagged near the end of his watch, when every moment had become a torment beyond endurance and the next one worse. Then the big man would appear and offer to relieve him a little early. Rap always refused, but always his partner would simply slide into the harder inboard position and row alongside until Rap knew that his own efforts had become mere show and Ballast was doing all the work. Rap, in fact, became a drag on the oar, but he made himself a promise that he would always keep up the pretense, and he never once released his grip before the bosun rang the bell.

Then came a watch when Ballast did not arrive to relieve him early, and the officers came at the bell. For a brief moment all oars were shipped and *Stormdancer* drifted, a lonely speck on a limitless ocean, visible only to the Gods. Trusting that They were watching, Captain Gnurr ritually thanked Them for sending him a new mariner and tipped a glass of wine over Rap's head. The officers shook his blood-soaked hand and the crew cheered. He was very grateful for the wine, because it would conceal any other shameful fluid that might be trickling down his cheeks.

Little Chicken had been a capable rower from the first, but no one bothered to honor him that way. He had made it look too easy.

The goblin's bench was port amidships, whereas Rap sat near the starboard bow, and the line of cabins stood between. Of course Rap's farsight was not blocked by mere cabins, and he took a mean pleasure in noting that the goblin's occult talent had not made him blister-proof—but Little Chicken probably enjoyed blisters.

Rap also knew that the viscount was failing to satisfy his young wife, and that the elderly bishop had the opposite problem with his. And he knew why the handsome young gentleman traveler, Sir Andor, so popular with both crew and passengers, took longer than the others to find his sea legs.

Andor had not been on board during the worst of the weather. Even in the calm, Sir Andor often pleaded squeamishness and retreated to his cabin. He sometimes even took his meals along with him, which seemed like odd treatment for seasickness.

More often than not, the man in Andor's cabin was Darad. The first time Rap farsaw that transformation, it frightened him, and made him angry. He suspected Andor was threatening him. He toyed with the idea of telling Gathmor and exposing the whole sequential gang. As he calmed down, he saw that a denunciation would be useless. Gathmor would never spy on his passenger and Andor would deny the charge. Rap knew who got believed when the two of them offered conflicting stories.

Much of the time, therefore, the occupant of Cabin One was a giant jotunn warrior, who did little except lie on his belly and squirm. His back was a mass of blisters, his eye swollen, and the bites on his arm tumescent and oozing. His agony would not improve his attitude toward Rap, but he did not need to suffer that way. He could simply call Andor back in his place and wait until one of the gang summoned him in some place where medical help was available. His innumerable scars showed that he had endured much healing in the past, and that was what he was doing now. Despite what Rap had been told by both Thinal and Sagorn, the five men did care about each other to some extent. Andor was giving Darad a chance to recover from his injuries, just as Andor's own arm was healing. When the cabal needed its fighter, he would be fit again.

Two weeks out of Milflor, the danger was extreme. Men were chanting the daily prayers with much greater verve than usual. The air stayed calm, the water barrels were almost dry. Gnurr cut the ration, and men began fainting at the oars—inevitably causing chaos and even injury. The next day the wind rose, but it came out of the north. *Stormdancer* wallowed and rolled, and the motion made rowing a worse torment than ever. Reluctantly Gathmor was forced to double up the men, two to an oar, and lack of sleep was added to the torture list; as was the salt spray that soaked every garment and bit into sun-scorched skin like acid. Rap suspected that all the men's efforts were fruitless and the ship was being driven backward. To run before the wind meant dying of thirst before they found Faerie again, if they ever did. They might die of thirst in any case.

On the sixteenth day the lookout saw smoke ahead. Gnurr himself came around with an extra allotment of water, but it was less than two swallows per man. By nightfall, the peaks of the Nogids were visible from the masthead.

The ensuing darkness seemed to last a whole lifetime. Rowers given a break would simply fall off the benches and lie where they landed until they were kicked awake to start rowing again. The wind had brought no clouds, and the stars shone bright and beautiful and merciless.

The next day was worse. The volcanic smoke was no longer in sight, but a fringe of brown islands along the northeast horizon was visible even from the benches. Cruelly, the wind had banked to the northwest, and *Stormdancer* was unmanageable in a crosswind. Rap had an oar to himself now, for the ordeal was taking its toll on the weaker men. When the fear of death itself could not inspire, then the threat of a beating would not, even if it came from Gathmor.

Fear worked on passengers, also. Rap's sole amusement of the whole day was to observe Andor bloodying his pretty hands on an oar. That was double irony, for Darad would be a much better rower. Hard to explain, though.

All day the islands drifted past. By afternoon, they were visibly drawing away, as the weakened crew lost its battle with the wind.

When the sun neared the western skyline, Gnurr handed around the last of the water and called for extra prayers. Those might be the last of the prayers, also. Inevitably morning would find *Stormdancer* out of sight of land, drifting away into the unknown ocean south of the Summer Seas.

As the prayers ended, the wind seemed to falter. The crew prayed all over again, forcing the words through cracked lips, and gradually—maddeningly slowly—the breeze freshened again and backed to the southwest. Smiles and laughter and cheers appeared among the holy words. The sail was raised, the oars pulled inboard, and soon the ship was dancing landward. The drab hills approached as the sky dimmed, exhausted men lay in heaps, and Gnurr and Gathmor brought out the charts.

4

A white bear had its teeth in Rap's shoulder and was shaking him bodily. He said, "What?" without opening his eyes. Why bother with eyes when there was no light? He knew it was Gathmor.

But Gathmor did not know that Rap knew that and he continued shaking until he was satisfied that Rap was awake. The ship was plunging and leaping, ropes creaking in a stiffening breeze.

"This farsight of yours, lad. What's your range?"

" 'Bout half a league, sir." Stupid question—why couldn't it have waited till morning?

"Thank the Gods! Come along, then."

Grumpily Rap rose and followed, stumbling aft over the sleeping men, but being gentler than the mate, who had no choice but just to walk on them in the dark. No one complained very loudly.

By the steering oar stood the master, old and battered, a proud vessel listing in a killer storm. But Gnurr was a jotunn; he would not go down without a fight. Mundane vision would hardly discern him, were it not for his silver hair, fluttering in the dark like a captive bird. The helmsman was almost invisible, and only two white-bandaged hands nearby defined the silent figure of Andor.

"You may save us all, lad, if you really have got farsight." Gathmor opened a case and pulled out a roll of vellum. "You've heard of the anthropophagi?" His voice was a dry croak.

"Aye, sir." Rap peered all around. Even to the west, the horizon was barely visible, and forward his eyes could only just make out the humped shapes of hills against the sky. His farsight could not reach those—he sensed nothing out there except waves breaking on a reef to starboard.

"We're still in danger. We're on a lee shore in a rising gale. We must find water before morning, and the natives are hostile."

"They really eat people, sir?" Rap had to force the words from his parched mouth. He was becoming more interested, less sleepy, but he had a pounding headache and he felt oddly fragile and unreal. He was shivering, and so were the others, fevered by the endless thirst.

"Yes. Now look here." Gathmor peered at his chart. He raised it almost to the end of his nose. Then he lowered it and seemed to slump back against the rail. "Evil take it! I can't even see well enough to show you."

"I can see it, sir."

"You can read?"

The mate's surprise was both insulting and oddly flattering. "Aye, sir."

Gathmor muttered what sounded like a prayer of thanks. "Well, look at this, then, if you really can." He thrust the chart at Rap. "We're approaching the channel between Inkralip and Uzinip, or so we think."

"Aye, sir." Rap was wondering foggily why Andor had gone away. It was Sagorn standing there in the dark, listening—erect and intent, holding tight to the rail. His sparse white hair blew free, like the captain's. Only Rap had noticed him.

"Well, man—look at the chart!" The mate was starting to

sound urgent, perhaps even desperate. He must know about the reef to starboard.

"I am looking, sir." Rap had not tried to unroll the scroll in that wind. "I've found Uzinip . . . Orphanlover Shoal . . . that's the surf over there, sir?" He pointed.

Gathmor's fist closed on Rap's shirt and twisted, hauling him closer, almost nose to nose. "You trying to tell me you can read a rolled chart in pitch darkness?"

"Aye, sir."

There was a stunned pause. Then Rap was restored to vertical and also thumped hard on a painfully burned, salt-scabbed shoulder. He staggered weakly and grabbed the rail for support.

"Right, faun. You may save us yet. Follow the channel. It branches. Veer to port—keep left, that is. Several small islands . . . Fort Emshandar . . . can you see it?"

"Aye, sir."

"Water, sailor! There's water there. There's Imperial soldiers there. The Gods have brought us to the only Imperial outpost in this stretch of the Nogids. Can you get us to the fort?"

Rap nodded, remembered it was dark, and said, "Aye, sir." Then he yawned, which seemed to make his headache worse. The channel looked like a tiny wormhole, but he didn't know much about charts. If Gathmor thought it was wide enough, likely it was. Fort Emshandar was on the far side of Uzinip, facing a much wider strait.

"You see where the chart says 'village'?"

"Aye, sir."

"That's the anthropophagi, except this chart's old, so they may have moved by now."

Instantly Andor stood in Sagorn's place. "Not probable! There's little water in these parts. The settlements will still be by the streams." That was Andor's voice and Sagorn's thinking, of course.

Gathmor growled angrily into the darkness, not seeing that the old sage had already replaced Andor again.

"Never mind, then," the mate said. "We'll creep by them, wherever they are. But it's narrow. This back door's not recommended but we have no choice. We'll have to sneak in quietly and make the fort before they know. Otherwise we'll be caught in the narrows and there'll be faun pie for breakfast. Coming out, we'll have a clear run to the north. All right?"

"Aye, sir. How close to the Orphanlover did you want to go, sir? We seem to be drifting that way."

Gathmor blasphemed.

Rap yawned and yawned. If he sat down, he would be asleep at once, so he lounged against the rail between the master and the first mate and he gave the orders. That would have been funny, had anyone felt like laughing. He told them when *Stormdancer* was entering the channel, and then the sail was lowered and oars were put to use. Winds in narrow passes, he was told, were not predictable. Gathmor put on his sixteen most skilled rowers, with oar blades and thole pins muffled. Out of all the rest of the crew, very few could even stand up, and among them only Ballast and Little Chicken would be capable of using weapons. If the anthropophagi attacked, they would find the larder door unguarded.

Only Rap noticed as Andor and Sagorn alternated in the darkness. The wily old scholar had contributed no more ideas.

The channel twisted to the right. It was much wider than it had looked on the chart. At first *Stormdancer* showed a dangerous desire to drift ashore in the crosswind, and Rap had to learn that he must make the crew row the ship *this way*, to make the scenery move at an angle *that way*. He held the chart in his hand, still rolled, slowly turning it to keep the picture the right way up. Then another bend brought calmer air and the ship began to behave more like a horse would.

His head drooped, his knees quivered. He forced himself to straighten up. This was much easier than driving a wagon down the hill in Krasnegar, but it was not easy enough to do in his sleep.

"There's a village over there!" The chart was correct so far. He wasn't sure that Gathmor could even see him pointing. There were no stars. The night was about as black as night could be.

"Ssh! Sound travels over water."

"Aye, sir," Rap said quietly. "We're getting too close this side, sir." The high walls of the valley had muffled the storm that would be battering the open sea by now, but ripples ahead must mean wind.

The mate leaned on the steering oar. "Current. You're doing great, lad."

"This can't be easy for you," Rap said, with sudden insight.

"Easy? *Easy?*" The jotunn's whisper was bitter. "Steering

my ship in the dark through the Nogids with a landlubber mongrel pup as pilot? I'd rather pull out my toenails. I mean that. Every nail. Slowly.''

"I'm sure you would, sir. A little bit to the left, sir.''

Gathmor shuddered and muttered, "Two points to port.'' He leaned on the oar.

The old captain had stretched out at Rap's feet, too weak to stand longer. He was either asleep or unconscious.

The silent progress was uncanny. Even within the ship, there was hardly a sound from the rowers. Perhaps these men had experience in sneaking around in the dark in boats, but it would be unwise to ask. They did not even have the coxswain piping the stroke for them. Likely they could hear the drumbeat in Rap's head—it felt loud enough to waken the anthropophagi.

Waves splashed on the shore, and the wind stirred trees on the higher slopes, but that was all. *Stormdancer* was going to pass very close to the village. A dog started to bark, and Rap quieted it—all part of the service. A man coughed on the shore. Nothing Rap could do about coughs. He wished he could cure headaches, though. His.

And his farsight was starting to play tricks, surely? "How much water does the ship need, sir?''

"Draft? About half a fathom is all.''

"Oh!'' Incredible—a fathom was a span. "That's all right then.''

Gathmor groaned. "You can see through water, too?''

"Aye, sir. At least two fathoms here.''

Water . . . drinking water . . . fresh water . . . *Gods be with us* . . .

"Where are we, lad?'' Nerves crackled in the mate's voice.

"Just rounding Uzinip.''

A moment later *Stormdancer* began to move uneasily in a stronger swell. Surf boomed somewhere ahead, and she came sweeping out of the narrow pass, turning the corner at an angle Rap had not expected, borne by the current into a strait whose far side he could not sense—it might be Zark, for all he knew.

And there were lights on the shore nearby, fires.

"That's it!'' Gathmor said. "The fort!'' He took a deep breath to yell his triumph, and Rap clapped a hand over his mouth just in time.

5

The crew rowed gently, holding the ship against the gusting breeze. Dead ahead, on a narrow meadow between hillside and beach, were the remains of Fort Emshandar. *Dead* ahead.

Rap had described the scene, but the sailors could make out most of it themselves. The great bonfires on the sand showed the dancing anthropophagi, while sounds of drums and chanting drifted over the waves, as did the rank odors from the smoking ruins of the stockade, and a stronger, stomach-churning scent of roast meat from the celebration. Large things were being cooked on spits.

"Can you see the water?" Gathmor asked grimly. He was keeping his voice low, but the wind would carry sound out to sea anyway.

"I think so, sir. In the ruins. A well, with a windlass. There's men there. No, they're women." Rap thought he could hear the windlass creaking, but that might be the turnspits on the beach.

"Doesn't matter." The mate thumped his fist on the rail in baffled fury. There were hundreds of the anthropophagi, and the jotnar were in no shape to fight anyway, whatever the odds.

Sagorn had been watching and listening, heedless that he might be noticed in the flicker of the bonfires. Now he became Andor again. "We must not linger. That fort must have had occult defenses. It would not have lasted a week in the Nogids without them."

"So?" Gathmor snarled. The other passengers had been sent to their cabins long ago. Anyone but Andor would have been.

"So the anthropophagi must have sorcerers of their own. They will have farsight, too."

The jotunn grunted agreement. "We're dead without water." Like them all, he was having trouble speaking. They were all shivering and staggering. The rowers would fail soon.

"There's a streambed," Rap croaked miserably. "Farther up the hill." Of course. That was why the fort had been built on this spot, and why its well had found water.

"There's a thousand cannibals between us and it."

"I can see in the dark, sir. But I can't swim."

Again the brutal hand thumped Rap's shoulder. "Who can,

with a bucket of water? The Gods sent you, lad. Do it, and you're a free man.''

Rap did not reply. If he didn't do it, he would be a dead one.

Stormdancer carried no dinghy and needed no fancy docks. Rap piloted her back along her previous course until the fires were out of sight. Farther would be safer, but the rowers could barely make way against the current being sent through the channel by the storm, and Rap was too weak to walk very far. One final spurt drove the bow up on the beach, and the men collapsed on top of their weaker companions. Without fresh water to revive them, they likely could not even push her off again.

The mate scrambled over the rail with a rope. Rap followed, clutching two buckets. The drop was not far, but he fell in a heap, struggling and spluttering in thigh-deep water. He swallowed a fair bit without meaning to, yet it felt good. The sailors had told him stories about seawater driving men mad, but perhaps a little wouldn't hurt in the short run, and there might not be any long run to worry about. The anthropophagi would not need to add salt to their Rap stew, that was all.

"Gods, it's dark!" Gathmor had blundered into a rock and was now tying the rope around it. "If I let go this cable I couldn't find the damn ship again. You still there?"

"Aye, sir."

"I'd come with you if I thought I could do a damn bit of good."

"I'm sure you would, sir."

"I'll try, if you want. If you hold my hand." The mate was suffering an attack of fallibility. Perhaps he had never before in his life had to admit that another man was better than he was at anything, and that must be hurting his jotunnish pride.

Rap said something reassuring as he staggered away across the sand. He was the seeing man in the land of the blind, but he kept remembering the warning that Sagorn had passed along by way of Andor's voice and memory—the anthropophagi might very well have sorcerers of their own.

They must have! The Nogids lay like a barricade across the road home from Faerie. Certainly Rap was not the first occult genius to be shipwrecked here. Adepts and even mages . . . not all would have died without telling their words of power. There might be many seeing men in this land of the blind.

Moreover—and the sudden insight felt more like a flicker of delirium than any sort of sane logic—down the centuries the Impire had launched dozens of campaigns to conquer the Nogids; so the sailors had told him. But the imps had never achieved more than a scattering of strongpoints, little forts like Emshandar, to succor the naval traffic. They were perpetually under seige, he had been told. Sooner or later they all got taken and sacked. Tonight was a case in point.

The legions' opponents, therefore, had not been mobs of primitive savages but the wardens of the west. The Nogids must lie in Zinixo's sector. They were a quarantine, a barrier defending Faerie itself from being overrun by the masses of the Impire. The Protocol kept East's legions at bay, and likely North's raiders, also. No occult defense the Impire put on its forts would last long when the warden of the west decided to clean house.

Tonight's anthropophagous treat came courtesy of the dwarf.

Rap's weakness appalled him. True, his clothes were soaked and clinging, but even so, he should not be shivering to such excess. He staggered, making far more noise than he should as he scrambled through the brush on the hillside.

Every few minutes he had to stop and rest. His head was pounding like a farrier's hammer, and all his muscles had turned to . . . no, not to water. Mud, maybe.

The shore flats were narrow: tide-washed sand, a strip of rocks, and then some scrub at the base of the slope. He knew he must climb well away from the beach before he rounded the curve in the hill that blocked his view of the anthropophagi—and blocked their view of him, also. The hill seemed unfairly steep, and the dry scrub was sharp and thorny and noisy. Just because his farsight didn't work through hills didn't mean that a sorcerer's wouldn't, but as he angled higher he began to hear the drums more clearly and see the flame-lit smoke roiling upward in the wind, and then sparks.

He took a farewell glance at *Stormdancer*, her prow almost clear of the water, and one thin thread of a cable curving down to a boulder. Gathmor sat morosely on that rock, sword in hand and totally blind. No one seemed to be moving on board. It was a ship of the dying.

Now Rap had reached the spur and he needed another rest, but he crouched low and forced himself to crawl through the prickly scrub until he had a clear view.

Once there had been a narrow stream valley notched into the hill. One side had collapsed ages ago, and the debris from the landslide now formed a little shelf on which Fort Emshandar had stood, a bulge on the shore. The rest of the gorge was still there, higher up the slope. It could not hold any great torrent, but surely there would be some water there? The Gods could not be so cruel as to make it completely dry?

Most of the anthropophagi were down by the fires. Not one of them wore as much as a string of beads. Few were still dancing. Many seemed to be feasting—*God of Vomit!*

Four chattering women were clustered around the well in the ruins of the fort just below Rap, so close that he could hear their laughter. He saw a whole pailful of water being tipped from the draw bucket into a pitcher, and the sight was a stab of pain to him. He wanted to leap up and run screaming down there. He quickly directed his attention farther seaward.

The shore below the fort was packed with canoes, dozens of them drawn up on the sand. Fuzzily Rap wondered if he could somehow damage those, to frustrate any pursuit when *Stormdancer* left. Then he knew he must be growing light-headed.

Yet he could detect no sentries anywhere, and the lack of them was an ominous hint that the cannibals might be relying on occult protection; and just as that thought occurred to him, his mental eye was caught by two anthropophagi who had left the victory feast and were running away from the firelight. They were running in his direction. For a freezing moment he thought they must be guardian sorcerers who had noticed him; then one of them seemed to trip and pull the other down on top of . . . of her. Oh, that! He sighed with relief and sent them a private blessing. Now he noticed other couples similarly engaged. Obviously the anthropophagi would not be indulging in that sort of celebration if they had any suspicion of enemies skulking nearby.

Deliberately, but shakily, he rose to his feet. Tiny whispers inside him said he should continue slithering through undergrowth, but no mundane eye could see him in this darkness, and no bush would hide him from sorcery.

His sodden boots were eating the skin off his toes, but he hobbled as fast as he could up the slope to the little gorge. He could hear no water running, but soon his farsight picked it out—slimy pools, small trickles. He stumbled down the rocks, remembering his arrival at the fairy village, when he had thought he was thirsty. He had not known what thirst was then. Oh, praise the Gods!

He stopped drinking before he made himself ill, but it was the hardest thing he had ever done. He had no time to let the first load settle and take on another. Well, he would be returning. He filled his two buckets and began staggering up the bank with them.

They were impossibly heavy. The rope handles cut his blistered hands, and he staggered with weariness, slopping more water into his already sodden boots. Almost all the anthropophagi had paired off, many not even bothering to leave the firelight. Apparently that was dessert. The drums had stopped. If he kept on swaying like this he'd arrive at *Stormdancer* with two empty buckets . . .

But he did reach the ship eventually. Gathmor was slumped over, holding his head as if it were about to fall off. His sword was thrust in the sand at his feet beside two empty buckets. Rap kicked a pebble and the sailor jumped a league in the air. He drank right from a bucket and afterward he muttered a prayer of thanks.

Then he said something else, but Rap was already heading back with the empties, going for more.

By his third trip, the drums had started again, and most of the lovers seemed to be back dancing and feasting. Anthropophagi must have remarkable stamina. Perhaps it came from their diet.

He felt a few spots of rain. The wind was backing.

He delivered his buckets and went back again. And again . . .

The fifth trip was a dangerous blur. Rain was falling heavily, and the wind was stronger. Even the distant surf sounded louder, so the storm was still increasing. Storm or not, the ship must leave before dawn. Rap was so unsteady now, slithering and stumbling, that he dropped one of his buckets coming down the hill. He handed over the other and fell to the sand.

"Need a break," he mumbled.

Gathmor had handed the precious cargo up to eager hands. There were people stirring on board now, revived by the water. "Everyone's had a drink, lad. You've done all you can."

Rap forced out the hateful words. "I'll do one more."

"No. You're beat! You've done great, though. Really shows the jotunn in you."

"How far to the next fort?"

"Gods know. Depends where we get blown."

Two buckets—even two half buckets—would mean very little water among seventy, but divided among the strongest rowers, it might make the difference between safe haven and shipwreck. Rap struggled to his feet, feeling as if he weighed more than the ship and all its crew together.

"One more," he insisted.

"No! Get aboard. That's enough."

Rap took up the buckets and walked away over the sand, and Gathmor could not have noticed at first that he had gone, for he was busy shouting orders to the crew.

Rap scrambled up the hill with his eyes tight closed against the streaming rain. The Gods were having fun, sending rain now. But Gathmor had been right, he was very close to his limits. He reeled with weariness, fighting for every step, waving the empty buckets around to keep his balance.

He tripped, fell, and rolled into a spiky bush. For a moment it was just pure heaven to lie there with his mouth open and the downpour washing his face. And he could sleep for days if he let himself.

Sleep? He sprang to wakefulness. He hadn't slept, had he?

Probably not, or not for more than a few minutes. But he had been awakened by shouting.

One quick scan around told him how bad things could become in just a few minutes. Dawn must be close, for the darkness was no longer impenetrable—he would have noticed that sooner had he kept his eyes open. He did not bother to hunt for his buckets. He was on his feet and running down the hill before he knew he had started to rise, and all the demons of the Evil were screaming in his ears.

It was a three-way race.

Stormdancer was leaving. The sailors clustered around the prow were heaving her seaward. The tide had gone out since she was beached, and the bosun's shouts rang through the night as he called time to the men. Every push moved the hull a fraction farther into the waves, but it was hard and desperate work for a sadly weakened crew.

Rap was staggering with weakness, windmilling down a thorny, tangled hillside. Only his occult ability to see in the dark let him avoid the roots and bushes and trees, but his magic was no help in keeping his balance. Rain had become a cloudburst, grass and dirt were slick and greasy. He slid and fell and rolled and scrambled up to do it all again; but his progress was agonizingly slow.

And racing along the sand were several hundred angry cannibals, all howling at the top of their lungs, all waving spears and bows, heading for the ship and already almost past their beached canoes, although others had turned aside to run out a few of those, planning to cut *Stormdancer* off if she escaped. That made it a four-way race, then.

As Rap reached the shore, a roar from the sailors announced that the ship was free, sliding away into the dark. Men had fallen headlong into the surf and now were scrambling up, grabbing one another's hands, grabbing also at the nets that had been hung over the bow for just this purpose.

As Rap reeled across the sand, the ship was already drifting off into the night, being caught now by the wind, trailing her struggling tangle of men like some strange marine weed.

He galloped into the waves, but the cannibals had seen him and their yells redoubled. He fell headlong, rose, fell again, and breathed water and choked and lurched forward, tripping repeatedly because the sea caught at his legs. His pursuers were moving much faster than he could and he was already almost out of his depth and *Stormdancer* was moving fast now, turning away, heeling as she escaped from the lee of the hill and the gale caught her.

Half a dozen anthropophagi were closing in on Rap, with a couple of giants in the lead. They were swimming while he just floundered, helpless in the waves, trying to run on tiptoe in the troughs, trying not to drown in the crests, being carried shoreward, but his farsight found the cable even as two huge hands reached out for him. He grabbed it just seconds before it could slither out of reach. The anthropophagite's fingers touched his shoulder, and then the rope whipped him away, burning his tattered hands, almost yanking his arms from their sockets, burying him under leagues of suffocating black water.

The tension eased; he knew he had only seconds before the next jerk, and it was not easy to think straight when farsight said you were four cubits underwater, but he managed to wrap the rope around one wrist before it pulled taut—and then it did and he shot through the sea like a fish. It slackened and he lashed fruitlessly, struggling to reach that surging, essential, breathable surface, but before he got there another heave on the rope sucked him along again, and deeper, spinning him giddily. If the sailors knew he was there they could haul him in, but they'd better do it soon . . .

5

Gathmor sent two youngsters over the side as the faun came within reach. They bent a line around his ankles and hauled him inboard bottoms up, so he'd jettison some of his bilge on the way.

Even so, he carried a cargo of seawater that would have floated a galleas. They worked him like a bellows to pump it out of him and get him breathing again.

But the seer's work was not over yet. The channel that had seemed so unending to his farsight was still only one of many in the archipelago. Even on a bare pole *Stormdancer* crossed it in a couple of hours, living up to her name, leaping and plunging against a sea anchor. If the sun came up, no one knew it, and the deluging rain cut visibility to less than a length. Neither Gnurr nor Gathmor could guess where the ship was by then; there were rocks out there, rocks and shoals and islets as uncountable as the stars of heaven, and only one man aboard could scry them.

With the tiniest sail the ship could hoist, still every blast seemed likely to unmast her. If that happened, she'd be a hulk, bearing her crew to the last weighing. And if she broached to, she'd be on her beam ends in seconds. It took four men to hold the steering oar, and she moved like a pig. Another three men kept the kid awake, walking him up and down, slapping his face, pouring rainwater into him—they had plenty of water now—and yelling in his ear. "There!" he would mumble, or "Rocks that way!" and then his head would droop again.

The mate reckoned afterward they'd likely gone through Eelskinner Gap by way of the Bunghole—a couple of times they'd had cliffs in view on both sides, and not much more than an oar's length away at that. It went on for half a lifetime, seemingly, but when nothing had shown up for an hour, they knew that they'd broken through into Dyre Channel itself, and by then they couldn't waken the faun anyway, so they rolled him in a blanket and laid him under a bench and said a prayer that he would live.

Water willy-nilly:
> I came like Water, and like Wind I go,
>
> Into this Universe, and *Why* not knowing
> Nor *Whence*, like Water willy-nilly flowing;
>   And out of it, As Wind along the Waste,
> I know not *Whither*, willy-nilly blowing.
>   Fitzgerald, *The Rubaiyat of Omar Khayyam*
>   (§29-30, 1879)

❰ ELEVEN ❱

Wilderness
were paradise

1

"This bread is remarkably good, Fooni," Azak said. He wiped one last fragment of bread around his bowl, popped it in his mouth, and simultaneously belched loudly. Inos winced. Such vulgarity was a compliment in Zark, she knew, but there were some local customs that she found harder to accept than others.

Azak and Inos, Kade and little Fooni—the four of them were sitting cross-legged on rugs, on the ground outside their tent, First Lionslayer and his family. The sun was setting, the temperature falling like a stooping falcon. The tents had been pitched in the lee of a steep rocky bank, but even there they all flapped and surged in the wind that howled through the pass. The night would be noisy; but Inos never had trouble sleeping these days.

Apparently Fooni was not going to comment on the bread.

"How fast it cools off!" Inos said, pulling her coat closed and fastening it. By day Gaunt Pass was a furnace, the rocky walls tossing the sun's heat back and forth. By night it felt like winter in Krasnegar. At sunset everyone donned warm mountain garb, heavy garments that Elkarath had purchased in the little foothill settlements during the past few weeks. She wondered if he would haul them all the way through the Central Desert to Ullacarn, or sell them again on the west side of the mountains. The big fleecy boots she had pulled on a few minutes ago might have crossed the range a dozen times already.

"Did your mother teach you to make such good bread, Fooni?" Azak inquired.

Inos shot him a puzzled glance. Why this sudden interest in cooking? He normally never bothered with trivia. The bread had not been specially good. In fact it had been poor stuff, flat and tasteless, made from a gritty meal paste spread on hot rocks. That and goat stew were standard fare for the camel folk. Tonight there had also been some sour wine as a special treat.

Hard bread and sour wine, distant laughter and the clanking of camel bells, braziers twinkling and a cithern twanging—these things were all very familiar to her now. Watch out for snakes in the bedding and scorpions anywhere; she was learning. Hair full of dried sweat, air full of flies. She could handle a camel quite adequately and erect a tent no floppier than her neighbors'.

Fooni was scowling and still saying nothing. Fooni was a miserable little pest, and Inos was planning to be rid of Fooni very shortly. She had served her purpose and soon could be sent off to travel with her great-grandfather, who would not have to tolerate her snide remarks and snappy temper.

Eastward, the first stars twinkled above blood-red crags. Gaunt Pass had turned out to be spectacular beyond Inos's farthest expectations. For days the caravan had been trekking over scrubby hills and through barren valleys, gradually losing altitude as it neared the western slopes of the Agoniste range, and yet all those hills and valleys had been mere wrinkles in the floor of the pass itself. On either hand a dreamscape of real mountains soared up in incredible cliffs and faces of rock to far-off icy peaks. The sheer scale of the scenery had astounded her. Her eye refused to comprehend it. It was a land for Gods, under a sky immeasurably huge.

Of course Kade enthused about this interesting experience, as she always did about anything, and for once Inos was inclined to agree with her. All her life she would remember this journey.

Everywhere were signs of a long and bloody history. Ruins of cities long forgotten sprawled in the mouths of tributary valleys; the wind wailed around derelict remains of castles on jutting spurs of the mountains. No one lived here now except goat herders, and perhaps bandits. She would have liked to have explored some of the ruins, but the caravan must keep moving.

If Azak slept at all, he must be doing so during the day, on his camel. If he did come to the tent, Inos never heard him. She suspected he prowled the campsite all night long. Early in the journey, he had worried only about petty pilfering in the settlements. In this lawless mountain land, all the lionslayers were becoming red-eyed and grumpy, and that was not from fear of fast-fingered village urchins.

Another spectacular belch rang through the twilight.

Inos discovered that her jaw had fallen open and she closed it quickly. That obscene noise appeared to have come from—

"Yes, the bread was delicious," Kade remarked softly.

Azak raised one eyebrow. He looked at Inos, then at Fooni.

"It wasn't me made it," Fooni muttered. "It was her!"

Azak coughed. "Congratulations, wife. Quite excellent."

"I didn't think it was much!" Fooni shouted. "Only bread! Too much salt! Any wife ought to be able to make better than that—my mother could! I can! What's so wonderful about a woman grinding meal and making rotten bread?" She leaped to her feet and went running off.

Inos watched her departure with satisfaction. "That child deserves a good spanking!"

Azak chuckled. "Why? Was she responsible for this atrocious bread?"

She glared. He grinned wickedly through his brigand's red beard. She glared harder, he began to laugh, then they laughed together, and even Kade joined in with a chuckle.

Inos had never heard Azak laugh in Arakkaran. Being a lionslayer must be less stressful than being a sultan. But this was her chance to dispose of the odious Fooni.

"No, I made the bread. However, these petty tantrums of hers are becoming very wearing! She snaps and gripes all the time."

"Ah! But you must make allowances for her."

"And what is that supposed to mean?"

"Lionslayers are romantic figures to a child of her years. Me especially, of course."

"You mean she . . . That's absurd! She's far too young!"

"No, she isn't," Azak said firmly.

Inos choked. "Forgive me! I keep forgetting that you are an expert in such matters! I suppose you have bedded several girls of her age?"

"Quite a few," he agreed complacently.

"Time for dishes!" Kade began gathering up the bowls and beakers in a hasty clatter.

"I'll do that, Aunt!"

"My turn," Kade insisted.

"Come walk with me, Inos." Azak rose, inhumanly tall against the sunset, holding out a hand.

Inos hesitated, then accepted when she saw that he was wearing thick sheepskin gloves. Just for a moment, some trick of the twilight and the heavy clothes and she could have sworn he was a winter-garbed jotunn. Some jotnar had red beards. He pulled her up effortlessly, then he took off at a run, and she found herself being hauled at high speed up the bank, as if being towed by a horse, rocks rattling and rolling under Azak's great boots.

When they reached the crest the wind struck them like a flying iceberg, and Inos staggered. Azak transfered his grip to her elbow to steady her. Below them, in the shelter of the slope, the braziers of the camp were spread in a long line like a string of fire jewels. At their backs, the sunset was drawing to a peaceful conclusion on the peaks.

"Idiots!" Azak said. "I tell them—and they camp all spread out like that! How can I defend them if they will not listen to common sense?"

"Can't the sheik make them?"

"Bah! He just smiles. He does not seem to care. How he has survived this journey so many times, I cannot imagine. The Gods tolerate his follies, it would seem."

Inos shivered at the bite of the wind, watching the long grass and wispy bushes writhe, as if in pain. Kade was plodding over to the spring, going to wash the pots. That was an excuse for a gossip, of course, or she would have made do with sand. Bells jingled in the distance, where the hobbled camels grazed.

"We've done it, haven't we?" she said. "Three weeks? There can't be any doubt now. Can there?"

Azak was studying her face instead of the scenery. "I expect so. There are very few passes, so I thought she might look for us here. But we seem to have slipped by . . ." He shrugged himself into silence, and gazed up at the stars.

"Why did you drag me up here?" she demanded, shivering.

"Is Krasnegar colder than this?"

She laughed. "This? There are times when you can spit ice in Krasnegar."

"Mmm," he said, noncommittally.

He did look like a jotunn in the twilight. It was his height, and the clothing. The distant peaks shone with ice, and ice also reminded her of home, although Krasnegar's hills were nothing like these ranges. A great adventure, this, but she was homesick still.

"Azak?"

"Mmm?"

"How long? When will we ever get to Hub?"

"Why? Are you not enjoying the journey?"

"Well, some of it. But I'm impatient! I hate this dawdling through Zark when terrible things may be happening. It's taking so long!"

He sighed. "I am enjoying it!" His grip on her elbow tightened. "Be patient, little one! The world moves slowly. The imperor may still not know anything about Krasnegar, unless the wardens have told him. Even the Imperial post takes weeks and weeks to cross the Impire. Armies rarely march more than eight leagues a day. You must learn to be patient."

Now it was she who said, "Mmm!" Then she asked again, "Why did you bring me up here? Because if you don't have—"

"To ask a question. Have you ever been in love, Inosolan?"

Love? Startled, she stared at him, but he was gazing at the last glimmer on the distant peaks. Alarm bells began to clamor in her mind.

"Once I thought I was. I'd been bewitched. I told you about Sir Andor."

"Just once?"

"Well, puppy love, maybe. There was a boy I was very fond of, when I was young. The one Rasha copied for that apparition she sent to haunt me, the first night on the trail, remember?"

Azak grunted. "I wondered why a stableboy upset you so much."

"Oh, no!" Inos said. "Don't start that! That was no stableboy! I can handle stableboys. It was a wraith, or seemed to be. Don't accuse me of—"

"Fooni is not the only one who has been snappish lately."

"Well, you're not getting enough sleep . . ." Mention of

Fooni roused Inos's temper again. The child herself was bad enough, and Azak's suggestion that she was lusting after him was pure barnyard disgusting. "But talk to the sheik. Mayhap he will include her with your wages when we reach Ulla-carn."

Azak turned to face her and took both her shoulders in his big hands. Huge hands, in their massive gloves. He stared intently at her for a moment and suddenly her heart started beating very hard.

"Love is an impish notion," he said. "It is not a Zarkian custom."

"I have noticed."

"I never thought it could happen to a djinn."

"I'm sure it doesn't."

"Yes, it does. I have fallen in love, Inos. Imagine such a thing happening to a sultan of Arakkaran!"

She dropped her eyes and said nothing. Oh, Gods!

"You once told me you would marry a goblin if your people's welfare required it."

"Er . . . Yes."

"You also said that any imp would be better than a goblin."

"I did?"

"You did."

She kept her eyes down and hoped the gloom hid her blushes. His grip on her shoulders was almost painful.

"How would you rank an imp and a djinn, Inosolan?"

"Azak! This is madness!"

"Yes, it is. But the poets say that all love is madness. The God of Lovers is the God of Fools, they say. Answer."

Answer how? Why had she let this take her unaware?

Because the idea was so absurd?

"Anything but a goblin," she admitted.

"So? A djinn also would be an outsider. Neither imps nor jotnar could object to a djinn. A royal djinn, Inos. A very suitable husband for a queen of Krasnegar."

"The climate would kill—"

"Heat has not killed you."

She tried to imagine Azak in Krasnegar and it was impossible. He would go mad with boredom. Would he kill off the burgesses if they annoyed him? Would he try to buy their daughters?

No, he wouldn't. Azak was not a fool. He had obviously thought about this. Now she recalled how he had been asking a lot of questions about Krasnegar lately. He had also been laughing a lot, and smiling a lot, and cracking jokes. She should have guessed.

And Kade must have, because Kade had been making some very odd remarks about Azak lately, very catty remarks for her.

"You have a kingdom of your own. A duty of your own."

"Arakkaran has many princes. Krasnegar has only one queen."

Why had she not foreseen this? And none of her Kinvale training had explained how to handle a giant barbarian swordsman intent on wooing. *Think, woman! Think!*

"What of your sons?"

"They can take their chances, as I did. My father died when I was seven. He was poisoned." After a moment, Azak added, "Or I could send for them, if you didn't mind."

God of Fools! She was trembling, and his grip on her shoulders would tell him that. Marry Azak? He was a barbarian! A peerless specimen of manhood, maybe, but a killer. Ruthless. Deadly.

"Azak, this is very sudden. I have never even considered such a possibility. It has never crossed my mind."

"Then why do you snap at Fooni so much?"

Incredible arrogance! "Because she is a nasty, ill-mannered little slut. Not because of you, I assure you! I was snapping at her, as you put it, the first day we met."

"Yes."

Azak thought she was jealous of Fooni? Nothing she could say would change that—she had never met a man so stubborn . . . or maybe one . . . Was she fated always to consort with obstinate men? She shied away from that line of thinking, and that comparison.

"What are you suggesting?" Her voice came out much too shrill.

"That when we go before the wardens to ask for justice, we go as man and wife. My curse lifted, your throne restored. I will relinquish Arakkaran for the woman I love."

Love? How to explain the problem tactfully? There wasn't any tactful way. Despite the chill of the wailing wind, she was sweating. "Love? Azak, Rasha's curse has deprived you of—"

He squeezed so hard that she yelped. His eyes seemed to flash in the dusk. His red beard bristled.

"Do you think I don't know the difference? Of course I need a woman. Desperately! I burn for the touch of a woman, my hands on her body, her flesh against mine. But what I feel for you is something else, something more, something I have never known till now. It is love! It is as the impish poets say, both joy and agony together. I can think of nothing else. I have eyes only for you. I am miserable except when I am with you. I will do anything, just to see you smile. This has never happened to me before."

Probably it had never happened because any other woman he had ever wanted had been his for the taking. Why had Inos not seen that this might happen? She had worried that she had no hold over Azak. Now she had too much of a hold over him. Love spurned could turn to hatred.

"I have never met a woman like you, Inos!" He was almost shouting. "That day you rode Evil, I could not believe it. I had not known a woman could behave like that. Your courage, your spirit—" He released her shoulders. "Why do you think I came?"

"Wh-what?"

"To tell the wardens that there is a sorceress in Zark?" He sneered. "Do you think I could not have trusted Kar with that message?"

"I . . ." Inos was speechless.

"And do you think I would have trusted Kar with *you*?"

Why had she not seen that? Blind, foolish, stupid—

Azak sank down on one knee. "Inosolan, my beloved, will you marry me?"

She muttered prayers to all the Gods. When had Azak last knelt to anyone? What would he do if she refused? His intensity terrified her. He was a killer. He was capable of anything. She might learn to love a hard man, a fighter, but only if he had some gentleness in him somewhere. And some respect for her womanhood. Azak had neither. A djinn? Who would reign in Krasnegar—the queen or her husband?

Azak's arrogance had no limits at all. He knew he was the ultimate male. He would never understand a woman refusing such a mate.

"Azak, when I marry, I must not jump into . . . I mean . . . Oh, Azak! Please stand up."

Reluctantly he rose, towering over her again.

Trust in love! the God had told her.

It was crazy, but it was also horribly logical. Azak was a

perfect solution to Krasnegar's problem. After all the trouble
with legionaries, and perhaps with jotnar, the city would need
a firmer rule than Holindarn's. The ideal monarch would be
strong, impartial, and experienced. Azak was all of those.
Gods!

Think, woman, think!

"Azak, there are too many things we don't know! Krasnegar
may have been seized by Kalkor, or taken over by the Impire,
or razed and butchered. The wardens may not want to help."
He started to speak and she shouted, "You expect me to marry
a man who can't even touch me? Who can't kiss me, or hold my
hand?"

He groaned, as if in pain. "A promise—"

"No! You are being unfair."

"Tell me that you care, then."

Not looking at him, Inos said, "I admire you. I am very
grateful for all your help, and I promise I will think very hard
about this. Anything more . . . I need time to think. Please,
Azak?"

He sighed, and shivered.

"I shall start spitting ice soon. Let's go down," she said.
"Yes."

He took her by the hand, and they started down the slope.

There were weeks and months of desert ahead of her and
Azak would be at her side all the way.

She did not love Azak ak'Azakar. Not now.

Could she learn to do so? Or could he persuade her? She
had watched wooing done at Kinvale, she had seen maiden
won against long odds. Hearts could be won, or won over.
Love Azak? She did not think she had ever known love, not
real love. Maybe if . . . but he had only been a stableboy.
What would Foronod and Yaltauri have said to a stableboy!
None of the eligible young men at Kinvale . . . Andor had
been a delusion.

In a daze, Inos stumbled at Azak's side as they descended the
rubbly slope, back to the tents.

What greater proof of love had any man ever offered a woman?
He would relinquish Arakkaran for her, leave his homeland, his
throne, his unbounded wealth and unlimited power . . . for her!
How could any woman refuse such a love?

Trust in love! the God had said, and at last she understood
that cryptic edict.

The God had been speaking of Azak, and Azak's love.

Wilderness were Paradise:
> A book of Verses underneath the Bough,
> A Jug of Wine, a Loaf of Bread—and Thou,
>   Beside me singing in the Wilderness—
> Oh, Wilderness were Paradise enow!
>
>   Fitzgerald, *The Rubaiyat of Omar Khayyam*
>   (§12, 1879)

◖ TWELVE ◗

Take the cash

1

"Think the Old Man's going to drop anchor?" Ogi whispered, his imp's nosiness making him twitch like a dog scenting rats. The captain had just gone by.

"Likely," Kani mumbled with his mouth full. "He looks almost as old as Rap, here."

They and a group of others were seated along the gangway, eating sausage and biscuit with their knees up and their backs against the cabins. Some were off duty; some, like Rap, were still too sick to work. On the benches before them, healthier men were rowing their hearts out, timing their stroke to the brutal swell for which Dyre Channel was famous.

The air was warm and still and muggy, with a thin drizzle keeping everything soaked, and clouds hanging just above the masthead. Even in the shelter of the awnings, water dripped everywhere. The storm had blown itself out before it smashed *Stormdancer* into the iron toes of the Mosweeps, but Rap had not been dry since he came back aboard; nor had anyone else. By nightfall they would reach Thuli Pan.

Rap was going to live. He was as weak as a sick chicken, still prone to sudden spasms of fever and ague, but definitely recovering. Some of the crew were in even worse shape, and everyone agreed that there was a sickness aboard, because no one wanted to admit to being felled by mere thirst and exhaustion; or even near drowning, as in Rap's case. No one had died. Most were on the mend.

And Rap had just been insulted, so he must give a suitable reply. He spoke around a wad of half-chewed sausage. "Kani . . . I wasn't eating, I'd feed your guts to the gulls."

The sailors considered the threat and decided it was adequate.

"Do it as soon as we get to Durthing," Ogi suggested. "He needs it. Four days now, maybe?"

"Five, more like," Ballast said in his guttural troll voice.

Kani wiped a glitter of rain off his silver mustache. "More. Number One says he's going to lay over a day or two in Thuli."

Everyone groaned. Rap ate in contented silence, knowing that someone would start explaining something to him shortly.

Kani did. "Some of the passengers may quit there. Can't say I'd blame them after this trip. That means looking for replacements, but most folk'd rather sail than go by galley, 'cept through the Nogids, see? Either way, we go on to Finrain. On Kith, see? We drop the rest there and carry on to Durthing."

Everyone sighed happily and began boasting of certain unbelievable experiences the female population of Durthing wanted, needed, and would soon receive.

"Good spot, Durthing," Ogi said, speaking only to Rap. "It's just a village. Not even a jetty there. We'll haul up on the beach and refit. Make momma happy, do some brawling, a bit of gardening. Durthing's all sailors. I'm almost the only imp there. Jotnar, and a few trolls, mostly."

Kani claimed to be pure jotunn, but he snooped and chattered like an imp. "And the Impire doesn't bother us," he said firmly. "No chains there! No clanking legionaries. Nice little spot. We can find you a girl. Hey, fellows—who do we fix Rap up with?"

Names were mentioned, and evidently became more and more unlikely, for each new one brought louder merriment. Even a couple of rowers joined in, calling out suggestions.

Rap just ate and smiled and tried not to remember that Durthing was on Kith, and Kith was another island. He wondered if he might possibly escape during the layover in Thuli, then decided he was too weak to walk to the edge of town. Any town, no matter how small.

His romantic future was soon forgotten, and talk returned to the captain's probable retirement. "The Old Man does drop anchor," Kani said, "then we put up Gathmor?"

Everyone agreed to that, and the argument broke out about a new first mate, and other promotions.

Ogi, though, turned again to Rap. "This one's been rough!

None of us can recall a worse trip.'' He dropped his voice as if being careful not to give offense—any imp who lived and worked with a shipful of jotnar would soon learn caution. ''We'll all be glad to see home this time; but in a month or so, we'll be ready to go again. It's a good life if you can stand these—'' His voice dropped to a whisper, ''—blue-eyed maniacs. A week or two at sea, over to Faerie and back. Week or two onshore. Usually it's dull as gutting fish, but the money's good. Five years, a man can buy a farm and a wife. And you're quick, lad. With that and your farsight you might even make an officer. You're half jotunn, after all.''

Rap mumbled noncommittally. He was sure now that escape from this Durthing place would turn out to be harder than it sounded, but he wasn't going to raise suspicion by asking. He leaned across Kani and Verg to grab another sausage. Build his strength up.

''Hey!'' Ballast boomed. The talk had changed subject yet again. ''The Mosweeps are the greatest mountains in all of Pandemia!''

''Greatest bilge!'' Kani mumbled, rubbing crumbs out of his mustache.

''Yeah—how would you know?'' asked Ogi. ''You've never seen 'em!''

''Nobody's ever seen them!''

''Not even Rap can see them!''

That remark won a brief guffaw all round. Rap just grinned. He was a seer, and *they didn't mind*! The matter was not usually mentioned, because sailors had a superstition against talking about magic, but they all knew about his power, obviously. Unlike the timid townsfolk of Krasnegar, these hardy sailors did not care that he could peer through walls or clothes. They had no privacy on board, anyway, so why did it matter? That discovery had touched him deeply. He was also something of a hero, which was another deliriously pleasant feeling. These tough seafolk had accepted him as one of themselves, and his freakish abilities didn't count against him at all.

It was a long time since he'd been one of a group.

He had friends again.

Someone whistled, and all eyes turned. ''Rap!'' shouted a voice. ''Report to Number One.''

Rap's insides lurched nervously. He handed the rest of his sausage to Ballast and scrambled to his feet. The sudden move made his head spin, and he had to steady himself against the cabin wall. Then he began making his way forward, cursing his wobbling knees. As he emerged from the shelter of the awnings, the rain felt like ice on his heated face. His fever was coming back.

Gathmor and Gnurr were waiting in the bow. The captain was slumped against the rail, looking haggard and about as ill as Rap was feeling. The mate was standing with feet apart, arms folded, glowering.

Rap came to a halt before him, spreading his own feet wide to balance on the tipping deck. "Sir?"

The deadly fog-gray eyes drilled through him. "Feeling better?"

"Aye, sir."

"Ready to pull your oar next watch?"

Rap's heart cringed at the thought, and he was afraid his shivering might be showing, but again he said, "Aye, sir."

The mate grunted. His silver hair was streaked down over his face almost to his walrus moustache. The ship pitched and rolled while he just stared. Then he began to unfasten his jerkin.

"You disobeyed an order."

Rap flinched. "Aye, sir."

"Look at me when I speak to you."

Rap looked up, although he didn't need to. Gnurr had his eyes half closed and did not seem to be paying much attention.

Gathmor hauled off the jerkin and dropped it on the desk, leaving himself bare-chested in the drizzle. "When a man does that," he said, biting the words, "I usually throw him overboard. *Look at me!*"

"Aye, sir."

"You believe me?"

Rap swallowed and said, "Yes, I do, sir." Jotnar often started quietly and then talked themselves up into manic frenzy. He could remember his friends Kratharkran and Verantor almost killing each other a few times as kids, and he'd lost his own temper once or twice, before he was old enough to control it. He wished he was in better shape to handle this, not so weak and shaky.

"Rarely, on a first offense, I just beat him until he's purple all over."

Why else would he strip down in the rain? "Aye, sir."

"Sometimes I do both."

Rap gave him the same reply. The sailor gripped the rail on either side of him. Muscles swelled and his knuckles showed white. He chewed his mustache for a moment.

"The tide was ebbing, dawn was coming, and it was raining. But you thought you knew better."

"I thought—"

"You're not *supposed* to think!"

"No, sir."

Pause. "And that line you caught was left there to keep her head to the wind. Not for you. I almost didn't have it pulled in."

"No, sir."

Another pause. The jotunn was breathing hard, shivering with fury. "Well? You got nothing to say? You disobeyed a direct order. That's mutiny, sailor! And you won't give me any reason why I shouldn't pulp you?"

"No, sir."

"No appeal for mercy?"

Rap had been studying the sodden planks again, but at that demand he looked up, met Gathmor's eye squarely, and said, "No." He knew that things were very dicey now, but he also knew jotnar, and to show his fear would be a fatal mistake. Then he found enough spit to add, "No excuses!" But all his insides were silently screaming, *Yes!*

"Evil take you!" For a moment Gathmor's lips tightened, turning pure white. "You could mention that you saved the ship again, later. That would help."

Rap felt a thin tremor of relief. "I won't beg, sir."

The mate seemed to take that as a challenge. His eyes narrowed, and Rap braced for the attack.

Then the captain seemed to waken. "Belay that!" he said quietly. "Quit hassling the boy! You're just mad because the whole crew started talking back." He turned dull eyes on Rap and pursed his lips in a hint of a smile. "Did you know that?"

"Sir?" Rap said blankly. He'd never spoken with Gnurr before.

"They didn't want to leave you."

Rap blinked stupidly, trying to comprehend an absurdity. The sailors had wanted to wait around for *him* when a million angry anthropophagi were about to descend on them?

Gathmor scowled. "I suppose no one else heard . . . All

right! But if you ever tell a soul—anyone at all, mind!—I'll kill you. I swear."

"Aye, I mean no—sir."

"Not a word! But as long as no one knows you flouted that order, I'll overlook it. Just this once."

"Thank you, sir. It won't happen again."

"No, it won't."

Suddenly the old captain laughed. "I told you he wouldn't scare easy!"

Gathmor grunted. "No, he didn't." He bent to retrieve his jerkin. With sudden anger, Rap realized that they'd been playing with him. Had Gathmor really been about to start a fight, he would have turned pale as ice, and he hadn't. They'd been testing.

For a long minute *Stormdancer* rolled and pitched, while the mate fastened buttons. Then he thrust aside his sodden hair with his fingers and sort of smiled. "But you did well. I said you'd be a free man. That stands."

He leaned back beside Gnurr, elbows on the drippy rail. Behind them the sea rolled in great gray hills and valleys. For a moment the two jotnar studied the greatly relieved faun.

The captain doubled over, racked by a spell of coughing. Then he straightened again, annoyed by his weakness. "It's not going to be much of a voyage, this one," he said hoarsely. "For one thing, it just about killed us. And it would have, but for you."

"Aye . . . I mean, I did what I could, sir."

"And for another, Number One blew all our profit on buying a couple of thralls. Thought he'd gone crazy."

"So did I," Gathmor growled sourly. "Forty-six imperials! Can't think what got into me."

Andor had, of course. Andor could make most people do anything. Rap scanned briefly, but Andor was not aboard. Darad was snoozing on his bunk, facedown. His back was healing.

Then the figure penetrated Rap's throbbing head. *"Forty-six imperials?"*

Gathmor scowled. "For you and your meaty friend. But it was worth it in the end."

"Er . . . thank you, sir." Forty-six imperials? Rap had never thought he'd be worth that much money, not to anyone. Even allowing half for Little Chicken . . . twenty-three?

"You like the life, don't you?"

"Aye, sir," Rap said politely—and truthfully.

Gathmor forced a thin smile and held out a horny hand to shake. "Welcome to the crew, sailor."

He seemed to mean well, he hardly squeezed at all.

Then the significance of that little ritual drove a spike of horror into Rap's conscience. Did the mate think he was promising to stay on, as one of *Stormdancer*'s hands? What about his quest for Inos? Had he just given his word to the sailor?

And if Rap was forced to settle down as a crewman, living in this Durthing place, then what would Little Chicken say? Or do? What happened to the goblin's destiny then, and how would he go about kidnapping—

Huh?

Rap scanned the ship again, then stared in shock at Gathmor. "The goblin?"

The mate scowled. "You mean you didn't know? He went after you."

Little Chicken? "He did?" Rap felt as if he'd been kicked in the stomach.

"When I ordered the men to float the ship, your buddy was the first to argue. I almost ran him through. Then he went tearing off, looking for you."

"Not my buddy," Rap muttered, and staggered over to slump on the rail beside Gnurr while the world turned cartwheels and his knees almost folded under him. He must have been putting the goblin out of his mind as a man might try to forget a debt or ignore an aching tooth. He hadn't noticed his absence.

Of course Little Chicken would not have wanted to leave the island without his chosen victim. The sailors insisted that no one ever escaped from the Nogids. Whole fleets could disappear there. Castaways had no chance at all. Rap stared unseeing at the foam-streaked sea rushing past below him.

Misunderstanding, the old captain laid a hand on his shoulder. "Death is a part of life, son," he said, "and the sea a demanding mistress. Sailors all know what it is to lose friends."

"If it makes you feel any better," Gathmor said sourly, "he disobeyed orders, also, and he didn't save the ship. In fact we needed his strength to push off, and he wasn't there, so even if he'd come back, I wouldn't have let him on. It was probably him who roused the anthros. Friendship can be carried—"

"He wasn't my friend!" Rap shouted. He straightened up to face them. "I hope he tasted delicious!"

That shocked the sailors into silence, while he struggled to take in all the implications of Little Chicken's death. The prophecy had been cheated by a freakish accident of weather and timing. The goblin king was not going to meet his destiny. Witch and warlock both—their foresight had failed them.

And the magic casement had been proved wrong, too! Not only was Rap not going to be tortured by the goblin, but if those prophecies had also been fallible, then he now had no reason to expect to be Inos's champion against Kalkor, or meet a dragon with Sagorn.

Whatever Rap did now, Inos would not be forced into marrying Little Chicken. Of course the witch might find another goblin prince for her.

But maybe Sagorn had been right—Rap was only a humble churl who did not belong in Inos's world of kings and imperors and sorcery. He was a faun, the old man had said, so he should be a hostler. But he was a jotunn, too. Jotnar were sailors by instinct.

Gathmor was scowling suspiciously at Rap's expression.

"Sir," Rap croaked, still clinging to the rail, "I haven't told you how I got to Faerie."

"If it's magic, I don't want to hear about it. Not now, not ever."

"But . . . I may bring bad luck, sir."

"You brought good luck," Gnurr said, with more authority than had shown so far. "You look beat, lad. Go greet your new partners."

"P-partners, sir?"

"Yes, partners!" Gathmor was grinning, which was astonishing—so astonishing that Rap could see nothing in the world but that huge grin under the great silver mustache and hardly noticed that he was shaking hands with the frail old captain, whose skin felt even hotter than his own. "They voted you in, sailor, as full partner. It won't mean much this voyage, because of what you cost, but from now on you get your share. Off with you—and try to stay warm."

It didn't make any sense. His head was throbbing, and waves of fever were tossing him like a tub in a storm. Moving on rubbery legs with the roll of the ship, Rap staggered away, and at once found himself encased in a mob of wet-smelling, noisy men, all crushing his hand and thumping his back, and half dragging him to his bench, raucously welcoming him and laughing. They'd all known why Gathmor had summoned him. They'd voted him a share. They wanted him as one of themselves. He thought he was going to vomit.

Little Chicken was dead. The casement had been wrong. Rap wasn't going to be butchered by the goblin. And he wasn't going to meet any dragons, or Kalkor, or be Inos's champion. He wasn't ever going to see Inos. Not even Andor could get him away from *Stormdancer* now. Andor's charm had limits—he couldn't charm this many men all at once. And eighty men had all paid an incredible fortune to buy a seer who could guide their vessel through the dark, and fog, and rocks.

They wanted him, and he felt good about that and couldn't do anything about the way they kept pumping his hands, both hands, and he couldn't tell them he didn't want to be their crewmate and he mustn't tell them about Inos and he was just babbling nonsense and no one was listening. They must think it was the fever talking, because someone was trying to wrap him in a damp blanket.

He hadn't been wanted like this for a long time. Or never.

But he didn't want to be wanted. He wanted to go and find Inos. Except that Inos didn't need him any more. She had a swordsman to protect her, a swordsman who shared her tent.

The sailors wanted him, and needed him.

They would keep him.

Escaping from goblins and imps and warlocks had been easy, compared to this. How could he escape from the sailors, when they had bound him with ties of friendship? He really didn't want all these new friends because he wanted to run away and that would betray their friendship and they'd talked back to Gathmor for his sake.

He had shaken their hands. No use saying he'd been too sick to understand—he'd shaken their hands. He was still shaking hands, trying to protest, and being shouted down in the celebration. He wanted to scream.

Trapped!

He was one of them now. He'd shaken hands.

He had given his word.

Take the cash:
> Some for the Glories of this World; and some
> Sigh for the Prophet's Paradise to come;
>   Ah, take the Cash, and let the Credit go,
> Nor heed the rumble of a distant Drum!

Fitzgerald, *The Rubaiyat of Omar Khayyam*
(§13, 1879)

❮ ABOUT THE AUTHOR ❯

Dave Duncan was born in Scotland in 1933 and educated at Dundee Hi2h School and the University of St. Andrews. He moved to Canada in 1955 and has lived in Calgary ever since. He is married and has three grown children.

After a thirty-year career as a petroleum geologist, he discovered that it was much easier (and more fun) to invent his own worlds than try to make sense of the real one.

DAVE DUNCAN

Fantasy Novels:

The Seventh Sword